MINDING FRANKIE

P9-CWE-625

Acclaim for

MINDING FRANKIE

"A comforting experience. . . . Warmhearted."
—*The Denver Post*

"Binchy's worldview is a large, benevolent one, and the reader is happier for it. . . . Bless her big Irish heart."
—*Minneapolis Star Tribune*

"Maeve Binchy has done it again [with] yet another warm tale of individual growth and human community, [in which] she assembles a large cast of characters and deploys them with her characteristic playfulness. . . . Binchy specializes in exploring human foibles without spelling them out in tiresome detail . . . There's a good chance that many readers, like this one, will consider *Minding Frankie* one of Binchy's best novels yet." —*BookPage*

"Solid, reliable, and comforting in its familiarity, delivering to Binchy fans what they have come to expect from her novels. . . . A reminder of the author's savvy ability to deliver what her loyal following has come to expect."
—*The Irish Times*

"Absorbing. . . . Teems with colorful characters whose concerns and connections are depicted with heart and humor. . . . New readers of Binchy will succumb to the appeal of the heartwarming tradition longtime fans love to love." —*The Free-Lance Star* (Fredericksburg, VA)

"All across America, Maeve Binchy fans will be kicking off their shoes, making a nice cup of tea, and curling up on the couch as they reenter Binchy's cozy world. The Irish author returns here to a charming Dublin milieu of favorite characters from past novels, with some important new ones." —*The Seattle Times*

Acclaim for

Maeve Binchy

"A remarkably gifted writer and a wonderful student of human nature." —*The New York Times Book Review*

"A modern-day women's writer in the Jane Austen sense." —*Standard-Times* (New Bedford, MA)

"Binchy makes you laugh, cry, and care. Her warmth and sympathy render the daily struggles of ordinary people heroic and turn storytelling into art." —*San Francisco Chronicle*

"An author of exceptional grace [with] a wickedly subtle sense of humor and a great deal of kindness." —*The Boston Globe*

"Maeve Binchy is a benevolent god of a novelist. . . . She can channel Irish voices with the best of them, and each of these voices has its own twisting story to tell . . . often with verve and humor." —*The Columbus Dispatch*

Maeve Binchy

MINDING FRANKIE

Maeve Binchy is the author of numerous best-selling books, including her most recent novel, *Heart and Soul*, in addition to *Whitethorn Woods*, *Nights of Rain and Stars*, *Quentins*, *Scarlet Feather*, *Circle of Friends*, and *Tara Road*, which was an Oprah's Book Club selection. She has written for *Gourmet*; *O, The Oprah Magazine*; *Modern Maturity*; and *Good Housekeeping*; among other publications. She and her husband, Gordon Snell, live in Dalkey, Ireland, and London.

www.maevebinchy.com

MINDING FRANKIE

Maeve Binchy

MINDING FRANKIE

ANCHOR BOOKS
A Division of Random House, Inc.
New York

FIRST ANCHOR BOOKS MASS-MARKET EDITION, DECEMBER 2011

The Library of Congress has cataloged the Knopf edition as follows:
Binchy, Maeve.
Minding Frankie / by Maeve Binchy. —1st U.S. ed.
p. cm.
1. Recovering alcoholics—Fiction. 2. Child rearing—Fiction.
3. Fatherhood—Fiction. 4. Families—Fiction. 5. Interpersonal relations—Fiction.
6. Community life—Ireland—Fiction. 7. City and town life—Ireland—Fiction.
8. Domestic fiction. I. Title.
PR6052.I7728M56 2011
823'.914—dc22
2010035999

Anchor ISBN: 978-0-307-47549-7

www.anchorbooks.com

Printed in the United States of America
10 9 8 7 6 5 4 3 2 1

For dear generous Gordon,
who makes life great every single day

MINDING FRANKIE

Chapter One

Katie Finglas was coming to the end of a tiring day in the salon. Anything bad that could happen had happened. A woman had not told them about an allergy and had come out with lumps and a rash on her forehead. A bride's mother had thrown a tantrum and said that she looked like a laughingstock. A man who had wanted streaks of blond in his hair became apoplectic when, halfway through the process, he had inquired what they would cost. Katie's husband, Garry, had placed both his hands innocently on the shoulders of a sixty-year-old female client, who had then told him that she was going to sue him for sexual harassment and assault.

Katie looked now at the man standing opposite her, a big priest with sandy hair mixed with gray.

"You're Katie Finglas and I gather you run this establishment," the priest said, looking around the innocent salon nervously as if it were a high-class brothel.

"That's right, Father," Katie said with a sigh. What could be happening now?

"It's just that I was talking to some of the girls who work here, down at the center on the quays, you know, and they were telling me . . ."

Katie felt very tired. She employed a couple of high school dropouts: she paid them properly, trained them. *What* could they have been complaining about to a priest?

"Yes, Father, what exactly is the problem?" she asked.

"Well, it *is* a bit of a problem. I thought I should come to you directly, as it were." He seemed a little awkward.

"Very right, Father," Katie said. "So tell me what it is."

"It's this woman, Stella Dixon. She's in hospital, you see . . ."

"Hospital?" Katie's head reeled. What *could* this involve? Someone who had inhaled the peroxide?

"I'm sorry to hear that." She tried for a level voice.

"Yes, but she wants a hairdo."

"You mean she trusts us again?" Sometimes life was extraordinary.

"No, I don't think she was ever here before. . . ." He looked bewildered.

"And your interest in all this, Father?"

"I am Brian Flynn and I am acting chaplain at St. Brigid's Hospital at the moment, while the real chaplain is in Rome on a pilgrimage. Apart from being asked to bring in cigarettes and drink for the patients, this is the only serious request I've had."

"You want me to go and do someone's hair in hospital?"

"She's seriously ill. She's dying. I thought she needed a senior person to talk to. Not, of course, that you look very senior. You're only a girl yourself," the priest said.

"God, weren't you a sad loss to the women of Ireland

when you went for the priesthood," Katie said. "Give me her details and I'll bring my magic bag of tricks in to see her."

"Thank you so much. I have it all written out here." Father Flynn handed her a note.

A middle-aged woman approached the desk. She had glasses on the tip of her nose and an anxious expression.

"I gather you teach people the tricks of hairdressing," she said.

"Yes, or more the *art* of hairdressing, as we like to call it," Katie said.

"I have a cousin coming home from America for a few weeks. She mentioned that in America there are places where you could get your hair done for near to nothing cost if you were letting people practice on you."

"Well, we do have a students' night on Tuesdays; people bring in their own towels and we give them a style. They usually contribute five euros to a charity."

"Tonight is Tuesday!" the woman cried triumphantly.

"So it is," Katie said through gritted teeth.

"So, could I book myself in? I'm Josie Lynch."

"Great, Mrs. Lynch—see you after seven o'clock," Katie said, writing down the name. Her eyes met the priest's. There was sympathy and understanding there.

It wasn't all champagne and glitter running your own hairdressing salon.

Josie and Charles Lynch had lived in 23 St. Jarlath's Crescent since they were married thirty-two years ago. They had seen many changes in the area. The corner shop had become a mini-supermarket; the old laundry, where sheets had been ironed and folded, was now a Laundromat, where people left big bags bulky with mixed clothes and asked for a service wash. There was now a proper medical practice with four doctors where once there had been just old Dr. Gillespie, who had brought everyone into the world and seen them out of it.

During the height of the economic boom, houses in St. Jarlath's Crescent had changed hands for amazing sums of money. Small houses with gardens near the city center had been much in demand. Not anymore, of course—the recession had been a great equalizer, but it was still a much more substantial area than it had been three decades ago.

After all, just look at Molly and Paddy Carroll, with their son Declan—a doctor—a real, qualified doctor! And just look at Muttie and Lizzie Scarlet's daughter Cathy. She ran a catering company that was hired for top events.

But a lot of things had changed for the worse. There was no community spirit anymore. No church processions went up and down the Crescent on the feast of Corpus Christi, as they used to. Josie and Charles Lynch felt that they were alone in the world, and certainly in St. Jarlath's Crescent, in that they knelt down at night and said the Rosary.

That had always been the way.

When they married they planned a life based on the maxim that the family that prays together stays together. They had assumed they would have eight or nine children, because God never put a mouth into this world that He didn't feed. But that wasn't to happen. After Noel, Josie had been told there would be no more children. It was hard to accept. They both came from big families;

their brothers and sisters had produced big families. But then, perhaps, it was all meant to be this way.

They had always hoped Noel would be a priest. The fund to educate him for the priesthood was started before he was three. Money was put aside from Josie's wages at the biscuit factory. Every week a little more was added to the post office savings account, and when Charles got his envelope on a Friday from the hotel where he was a porter, a sum was also put into the post office. Noel would get the best of priestly educations when the time came.

So it was with great surprise and a lot of disappointment that Josie and Charles learned that their quiet son had no interest whatsoever in a religious life. The Brothers said that he showed no sign of a vocation, and when the matter had been presented to Noel as a possibility when he was fourteen, he had said if it was the last job on earth he wouldn't go for it.

That had been very definite indeed.

Not so definite, however, was what he actually *would* like to do. Noel was vague about this, except to say he might like to run an office. Not work in an office, but run one. He showed no interest in studying office management or bookkeeping or accounting or in any areas where the careers department tried to direct him. He liked art, he said, but he didn't want to paint. If pushed, he would say that he liked looking at paintings and thinking about them. He was good at drawing; he always had a notebook and a pencil with him and he was often to be found curled up in a corner sketching a face or an animal. This did not, of course, lead to any career path, but Noel had never expected it to. He did his homework at the kitchen table, sighing now and then, but rarely ever excited or enthusiastic. At the parent-teacher meetings Josie and Charles had inquired about this. They wondered, Does anything at school fire him up? Anything at all?

The teachers were at a loss. Most boys were unfathomable around fourteen or fifteen but they had usually settled down to do something. Or often to do nothing. Noel Lynch, they said, had just become even more quiet and withdrawn than he already was.

Josie and Charles wondered, Could this be right?

Noel was quiet, certainly, and it had been a great relief to them that he hadn't filled the house up with loud young lads thumping one another. But they had thought this was part of his spiritual life, a preparation for a future as a priest. Now it appeared that this was certainly not the case.

Perhaps, Josie suggested, it was only the Brothers' brand of religious life that Noel objected to. In fact, he might have a different kind of vocation and want to become a Jesuit or a missionary?

Apparently not.

And when he was fifteen he said that he didn't really want to join in the family Rosary anymore; it was only a ritual of meaningless prayers chanted in repetition. He didn't mind doing good for people, trying to make less fortunate people have a better life, but surely no God could want this fifteen minutes of drone drone drone.

By the time he was sixteen they realized that he had stopped going to Sunday Mass. Someone had seen him up by the canal when he was meant to have been to the early Mass up in the church on the corner. He told them that there was no point in his staying on at school, as there was nothing more he needed to learn from them. They were hiring office staff up at Hall's, the big builders' merchants, and they would train him in office routine. He might as well go to work straightaway rather than hang about.

The Brothers and the teachers at his school said it was always a pity to see a boy study and leave without a qualification, but still, they said, shrugging, it was very hard trying to interest the lad in anything at all. He seemed to be sitting and waiting for his schooldays to end. Could even be for the best if he left school now. Get him into Hall's; give him a wage every week and then they might see where, if anywhere, his interest lay.

Josie and Charles thought sadly of the fund that had been growing in the post office for years. Money that would never be spent making Noel into a reverend. A kindly Brother suggested that maybe they should spend it on a holiday for themselves, but Charles and Josie were shocked. This money had been saved for God's work; it would be spent on God's work.

Noel got his place in Hall's. He met his work colleagues but without any great enthusiasm. They would not be his friends and companions any more than his fellow students at the Brothers had become mates. He didn't *want* to be alone all the time, but it was often easier.

Over the years Noel had arranged with his mother that he would not join them at meals. He would have his lunch in the middle of the day and he would make a snack for himself in the evening. This way he missed the Rosary, the socializing with pious neighbors and the interrogation about what he had done with his day, which was the natural accompaniment to mealtimes in the Lynch household.

He took to coming home later and later. He also took to visiting Casey's pub on the journey home—a big barn of a place, both comforting and anonymous at the same time. It was familiar because everyone knew his name.

"I'll drop it down to you, Noel," the loutish son of the house would say. Old Man Casey, who said little but noticed everything, would look over his spectacles as he polished the beer glasses with a clean linen cloth.

"Evening, Noel," he would say, managing to combine the courtesy of being the landlord with the sense of disapproval he had of Noel. He was, after all, an acquaintance of Noel's father. It was as if he were glad that Casey's was getting the price of the pint—or several pints—as the night went on but as well as this he seemed disappointed that Noel was not spending his wages more wisely. Yet Noel liked the place. It wasn't a trendy pub with fancy prices. It wasn't full of girls giggling and interrupting a man's drinking. People left him alone here.

That was worth a lot.

When he got home, Noel noticed that his mother looked different. He couldn't work out why. She was wearing the red knitted suit that she wore only on special occasions. At the biscuit factory where she worked they wore a uniform, which she said was wonderful because it meant you didn't wear out your good garments. Noel's mother didn't wear makeup so it couldn't be that.

Eventually he realized that it was her hair. His mother had been to a beauty salon.

"You got a new hairdo, Mam!" he said.

Josie Lynch patted her head, pleased. "They did a good

job, didn't they?" She spoke like someone who frequented hairdressing salons regularly.

"Very nice, Mam," he said.

"I'll be putting a kettle on if you'd like a cup of tea," she offered.

"No, Mam, you're all right." He was anxious to be out of there, safe in his room. And then Noel remembered that his cousin Emily was coming from America the next day. His mother must be getting ready for her arrival. This Emily was going to stay for a few weeks, apparently. It hadn't been decided exactly how many weeks. . . .

Noel hadn't involved himself greatly in the visit, doing only what he had to, like helping his father to paint her room and clearing out the downstairs storage room, where they had tiled the walls and put in a new shower. He didn't know much about her; she was an older person, in her fifties, maybe, the only daughter of his father's eldest brother, Martin. She had been an art teacher but her job had ended unexpectedly and she was using her savings to see the world. She would start with a visit to Dublin, from where her father had left many years ago to seek his fortune in America.

It had not been a great fortune, Charles reported. The eldest brother of the family had worked in a bar, where he was his own best customer. He had never stayed in touch. Any Christmas cards had been sent by this Emily, who had also written to tell first of her father's death and then her mother's. She sounded remarkably businesslike and said that when she arrived in Dublin she would expect to pay a contribution to the family expenses and that since she was letting her own small apartment in New York during her absence, it was only fair. Josie and Charles were also reassured that she seemed sensible and had promised not to be in their way or looking for entertainment. She said she would find plenty to occupy her.

Noel sighed.

It would be one more trivial happening elevated to high drama by his mother and father. The woman wouldn't be in the door before she heard all about his great future at Hall's, about his mother's job at the biscuit factory and his father's role as a senior porter in a very grand hotel. She would be told about the moral decline in Ireland, the lack of attendance at Sunday Mass and that binge drinking kept the emergency departments of hospitals full to overflowing. Emily would be invited to join the family Rosary.

Noel's mother had already spent considerable time debating whether they should put a picture of the Sacred Heart or of Our Lady of Perpetual Succour in the newly painted room. Noel had managed to avoid too much further discussion of this agonizing choice by suggesting that they wait until she arrived.

"She taught art in a school, Mam. She might have brought her own pictures," he had said, and amazingly his mother had agreed immediately.

"You're quite right, Noel. I have a tendency to make all the decisions in the world. It will be nice having another woman to share all that with."

Noel mildly hoped that she was right and that this woman would not disrupt their ways. This was going to be a time of change in their household anyway. His father was going to be retired as porter in a year or two. His mother still had a few more years in the biscuit factory but she thought she might retire also and keep Charles company, with the two of them doing some good works. He hoped that Emily would make their lives less complicated rather than more complicated.

But mainly he gave the matter very little thought.

Noel got by well by not thinking too deeply on anything: not about his dead-end job in Hall's; not about the hours and money he spent in Old Man Casey's pub; not about the religious mania of his parents, who thought that the Rosary was the answer to most of the world's problems. Noel would not think about the lack of a steady girlfriend in his life. He just hadn't met anyone, that's all it was. Nor indeed did he worry about the lack of any kind of mates. Some places were easy to find friends. Hall's wasn't one of those places. Noel had decided that the very best way to cope with things not being so great was not to think about them at all. It had worked well so far.

Why fix things if they weren't broken?

Charles Lynch had been very silent. He hadn't noticed his wife's new hairdo. He hadn't guessed that his son had drunk four pints on the way home from work. He found it hard to raise any interest in the arrival next morning of his brother Martin's daughter, Emily. Martin had made it clear that he had no interest in the family back home.

Emily had certainly been a courteous correspondent over the years—even to the point of offering to pay her bed and board. That might come in very useful indeed these days. Charles Lynch had been told that morning that his services as hotel porter would no longer be needed. He and another "older" porter would leave at the end of the month. Charles had been trying to find the words to tell Josie since he got home, but the words weren't there.

He could repeat what the young man in the suit had said to him earlier in the day: a string of sentences about it being no reflection on Charles or his loyalty to the hotel. He had been there, man and boy, resplendent in his uniform and very much part of the old image. But that's exactly what it was—an old image. The new owners were insisting on a new image, and who could stand in the way of the march of progress?

Charles had thought he would grow old in that job. That one day there would be a dinner for him where Josie would go and wear a long frock. He would be presented with a gold-plated clock. Now none of this was going to happen.

He was going to be without a job in two and a half weeks' time.

There were few work opportunities for a man in his sixties who had been let go from the one hotel where he had worked since he was sixteen. Charles Lynch would have liked to have talked to his son about it all, but he and Noel didn't seem to have had a conversation for years now. If ever. The boy was always anxious to get to his room and resisted any questions or discussions. It wouldn't be fair to lay all this on him now.

Charles wouldn't find a sympathetic ear or any font of advice. Just tell Josie and get it over with, he told himself. But she was up to high doh about this woman coming from America. Maybe he should leave it for a couple of days. Charles sighed again about the bad timing of it all.

Dear Emily,

I wish that you hadn't decided to go to Ireland. I will miss you greatly.

I wish you had let me come and see you off . . . but then you were always one for the quick, impulsive decision. Why should I expect you to change now?

I know that I *should* say that I hope you will find all your heart's desire in Dublin, but in a way I don't want you to. I want you to say it was wonderful for six weeks and then for you to come back home again.

It's not going to be the same without you here. There's an exhibit opening and it's just up the street and I can't bring myself to go to it on my own. I won't go to nearly as many theater matinees as I did with you.

I'll collect your rent every Friday from the student who's renting your apartment. I'll keep an eye open in case she is growing any attitude-changing substances in your window boxes.

You must write and tell me all about the place you are staying—don't leave anything out. I am so glad you will have your laptop with you. There will be no excuse for you not to stay in touch. I'll keep telling you small bits of news about Eric in the suitcase store. He really IS interested in you, Emily, whether you believe it or not!

I'll hear all about your arrival in the land of the
Shamrock when you get your laptop up and running
and read this.

Love from your lonely friend,
Betsy

Hi, Betsy,

What makes you think that I would have to wait to get
to Ireland to hear from you? I'm at Kennedy Airport
and the machine works.

Nonsense! You won't miss me—you and your fevered
imagination! You will have a thousand fantasies. Eric
does not fancy me, not even remotely. He is a man of
very few words and none of them are small talk. He
speaks about me to you because he is too shy to
speak to you. Surely you know that?

I'll miss you too, Bets, but this is something I have to
do.

I swear that I will keep in touch. You'll probably get
twenty e-mails from me every day and wish you hadn't
encouraged me!

Love,
Emily

"I wonder, should we have gone out to the airport to meet her?" Josie Lynch said for the fifth time next morning.

"She said she would prefer to make her own way here," Charles said, as he had on the previous four occasions.

Noel just drank his mug of tea and said nothing.

"She wrote and said the plane could be in early if they got a good wind behind them." Josie spoke as if she were a frequent flyer herself.

"So she could be here any time . . . ," Charles said with a heavy heart. He hated having to go in to the hotel this morning knowing that his days there were numbered. There would be time enough to tell Josie once this woman had settled in. Martin's daughter! He hoped that she hadn't inherited her father's great thirst.

There was a ring at the doorbell. Josie's face was all alarm. She snatched Noel's mug of tea from him and swept up the empty eggcup and plate from in front of Charles. Patting her new hairdo again, she spoke in a high, false voice.

"Answer the door please, Noel, and welcome your cousin Emily in."

Noel opened the door to a small woman, forty-something, with frizzy hair and a cream-colored raincoat. She had two neat red suitcases on wheels. She looked entirely in charge of the situation. First time in the country and she had found St. Jarlath's Crescent with no difficulty.

"You must be Noel. I hope I'm not too early for the household."

"No, we were all up. We're about to go to work, you see, and you are very welcome, by the way."

"Thank you. Well, shall I come in and say hello and good-bye to them?"

Noel realized that he might have left her forever on the doorstep, but then he was only half awake. It took him until about eleven a.m., when he had his first vodka and Coke, to be fully in control of the day. Noel was absolutely certain that nobody at Hall's knew of his morning injection of alcohol and his midafternoon booster. He covered himself very carefully and always allowed a bottle of genuine Diet Coke to peek out of his duffel bag. The vodka was added from a separate source when he was alone.

He brought the small American woman into the kitchen, where his mother and father kissed her on the cheek and said this was a great day that Martin Lynch's daughter had come back to the land of her ancestors.

"See you this evening then, Noel," she called.

"Yes, of course. I might be a bit late. Lots of things to catch up on. But settle in well. . . ."

"I will, and thank you for agreeing to share your home with me."

He left them to it. As he pulled the door behind him he could hear the pride in his mother's voice as she showed off the newly decorated downstairs bedroom. And he could hear his cousin Emily cry out that it was just perfect.

Noel thought his father had been very quiet today and last night. But then he was probably just imagining it. His father didn't have a care in the world, just as long as they made a fuss of him in that hotel and while he was sure there would be the Rosary every evening, an annual visit to Lourdes to see the shrine and talk of going farther afield one day, like maybe Rome or the Holy Land. Charles Lynch was lucky enough to be a man who was content with things the way they were. He didn't need to numb himself against the dead weight of days and nights by spending long hours drinking alcohol in Old Man Casey's.

Noel walked to the end of the road, where he would catch his bus. He walked as he did every morning, nodding to people but seeing nothing, noting no details about his surroundings. He wondered mildly what that busy-looking American woman would make of it all here.

Probably she would stick to it for about a week before she gave up in despair.

At the biscuit factory Josie told them all about the arrival of Emily, who had found her own way to St. Jarlath's Crescent as if she had been born and reared there. Josie said she was an extremely nice person who had offered to make the supper for everyone that night. They were just to tell her what they liked and didn't like and point her to the market. She didn't need to go to bed and rest, apparently, because she had slept overnight on the plane coming over. She had admired everything in the house and said that gardening was her hobby so she would look out for a few plants when she went shopping. If they didn't mind, of course.

The other women said that Josie should consider herself lucky. This American could have easily turned out to be very difficult indeed.

At the hotel, Charles was his normal, pleasant self to everyone he met. He carried suitcases in from taxis, he directed tourists out towards the sights of Dublin, he looked up the times of theater performances, he looked down at the sad face of a little fat King Charles spaniel that had been tied to the hotel railing. Charles knew this little dog: Caesar. He was often attached to Mrs. Monty—an eccentric, titled old lady who wore a huge hat and three strands of pearls, a fur coat and nothing else. If anyone angered her, she opened her coat, rendering them speechless.

The fact that she had left the dog there meant she must have been taken into a psychiatric hospital. If the past was anything to go by, she would discharge herself from the hospital after about three days and come to collect Caesar and take him back to his unpredictable life with her.

Charles sighed.

Last time, he had been able to conceal the dog in the hotel until Mrs. Monty came back to get him, but things were different now. He would take the dog home at lunchtime. Josie wouldn't like it. Not at all. But St. Francis had written the book as far as animals were concerned. If it came to a big, dramatic row Josie wouldn't go against St. Francis. He hoped that his brother's daughter didn't have any allergies or attitudes towards dogs. She looked far too sensible.

Emily had spent a busy morning shopping. She was surrounded by food when Charles came in. Immediately, she made him a mug of tea and a cheese sandwich.

Charles was grateful for this. He had thought that he was about to miss lunch altogether. He introduced Emily to Caesar and told her some of the story behind his arrival in St. Jarlath's Crescent.

Emily Lynch seemed to think it was the most natural thing in the world. "I wish I had known he was coming. I could have gotten him a bone," she said. "Still, I met that nice Mr. Carroll, your neighbor. He's a butcher. He might get me one." She hadn't been here five minutes and she had got to know the neighbors!

Charles looked at her with admiration. "Well, aren't you a real bundle of energy," he said. "You took your retirement very early for someone as fit as you are."

"Oh, no, I didn't choose retirement," Emily said, as she trimmed the pastry crust around the pie. "No, indeed, I loved my job. They let me go. Well, they said I *must* go, actually."

"Why? Why did they do that?" Charles was shocked.

"Because they thought that I was old and cautious and always very much the same. It was a question of my being the old style. The old guard. I would take children to visit galleries and exhibits. They would have a sheet of paper with twenty questions on it and they would spend a morning there trying to find answers. I thought that it gave them a great grounding in how to look at a picture or a sculpture. Well, I thought so, anyway. Then came this new principal, a child himself, with the notion that teaching art was all about free expression. He really wanted a recent graduate who knew how to do this. I didn't, so I had to go."

"They can't sack you for being mature, surely?" Charles was sympathetic. His own case was different. He was the public face of the hotel, they had told him, and these times meant the hotel's face must be a young face. That was logical in a cruel sort of way. But this Emily wasn't old. She wasn't fifty yet. They must have laws against that kind of discrimination.

"No, they didn't actually say I was dismissed. They just kept me in the background doing filing, away from the children, out of the art studio. It was unbearable, so I left. But they had forced me to go."

"Were you upset?"

"Oh, yes, at the start. I was very upset indeed. It kind of made nothing of all the work I had done for years. I had gotten accustomed to meeting people at art galleries who often said, 'Miss Lynch, you started off my whole interest in art,' and so I thought it was all written off when they let me go. Like saying I had contributed nothing."

Charles felt tears in his eyes. She was describing exactly his own years as porter in the hotel. Written off. That's what he felt.

But Emily had cheered up. She put twirly bits of pastry on top of the pie and cleared the kitchen table swiftly. "But my friend Betsy told me that I was crazy to sit sulking in my corner. I should resign at once and set about doing what I had really wanted to do. Begin the rest of my life, she called it."

"And did you?" Charles asked. Wasn't America a wonderful place! *He* wouldn't be able to do that here—not in a million years.

"Yes, I did. I sat down and made a list of what I wanted to do. Betsy was right. If I had gotten a post in some other school maybe the same thing would have happened. I had a small savings account, so I could afford to be without paid work for a while. Trouble was I didn't know exactly what I wanted to do, so I did several things.

"First I took a cooking course. Tra-la-la. That's why I can make a chicken pie so quickly. And then I went to an intensive course and learned to use computers and the Internet properly so I could get a job in any office if I wanted to. Then I went to this garden center where they had window-box and planter classes. So now that I am full of skills I decided to go and see the world."

"And Betsy? Did she do that too?"

"No. She already understood the Internet and she doesn't want to cook because she's always on a diet, but she did share the window-box addiction with me."

"And suppose they asked you back to your old job. Would you go?"

"No. I can't now, even if they *did* ask. No, these days I'm much too busy," Emily said.

"I see." Charles nodded. He seemed about to say something else but stopped himself. He fussed about getting more milk for the tea.

Emily knew he wanted to say something; she knew how to listen. He would say it eventually.

"The thing is," he said slowly and with great pain, "the real thing is that these new brooms which are meant to be sweeping clean, they sweep away a lot of what was valuable and important as well as sweeping out cobwebs or whatever. . . ."

Emily saw it then. This would have to be handled carefully. She looked at him sympathetically. "Have another mug of tea, Uncle Charles."

"No, I have to get back," he said.

"Do you? I mean think about it for a moment, Uncle Charles. Do you have to? What more can they do to you? I mean that they haven't done already. . . ."

He gave her a long, level look.

She understood.

This woman he had never met until this morning realized, without having to be told, exactly what had happened to Charles Lynch. Something that his own wife and son hadn't seen at all.

The chicken pie that evening was a great success. Emily had made a salad as well. They talked easily, all three of them, and Emily introduced the subject of her own retirement.

"It's just amazing—the very thing you most dread can turn out to be a huge blessing in disguise! I never realized until it was over that I spent so much of my life on trains and crosstown buses. No wonder there were no hours left to learn the Internet and small-scale gardening."

Charles watched in admiration. Without ever appearing to have done so, she was making his path very smooth. He could tell Josie tomorrow, but maybe he would tell her now, this very minute.

It was much easier than he would ever have believed possible. He explained slowly that he had been thinking for a long time about leaving the hotel. The matter had come up recently in conversation and, amazingly, it turned out that it would suit the hotel too and so the departure would be by mutual agreement. All he had to do now was make sure that he was going to get some kind of reasonable compensation.

He said that for the whole afternoon his head had been bursting with ideas for what he would like to do.

Josie was taken aback. She looked at Charles anxiously in case this was just a front. Perhaps he was only blustering when inside he was very upset. But inasmuch as she could see he seemed to be speaking from the heart.

"I suppose it's what Our Lord wants for you," she said piously.

"Yes, and I'm grabbing it with both hands." Charles Lynch was indeed telling the truth. He had not felt so liberated for a long time. Since talking to Emily today at lunchtime, he had begun to feel that there was a whole world out there.

Emily moved in and out, clearing dishes and bringing in some dessert, and from time to time she entered the conversation easily. When her uncle said he had to walk Mrs. Monty's dog until she was released from wherever she was, Emily suggested that Charles could mind other people's dogs as well.

"That nice man Paddy Carroll, the butcher, has a huge dog named Dimples who needs to lose at least ten pounds," she said enthusiastically.

"I couldn't ask Paddy for money," Charles protested.

Josie agreed with him. "You see, Emily, Paddy and Molly Carroll are neighbors. It would be odd to ask them to pay Charles to walk that big foolish dog. It would sound very grasping."

"I see that, of course, and you wouldn't want to be grasping, but then again he might see a way to giving you some lamb chops or best ground beef from time to time." Emily was a great believer in barter, and Charles seemed to think that this was completely possible.

"But would there be a real job, Emily, you know, a *profession,* a life like Charles had in the hotel, where he was a person that mattered?" Josie asked.

"I wouldn't survive just with dog walking alone, but maybe I could get a job in a kennel—I'd really love that," Charles said.

"And if there was anything else that you had both *really* wanted to do?" Emily was gentle. "You know, I so enjoyed looking up all my roots and making a family tree. Not that I'm suggesting that to you, of course."

"Well, do you know what we always wanted to do?" Josie began tentatively.

"No. What is that?" Emily was interested in everything so she was easy to talk to.

Josie continued. "We always thought that it was a pity that St. Jarlath was never properly celebrated in this neighborhood. I mean our street is called after him, but nobody you'd meet knows a thing about him. Charles and I were thinking we might raise money to erect a statue to his memory."

"A statue to St. Jarlath! Imagine!" Emily was surprised. Perhaps she had been wrong to have encouraged them to be freethinkers. "Wasn't he rather a long time ago?" She was careful not to throw any cold water on Josie's plan, especially when she saw Charles light up with enthusiasm.

Josie waved this objection away. "Oh, that's no problem. If he's a saint, does it matter if he died only a few years back or in the sixth century?"

"The *sixth* century?" This was even worse than Emily had feared.

"Yes, he died around A.D. 540 and his Feast Day is June sixth."

"And that would be a very suitable time of the year for a little procession to his shrine." Charles was busy planning it all already.

"And was he from around these parts?" Emily asked. Apparently not. Jarlath was from the other side of the country, the Atlantic coast. He had set up the first archdiocese of Tuam. He had taught other great holy men, even other saints: St. Brendan of Clonfert and St. Colman of Cloyne. Places that were miles away.

"But there was always a devotion to him here," Charles explained.

"Why would they have named the street after him otherwise?" Josie wanted to know.

Emily wondered what would have happened if her father, Martin Lynch, had stayed here. Would he have been a simple, easily pleased person like Charles and Josie instead of the discontented drunk that he had turned into in New York? But all this business about the saint who had died miles away, hundreds of years ago, was a fantasy, surely?

"Of course, the problem would be raising the money for this statue *and* actually earning a living at the same time," Emily said.

That was apparently no problem at all. They had saved money for years, hoping to put it towards the education of Noel as a priest. To give a son to God. But it hadn't taken. They always intended that those savings be given to God in some way, and now this was the perfect opportunity.

Emily told herself that she must not try to change the world. No time now to consider all the good causes that that money could have gone towards—many of them even run by the Catholic Church. Emily would have preferred to see it all going to look after Josie and Charles, and give them a little comfort after a life of working long, hard hours for little reward. They'd had to endure what to them must have been a tragedy—their son's vocation "hadn't taken," to use their own words. But there were some irresistible forces that could never be fought with logic and practicality. Emily Lynch knew this for certain.

Noel had been through a long, bad day. Mr. Hall had asked him twice if he was all right. There was something behind the question, something menacing. When he had asked for the third time, Noel inquired politely why he was asking.

"There was an empty bottle which appears to have contained gin before it was empty," Mr. Hall said.

"And what has that to do with me and whether I'm all right or not?" Noel asked. He was confident now, emboldened, even.

Mr. Hall looked at him long and sternly from under his bushy eyebrows. "That's as may be, Noel. There's many a fellow taking the plane to some faraway part of the world who would be happy to do the job you are meant to be doing." He walked off and Noel saw other workers look away.

Noel had never known Mr. Hall like this—usually there was a kindly remark, some kind of encouragement about continuing in this work of matching dockets to sales slips, of looking through ledgers and invoices and doing the most lowly clerk duties imaginable.

Mr. Hall seemed to think that Noel could do better and had made many positive suggestions in earlier days. Times when there was some hope. But not now. This was more than a reprimand; it was a warning. It had shaken him, and on the way home he found his feet taking him into Casey's big, comforting pub. He vaguely recalled hav-

ing had one too many the last time he'd been here but he
hesitated for only a moment before going in.

Mossy, the son of Old Man Casey, looked nervous.
"Ah, Noel, it's yourself."

"Could I have a pint, please, Mossy?"

"Ah, now, that's not such a good idea, Noel. You know
you're barred. My father said . . ."

"Your father says a lot of things in the heat of the moment. That barring order is long over now."

"No, it's not, Noel. I'm sorry, but there it is."

Noel felt a tick in his forehead. He must be careful
now.

"Well, that's his decision and yours. As it happens, I
have given up drink and what I was actually asking for
was a pint of lemonade."

Mossy looked at him openmouthed. Noel Lynch off
the liquor? Wait till his father heard this!

"But if I'm not welcome in Casey's, then I'll have to
take my custom elsewhere. Give my best to your father."
Noel made as if to leave.

"When did you give up the gargle?" Mossy asked.

"Oh, Mossy, that's not any of your concern these days.
You must go ahead serving alcohol to folks here. Am I interfering with your right to do this? I am most definitely
not."

"Wait a minute, Noel," Mossy called out to him.

Noel said he was sorry but he had to go now. And he
walked, head high, out of the place where he had spent so
much of his leisure time.

There was a cold wind blowing down the street as
Noel leaned against the wall and thought over what he
had just said. He had spoken only in order to annoy

Mossy, a foolish, mumbling mouthpiece for his father's decisions. Now he had to live with his words. He could never drink in Casey's again.

He would have to go to that place where Declan Carroll's father went with his huge bear of a dog. The place where nobody had friends or mates or people they met there. They called them "Associates." Muttie Scarlet was always about to confer with his Associates over the likely outcome of a big race or a soccer match. Not a place that Noel had enjoyed up to now.

Wouldn't it be much easier if he really *had* given up drink? Then Mr. Hall could find whatever bottles he liked. Mr. Casey would be regretful and apologetic, which would be a pleasure to see. Noel himself would have all the time in the world to go back to doing the things he really wanted. He might go back and get a business certificate so as to qualify for a promotion. Maybe even move out of St. Jarlath's Crescent.

Noel went for a long, thoughtful walk around Dublin, up the canal, down through the Georgian squares. He looked into restaurants where men of his own age were sitting across tables from girls. Noel wasn't a social outcast, he was just in a world of his own making where these kind of women were never available. And why was this? Because Noel was too busy with his snout in the trough.

It would not be like this anymore. He was going to give himself the twin gifts of sobriety and time: much more time. He checked his watch before letting himself into Number 23 St. Jarlath's Crescent. They would all be safely in bed by now. This was such an earthshaking decision he didn't want to muddy it all up with conversation.

He was wrong. They were all up, awake and alert at

the kitchen table. Apparently his father was going to leave the hotel where he had worked all his life. They appeared to have adopted a tiny King Charles spaniel called Caesar, with enormous eyes and a soulful expression. His mother was planning to work fewer hours at the biscuit factory. His cousin Emily had met most of the people in the neighborhood and become firm friends with them all. And, most alarming of all, they were about to start a campaign to build a statue to some saint who, if he had ever existed, had died fifteen hundred years ago.

They had all been normal when he left the house this morning. What could have happened?

He wasn't able to manage his usual maneuver of sliding into his room and retrieving a bottle from the box labeled ART SUPPLIES, which contained mainly unused paintbrushes and unopened bottles of gin or wine.

Not, of course, that he was ever going to drink them again.

He had forgotten this. A sudden, heavy gloom settled over him as he sat there trying to comprehend the bizarre changes that were about to take place in his home. There would be no comforting oblivion afterwards, instead, it would be a night of trying to avoid the ART SUPPLIES box or maybe even pouring the contents down the hand basin in his room.

He struggled to make out what his father was talking about: walking dogs, minding pets, raising money, restoring St. Jarlath to his rightful place. In all his years of drinking, Noel had not come across anything as surreal and unexpected as this scene. And all this on a night when he was totally sober.

Noel shifted in his seat slightly and tried to catch the

eye of his cousin Emily. She must be responsible for all this sudden change of heart: the idea that today was the first day of everybody's life. Mad, dangerous stuff in a household that had known no change for decades.

In the middle of the night, Noel woke up and decided that giving up drink was something that should not be taken lightly or casually. He would do it next week, when the world had settled down. But when he reached for the bottle in the box, he felt, with a clarity that he had not often known, that somehow next week would never come. So he poured the contents of two bottles of gin down his sink, followed by two bottles of red wine.

He went back to bed and tossed and turned until he heard his alarm clock the next morning.

In her bedroom, Emily opened her laptop and sent a message to Betsy:

> I feel that I have lived here for several years and yet I have not spent one night in the country!

> I have arrived at a time of amazing change. Everyone in this household has begun some kind of journey. My father's brother was fired from his job as a hotel porter and is now going to go into a dog-walking business, his wife is hoping to reduce *her* hours at her place of employment and set up a petition to get a statue erected to a saint who has been dead for—wait for it— fifteen hundred years!

The son of the house, who is some kind of recluse, has chosen this, of all days, to give up his love affair with alcohol. I can hear him flushing bottles of the stuff down the drain in his bedroom.

Why did I think it would be peaceful and quiet here, Betsy? Have I discovered *anything* about life or am I condemned to wander the earth learning little and understanding nothing?

Don't answer this question. It's not really a question, more a speculation. I miss you.

Love,
Emily

Chapter Two

Father Brian Flynn could not sleep in his small apartment in the heart of Dublin. He had just heard that day that he had only three weeks to find a new place to stay. He hadn't many possessions, so moving would not be a nightmare. But neither had he any money to speak of. He couldn't afford a smart place to live.

He hated leaving this little flat. His pal Johnny had found him this entirely satisfactory place to live, only minutes from his work in the immigrant center, and only seconds from one of the best pubs in Ireland. He knew everyone in the area. It was worrying to have to move.

"Couldn't the Archbishop find you a place?" Johnny was unsympathetic. He himself was going to move into his girlfriend's place. This wasn't a solution open to a middle-aged Catholic priest. Johnny was in the habit of saying to anyone who would listen that a man must be certifiably mad to be a priest in this day and age and the least the Archbishop of Dublin could do was provide lodgings for all these poor eejits who had given up anything that mattered in life and went around doing good day and night.

"Ah, it's not really the Archbishop's job. He has more important things to do," Brian Flynn said, "but it should be no trouble to find a place."

It was proving more troublesome than he had thought possible. And there were only twenty days to go.

Brian Flynn could not believe the amounts people were asking as rent. Surely they could never get sums like that? In the middle of a recession as well! Other things kept him awake too. The appalling priest who had broken his leg in Rome falling down the Spanish Steps and who was *still* out there eating grapes in an Italian hospital. Father Flynn was therefore *still* acting chaplain in St. Brigid's Hospital, with all the many complications that this added to his life.

He kept hearing reports from his old parish in Rossmore. His mother, who was already fairly confused and in a home for the elderly, was thought to have seen a vision, but it turned out she was talking about the television, and everyone in the old people's home was greatly disappointed.

He found himself increasingly brooding about the meaning of life now that he had to see so much of the end of life in St. Brigid's. Look at that poor girl Stella who seemed to like him just because he had arranged for a hairdresser to come in and visit her. She was pregnant as well as dying. She had lived a short and vaguely unsatisfactory life but then she told him that almost everyone else did as well. She seemed not even marginally interested in preparing to meet her Maker, and Father Flynn was always very firm about this; unless the patients brought the matter up themselves, it wasn't mentioned. They knew what his job description was, for heaven's sake. If they wanted intervention made, prayers said or sins forgiven, then he would do that; otherwise he wouldn't mention the topic.

He and Stella had had many good conversations about single-malt whiskey, about the quarterfinals in the soccer World Cup, about the unequal division of wealth in the world. She said that she had one more thing to do before she was off to the next world, whatever it might bring. Just one thing. But she had a sort of hope that it was all going to work out all right. And could Father Flynn kindly ask that nice hairdresser to come again fairly soon? She needed to look well when she did this one last thing.

Father Flynn paced his small apartment with the soccer posters nailed to the wall to cover the damp patches. Maybe he would ask Stella did she know anywhere for him to live. It might be tactless since he *was* going to live and she wasn't, but it would be better than looking into her ravaged face and haunted eyes and trying to make sense of it all.

In St. Jarlath's Crescent, Josie and Charles Lynch whispered long and happily into the night. Imagine—this time last night they hadn't even met Emily and now their lives had been turned right around. They had a dog, they had a lodger and, for the first time in months, Noel had sat and talked to them. They had begun a campaign to have St. Jarlath recognized properly.

Things were better on every front.

And, amazingly, things continued well on every front.

A message came to the hotel from a psychiatric hospital saying that Caesar's mother, Mrs. Monty, was unavoidably detained there and that she hoped Caesar was being adequately looked after. The hotel manager, bewildered by this, was relieved to know that the matter was all in hand and somewhat embarrassed to learn that the rescuer had been that old porter he had just made redundant. Charles Lynch seemed to bear him no ill will but let slip the fact that he was looking forward to some kind of retirement ceremony. The manager made a note to remind himself or someone to organize something for the fellow.

At the biscuit factory they were surprised to hear that Josie was going to work part-time and raise money for a statue to St. Jarlath. Most of the others who worked with her were desperate to hold on to their jobs at any cost.

"We'll have to give you a great sendoff when you finally retire, Josie," one of the women said.

"I'd really prefer a contribution to the St. Jarlath's statue fund," Josie said. And there was a silence not normally known in the biscuit factory.

Noel Lynch found the days endless in Hall's Builders' Merchants. The mornings were hard to endure without any alcohol. The nice fuzzy afternoons were gone and replaced now by hours of mind-numbing checking of delivery dockets against sales slips. His only pleasure was leaving a glass of mineral water on his desk and watching from the distance as Mr. Hall either smelled it or tasted it.

Noel could see only too well that his job could easily be done by a not-very-bright twelve-year-old. It was hard to know how the company had survived as long as it had. But in spite of everything he stuck to it, and before too long he was able to chalk up a full week without alcohol.

Matters were much helped by Emily's presence at Number 23. Every evening there was a well-cooked meal served at seven o'clock and, with no long evenings to spend in Casey's bar, Noel found himself sitting at the kitchen table eating with his parents and cousin.

They fell into an easy routine: Josie set the table and prepared the vegetables, Charles built up the fire and helped Noel to wash up. Emily had even managed to put off the Rosary on the grounds that they all needed this joint time to plan their various crusades, such as what strategy they should use to get the fund-raising started for St. Jarlath's statue and how Emily could go out and earn a living for herself and where they would find dogs for Charles to walk and if Noel should do night classes in business or accountancy in order to advance himself at Hall's.

Emily had, in one week, managed to get more information out of Noel about the nature of his work than his parents had learned in years. She had even been able to collect brochures, which she went over with Noel. This course looked good, but rather too general; the other looked more specific, but might not be relevant to his work at Hall's. Little by little, she had learned of the mundane clerical officer–type work Noel did all day—the matching of invoices, paying of suppliers and gathering of expenditure data from departments at the end of the month. She discovered that there were young fellows in the company who had "qualifications," who had a degree or a diploma, and they climbed up what passed for a corporate ladder in the old-fashioned builders' providers store that was Hall's.

Emily spent no time regretting time wasted in the past or wrong decisions or Noel's wish to leave his school and not continue with education. When they were alone one night, she said to him that the whole business of beating a dependency on alcohol was often a question of having adequate support.

"Did I ever tell you that I was battling against alcohol?" Noel asked her.

"You don't need to, Noel. I'm the daughter of an alcoholic. I know the territory. Your uncle Martin thought he could do it on his own. We lived through that one."

"Maybe he didn't choose AA. Maybe he wasn't a social man. He could have been a bit like me and didn't want a lot of other people knowing his business," Noel said in his late uncle's defense.

"He wasn't nearly as good a man as you are, Noel. He had a very closed mind."

"Oh, I think I have a closed mind too."

"No, you don't. You'll get help if you need it. I know you will."

"It's just I don't go along with this thing 'I'm Noel. I'm an alcoholic' and then they all say, 'Ho, Noel' and I'm meant to feel better."

"People have felt better for it," Emily said mildly. "They have a great success rate."

"It's all a matter of 'me and my illness'; it's making it so dramatic for them all, as if they are heroes of some kind of thing that's working itself out onstage."

Emily shrugged. "So AA doesn't do it for you. Fine. One day you might need them. They will still be there, that's for sure. Now let's look at these courses. I know what CPA means, but what are ACA and ACCA? Tell me the difference between them and what they mean."

And Noel could feel his shoulders relaxing. She wasn't going to nag him. That was the main thing. She had moved on and was asking his advice on other matters. Where could she get timber to make window boxes? Would his father be able to make them? Where might Emily get some regular paid work? She could run an office easily. Would it be a good idea to get a washing machine for the household, as they were all going to be so busy raising money for St. Jarlath's statue?

"Emily, you don't think that will really happen—the statue business, do you?"

"I was never more sure of anything in my life," Emily said.

Katie Finglas went to the hospital again. Stella Dixon looked worse than before: her face thin, her arms bony and her round stomach more noticeable.

"This has got to be a really good hairdo, Katie," Stella said, as she inhaled the cigarette down to her toes. As usual, the other patients kept watch in case a nurse or hospital official should come by and catch Stella in the act.

"Have you set your eye on someone?" Katie asked. She wished that she could take a group of her more difficult clients into this ward so they could see the skin-and-bones woman who knew nothing ahead of her except the certainty that she would die shortly after they did the cesarean section to remove her baby. It made their problems so trivial in comparison.

Stella considered the question. "It's a bit late for me to have my eye on anyone at this stage," she said. "But I *am* asking someone to do me a favor, so I have to look normal, you know, not mad or anything. That's why I thought a more settled type of hairstyle would be good."

"Right, we'll make you look settled," Katie said, taking out the plastic tray that she would put over the hand basin to wash Stella's thin, frail-looking head with its pre-Raphaelite mass of red curly hair. She had styled it already, but the curls kept coming back as if they had decided not to take any notice of the diagnosis that the rest of her body was having to cope with.

"What kind of a favor is it?" she asked, just to keep the conversation going.

"It's the biggest thing you could ever ask anyone to do," Stella said.

Katie looked at her sharply. The tone had changed and suddenly the fire and life had gone out of the girl who had entertained the ward and made people smuggle her in packets of cigarettes and do sentry duty so that she would not be discovered.

"Call for you, Noel," Mr. Hall said. Nobody ever telephoned Noel at work. The few calls he got came in through his cell phone. He went to Mr. Hall's office nervously. This was a time he would normally have had a drink; it was the low time of morning and he always liked a drink to help him cope with an unexpected event.

"Noel? Do you remember me, Stella Dixon? We met at the line dancing night last year."

"I do, indeed," he said, pleased. A lively redhead who could match him drink for drink. She had been good fun. Not someone he would want to meet now, though. Too interested in the gargle for him to meet up with her these days. "Yes, I remember you well," he added.

"We sort of drifted away from each other back then," she said.

It had been a while back. Nearly a year. Or was it six months? It was so hard to remember everything.

"That's right," Noel said evasively. Almost every friendship he had sort of drifted away, so there was nothing new about this.

"I need to see you, Noel," she said.

"I'm afraid I don't go out too much these days, Stella," he began. "Not into the old line dancing, I'm afraid."

"Me neither. I'm in the oncology ward of St. Brigid's, so in fact I don't go out at all."

He focused on trying to remember her: feisty, jokey, always playing it for a laugh. This was shocking news indeed.

"So would you like me to come and see you sometime? Is that it?"

"Please, Noel, today. At seven."

"Today . . . ?"

"I wouldn't ask unless it was important."

He saw Mr. Hall hovering. He must not be seen to dither. "See you then, Stella," he said, and wondered what on earth she wanted to see him about. But, even more urgently, he wondered how he could approach a cancer ward to visit a woman he barely remembered. *And* approach her without a drink.

It was more than any man could bear.

The corridors of St. Brigid's were crowded with visitors at seven o'clock. Noel threaded his way among them. He saw Declan Carroll, who lived up the road from him, walking ahead of him and ran to catch him up.

"Do you know where the female oncology ward is, Declan?"

"This lift over here will take you to the wing. Second floor." Declan didn't ask who Noel was visiting or why.

"I didn't know there were so many sick people," Noel said, looking at the crowds.

"Still, there's lots that can be done for them these times compared to when our parents were young." Declan was always one for the positive view.

"I suppose that's the way to look at it, all right," Noel agreed. He seemed a bit down, but then Noel was never a barrel of laughs.

"Right, Noel. Maybe I'll see you for a pint later? In Casey's, on our way home?"

"No. As a matter of fact, I don't drink anymore," Noel said in a tight little voice.

"Good man, yourself."

"And, anyway, I was actually barred from Casey's."

"Oh, well, to hell with them then. Big barn of a place anyway." Declan was being supportive, but he had a lot on his mind. Their first baby was due in the next several weeks and Fiona was up to high doh over everything. Plus his mother had knitted enough tiny garments for a multiple birth even though they knew they were going to have only one baby.

He could have done with a nice, undemanding pint

with Noel. But that was obviously not on the cards now.
He sighed and went purposefully towards a patient who
was busy making plans to come out of hospital soon and
wanted Declan to try to hurry up the process. The man's
diagnosis said that he would never leave the hospital,
sooner or later, and would die there within weeks. It was
hard to rearrange your face to see something optimistic in
this, but somehow Declan managed it.

It went with the territory.

There were six women in the ward. None of them had
great, tumbling red curly hair.

One very thin woman in the corner bed was waving at
him.

"Noel, Noel, it's Stella! Don't tell me I've changed *that*
much!"

He was dismayed. She was skin and bone. She had
clearly made a huge effort: her hair was freshly washed
and blow-dried, she had a trace of lipstick on and she wore
a white Victorian nightdress with a high neck and cuffs.
He remembered her smile, but that was all.

"Stella. Good to see you," he mumbled.

She swung her thin legs out of the bed and gestured
for him to pull the curtains around them.

"Any ciggies?" she whispered hopefully.

"In *here*, Stella?" He was shocked.

"Particularly in here. Well, you obviously didn't bring
me any, so reach me my sponge bag there. The other girls
will keep watch."

He looked on, horrified, as she pulled a cigarette from

behind her toothpaste, lit it expertly and made a temporary ashtray out of an old envelope.

"How have you been?" he asked and instantly wished he hadn't. Of course she hadn't been well—otherwise why was she wasting away in front of his eyes in a cancer ward? "I mean, how are things?" he asked, even more foolishly.

"Things have been better, Noel, to be honest."

He tried to imagine what Emily might say in the circumstances. She had a habit of asking questions that required you to think.

"What's the very worst thing about it all, Stella?"

She paused to think, as he had known she would.

"I think the very worst thing is that you won't believe me," she said.

"Try me," he said.

She stood up and paced the tiny cubicle. It was then he realized that she was pregnant. Very pregnant. And at exactly that moment she spoke to him.

"I was hoping not to have to bother you about this, Noel, but you're the father. This is your baby."

"Ah, no, Stella, this is a mistake. This didn't happen."

"I know I'm not *very* memorable, but you must remember that weekend."

"We were wasted that weekend, both of us."

"Not too drunk to create a new life, apparently."

"I swear it can't be me. Honestly, Stella, if it were, I would accept . . . I wouldn't run away or anything . . . but . . . but . . ."

"But what, exactly?"

"There must have been lots of other people."

"Thanks a lot for that, Noel."

"You know what I mean. An attractive woman like you must have had lots of partners."

"I'm the one who knows. Do you honestly think I would pick *you* out of a list of candidates? That I'd phone you, a drunk in that mausoleum where you work, in some useless job? You live with your parents, for God's sake! Why would I ask *you*, of all people, to be the father of my child if it wasn't true?"

"Well, as you said yourself, thanks a lot for that." He looked hurt.

"So you asked me what would be the worst thing. I told you and now the worst *has* happened. You don't believe me." She had a defeated look.

"It's a fantasy. It didn't happen. I'd remember. I haven't slept with that many women in my life, and what good would I be to you anyway? I am, as you say, a useless drunk with a non-job in Hall's, living with my mother and father. I'd be no support to you. You'll be able to bring this child up fine, give him some guts, fight his battles for him, more than I would ever do. Do it yourself, Stella, and if you think I should make some contribution, and I don't want you to be short, I could give you something— not admitting anything—just to help you out."

Her eyes blazed at him.

"You are such a fool, Noel Lynch. Such a stupid fool. I won't bloody well be here to bring her up. I'm going to die in three or four weeks' time. I won't survive the operation. And the baby is not a boy, by the way, she's a girl, she's a daughter, her name is Frankie. That's what she's going to be called: Frances Stella."

"This is only a fantasy, Stella. This illness has made you very unhinged."

"Ask any of them in the ward. Ask any of the nurses. Wake up to the real world, Noel. This is happening. We have to do something about it."

"I can't raise a child, Stella. You've already listed all the things against it. Whatever chance she's going to have, it can't be with me."

"You're going to *have* to," Stella said. "Otherwise she'll have to go into care. And I'm not having that."

"But that would be the very best for her. There are families out there who are dying to have children of their own . . . ," he began, blustering slightly.

"Yes, and some other families, like the ones I met when I was in care, where the fathers and the uncles love to have a little plaything in the house. I've been through it all and Frankie's not going to have to cope with it just because she will have no mother."

"What are you asking me to do?"

"To mind your daughter, to give her a home and a secure childhood, to tell her that her mother wasn't all that bad. Fight her battles. The usual things."

"I can't do it." He stood up from his chair.

"There's so much to discuss . . . ," Stella began.

"It's not going to happen. I'm so sorry. And I'm really sorry to know how bad your illness is, but I think you're painting too black a picture. Cancer can be cured these days. Truly it can, Stella."

"Good-bye, Noel," she said.

No matter how often he said her name she would not turn towards him.

He walked to the door and looked around once more. She seemed to have shriveled even further. She looked tiny as she sat there on her bed. He fancied that the other women in the ward had heard most of their conversation. They looked at him with hostility.

On the bus home Noel realized that there was no way he could force himself to sit at the kitchen table eating a supper that Emily would have kept warm for him. Tonight was not a time to sit and talk about saints and statues and fund-raising and accountancy and business management classes. Tonight was a night to have three pints in some pub and forget everything. He headed for the pub where Paddy Carroll, Declan's father, took his huge Labrador dog every night. With any luck, at this time of night Noel might get away without being spotted.

The beer felt terrific. Like an old friend.

He had lowered four pints before he realized it.

Noel had hoped that he might have lost the taste for it, but that hadn't happened. He just felt a great sense of irritation and annoyance with himself that he had denied himself this familiar and friendly relaxation. Already he was feeling better. His hand had stopped shaking, his heart wasn't pounding as it had been.

He *must* stay clear and focused.

He would have to go back to St. Jarlath's Crescent and take up some semblance of ordinary life. Emily would, of course, see through him at once, but he could tell her later. Much later. No need to announce everything to everyone all at once. Or maybe no need to announce anything at all. It was, after all, some terrible mistake. Noel would *know* if he had fathered a child with that girl.

He would *know* it.

It had to have come from her mind having been af-

fected by this cancer. Anybody normal would not have se-
lected Noel, of all people, as the father of their child. Poor
Stella was far from normal and he pitied her, but this was
ludicrous.

It could not be his child.

He waved away the suggestion of a fifth pint and
moved purposefully towards the door.

He didn't see Declan Carroll having a drink with his
father and looking curiously at the man who had claimed
to have given up alcohol but who had just downed four
pints of beer at racing speed.

Declan sighed.

Whatever Noel had heard at the hospital, whoever he
had visited, it had not made him happy.

Paddy Carroll patted his son's hand.

"In a matter of weeks it will all be behind you. You'll
have a great little son and the waiting bit will be forgotten."

"Yes, Dad. Tell me what it was like when Mam was expecting me."

"I don't know how I survived it," Declan's father said,
and told the old, familiar story again from the point of
view of the father of the baby.

The mother's role in the birth had been merely minimal, apparently.

Noel had only opened his mouth when Emily looked up
at him sharply. It was as if she had called the meeting to
order.

"We're all tired now, it's late. Not a good time to discuss the running of a thrift shop."

"A what?" Noel shook his head as if that would some-how settle the collection of thoughts and ideas that were nestling in it. His parents looked disappointed. They were being carried along by the enthusiasm of Emily's planning and they were sorry to see it being cut short.

But Emily was adamant. She had the whole household ready for bed in no time.

"Noel, I saved you some Italian meatballs."

"They were just delicious," Josie said. "Emily can turn her hand to anything."

"I don't think I really want anything. I stopped on the way home, you see . . . ," Noel began.

"I did see," Emily said, "but these are good for you, Noel. Go on into your room and I'll bring a tray in to you in five minutes."

There was no escape.

He sat there waiting for her and the storm that would follow. Oddly there was no storm. She never mentioned the fact that he had taken up drinking again. And Emily had been right—he *did* feel better when he had something to eat. She was clearing up and about to go when she asked sympathetically if it had been a bad day.

"The worst ever," he said.

"Mr. Hall?"

"No, he was fine. Just something mad and upsetting happened later on in the day. That's why I went back to the pints."

"And did that help?" She seemed genuinely interested.

"At first it did a bit. It's not working now and I'm just annoyed with myself for staying off it for all those days and nights and now running straight back when I get a bit of an upset."

"Did you sort out the upset?" She was completely non-judgmental. She looked at him, inviting him to share whatever it was, but she would have left if there was no information to hear.

"Please sit down, Emily," Noel begged, and he told the whole story, haltingly and with a lot of repetition. Mainly he said that he could not have fathered a child without remembering it.

"I have so little sex, Emily, that I'm not likely to forget the little bit I *do* have."

She was very still as she sat and listened to him. Her face changed from time to time. It was concerned and distressed when she heard how gaunt and painful Stella's face had become. She inclined her head to show sympathy as Noel told how Stella had said that if she were to choose a father from anyone in the world he would be the very last choice—a drunk who was a loser and still lived with his parents.

It was only when Noel came to the end of his tale, when he got to the part where he had walked away from Stella, the hospital and the problem, that Emily's face became confused.

"Why did you do that?" she asked.

"Well, what else could I do?" Noel was surprised. "It has nothing to do with *me.* There's no point in my being there—it's adding to the whole charade. The girl's head is unhinged."

"You walked out and left her there?"

"I *had* to, Emily. You know what a tightrope I'm walking. Things are quite bad enough already without inviting the Lord knows what kind of fantasies in on top of me."

"You say that things are bad enough for you, Noel? Right?"

"Well, they *are* bad." He sounded defensive.

"Like you have terminal cancer?" she asked him. "Like you were abused when you were in foster care? Like you are going to be dead a month from now, before you see the only child you will ever have? No, indeed, Noel, none of these things has happened to you, yet you just said things are very bad for *you.*"

He was stricken.

"That's all you think. You think how things are for *you*, Noel. Shame on you," she said, her face full of scorn. This was the nearest he had come to having a best friend and now she was turning against him.

"Emily, please sit down. You asked me what was wrong, so I told you."

"Yes, you did, Noel." She made no movement to sit down.

"So? Won't you stay and discuss it?"

"No. Why should I join in this charade, as you call it? Don't make faces at me, Noel. These are your words. Why should I not think of the perilous tightrope that *I* am walking in my life? I'm sorry, but everyone in all this is becoming . . . what did you call it— 'unhinged in the head'? Why should I let people surround me with their fantasies?" She was almost at the door.

"But they're not fantasies, Emily. It's what happened."

"That's right. They're not fantasies. It's what actually happened. But hey, what the hell? It's got nothing to do with *you*, Noel. Good night. I'm sorry, but that is all I feel capable of saying." And she was gone.

He had thought that this day just couldn't get any

worse. That's why he had told her. In a few short hours two women had turned away from him in disgust.

And somehow it had made the day worse than ever.

Betsy,

There is a drama unfolding here which we would have considered compelling when we were kids and went to the movies on Saturday afternoons. But oddly it's too sad to talk about just now. I will tell you how it turns out.

OF COURSE you should go out with Eric! I told you a hundred times he is not interested in me. He just said that as a devious way of getting to know you better.

I know! I know! But the longer I live, the more crazy I think everyone is.

Love,
Emily

Katie Finglas was locking up the hair salon. It had been a long day and she was tired. It was Garry's night out. Once a week he and a group of the lads kicked a ball around a pitch and planned strategy for the year.

Katie would have loved to have gone home and had a long bath while he made them some French onion soup. Then they could have sat by the fire and talked about the big decision they had to make. People thought that Katie and Garry had plenty of time to talk to each other all day since they worked together in the salon. Little did people know how rarely they had a chance to snatch a five-minute coffee together. And then there were always people within earshot and it was impossible for Katie and Garry to talk about their plans.

So she was looking forward to a proper discussion. One where they would put all the arguments on one side and then the other. They would list the reasons why they *must* lease the flat over their salon: they needed to expand, they had no storage place, they had no proper staff areas, they would be able to install little manicure stations and could fit in tables and mirrors for at least six more customers, how it would mean that they would be able to compete on equal ground with the successful health and beauty salons in Dublin.

It was too much to take on. Too big and spread out so they would use only half the space upstairs. And just suppose they *did* do it— then they would have to do up some of the rooms and sublet them in order to try to get a return on their money. And just suppose that they did rent them—what kind of people would they get? Suppose they turned out to be the tenants from hell, making a lot of noise and leaving litter, making nonsense of all Katie and Garry's hard work?

Katie sighed as she set the alarm outside her premises. Across the street she saw Father Flynn, that cheerful priest from the center down the road, the one who had introduced her to poor Stella Dixon up in St. Brigid's.

Stella had said that she didn't normally have a lot to say for the clergy, but Brian Flynn was a very decent fellow and didn't go on about sin and redemption and things.

He did what a priest should do—he brought her cigarettes and did little jobs for people.

Katie called out to him and was delighted when he suggested they go for a coffee in a small Italian place on the corner.

Father Flynn spoke briefly and testily about his friend the priest who had fallen down the Spanish Steps and was still malingering in Rome. He also spoke about his greedy landlord, who had evicted him, and how it was impossible for a man of simple lifestyle, like himself, to discover any kind of budget accommodation.

"I'm such an undemanding person, really," Brian Flynn said, full of self-pity. "If people only *knew* how little I want in terms of style or comfort."

Katie looked at him thoughtfully across her cappuccino. "Exactly *how* undemanding?" she asked. She suddenly saw a solution to everything.

Father Flynn would be the perfect tenant.

"Finish up your coffee there and come with me," she said, draining her cup and heading back to the salon that she had just locked up.

By the end of the month, he had moved into his new home. His friend Johnny had put up a few bookshelves for him and Katie's husband had found him a secondhand fridge where he could keep his milk, butter and the odd can of beer. His only duty was to make sure that he locked the salon properly and put on the burglar alarm whenever he left the premises after hours. It suited everyone perfectly.

Chapter Three

Noel couldn't believe that Emily, who had recently been part of his every waking moment at St. Jarlath's Crescent, now seemed to have disappeared completely.

"Where is she?" he asked his mother on the morning after Emily had left his room in scorn and disgust. "It's not like Emily to miss breakfast."

"Oh, she's gone to find a premises for the charity shop," Josie Lynch replied, confident that Emily would have one before the day was out. There was nothing that woman couldn't do.

"She took Caesar with her. She's going to make inquiries for me about dog-walking opportunities as well." Charles was pleased too. "She said she'd have more credibility if she was accompanied by a dog herself when she went looking for business."

"She'll be back after lunch, Noel, if you wanted her for anything," Josie said. "She's going to the market for our supper later. What *did* we do before she came to stay?"

Noel hadn't known Emily to be out of the house for

two meals in one day. Not since she had arrived. There was only one explanation. She was avoiding him.

He did try to stay off drink when he was at work, but the sharp pain of Stella's situation and Emily's shocked revulsion kept coming back to him as the day crawled along. When it came to midafternoon he could bear it no more and made an excuse to go out and get some more stationery supplies. He bought a half-bottle of vodka and decanted it into a bottle that already had a fizzy orange drink in it. As he drank mug after mug of it he felt the strength coming back to him and the pain receding. The familiar blur came down like a thick, comforting shawl.

Noel now felt able to face the afternoon again; but what didn't go away was the feeling that he was a loser who had let down three people: the dying Stella, his strong cousin Emily and an unborn child called Frankie, who could not possibly be his daughter.

But he should have handled it very differently.

Emily was in the Laundromat with Molly Carroll. She had brought towels for a service wash but actually she was there on a mission. On a previous visit she had noticed two large sheds that were not in use. They might form the basis of the new thrift shop that would help raise money for the statue. She had to take it one step at a time: find out who actually owned the premises first.

It had turned out to be much simpler than she had feared. Molly and Paddy Carroll had bought the sheds some years back when the owner had had some pressing gambling debts and was anxious for a quick sale. They had never needed the unused part of the premises but had been loath to sell it in case someone built a noisy take-away food outlet.

Molly thought that a thrift shop would be perfect. She and Emily toured the place and decided to put shelves here and clothes rails there. They would have a second-hand book section and Emily said she could grow a few plants from seed and sell them too. Together they made a list of people to approach, those who might give a few hours every week to working in the charity shop.

Molly knew a man who had the unlikely name of Dingo. He was a decent soul and would help them with his van, collecting things or stacking them. Emily had met several women who said they would be happy to help, but were a little anxious in case they wouldn't be able to manage the till properly. Emily said she would check what permits they might need and if they had to apply for a change of premises; she promised she would deliver a fully planted window box to the Laundromat the following week to celebrate the whole deal. Molly said her husband Paddy's friend had a lot of Associates in the pub who could do the refurbishments.

They decided to call the place St. Jarlath's Thrift Shop, and Molly said it would be great to be partly in charge because if a nice jacket came in she could get first crack at it. Emily left with the air of someone who had completed a difficult and complicated assignment.

She stopped at a fishmonger and bought some smoked cod. Charles and Josie had not been great fish lovers or salad eaters when she arrived but, little by little, she was changing their ways. It was a pity that she couldn't do anything to direct Noel, but the boy had built a shield about himself that even she couldn't penetrate.

"Is there anything I can get you, Stella?" Father Flynn had brought her the usual pack of cigarettes.

"Not much, Brian, but thanks all the same." She looked very down, not her usual gutsy self.

He hesitated asking any more. The future was bleak for her. What helpful words could he find?

"Any visitors?" he asked.

Stella's eyes were dull. "No visitors to speak of," she said, and as he looked at her with sympathy and with the realization he had no comfort to give, he saw for the first time a tear in her eye.

"I'm no good with words, Stella," he began.

"You're fine with words, Brian, and with getting me fags and a hairdresser—for all the bloody use it was."

"Your hair looks very nice," he said hopelessly.

"Not nice enough to make that no-hoper believe me."

"Believe you about what, exactly?" Brian was confused.

"That he was the father of my child. He said he couldn't remember having sex with me. That was nice, wasn't it?"

"Ah, God, Stella, I'm so sorry." There was real compassion in his face.

"It was probably my own fault. I told him all wrong. He's a bit drinky, as I was indeed myself, and he couldn't face it. He ran out of here. *Ran*, I tell you."

"Maybe he'll come back when he sees sense."

"He won't—he literally doesn't remember. He's not making it up." She sounded resigned, defeated.

"Could you get a DNA test to prove he's the father?"

"No. I thought about it, but if he doesn't remember

being there at her conception, there's no point in asking him to be a father to her. No, she'll have to take her chances like the rest of us."

"Would it help if I had a word with him?" Brian Flynn felt that he should offer anyway.

"No, Brian, thanks, but no. If he ran when I told him, he would go into orbit if I sent a priest after him." For a moment, there was a flash of the old Stella.

After supper that night in St. Jarlath's Crescent Emily was busy explaining her day's negotiations with Molly Carroll. Charles and Josie were drinking in every word.

Charles had news too. There would be a good-bye celebration for him in a few weeks' time at the hotel— finger food, wine and beer, and a presentation. And would you believe who wanted to come to it, but Mrs. Monty—who was really Lady something. The woman who wore a fur coat, a big hat and pearls and nothing else: the hotel manager was very nervous about letting her in.

Mrs. Monty was now going into a residential home where, sadly, Caesar would not be welcome; and since Charles had agreed to take him, she wanted to thank the kind employee who had given the little spaniel such a good home. She was also going to make a donation to a charity of his choice. It would be a wonderful start to the fund-raising.

Charles was allowed to bring a small number of family and friends. As well as Josie, Emily and Noel, he thought he would invite Paddy and Molly Carroll and the Scarlets, Muttie and Lizzie.

"Will Noel be able to come, do you think?" Emily's voice was slightly tart.

"Well, here he comes now—we can ask him!" Josie cried out happily.

Noel listened carefully, arranging his face in various receptive expressions as the excitement of the good-bye celebrations was revealed.

Emily knew the technique: she recognized it from her father. It was a matter of saying as little as possible and therefore cutting down on the possibility of being discovered to be drunk.

Eventually he had to speak. Slowly and carefully he said that he would be privileged to be part of the ceremony.

"It would be great to be there when they are honoring you," he said to his father.

Emily bit her lip. At least he had been able to respond adequately. He had managed not to rain on his father's parade.

"There's some lamb stew left, Noel. I'll heat it and bring it up to you," she said, giving him permission to leave before his mask of sobriety collapsed.

"Thank you, Emily, I'd love that," he said and fled to his room after shooting a grateful look in her direction.

When she went in with the tray, he was sitting in his chair with tears streaming down his face.

"Oh, Lord, Noel, what is it?" she asked, alarmed.

"I'm utterly *useless,* Emily. I've let everyone down. What's the use of my going on, waking in the morning and going to bed at night? What good does it serve?"

"Have your supper, Noel. I brought you a pot of coffee as well. We have to talk."

"I thought you didn't talk to me anymore," he said with a great sniff and wiping his eyes.

"I thought that *you* were avoiding *me*," she said.

"I didn't want to come home and have you being cold and distant. I don't have any friends, Emily. I have no one at all to turn to. . . ." His voice sounded lost and frightened.

"Eat your supper, Noel. I'll be here," she said. And she was there while he told her how despairing he was and what a hopeless father he would be to any child.

She listened and then said simply, "I hear all that and you may well be right. But then again it might be the making of you, *and* Frankie. She might make you into the kind of person you want to be."

"They'd never let me keep her . . . the social welfare people . . ."

"You'll need to show them what you're made of."

"It's better they don't know," Noel said.

"Please, Noel, no self-pity. Think—think what you should do next. A lot of lives will be affected by it."

"I couldn't bring the child here," he said.

"It was time for you to move on anyway." Emily was as calm as if they were discussing what to have for lunch tomorrow, rather than Noel's future.

Next morning, Stella looked up from the magazine she was reading as a shadow fell on her bed. It was Noel, carrying a small bunch of flowers.

"Well, hello!" she said. "How did you get in? It isn't visiting time."

"Am I interrupting you?" he asked.

"Yes, I'm reading about how to put more zing back into my marriage, as if I knew what either zing or marriage was!"

"I came here to ask you to marry me," he said.

"Oh, Christ, Noel, don't be such an eejit. Why would I marry you? I'll be dead in a few weeks' time!"

"You wouldn't say the baby was mine if it wasn't. I would be honored to try to bring her up."

"Listen, marriage was never part of it." Stella was at a complete loss.

"I thought that's what you wanted!" He was perplexed now.

"No. I wanted you to look after her, to be a dad for her, to keep her out of the lottery of the care system."

"So will we get married, then?"

"No, Noel, of course we won't, but if you *do* want to talk about looking after her, tell me why and how."

"I'm going to change, Stella."

"Right."

"No, I am. I was up all night planning it. I'm going to go to AA today, admit I have a drink problem, and then I'm going to enroll to do a business course at a college and then I'm going to find a flat where I can bring up the baby."

"This is all so sudden. So spur-of-the-moment. Why aren't you at work today anyway?"

"My cousin Emily has gone to Hall's to say I have a personal crisis today and that I will make up the time next week by going in one hour earlier and staying one hour later every day."

"Does Emily know about all this?"

"Yes. I had to tell someone. She was very cross with me for walking out on you."

"You didn't walk, Noel. You ran."

"I am so sorry. Believe me. I *am* sorry."

"So what has changed?" She wasn't hostile, just interested.

"I want to amount to something. To do something for someone before I die. I'll be thirty soon. I've done nothing except dream and wish and drink. I want to change that."

She listened in silence.

"So tell me what you'd like if you don't want us to get married?"

"I don't know, Noel. I'd like things to have been different."

"So do most people walking around. They all wish things had been different," he said sadly.

"Then I'd like you to meet Moira Tierney, my social worker, tomorrow evening. She's coming in to discuss what she calls 'the future' with me. A fairly short discussion."

"Could I bring Emily in? She said she'd like to come and talk to you anyway."

"But is she going to be a nanny figure? Always there hovering, making all the decisions?"

"No, she'll be going back to America soon, I think, but she *has* made me see things more clearly."

"Bring her in, then. Is she dishy? Could you marry *her,* maybe?" Stella was mischievous again.

"No! She's as old as the hills. Well, fifty or forty-five or something, anyway."

"Bring her in, then," Stella said, "and she's going to have to talk well to deal with Moira."

He leaned over and put the flowers in a glass.

"Noel?"

"Yes?"

"Thanks, anyway, about the marriage proposal and all. It wasn't what I had in mind but it was decent of you."

"You might still change your mind," he said.

"I have a tame priest in here. A very nice fellow. He could do it if we were pushed, but actually I'd prefer not to."

"Whatever you think," he said, and touched her gently on the shoulder.

"Before you go, one thing . . . how *did* you get in outside visiting hours?"

"I asked Declan Carroll. He lives on my road. I said I needed a favor, so he made a phone call."

"He and his wife are having a baby at the same time as I am," Stella said. "I always thought the children might be friends."

"Well, they might easily be friends," Noel said.

When he looked around from the door he saw she was lying back in her bed, but she was smiling and seemed more relaxed than before.

He set out then to face what was going to be the most challenging day of his life.

It was hard to go into the building where the lunchtime AA meeting was taking place. Noel stood for ten minutes in the corridor watching men and women of every type walking down to the door at the end.

Eventually he could put it off no longer and followed them in.

It was still very unreal to him but, as he had said to

Emily, he had to get his head around the fact that he was a father and an alcoholic.

He had faced the first and he could still recall the glow in Stella's face this morning. *She* hadn't thought he was a loser and a hopeless father for her baby.

Now he had to face the drinking.

There were about thirty people in the room. A man sat at a desk near the door. He had a tired, lined face and sandy hair. He didn't look like a person who was a heavy drinker. Maybe he was just part of the staff.

"I would actually like to join," Noel said to him, hearing, as he spoke, his own voice echoing in his ears.

"And your name?" the man asked.

"Noel Lynch."

"Right, Noel. Who referred you here?"

"I'm sorry? Referred?"

"I mean, are you coming here because of a treatment center?"

"Oh, heavens no. I haven't been having any treatment or anything. I just drink too much and I want to cut it down."

"We try to encourage each other to cut it out completely. Are you aware of that?"

"Yes, if that were possible, I would be happy to try."

"My name is Malachy. Come on in," the man said. "We're about to begin."

Later in the day Noel had to do his third confrontation.

Emily had made an appointment for him with a college admissions supervisor. He was going to sign up for a business diploma, which included marketing and finance, sales and advertising. The fees, which would have been well beyond him, were going to be paid by Emily. She said it was an interest-free loan. He would repay it when he could.

She had assured him that this was exactly what she wanted to do with her savings. She saw it as an investment. One day when he was a rich, successful man he would always remember her with gratitude and look after her in her old age.

The admissions supervisor confirmed that the fees had been paid and that the lectures would start the following week. Apart from the lectures, Noel would be expected to study on his own for at least twelve hours a week.

"Are you married?" the supervisor asked.

"No, indeed," and then almost as an afterthought Noel said, "but I'll be having a baby in a couple of weeks."

"Congratulations, but you had better get a good bit of the groundwork in before the child arrives," said the admissions supervisor, a man who seemed to know what he was talking about.

That evening at supper Josie was eager to discuss the thrift shop and its possible opening date. She was excited and alive.

Charles was in high good form too. He wasn't going to have to give Caesar back to Mrs. Monty, he was going to have this big celebration at the hotel, he had more plans for dog walking and dog exercising and he had been to a local kennel.

But before the conversation could go down either route—thrift shop or dog walking—Emily spoke firmly.

"Noel has something important to talk to us about, perhaps before we make any more plans."

Noel looked around him, trapped.

He had known that this was coming. Emily said they could not live in a shadowy world of lies and deception.

Still, he had to tell his parents that they were about to become grandparents, there was no marriage included in the plans and he would be moving into a place of his own.

It was not news he was going to find easy to break. Emily had suggested that he might pause before using the same opportunity to tell them that he was joining Alcoholics Anonymous and that he was registering as a student at the college.

She wondered whether it might not be too much for them.

But when he began his tale, sparing nothing but telling it all as it had unfolded, he felt it was easier and more fair to tell them everything.

He went through it as if he were talking about someone else, and he never once caught their eye as the story went on.

First he told of the message from the hospital, his two meetings with Stella, and her news—which he had refused to believe at first but realized must be true; then he told of his intention to meet the social worker and plan for the future of the baby girl, whose birth would also involve her mother's death.

He told them how he had tried to give up drinking on his own and had not succeeded, that he now had a sponsor in AA called Malachy and would attend a meeting every day.

He told them that his job in Hall's had been depressing and that he was constantly passed over while younger and less experienced staff were appreciated because they had diplomas or degrees.

At this point he realized his parents had been very silent, so he raised his eyes to look at them.

Their faces were frozen with horror at the story he was telling.

Everything they had feared might happen in a godless world *had* happened.

Their son had enjoyed sex outside marriage and a child had resulted and he was admitting a dependency on alcohol even to the point of getting help from Alcoholics Anonymous!

But he would not be put off. He struggled on with the explanations and his plans to get out of the situations he had brought on himself.

He accepted that it was all his own fault.

He blamed no outside circumstances.

"I feel ashamed telling you all this, Mam and Da. You have lived such good lives. You wouldn't even begin to understand, but I got myself into this and I'm going to get myself out of it."

They were still silent so he dared to look at them again.

To his amazement they both had some sympathy in their faces.

His mother's eyes were full of tears, but there were no recriminations. No mention of sex before marriage, only concern.

"Why did you never tell us this, son?" His father's voice was full of emotion.

"What could you have said? That I was a fool to have left school so early? Or that I should put up with it. You were happy at work, Da. You were respected. That's not the way it is at Hall's."

"And the baby?" Josie said. "You had no idea this Stella was expecting your child?"

"None in the wide world, Ma," Noel said. And there was something so bleak and honest in his tone that everyone believed him.

"But the drink thing, Noel . . . are you sure that it's bad enough for you to be going to the AA?"

"It is, Da, believe me."

"I never noticed you drunk. Not once. And I'm well used to dealing with drunk people up at the hotel," his father said, shaking his head.

"That's because you're normal, Da. You don't expect people to come back from work half-cut, having spent two hours in Casey's."

"That man has a lot to answer for." Charles shook his head with disapproval for Old Man Casey.

"He didn't exactly open my mouth and force it down," Noel said.

Emily spoke for the first time.

"So we are up to speed on Noel's plans now. It's going to be up to us to give him all the support we can."

"You *knew* all this?" Josie Lynch was shocked and not best pleased.

"I only knew because I can recognize a drunk at fifty feet. I've had a lifetime of knowing when people are drunk. We don't talk about him much, I know, but my father was one very unhappy man and he was miles from home with no one to help him or advise him when he had made one wrong decision that wrecked his life."

"What decision was that?" Charles asked.

This evening was full of shocks.

Since Emily's arrival there had been no mention of the late Martin Lynch's drinking.

"The decision to leave Ireland. He regretted it every day of his life."

"But that can't be right. He lost total interest in us. He never came home." Charles was astonished.

"He never came home, that's true, but he never lost interest. He probed it as if it were a sore tooth. All he *could* have done if only he had stayed here. All of it fantasy, of course, but still, if he'd had someone to talk to . . ." Her voice trailed away.

"Your mother?" Josie asked tentatively.

"No joy there, I'm afraid. She never understood what a hold drink had on him. She just told him to stay away from it, as if it were a simple thing to do."

"Could you not talk to him? You're great at talking to people," Charles said admiringly.

"No, I couldn't. You see, my father didn't have the basic decency that Noel here has. He could not accept that in the end it was all up to him. He wasn't half the man Noel is."

Josie, who had in the last half hour been facing the whole range of disgrace, mortal sin and shame, found some small comfort in this praise.

"You think that Noel will be able to do all this?" she asked Emily pitifully, as if Noel were not even there.

"It's up to us to help him, Josie," Emily said as calmly as if they were discussing the menu for tomorrow's supper.

And even to Noel it didn't seem quite as impossible as it had when he had begun his explanation.

———

"Stella, I'm Emily, Noel's cousin. Noel's gone to get you some cigarettes. I came a little early in case there's anything I should know before the social worker comes."

Stella looked at the businesslike woman with the frizzy hair and the smart raincoat. Americans always dressed properly for the Irish weather. Irish people themselves were constantly being drenched with rain.

"I'm pleased to meet you, Emily. Noel says you are a rock of sense."

"I don't know that I am." Emily seemed doubtful. "I came over on a whim to learn about my late father's background. Now I seem to be up to my neck in organizing a statue for some saint who has been dead for centuries. Hardly a rock of sense . . ."

"You're very good to take all this on as well." Stella looked down somewhat ruefully at the bump in her stomach.

"You have enough problems to think about," Emily said, her voice warm and sympathetic.

"Well, this social worker is a bit of a madam. You know, interested in everything, believing nothing, always trying to trip you up."

"I suppose they have to be a bit like that on behalf of the child," Emily murmured.

"Yes, but not like the secret police. You see, I sort of implied that Noel and I were more of an item than we are. You know, in terms of seeing each other and everything."

"Sure." Emily nodded approvingly. It made sense.

There was no point in Stella telling a social worker that she hardly knew the least thing about the father of the child she was about to have.

It wouldn't look good from the start.

"I'll help to fill you in on all that," Emily said.

At that moment Noel came in, closely followed by Moira Tierney.

She was in her early thirties with dark hair swept back with a red ribbon. If not for her frown of concentration, she would have been considered attractive. But Moira was too busy to consider looking attractive.

"You are Noel Lynch?" she said briskly and without much enthusiasm.

He began to shuffle and appear defensive.

Emily moved in quickly. "Give me your parcels, Noel. I know you want to say hello to Stella properly." She nudged him towards the bed.

Stella held up her thin arms to give him an awkward combination of a hug and a peck on the cheek.

Moira watched suspiciously.

"You and Stella don't share a home, Mr. Lynch?" Moira said.

"No, not at the moment," he agreed apologetically.

"But there are active plans going ahead so that Noel can get a place of his own to raise Frankie," Emily said.

"And you are . . . ?" Moira looked at Emily inquiringly.

"Emily Lynch. Noel's cousin."

"Are you the only family he has?" Moira checked her notes.

"Lord, no! He has a mother and father, Josie and Charles . . . ," Emily began, making sure that Stella could hear the names as well.

"And they are . . . ?" Moira had an irritating habit of asking a question the wrong way round, as if she were making some kind of disapproving statement.

"They are at home organizing a fund to erect a statue to St. Jarlath in their street."

"St. *Jarlath*?" Moira was bewildered.

"I know! Aren't they wonderful? Well, you'll meet them yourself. They'll be in tomorrow to see Stella."

"They will?" Stella was startled.

"Of course they will." Emily sounded more confident than she felt.

Josie would take a lot of convincing before she arrived to see the girl who was no better than she should be. But Emily was working on it and the important thing just now was to let the social worker see that there was strong family support.

Moira absorbed it all as she was meant to.

"And where do you intend to live, Mr. Lynch, if you *are* given custody of the child?"

"Well of course he will have custody of the child," Stella snapped. "He's the child's father. We are all agreed on that!"

"There may be circumstances which might challenge this." Moira was prim.

"What kind of circumstances?" Stella was angry now.

"A background of alcohol abuse, for one thing," Moira said.

"Not from me, Noel," Stella said apologetically.

"Naturally, we make inquiries," Moira said.

"But that is all under control now," Emily said.

"Well, that will be looked into," Moira said in a clipped voice. "What kind of accommodation were you thinking of, Mr. Lynch?"

Emily spoke again. "Noel's family have been discussing nothing else but accommodation. We are looking at this apartment in Chestnut Court. It's a small block of flats not far away from where he lives now."

"Would it not be preferable to start the child off living with a ready-made family in er . . . St. Jarlath's Crescent?"

"Well, you see . . . ," Noel began.

"You see, Moira, you are very welcome to come and visit Noel's home at any time, but you will realize that it's entirely unsuited for a baby. The places in Chestnut Court are much more child-friendly. The one we are all interested in is on the ground floor. Would you like to see a picture of it here . . ."

Moira didn't seem as interested as she might have been. She was looking at Noel and seemed to spot the surprise on his face.

"What do *you* think of this as a place to move to?" she asked him directly.

Stella and Emily waited anxiously.

"As Emily said, we have talked through so many ideas and this one seems to be the most suitable so far."

Moira nodded as if in agreement, and if she heard the breath of relief from the two women, she gave no sign.

There were questions then about the rent that would be paid and the babysitting support that would be available, seeing that Noel would be at work all day.

And soon it was over.

Emily made one last statement to show how reliable her cousin Noel was.

"I don't know whether you realize that Noel is very anxious to marry Stella. He has proposed to her, but Stella would prefer not to. This is the attitude of a committed person, someone who would be reliable and responsible."

"As I said, Ms. Lynch, there are some formalities that

have to be gone through. I will have to talk about it with my team and then the last word will be with the supervisor."

"But the first and most influential word will be from *you*, Moira," Emily said.

Moira gave one of her brisk little nods and was gone.

Stella waited till she was out of the ward before she started to celebrate. With a flick of her wrist she pulled the curtains and produced the cigarettes.

"Well done to the pair of you," she said, looking from Noel to Emily and back. "We have Madam Moira on the run!"

"We still have a way to go," Emily said, and they settled down to discuss further strategies.

And they continued to do this for the next few weeks. Every aspect of the effort to turn Noel into a father was discussed.

Josie and Charles were introduced to Stella and, after some awkward shuffling at the start, they found an astonishing amount of common ground. Both Noel's parents and Stella herself seemed entirely convinced that shortly Stella would be going to a better place. There was no pretense that she might recover.

Josie talked wistfully of Stella going to meet Our Lord fairly soon and Charles said that if Stella were to meet St. Jarlath, she could pass on the news that the statue would indeed be erected but it might take a little longer than they had once believed possible. They had helped by paying a deposit on the flat in Chestnut Court. St. Jarlath's image might have to wait a little, but it would happen.

"Wouldn't he be able to see that already?" Stella asked.

"Yes, I imagine he would," Charles agreed. "But it would be no harm to give him a personal message."

Noel felt ashamed that his parents took this whole idea of an afterlife so casually. They really and truly saw heaven as some kind of a big park where they would meet everyone.

Stella rolled her eyes a bit at the whole notion, but she didn't seem put out by it either. She was game to take a message to any old saint just to keep the show on the road.

But they also made plans on a more practical level. Chestnut Court was only a seven-minute walk from St. Jarlath's Crescent. Noel could wheel the baby around to his parents' home before work each morning; Josie and Charles would look after Frankie until lunchtime. Then she would go for the afternoon either to Molly Carroll's house or to this couple called Aidan and Signora, who looked after their grandchild; to Dr. Hat, who had retired recently and found time hanging heavy on his hands; or to Muttie and Lizzie Scarlet, who, quite apart from their own children, had raised twins who were no blood relations to them at all.

The three evenings a week when Noel would be at his evening classes would be covered as well. For a time Emily would go to the new apartment in Chestnut Court and do her paperwork. Noel would return after his lectures and she would cook him a meal. He had started getting lessons from the district nurse on what he would need in the new flat to welcome the baby and had been shown how to prepare a feed and the importance of sterilizing bottles. Declan Carroll's wife, Fiona, had sent a message to say that she had already received a baby's layette that would be enough for sextuplets. Stella and Noel *must* help her out and get the garments worn; their babies would arrive at around the same time. What could be more luck?

Noel was swept along in the whirl of activity of it all.

The thrift shop was up and running; he and his father had painted it to Emily and Josie's satisfaction and already people had begun to donate items to be sold. Some of these would be useful for Noel's new flat, but Emily was adamant: a fair price must be paid for them. The money was for St. Jarlath, not to build a comfortable lifestyle for Noel.

He had little time alone with Stella. There were so many practicalities to be sorted out. Did Stella want the child to be brought up as a Catholic?

Stella shrugged. The child could abandon it once she was old enough. Possibly to please Josie and Charles, there should be a baptism and First Holy Communion and all, but nothing too "Holy Joe."

Were there *any* relations on Stella's side whom she might want to involve?

"None whatsoever." She was clipped and firm.

"Or anyone at all from the various foster homes from the past?"

"No, Noel, don't go there!"

"Right. It's just that when you're gone, I'll have no one to ask."

Her face softened. "I know. Sorry for snapping at you. I'll write her a letter telling her a bit about myself and about you and how good you've been."

"Where will you leave the letter?" Noel asked.

"With you, of course!"

"I mean, if you wanted to leave it in a bank or something . . . ," Noel offered.

"Do I look to you like someone who has a bank account, Noel? Please . . ."

"I wish you weren't going to leave, Stella," he said, covering her thin hand with his.

"Thanks, Noel. I don't want to go either," she said. And they sat there like that until Father Flynn came in for a visit. He took in the scene and the hand-holding, but made no comment.

"I was just passing," he said foolishly.

"Well, I was on my way anyway, Father." Noel stood up to leave.

"Maybe you could stay a minute, Noel. I wanted Stella to tell me what, if anything, she wanted for her funeral."

The question didn't faze Stella at all.

"Listen, Brian, ask Noel's family what *they* want. I won't be here. Let them have whatever is easiest."

"A hymn or two?" Brian Flynn asked.

"Sure, why not. I'd like a happy clappy one. You know, like a gospel choir, if possible."

"No problem," Father Flynn said. "And burial or cremation or body to science?"

"Don't think my body would tell anyone anything they didn't know already." Stella considered it. "I mean, if you smoke four packs a day, you get cancer of the lung. If you drink as much as I did, then you get cirrhosis of the liver. There isn't a part of me sound enough for a transplant, but what the hell . . . it could be an awful warning." Her eyes were very bright.

Brian Flynn swallowed.

"We don't talk about this sort of thing much, Stella, but do you want a Requiem Mass?"

"That's the one with all the bells and whistles, isn't it?"

"It gives a lot of people comfort," Father Flynn said diplomatically.

"Bring it on then, Brian," she said good-humoredly.

Chapter Four

Lisa Kelly had been very bright at school; she had been good at everything. Her English teacher encouraged her to do a degree in English literature and aim for a post in the university. Her sports teacher said that with her height—by the age of fourteen she was already nearly six feet tall—she was a natural and she could play tennis or hockey, or both, for Ireland. But when it came to it, Lisa decided to go for art. Specifically for graphic art.

She graduated from that, first in her year, and was instantly offered a position in one of the big design firms in Dublin. It was at that point that she should have left the family home.

Her younger sister, Katie, had gone three years previously, but Katie was very different. No child genius, only barely able to keep up with the class, Katie had taken a holiday job in a hairdresser's and found her life's calling. She had married Garry Finglas and together they had set up a smart salon that had gone from strength to strength. She loved to practice on Lisa's long honey-colored hair, blow-drying it and then styling it into elegant chignons and pleats.

Their mother, Di, had been very scornful about it all. "Touching people's dirty heads!" she had exclaimed in horror.

Their father, Jack Kelly, barely commented on Katie's career, any more than he had on Lisa's work.

Katie had begged Lisa to leave home. "It's not like that out in the real world, not awful silences like Mum and Dad have. Other people don't shrug at each other the way *they* do, they *talk*."

But Lisa had waved this away. Katie had always been oversensitive about the atmosphere at home. When Katie went out to friends' houses, she returned wistfully talking about happy meals at kitchen tables, places where mothers and fathers talked and laughed and argued with their children and their friends. Not like their home, where meals were eaten in silence and accompanied by a series of shrugs. And anyway, Katie had always been easily affected by people's moods. Lisa was different. If Mum was distant, then *let* her be distant. If Dad was secretive, then what of it? It was just his way.

Dad worked in a bank, where, apparently, he had been passed over for promotion; he didn't know the *right* people. No wonder he was withdrawn and didn't want to make idle chitchat. Lisa could never interest him in anything she did; if ever she showed him one of her drawings from school, he'd shrug, as if to say, "So what?"

Her mother was discontented, but she had reason to be. She worked in a very upmarket boutique, where rich, middle-aged women went to buy several outfits a year. She herself would have looked well in those kinds of clothes, but she could never have afforded them; so instead she helped to fit plumper women into them and arranged for seams to be let out and for zip fasteners to be lengthened. Even with a very generous staff discount, the clothes were way out of her league. No wonder she looked at Dad with disappointment. When she had married him at the age of eighteen he had looked like a man who was going somewhere. Now he went nowhere except to work every morning.

Lisa went to her office and worked hard all day. She had lunch with colleagues at places that were high in style and low in calories. But it was at a private lunch for a client that Lisa met Anton Moran: it was one of those moments that was frozen forever in her mind.

Lisa saw this man crossing the room, pausing at each table and talking easily with everyone. He was slight and wore his hair quite long. He looked confident and pleasant without being arrogant.

"Who's *he*?" she gasped to Miranda, who knew everyone.

"Oh, that's Anton Moran. He's the chef. He's been here for a year, but he's leaving soon. Going to open his own place, apparently. He'll do well."

"He's gorgeous," Lisa said.

"Get to the end of the line!" Miranda laughed. "There's a list as long as my arm waiting for Anton."

Lisa could see why. Anton had style like she had never seen before. He didn't hurry, yet he moved on from table to table. Soon he was at theirs.

"The lovely Miranda!" he exclaimed.

"The even lovelier Anton!" Miranda said archly. "This is my friend Lisa Kelly."

"Well, hello, Lisa," he said, as if he had been waiting all his life to meet her.

"How do you do?" Lisa said and felt awkward. Normally she knew what to say, but not this time.

"I'll be opening my own place shortly," Anton said. "Tonight is my last night here..I'm going round giving my cell phone number to everyone and I'll expect you all to be there. No excuses now." He handed a card to Miranda and then gave one to Lisa.

"Give me a couple of weeks and I'll give you the details. They'll all know I must be doing *something* right if you two gorgeous girls turn up there," he said, looking from one to the other. It was an easy patter. He might be going to say something similar at the next table.

But Lisa knew that he had meant it. He wanted to see her again.

"I work in a graphic design studio," Lisa said suddenly, "in case you ever need a logo or any designs?"

"I'm sure I will," Anton said. "I'm certain I will, actually." And then he was gone.

Lisa remembered nothing about the rest of the meal. She yearned to go to Miranda's flat and talk about him all night, check that he wasn't married, that he didn't have a partner. But Lisa had survived life so far by remaining a little aloof. She didn't go to stay with friends, as she didn't want to invite them home to her house. She didn't want to wear her heart on her sleeve and confide to someone gossipy like Miranda about Anton. She would get to know him herself in her own time. She would design him a logo that would be the talk of the town.

The important thing was not to rush it, not to make any sudden moves.

She thought about him way into the night. He wasn't conventionally handsome but he had a face that you wouldn't forget. Intense dark eyes and a marvelous smile. He had a grace like you'd expect in an athlete or a dancer.

He must be spoken for. A man like that wouldn't be available. Surely?

She was taken aback when he telephoned her the next day.

"Good. I found you," he said, sounding pleased to hear her voice.

"How many places did you try?"

"This is the third. Will you have lunch with me?"

"Today?"

"Well, yes, if you're free. . . ." And he named Quentins, one of the most highly regarded restaurants in Dublin.

Lisa had been going to have lunch with Katie. "I'm free," she said simply. Katie would understand. Eventually.

Lisa went to her boss, Kevin.

"I'm going to have lunch with a very good contact. A man who is about to open his own business and I was wondering . . ."

" . . . if you can take him to an expensive restaurant—is that it?" Kevin had seen it all, heard it all.

"No. Certainly not. *He's* paying. I thought I might offer him a glass of champagne and that I might go an hour early so that I can get my hair done and present a good image of the agency."

"Nothing wrong with your hair," Kevin grumbled.

"No, but better to make a good impression than a sort of half-hearted one."

"All right—do we have to pay for the hairdo as well?"

"No way, Kevin. I'm not greedy!" Lisa said and ran off before he could think about this.

She raced out to buy a large potted plant for Katie and turned up at the salon.

"So this is a consolation prize. You're canceling lunch!"

"Katie, *please* understand."

"Is it a man?" Katie asked.

"A man? No, of course not. Well, he is a man, but it's a business lunch and I can't get out of it. Kevin is on his knees to me. He even let me have time off so that I could have my hair done."

"What do you want done? Apart from bypassing the line of people who actually made bookings?"

"I beg you, Katie . . ."

Katie called to an assistant. "Could you take Madam to a basin and use our special shampoo? I'll be with you in a moment."

"You're too good . . . ," Lisa began.

"I know I am. It's always been my little weakness, being too good for this world. I wish it *were* for a man, you know, Lisa. I'd have done something special."

"Let's pretend it *is* for a man," Lisa begged.

"If it was a man who would get you out of that house, I'd do it for nothing!" Katie said, and Lisa smiled to herself. She yearned to tell her sister, but a lifetime of keeping her own counsel intervened.

"You look very elegant," Anton said as he stood up to greet Lisa at Quentins.

"Thank you, Anton. You don't look as if you made too late a night of it yourself."

"No, indeed. I just gave my phone number to everyone in the restaurant and then went home to my cup of cocoa and my narrow little bed." He smiled his infectious smile, which would always manage to get a return smile. Lisa didn't know what she was smiling at—cocoa, a narrow little bed, an early night. . . . But it must mean that he was giving her signals that he was available.

Should she send back a similar signal or was it too early? Too early, definitely.

"I told my boss I was coming here for lunch with a man who was going into business on his own and he said that I should offer you a glass of champagne on the company."

"What a civilized boss," Anton said admiringly as Brenda Brennan, the proprietor, came over. She knew Anton Moran already. He had worked in her restaurant a while ago. He introduced Lisa to Brenda. "Lisa's company is buying us a glass of champagne each, Brenda, so could we have your delightful house sparkling to start us off, with a receipt for that to Lisa, and the rest of the meal is on me."

Brenda smiled. Her look said she had seen Anton here with several ladies before.

Lisa felt a stab of hurt, which surprised her. In twenty-five years she had never known such a feeling. It was envy, jealousy and resentment all rolled into one. This was completely ludicrous.

It wasn't as if she were a starry-eyed teenager. Lisa had had many boyfriends, and some of them had been lovers. She had never felt a really strong attraction to any of these men. But Anton was different.

His hair looked soft and silky, and she longed to reach

across the table and run her hands through it. She had the most absurd wish to have his head on her shoulder while she stroked his face. She must shake herself out of this pretty sharpish and get back to the business of designing a look and styling a logo for his new company.

"What will you call the new place?" she asked, surprised that she could keep so calm.

"Well, I know it's a bit of an ego trip, but I was thinking of calling it Anton's," he said. "But let's order first. They have a really good cheese soufflé here. I should know—I made enough of them in my time!"

"That would be perfect," Lisa said. This could not be happening. She was falling in love for the very first time.

Back at the office Kevin asked her, "Any luck with Golden Boy?"

"He's very personable, certainly."

"Did you give him any outline and our rates?" Kevin was anxious there would be no gray areas.

"No—that will come later." Lisa was almost dreamy as she thought of Anton and how he had kissed her cheek when they parted.

"Yeah, well, as long as he understands it doesn't come free because he's a pretty boy," Kevin said.

"How do you know that he's a pretty boy?" Lisa asked.

"You just said that he was personable and I think he was the same guy that my niece had a nervous breakdown over."

"Your niece?"

"Yes. My brother's daughter. She went out with a chef called Anton Moran once. Nothing but tears and tantrums, then she drops out of college, *then* she goes to face him down about it all and he's gone off cooking on a cruise ship."

Lisa's heart felt like lead. Anton had told her of his wonderful year onboard a luxury liner.

"I don't think it could have been the same person." Lisa's tone was cold.

"No, maybe not . . . probably not . . ." Kevin was anxious for the least trouble possible. "Just as long as he knows he's getting nothing for free from us."

Lisa knew with a terrible certainty that there would be a lot of trouble ahead. Anton had barely the money to cover the deposit on his premises. He was relying on outstanding restaurant reviews to meet the mortgage payments and the expenses of doing the place up. He had given no thought whatsoever to the cost of a graphic artist and a campaign.

The site for the restaurant was perfect: it was in a small lane just a few yards off a main road, near to the railway station, a tram route and a taxi rank. He had suggested a picnic. Lisa brought cheese and grapes, Anton brought a bottle of wine.

They sat on packing cases and he described his great plans. She hardly took in any of them as she watched his face. His sense of excitement was contagious.

By the time they had finished the cheese and grapes she knew that she would leave Kevin and set up on her own. Perhaps she could move in with Anton, work with him—they could build the place together—but she must not rush her fences. However hard it was, she mustn't look overeager.

Anton had mentioned very little about his private life.

His mother lived abroad, his father lived in the country and his sister lived in London. He spoke well of everyone and badly of no one. She *mustn't* ask him about Kevin's niece. She must hassle him about nothing. She knew that he was totally right—this place was going to be a huge success and she wanted to be part of it and in at the very start.

She gave a sigh of pure pleasure.

"It's good, that wine, isn't it?" he said.

It might as well have been turpentine. She couldn't taste it. But she mustn't let him know at this early stage that she was sighing with pleasure at the thought of a future with him.

It would be lovely to have someone to tell—someone who would listen and ask, What did you do then? What did he say to that? But Lisa had few close friends.

She couldn't tell anyone at work, that was for sure. When she left Kevin's studio she wanted no one to suspect why. Kevin might become difficult and say she had met Anton on *his* time and that he had stood them the glasses of champagne that had clinched the deal.

Once or twice he had asked her if "Anton pretty boy" had got any further along the line in his decision-making. Lisa shrugged. It was impossible to know, she had said vaguely. You couldn't rush people.

Kevin agreed. "Just so long as he's not getting anything for free," he warned several times.

"Free? You *must* be joking!" Lisa said, outraged at the very idea.

Kevin would have been astonished had he known just how long Lisa had spent with Anton and how many drawings she had shown him to establish a logo for his new venture. At that moment she had concentrated on the colors of the French flag, and the *A* of *Anton* was a big curly, showy letter. It could not be mistaken for anything else. She had done drawings and projections, shown him how this image would appear on a restaurant sign, on business cards, menus, table napkins and even china.

She had spent every single evening with Anton—sometimes sitting on the packing cases, sometimes in small restaurants around Dublin, where he was busy seeing what worked and what didn't. One night, he did a shift at Quentins to help them out and invited Lisa to have a meal there at a staff discount. She sat proudly, looking out from her booth, grateful that she had met this man who was now quite simply the center of her whole life. Then and there she had definitely decided to leave Kevin's office and set up business on her own.

She would shortly leave the cold, friendless home where she lived now, but would wait until Anton suggested that she move in with him. He would ask her soon.

The whole business had been brought up for discussion. As early as their fifth date he had made the first move.

"It's a great pity to go back alone to my narrow bed . . . ," he had said, his voice full of meaning as he ran his hands through her long hair.

"I know, but what are the alternatives?" Lisa had asked playfully.

"I suppose you could invite me home to *your* narrow bed?" he offered as a solution.

"Ah, but I live with my parents, you see. That kind of thing couldn't happen," she said.

"Unless you were to get your own place, of course," he grumbled.

"Or we were to explore *your* place?" Lisa said.

But he didn't go down that road. Yet.

When he brought the matter up again it was in connection with a hotel. A place thirty miles from Dublin where they might have dinner, steal some ideas for the new restaurant and stay the night.

Lisa saw nothing wrong with this plan, and it all worked out perfectly. As she lay in Anton's arms she knew she was the luckiest girl in the whole world. Soon she was going to be living and working with the man she loved. Wasn't this what every woman in the world wanted?

And it was going to happen to her, Lisa Kelly.

"I always knew you would fly the coop one day," Kevin said. "And you have been restless for the last couple of weeks. I guessed you were planning something."

"I was very happy here," Lisa said.

"Of course you were. You're very good. You'll be good anywhere. Have you decided where to go yet?"

"On my own," Lisa said simply.

"Not a good idea in this economic climate, Lisa," Kevin advised her.

"*You* took the risk, Kevin, and look how it paid off for you. . . ."

"It was different. I had a rich father and a load of contacts."

"I have a little savings and I'll make the contacts," Lisa said.

"You will in time. Have you an office?"

"I'll start from home."

"The very best of luck to you, Lisa," he said, and she managed to get out before he asked her was there any news of Anton.

Kevin, however, knew all about the place Anton had in Lisa's life and the reason for her move. He had spent a weekend in Holly's Hotel in County Wicklow and Miss Holly, forever anxious to give her customers news of one another, mentioned that one of his colleagues, Ms. Kelly, had stayed there the previous night.

"With a very attractive young man. Most knowledgeable about food, he was out in the kitchens talking to the chef."

"Was his name Anton Moran?" Kevin asked.

"That's the very man." Miss Holly clapped her hands. "He even asked us for the recipe for our special orange sauce that the chef makes with Cointreau and walnuts. Normally Chef won't tell anyone, but he told Mr. Moran because he was going to cook it for his parents."

"I'll bet he was," Kevin said grimly. "And did they share a room?"

Miss Holly sighed. "Of course they did, Kevin. But that's today for you. If you tried to apply any standards these days you'd be laughed out of business!"

Kevin thought of his niece, who was still in fragile health, and he shivered a little for what might lie ahead for Lisa Kelly, one of the brightest designers he had ever come across.

————

Lisa wondered were there other homes in Dublin like hers, where the communication was minimal, the conversation limited and the goodwill nonexistent. Her parents talked to each other in heavy sighs and to her hardly at all.

Every Friday, Lisa left her rent on the kitchen dresser. This entitled her to her room and to help herself to tea and coffee. No meals were served to her unless she were to buy them herself.

Lisa wasn't looking forward to telling her parents that shortly there would be no salary coming in, and therefore the rent would be hard to pay. She was even less enthusiastic about telling them that she would be using her bedroom as an office. In theory, they might offer her the formal dining room, which was never used and would have made a perfectly presentable business surrounding. But she knew not to push things too far.

Her father would say they weren't made of money. Her mother would shrug and say they didn't want strangers traipsing in and out of the place. Better do it little by little. Tell them about the job first, then gradually introduce the need to bring clients to the house as they got used to the first situation.

She wished over and over that Anton was less adamant about their living arrangements. He said that she was lovely, the loveliest thing that had ever happened to him. If this was so, why would he not let her come to live with him?

He had these endless excuses: it was a lads' place— he just had a room there, he didn't pay for it, instead he cooked for the lads once a week and that was his rent, he couldn't abuse their hospitality by bringing in someone else. Anyway, it would change the whole atmosphere of the place if a woman were to come into it.

He had sounded a little impatient. Lisa didn't mention it again. There was no way she could afford a place to live. There were new clothes, picnic meals and the two occasions she pretended to have got hotel vouchers in order to spirit him off for a night of luxury. All this had cost money.

Once or twice she wondered whether Anton might possibly be cheap? A bit *careful* with money, anyway? But no, he was endearingly honest.

"Lisa, my love, I'm a total parasite at the moment. Every euro I earn doing shifts I have to put away towards the cost of setting the place up. I'm a professional beggar just now, but in time I'll make it up to you. When you and I are sitting in the restaurant toasting our first Michelin star, *then* you'll think it was all worthwhile."

They sat together in the new kitchen, which was coming to life under their eyes. Ovens, refrigerators and hot plates were springing up around them. Soon the work would begin on the dining room. They had agreed on the logo and it was being worked into the rugs that would be scattered around the wooden floors. The place was going to be a dream, and Lisa was part of it.

Anton was only mildly surprised that she had left Kevin. He had always assumed that she would one day. He was less enthusiastic, however, about the notion that she might move into one of the spare rooms in the new building.

"I could make a bed-sitter out of *this* room and my office out of *that* one." Lisa pointed out two rooms down the corridor off the new kitchen.

"This one's the cold room and that's for linen and china," he said impatiently.

"Well, eventually, but I have to have *somewhere* to work and we agreed that I should help with the marketing as well . . . ," she began, but he started to look cross again so she dropped it.

It had to be home.

The reception was more glacial than she had expected.

"Lisa, you are twenty-five years of age. You have been well educated—expensively educated. Why can't you find a place to live and work like other girls do? Girls with none of your advantages and privileges . . ." Her father spoke to her as if she were a vagrant who had come into his bank and asked to sleep behind the counter.

"Even poor Katie, and Lord knows she never achieved much, she's at least able to look after herself," Lisa's mother said witheringly of her other daughter.

"I thought you'd be pleased that I was going out on my own," Lisa said. "I'm even thinking of taking some classes, on starting your own business and the like. I'm showing initiative."

"Mad is more like it. These days anyone who has a job holds on to it instead of throwing it up on a whim," her father said.

"And no rent for the foreseeable future," her mother sighed. "*And* you'll want the heating on during the day when there's no one else at home. *And* you want businesspeople filing in and out of this house. No, Lisa, it's not on."

"If we were to let your room to a stranger, we could get a proper rent for it," her father added.

"What about the dining room? I could put shelves and a filing system into it . . . ," Lisa began.

"And ruin the lovely dining room? I think not," her mother said.

"Why don't you forget the whole idea and stay where you are . . . in the agency," her father suggested, his tone slightly kinder as he saw her distressed face. "Do that, like a good girl, and we'll say no more about any of this."

Lisa didn't trust herself to speak anymore. She walked quickly to the front door and left the house.

She didn't *care* about money. She didn't *mind* working hard, and even though she hated self-pity she did begin to feel that the world was conspiring against her. Her own family were so unsupportive and her boyfriend impervious to any signals and hints. He *was* her boyfriend, wasn't he? He had mentioned no other woman and he had said she was lovely. Admittedly, he hadn't said he loved her, but being lovely was the same thing.

Lisa caught sight of herself in a shopwindow: she looked hunched and defeated.

This would never do. She brushed her hair, put on more makeup and held her shoulders back and strode confidently along to Anton's, to the place where a great restaurant was about to rise from the rubble and confusion that was currently there.

Later she would think about where to live and where to work. Tonight she would just drop into the gourmet shop and buy some smoked salmon and cream cheese. She wouldn't weary him with her problems. She would hate to see that impatient frown again on his handsome face.

To her great annoyance there were eight people there

already, including her friend Miranda, who had been the one to introduce her to Anton in the first place. They were sitting around eating very gooey-looking pizza.

"Lisa!" Anton managed to sound delighted, welcoming and surprised at the same time, as if Lisa didn't come there every evening.

"Come on in, Lisa, and have some pizza. Isn't Miranda clever? She found *exactly* what we all wanted."

"Very clever," Lisa said through her teeth. Miranda, who looked slim like a greyhound but who ate like a hungry horse, was sitting on the ground in her pencil-slim jeans, wolfing down pizza as if she had known no other food. Some of the men were people who shared Anton's flat. The other girls were glamorous and suntanned. They looked as if they were auditioning for a musical.

None of them was broke, in debt, with nowhere to live and nowhere to work. Lisa wanted to run away and go and cry somewhere, big heaving sobs. But where could she go? She had nowhere, and this, after all, was where she wanted to be.

She slipped the smoked salmon and cream cheese into one of the fridges and came to join them.

"Anton has been singing your praises," Miranda said when she looked up momentarily from the huge pizza she was devouring. "He says you are a genius."

"That's going a bit far." Lisa smiled.

"No, it's the truth," Anton assured her. "I was telling them all about your ideas. They said I was very lucky to get you."

These were the words she had wanted to hear for so long. Why did it not seem as real and wonderful as she had hoped?

Then he said, "Everyone is here to give some ideas about marketing, so let's start straightaway. Lisa, you first . . ."

Lisa didn't want to share her ideas with this cast. She didn't want their approval or their dismissal.

"I'm last in—let's hear what everyone else has to say." She gave a huge smile at the group.

"Sly little fox," Miranda whispered, but loudly enough to be heard.

Anton didn't seem disturbed. "Right, Eddie, what do you think?" he began.

Eddie, a big bluff rugby player, was full of ideas, most of them useless. "You need to make this place a focus for the rugby set, somewhere people would lunch on the days of an International."

"That's about four days a year," Lisa heard herself say.

"Well, yes, but you could host fund-raisers for various rugby clubs," he said.

"Anton wants to *make* money, not give it away at this stage," Lisa said. She knew she sounded like someone's nanny or mother, but honestly . . .

A girl called April said that Anton could have wine appreciation classes there, followed by a dinner serving some of the most popular choices of the evening. It was so ludicrous as a moneymaker that Lisa hardly believed anyone would take it seriously, yet they were all eager and excited.

"Where's the profit?" she asked icily.

"Well, the wine manufacturers would sponsor it," April said, annoyed.

"Not until the place is up and running, they won't," Lisa said.

"Anton could have fashion shows here," Miranda suggested.

Everyone looked at Lisa to see how she would knock this one down, but she was careful. She had been too snide already.

"That's a good idea, Miranda. Have you any designers in mind?"

"No, but we could think up a few," Miranda said.

"I think it would take from the meal itself," Anton said.

"Yes, maybe you're right." Miranda didn't care; she was there only for the laughs and the pizza anyway.

"What do *you* think, Lisa? Do you have a background in marketing and business as well as graphic art?"

"No, I don't, April. In fact, I've just decided to do an evening course in management and marketing. The term starts next week, so at the moment all I have is my instinct." Lisa even managed a smile.

"Which says . . . ?" April was obviously keen.

"Just as Anton says, that the food is going to be extraordinary and everything else is second to that." She had surprised herself with the announcement about the evening class. She'd had the vague notion that such a thing would be a good idea, but being challenged by April had made up her mind. She was going to do it. She'd show them.

"You didn't tell me you were going back to college," Anton said when the others had all left. It had been touch and go as to whether April would *ever* leave, but somehow she

realized that Lisa would outstay her and she did go grudgingly.

"Ah, there's lots of things I don't tell you, Anton," she
said, scooping the glutinous pizza and paper plates into a
refuse bag.

"Not too many, I hope," he said.

"No, not *too* many," Lisa agreed. This was the way it
had to be played. She knew that now.

She signed on for the business diploma the next day. They
were very helpful in the college and she gave them a check
that was the very last of her savings.

"How will you support yourself?" the tutor asked her.

"It will be hard, but I'll manage," she said with a bright
smile. "I have one client already, so that's a start."

"Good. That will keep you solvent," the tutor said,
pleased.

Lisa wondered what he would say if he knew that the
one client wasn't going to pay a cent for the job she was
doing and that he was costing her a fortune because he
liked a woman to smell of expensive perfume and have
lacy underwear, but because he was putting everything he
had into the business he was unable to buy her any of
these things.

At her first lecture, she sat beside a quiet man called
Noel Lynch, who seemed very worried about it all.

"Do you think it will help us, all this?" he asked her.

"God, I don't know," Lisa said. "You always hear successful people saying that qualifications don't matter, but
I think they do because they give you confidence."

"Yes. I know. That's why I'm doing it too. But my cousin is paying my fees and I wouldn't want her to think it was a waste. . . ."

He was a gentle sort of fellow. Not smart and lively and vibrant like Anton's friends, but restful.

"Will we go and have a drink afterwards?" she asked him.

"No, if you don't mind. I'm actually a recovering alcoholic and I don't find myself at ease in a pub," he said.

"Well, coffee then?" Lisa said.

"I'd like that," Noel said with a smile.

Lisa went back to the bleak terraced house that she had called home for so long. *Why* was Anton so against her moving into his premises? It made absolute sense for her to be there, and once settled she could persuade him to give up his ludicrous bachelor existence with the others. After all, they were still on the prowl, while he had everything sorted: his own restaurant, his own girlfriend. What *was* the point in keeping up the charade of all being men about town?

If she could have gone back to the restaurant now and told him about the introductory lecture, it would have been great.

Mother was out somewhere and Father was watching television. He barely looked up as she came in.

"It went very well," she said to him.

"What did?" He looked up, startled.

"My first lecture at the college."

"You have qualifications already: a career, a job. This

is just some kind of a *figario* you are taking." He went back to the television.

Lisa felt very, very lonely. Everyone in that lecture hall tonight had someone to talk to about it. Everyone except her.

Anton was out tonight. He and the flatmates were going to some reception, not that he would have been *very* interested, but he would have listened for a little bit anyway.

Katie would have cared, but Katie and Garry had gone away on a long weekend to Istanbul. It seemed a very long way to go just for three nights, but they were highly excited about it and regarded it as one of the great explorations of all time.

There were no other friends. None who cared. What the hell? She would call Anton. Nothing heavy, nothing clinging, just to make contact. He answered immediately.

There was a lot of noise in the background and he had to shout.

"*Lisa,* great. Where are you?"

"I'm at home."

"Oh, I thought you'd be here," he said, and he actually sounded disappointed.

Lisa brightened a little. "No, no, I was at my first lecture tonight."

"Oh, that's right. Well, why don't you come along now?"

"What is it, exactly?"

"No idea, Lisa, just lots of fun people. Everyone's here."

"You must know what it is."

She could hear him frown. Even over the phone.

"Love, I don't know who's running it, some magazine company, I think. April invited us. She said there was un-limited champagne and unlimited chances to meet people, and she was right."

"April asked you."

"Yes, she's part of the PR for it all. I was expecting you to be here too. . . ."

"No, honestly, I have to dash," she said and got off the phone just before she began to weep as if she were never going to stop crying ever again.

Katie came back from Istanbul and called Lisa to say she had a present for her. "How was it at the college?" she asked.

"You remembered?" Lisa was amazed. Nobody else had asked.

"I got you a terrific present at the bazaar," Katie said. "You'll love it!"

Lisa felt a prickling behind her nose and eyes.

She never remembered getting Katie a present from anywhere. "That's lovely," she said in a small voice.

"Will you come over this evening? Garry and I will bore you to death about all we saw."

Normally Lisa might have said that she'd have loved to but she had a million things to do. But she surprised both herself and her sister by saying that there was noth-ing she would like better.

"Brian might come as well, but he's no trouble."

"Brian?"

"Our tenant. We gave him the two rooms upstairs. I told you about him."

"Oh, yes, of course you did." Lisa felt guilty. Katie had indeed been wittering on about someone coming to live upstairs. She wished she had thought of asking for the rooms herself, but as usual the timing had been all wrong.

"You're not trying to set me up with this Brian, are you?" she asked.

"Hardly! He's a priest and he's nearly a hundred!"

"No!"

"Well, fifty anyway. Not about to break his vows. Anyway, don't you *have* a fellow?"

"Not really," Lisa said, admitting it for the first time to herself.

"Of course you do," Katie said briskly. "Anyway, I'm glad you're free tonight—come around seven-thirty."

Lisa was free that night. She had been free the night before, and the night before that. It had been three days since Anton had gone to April's party. Lisa was waiting for him to contact her.

Waiting and waiting.

Brian Flynn turned out to be a very decent man and great company. He told them about his mother, who had dementia but seemed quite content and happy in whatever world she lived in. How his sister had married a man called Skunk, how his brother had left one wife and fled from one girlfriend.

He told them about a holy well that he didn't rate very highly and about the immigrant center where he worked now and how he had a lot of respect for the people there.

Occasionally, he asked Katie and Lisa about their family. They both made excuses to get onto other subjects, so he either gave up or realized this was not an area where they were comfortable.

Garry talked cheerfully about his parents and how his father had originally said that being a hairdresser was only a job for "nancy" boys, but had slightly softened in his view over the years.

He told them about the time he had gone to the zoo on his birthday when he was seven and his parents had told the elephant that he was the best boy in the country, and they told him that the elephant would never forget this because elephants don't forget. And to this day Garry always thought that the elephant remembered.

They smiled at the notion.

Lisa wondered why she had ever thought Garry plodding. He was just decent. And romantic too. He showed them pictures on his phone of Katie with her hair blowing as they went for a cruise on the Bosporus and another of her with minarets in the background. But he hardly saw anything except her face.

"Katie looks so happy," he said over and over.

"And do you have a young man of your own?" Brian Flynn asked Lisa unexpectedly.

"Sort of," Lisa answered him truthfully. "There is a man I fancy a lot, but I don't think he is as serious as I am about it."

"Oh, men are fools, believe me," Brian Flynn said with the voice of authority. "They have no idea what they want. They are much more simple than women think, but more confused as well."

"Did you ever love anyone? I mean before you joined up . . . ," Lisa asked.

"No, nor after either. I'd have been a useless husband

anyway. By the time they end this celibacy thing for priests, I'll be too old to get involved with anyone and that's probably all for the best."

"Is it lonely?"

"No more than any other life," he said.

As Lisa walked home from Katie's house she took a detour that brought her past Anton's. There were lights on upstairs in the room he was going to have as his office. She yearned to go in, but was too afraid of what she might find. April with her legs stretched out on his desk, Miranda sitting on the floor and any number of others. She went home in the dark and let herself into the house where there were no lights and no hints as to whether anyone was at home or not.

Just silence.

Next morning, she got a text from Anton: WHERE ARE YOU? I AM LOST WITHOUT YOU TO ADVISE ME AND SET ME ON TARGET AGAIN. I'M LIKE A JELLY-FISH WITH NO BACKBONE. WHERE DID YOU GO, LOVELY LISA? A TOTALLY ABANDONED ANTON

She forced herself to wait two hours before replying, then she wrote: I WENT NOWHERE. I AM ALWAYS HERE. LOVE LISA

Then he wrote: DINNER HERE? 8PM? DO SAY YES.

Again, she forced herself not to reply at once. It was so silly, all this game playing, yet it appeared to work. Eventually she texted: DINNER AT 8 SOUNDS LOVELY.

She made no offer to bring cheese or salmon or artichoke hearts. She couldn't afford them, for one thing, and for another he was inviting *her*—he must remember that.

He had, of course, expected she would bring something to eat. She realized that when he went to the freezer to thaw out some frozen Mexican dishes, but she sat and sipped her wine, smiling, and asked him all about the business. She didn't mention the reception that April had invited him to. She only asked had he made any new contacts to help him with the launch.

He seemed slightly distracted as he prepared the meal. He was his usual efficient self, expertly slicing avocado, deseeding chilies and squeezing limes over prawns as a starter, but his mind was somewhere else. Eventually he got around to what he wanted to say.

"Have I annoyed you, Lisa?" he asked.

"No, of course not."

"Are you sure?"

"Well, obviously I am. Why do you think you did?"

"I don't know. You're different. You don't call me. You didn't bring anything for dinner. I didn't know if you were trying to say something to me . . ."

"Like what?"

"Like you're pissed off with me or something?"

"But why should I be? You invited me to dinner and I'm here. I'm having a lovely time."

"Oh, good. It's just a feeling I had. . . ." He seemed totally satisfied.

"Fine. So that's out of the way," she said cheerfully.

"I mean I value you, Lisa. We're not joined at the hip

or anything, but I really do appreciate all you've done to help me get started. . . ." He paused.

She looked at him expectantly, not helping him out.

"So, I suppose I was afraid that there had been a misunderstanding between us, you know."

"No, I don't know. What kind of a misunderstanding?"

"Well, that you might be reading more into it than there is."

"Into what, Anton? You're talking in code."

"Into . . . well, into our relationship," he said eventually.

She felt the ground slip away from her and had to struggle hard to sound normal.

"It's fine, isn't it?" Lisa said, hearing her own voice as if from very far away.

"Sure. It's just me being silly. I mean it's not a commitment or anything . . . exclusive like that."

"We sleep together," Lisa said bluntly.

"Yes, we have, of course, and will again, but I don't ask you about who you meet after the lectures at your college. . . ."

"No, of course not."

"And you don't ask me about where I go and who I meet. . . ."

"Not if you don't want me to."

"Oh, Lisa, don't take an attitude." He was definitely frowning now.

The food tasted like lumps of cardboard. Lisa could barely swallow it.

"Will I make you a margarita? You're only nibbling at your food." Anton feigned concern.

Lisa shook her head.

"So cheer up then, and let's talk about the launch. April has all her people working on it."

"So what's left to talk about, then?" She knew she sounded childish and mutinous but she couldn't help it.

"Oh, Lisa, don't turn into one of those whining women. *Please*, Lisa . . ."

"Does this relationship, as you call it, mean anything to you? Anything at all?"

"Of course it does. It's just that I've taken a huge risk, I'm scared shitless that I'm going to fall on my face in this new venture, juggling a dozen balls in the air, just ahead of the posse in terms of debt and I haven't the *time* to think of anything seriously yet like . . . you know . . . permanent things." He looked lost and confused.

She hesitated. "You're right. I'm just tired and intense because I'm doing too much. I think I *would* like a margarita. Will you put salt around the rim of the glass?"

He brightened up at once.

Maybe that priest who lived over Katie and Garry was right: men *were* simple. And to please them, you had to be equally simple in return. She beat down her feeling of panic and was rewarded with one of Anton's great smiles.

The evening classes were going well. Lisa was actually much more interested than she had expected to be. She *was* quick, she realized.

Noel told her that she was the first in the group to understand any concept. He felt slow and was tempted to give up, but life in his job was so dreary and dull and he had no qualifications; this would give him the confidence and clout he needed.

She learned about him during their coffee breaks. He said the classes and his AA meetings were his only social outings of the week.

He was a placid person and didn't ask many questions about Lisa's life. Because of this, she told him that her parents had always seemed to dislike each other greatly and that she couldn't understand why they stayed together.

"Probably for fear of finding a worse life," Noel said glumly, and Lisa agreed that this might well be true.

He asked her once did she have a fellow and she had replied truthfully that she loved someone but it was a bit problematical. He didn't want to be tied down so she didn't really know where she was.

"I expect it will sort itself out," Noel said, and somehow that was fairly comforting.

And Noel was right, in a way. It sort of sorted itself out.

Lisa never called around to Anton without letting him know she was on her way. She took an interest in all he was doing and made no more remarks about April's involvement in anything. Instead, she concentrated on making the cleverest and most eye-catching invitations to the pre-launch party.

There was no question of her getting anything new to wear. There wasn't any money to pay for an outfit. She confided this to Noel.

"Does it matter all that much?" he asked.

"It does a bit because if I thought I looked well I'd behave well, and I know this sounds silly, but a lot of the people who will be there sort of judge you by what you wear."

"They must be mad," Noel said. "How could they not take notice of you? You look amazing, with your height and your looks—that hair . . ."

Lisa looked at him sharply, but he was clearly speaking sincerely, not just trying to flatter her. "Some of them are mad, I'm sure, but I'm being very honest with you. It's a real pain that I can't get anything new."

"I don't like to suggest this but what about a thrift shop? My cousin sometimes works in one. She says she often gets designer clothes in there."

"Lead me to it," Lisa said with a faint feeling of hope.

Molly Carroll had the perfect dress for her. It was scarlet with a blue ribbon threaded around the hem. The colors of Anton's restaurant and the logo she had designed.

Molly said the dress could have been designed just for her. "I'm not very up-to-date in fashion," she said, "but you'll certainly stop them in their tracks in this one."

Lisa smiled with pleasure. It *did* look good.

Katie treated her to a wash and blow-dry and she set out for the party in high good spirits. April was there in a very official capacity, welcoming people in.

"Great dress," April said to Lisa.

"Thanks," Lisa said. "It's vintage," and went to find Anton.

"You look absolutely beautiful," he said when he caught sight of her.

"It's *your* night. How's it going?" Lisa asked.

"Well, I've been working for two days on all these canapés but you wouldn't think it was my night. April be-

lieves it's hers. She's insisting on being in every picture."
Just then a photographer approached them.

"And who's this?" he asked, nodding at Lisa.

"My brilliant designer and stylist, Lisa Kelly," responded Anton instantly.

The photographer wrote it down, and out of the corner of her eye Lisa could see April's disapproval. She smiled all the more broadly.

"You're really gorgeous, you know." Anton was admiring Lisa openly. "And you wore my colors too."

She savored the praise. She knew there would be times when she would play this scene over and over again in her mind. But she mustn't dwell on herself and her dress.

Lisa blessed Noel and his cousin Emily's thrift shop. She had paid so little for this outfit and she was one of the most elegant women in the room. More photographers were approaching her. She must try to look as though she wanted to deflect attention from herself.

"There's a great crowd here," Lisa said. "Did all the people you wanted turn up?" Across the room she saw that April had a face like a sour lemon. "But I mustn't monopolize you," she added as she slipped away, knowing that he was looking after her as she went to mingle with the other guests.

Miranda was slightly drunk.

"I think it's game, set and match to you, Lisa," she said unsteadily.

"What do you mean?" Lisa asked innocently.

"Oh, I think you've knocked April into Also-Ran. . . ."

"What?"

"It's a saying, you know, in a horse race. There's the winner and there's Also-Ran, meaning the ones that didn't win."

"I know what it *means*," Lisa said, "but what do *you* mean?"

"I think you have the single, undivided attention of Anton Moran," Miranda said. It was a complicated phrase to finish and she sat down after the effort.

Lisa smiled. What should she do now? Try to outstay April or leave early? Hard though it was to do, she decided to leave early.

His disappointment was honey to her soul.

"You're never going? I thought you were going to sit down with me afterwards and have a real postmortem."

"Nonsense! You'll have lots of people. April, for example."

"Oh, God, no. Lisa, rescue me. She'll be talking of column inches of coverage and her biological clock."

Lisa laughed aloud. "No, Anton, of course she won't. See you soon. Call me and tell me how it all went." And she was gone.

There was a bus at the end of the lane and she ran to catch it. It was full of tired people going home late from work. She felt like a glorious butterfly in her smart dress and high heels, while they all looked drab and colorless. She had drunk two cocktails, the man she loved had told her that she was gorgeous and wanted her to stay.

It was only nine o'clock at night. She was a lucky, lucky girl. She must never forget this.

Chapter Five

For Stella Dixon the time just flew by: there was so much to see to every day. There was a lawyer to talk to, a nurse from the health authorities, another nurse—this time from the operating theater—who tried to explain the procedure (though Stella was having none of it; she was far too busy, she said). Once she got her anesthetic "that would be curtains" for her. While she was still here she had to try to deal with everything.

Her doctor, Declan Carroll, came in to see her regularly. She asked after his wife.

"Maybe the babies will get to know each other," Stella had said wistfully one day.

"Maybe. We'll have to work on it." He was a very pleasant young man.

"You mean *you* will have to work on it," she said with a smile that broke his heart.

———

For Noel there weren't enough hours in the day either. Anytime that he was not slaving in Hall's, going to twelve-step meetings or catching up on his studies, he spent surfing the net for advice on how to cope with a new baby. He had moved into his new place in Chestnut Court and was busy making preparations for her arrival.

He had AA meetings every day, since the thought that most things could be sorted out by several pints and three whiskeys was always with him. He managed to stay away from the bar at his father's retirement party. There wasn't a dry eye in the place as they presented a watch to Charlie that he said he would wear every day.

Noel began to wonder how he had ever found time to drink.

"Maybe I'm nearly over it," he said hopefully to Malachy, whom he had met on his first visit and who was now his sponsor at AA.

"I don't want to be downbeat, but we all feel this in the early days," Malachy warned him.

"It's not really early days. I haven't had a drink for twenty-one days," Noel said proudly.

"Fair play to you, but I am four years dry and yet if something went seriously wrong in my life I know only too well where I would *want* to find a solution. It would solve everything for a couple of hours and then I'd have to start all over again . . . as hard as the first time, only worse. . . ."

For Brian Flynn the days flew by as well. He adapted perfectly to his new living quarters and began to think that he had always lived over a busy hair salon. Garry cut his hair for him and tamed the red-gray thatch into a reasonable shape. They said he was better than any security firm and that the fact that he lived there was a deterrent to intruders.

He left each morning for the immigrant center where he worked; as he passed through the salon he encountered many ladies in varying degrees of disarray and marveled to himself how they endured so much in the cause of beauty. He would greet them pleasantly, and Katie always introduced him as the Reverend Lodger Upstairs.

"You could hear confessions here, Brian, but I think you'd be electrified by what they'd tell you," Katie said cheerfully.

She had discovered that even in the middle of a recession, women were more anxious than ever to have their hair done. It kept them sane, somehow, and feeling in control.

For Lisa Kelly the time crawled by.

She was finding it difficult to get decisions made about her designs for Anton's restaurant, as a decision meant money being spent. Although the restaurant was open and full to bursting every night, there was still no verdict on whether to use her new logos and style on the tableware. Instead, she was concentrating on her coursework and giving Noel a hand.

Noel had undergone some amazing conversion; when Lisa heard about his plan to take on a baby, she thought it was a fantasy. She had felt sure he would never be able to cope with a job, a college course and a newborn: it was too much to ask from one person, especially someone who was weak and shy like Noel. However, she was beginning to change her mind.

Noel had surprised her, and in a way she almost envied him. He was so dedicated to all that he was doing. Everything was new for him. He had a whole new life ahead, while Lisa felt that it was forever more of the same. Of course it was all still theoretical; the baby wasn't even born yet. But he was preparing as much as he could to be a father. His notes always had lists scribbled in the margins: *nappy-rash cream, baby wipes,* they would say. *Four bottles, bottle brush, nipples, steriliser* . . .

Her parents were still living in their icy, uncaring way, sharing a roof but not a bedroom, not a dining table, not any leisure time. They had no interest in Lisa or her life, any more than they cared how Katie fared with Garry in the salon. It was just casual indifference, not amazing hostility, that existed between them as a couple. One had only to come into a room for the other to leave it.

Lisa had never been able to pin Anton down: there was always *this* conference and *that* sales meeting and *this* television appearance and *that* radio interview. She had never seen him alone. The pictures of her and Anton together had given way to shots of him with any number of beautiful girls; though she would have heard if he had any new real girlfriend. It would have been in the Sunday papers. That was the way Anton attracted publicity—he gave free drinks to columnists and photographers and they always snapped him with several beautiful women and gave the impression that he was busy making up his mind among them all.

And it wasn't as if he had abandoned her or was ignoring her, Lisa reminded herself. A day didn't pass without a text message from Anton. Life was so busy, he would text. They had a rock band in last night, they were going to do a society wedding, a charity auction, a new tasting menu, a week of Breton specialties. Nowhere any mention of Lisa or her designs and plans.

Then, just as she was about to face the fact that he had left her, he wrote about this simply beautiful restaurant he had heard of in Honfleur, where the seafood was to die for. They *must* sneak away there for a weekend of self-indulgence soon. No date was fixed—just the word "soon," and when she was starting to think that it meant "never," he said that there was a trade fair next month in Paris that they could both go to and fish for ideas and *then* run off to Honfleur. They might even dream up a whole Normandy season for the restaurant while they were there.

It was an unsettling life, to say the least.

Lisa couldn't seem to get on with other work. She kept changing or improving the proposals she had done for Anton—ideas that had never been discussed or even acknowledged.

She was doing all right at school. Nothing like Noel, of course. *That* man was like something possessed. He said that he made do with four and a half hours' sleep. He laughed it off, saying that he would probably get less when the new baby arrived. He was so calm and accepting about it all.

"Did you love her, this Stella?" Lisa had asked.

"I think 'love' is too strong a word. I like her a lot," he replied, struggling to be honest.

"She must love you, then, to leave you in charge," Lisa said.

"No, I don't think she does. I think she trusts me. That's all."

"Well, that's a big part of life. If you trust someone, you're halfway there," Lisa said.

"Do you trust this Anton you talk about?"

"Not really," Lisa said, with a face that closed the door on any further conversation about the topic.

Noel shrugged. He was off anyway up to the hospital to visit Stella.

Three days later, Declan Carroll was in the delivery room holding Fiona's hand as she groaned and whimpered.

"Great, girl. Just three more. . . . Just three . . ."

"How do you know it's only three?" gasped Fiona, red-faced, her hair damp and stuck to her forehead.

"Trust me, I'm a doctor," Declan said.

"You're not a woman, though," Fiona said, teeth gritted and preparing for another push.

But he was right—there were only three more. Then the head of his son appeared and he began to cry with relief and happiness.

"He's here," he said, placing the baby in her arms. He took a photograph of them both and a nurse took a picture of all three of them.

"He'll hate this when he grows up," Fiona said, and John Patrick Carroll let out a wail in agreement.

"Only for a while and then he'll love it," said Declan, who had had his fair share of a mother who showed pictures of him to total strangers at the Laundromat where she worked.

He left the delivery ward of St. Brigid's and headed for oncology. He knew what time Stella was going down for surgery and he wanted to be there as moral support.

They were just putting her on the trolley.

"Declan!" she said, pleased.

"Had to come and wish you well," he said.

"You know Noel. And this is his cousin Emily." Stella was totally at ease, as if she were at a party instead of about to make the last journey of her life.

Declan knew Emily already, as she came regularly to the group practice where he worked. She filled in at the desk as a receptionist or made the coffee or cleaned the place. It was never defined exactly what she did except that everyone knew the place would close down without her. She also helped his mother in the Laundromat from time to time. No job seemed too menial for her, even though she had a degree in art history. He tried to think about her as they stood in a little tableau waiting for Stella to be wheeled to the operating theater. It helped to concentrate on the living rather than on Stella, who would not be in their number for much longer.

"Any news of *your* baby yet, Declan?" Stella asked.

Declan decided against telling her of his great happiness with his brand-new son. It would make things even worse for the woman who would never see her own child.

"No, not a sign," he lied.

"Remember they are to be friends," Stella urged him.

"Oh, that's a promise," said Declan.

Just at that moment the ward sister came in. She smiled when she saw Declan.

"Congratulations, Doctor, we hear you've had a beautiful baby boy!"

He looked like something trapped in the headlights of an approaching car. He could not deny his son, nor could he pretend to be surprised when it would be known that he was there for the birth.

He had to face it.

"Sorry, Stella. I didn't want to be gloating."

"No, you wouldn't ever do that," she said. "A boy! Imagine!"

"Yes, we didn't know. Not until he was born."

"And is he perfect?"

"Thank God."

And then she was wheeled out of the ward, leaving Noel, Emily and Declan behind.

Frances Stella Dixon Lynch was delivered by cesarean section on October 9 at seven p.m. She was tiny, but perfect. Ten tiny, perfect fingers, ten tiny, perfect toes and a shock of hair on her tiny, perfect head. She frowned at the world around her and wrinkled her tiny nose before opening her mouth and wailing as if it were already all too much.

Her mother died twenty minutes later.

The first person Noel telephoned was Malachy. "I can't live through this night without a drink," he told him. Malachy said he would come straight to the hospital. Noel was not to move until he arrived.

The women in the ward were full of sympathy. They

arranged that he get tea and biscuits, which tasted like sawdust.

There was a small bundle of papers in an elastic band on her locker. The word NOEL was on the outside. He read them through with blurred eyes. One was an envelope with FRANKIE written on it. The others were factual: her instructions about the funeral, her wishes that Frankie be raised in the Roman Catholic faith for as long as it seemed sensible to her. And a note dated last night.

> *Noel, tell Frankie that I wasn't all bad and that once I knew she was on the way I did the very best for her. Tell her that I had courage at the end and I didn't cry my eyes out or anything. And tell her that if things had been different you and I would both have been there to look after her. Oh—and that I'll be looking out for her from up there. Who knows? Maybe I will.*
> *Thanks again,*
> *Stella*

Noel looked down at the tiny baby with tears in his eyes. "Your mam didn't want to leave you, little one," he whispered. "She wanted to stay with you, but she had to go away. It's just you and me now. I don't know how we're going to do it, but we'll manage. We've got to look after each other." The baby looked at him solemnly as though concentrating on his words in order to commit them to memory.

Baby Frances was pronounced healthy. A collection of people came to visit her as she lay there in her little crib. Noel, who took time off from work, came every day. Moira Tierney, the social worker, showed up at odd times, asking too many questions. Emily brought Charles and Josie to see their grandchild, and they visibly melted at the sight of the baby. They seemed to have completely forgotten their earlier condemnation of sex without marriage, and Josie was even seen to lift the child in her arms and pat the baby's back.

Lisa Kelly visited a couple of times, as did Malachy. Mr. Hall came from Noel's workplace; even Old Man Casey came and said that Noel was a sad loss to his bar. Young Dr. Declan Carroll came in carrying his own son and introduced the babies formally to each other.

Father Brian Flynn came in and brought Father Kevin Kenny with him. Father Kenny, still on one crutch, was eager to take up his role as hospital chaplain again. He seemed slightly put out that Father Flynn had been so warmly accepted as his replacement. Many people seemed to know him and called him Brian in what Father Kenny thought of as a slightly overfamiliar way. He had obviously been involved in every stage of the unfortunate woman's pregnancy and the birth of the motherless baby who lay there looking up at them. Father Kenny assumed that they were there to arrange a baptism and started to clear his throat and talk about the technicalities.

But no, Father Flynn had brushed that away swiftly. The baby's grandparents were extraordinarily devout people and they would discuss all that sort of thing at a later time.

Charles and Josie Lynch's neighbor Muttie Scarlet

came to pay his respects to the child. He was in the hospital anyway, he said, on business, and he thought he would take advantage of the occasion to visit the baby.

And eventually Noel was told that he could take his baby daughter home to his new apartment. It was a terrifying moment. Noel realized that he was about to stop being a visitor and become entirely responsible for this tiny human being. How was he going to remember all the things that needed to be done? Supposing he dropped her? Poisoned her? He couldn't do it, he couldn't be responsible for this baby, it was ludicrous to ask him. Stella had been mad, she was ill, she didn't know what she was doing. Someone else would have to take over, they'd have to find someone else to look after her baby—*her* baby, nothing to do with him at all. He had a sudden urge to flee, to run down the corridor and out into the street, and to keep on running until the hospital and Stella and Frankie and all of them were just a memory.

Just as his feet were starting to turn towards the doorway, the nurse arrived with Frankie, wrapped in a big pink shawl.

She looked up at him trustingly, and suddenly, from nowhere, Noel felt a wave of protectiveness almost overwhelm him. This poor, helpless baby had no one else in the world. Stella had trusted him with the most precious thing she ever had, the child she knew she wouldn't live to see. Nervously, almost shyly, he took the baby from the nurse.

"Little Frankie," he said to the tiny baby. "Let's go home."

Emily had said she would come to stay with him for a few days to tide him over the most frightening bits. There were three bedrooms in the apartment, two reasonably sized and one small one, which was to be Frankie's, so she would be perfectly comfortable. The visiting nurse came every couple of days but even so, there were so many questions.

Was that horrible-colored mess in the baby's nappy normal, or did she have something wrong with her? How could anyone so very small need to be changed ten times a day? Was that breathing normal? Did he dare go to sleep in case she stopped?

How on earth did anyone manage to get all those snaps on a baby's sleep suit in the right places? Was one blanket too much or too little? He knew she mustn't be allowed to get too cold, but the pamphlets were full of terrible warnings about the dangers of overheating.

Bath times were a nightmare. He knew to test the temperature of the water with his elbow, but would a mother's elbow signal a different temperature from his? Emily needed to come to test the water as well.

She was kept busy: she would do the laundry and help him prepare the bottles and they could read the hospital notes and the baby books and consult the Internet together. They would take the baby's temperature and make sure they had supplies of nappies, wipes, newborn formula. So much of it and so expensive. How did anyone cope with all this?

How did anyone learn to identify what kind of crying meant hunger, discomfort or pain? To Noel all crying sounded the same: piercing, jagged, shrill, drilling through the deepest, most exhausted sleep. No one ever told you how tiring it was to be up three, four times every night, night after night. After three days he was near to weeping with fatigue; as he walked up and down with his daughter trying to burp her after her third feed of the night, he found himself stumbling against furniture, almost incapable of remaining upright.

Emily found him asleep in an armchair. "Don't forget you have to go to the center every week."

"They're not taking any chances with me," Noel said.

"It's the same for everyone. They call it the Mothers and Babies Group, but more and more it can be Fathers and Babies." Emily was practical.

"It's not just that they think I'm a bit of a risk—past history of drinking and all that?" Noel asked.

"No. Don't be paranoid. And aren't you a shining example of what people can achieve."

"I'm terrified, Emily."

"Of course you are. So am I, but we'll manage."

"You won't go back to America and leave me here all on my own. . . ."

"No plans to do that, but I think you should set up some kind of a system for yourself from the very start. Like going to your mother and father for lunch on a Sunday every week."

"I don't know . . . *Every* week?"

"Oh, at least, and in time you should offer to take Declan and Fiona's baby one evening a week to give them a night off. They'll do the same for you."

"You definitely sound as if you're going to jump ship and you're just building me up some support to keep me going," Noel said.

"Nonsense, Noel. But you have to learn to do it without me. You'll be on your own soon." Emily had no plans to go back to New York for a while, but she must be practical and get this show properly launched on the road.

Father Flynn found a gospel choir, which sang at the funeral Mass down at his church at the welcome center for immigrants. Twins called Maud and Simon, who seemed to be related to Muttie Scarlet, prepared a light lunch in the hall next door. There were no orations or speeches. Declan and Fiona sat next to Charles and Josie; Emily had the bag of baby essentials while Noel held Frankie wrapped in a warm blanket.

Father Flynn spoke simply and movingly about Stella's short and troubled life. She had died, he said, leaving behind a very precious legacy. Everyone who had come to know and care for Stella would support Noel as he provided a home for their little daughter. . . .

Katie was there with Garry and Lisa. She had only recently found out that Lisa was on the same course as Noel and had begun at the same time. They knew each other, had had coffee together once or twice; Lisa knew the story. Katie had hoped that Lisa would learn something from Noel—like that it was totally possible to get up and leave the safety of the family home. Home was not a healthy place to be, Katie thought, but there was no talking to Lisa, beautiful and restless as she had always been. Katie noticed that Lisa, for once, was not being distant and withdrawn as she so often was. Instead she was being helpful, offering to pass plates of food or pour coffee. She was talking to Noel in terms of practicalities.

"I'll help you whenever I can. If you have to miss any lectures I'll give you the notes," she offered.

"People are being very kind," Noel said. "Kinder than I ever expected."

"There's something about a baby," Lisa said.

"There is indeed. She's so very small. I don't know if I'll be able . . . I mean, I'm pretty clumsy."

"All new parents are clumsy," Lisa reassured him.

"That's the social worker over there. Moira," he said with a nod in her direction.

"She's got a very uptight little face," Lisa said.

"It's a very uptight job. She's always coming across losers like me."

"I don't think you're a loser—I think you're bloody heroic," Lisa said.

Moira Tierney had always wanted to be a social worker. When she was very young she had thought she might be a nun, but somehow that idea had changed over the years. Well, nuns had changed, for one thing. They didn't live in big, quiet convents chanting hymns at dawn and dusk anymore. There were no bells ringing and cloisters with shadows. Nuns, more or less, *were* social workers these days, without any of the lovely ritual and ceremony.

Moira was from the west of Ireland, but now she lived alone in a small apartment. When she first came to Dublin, she went home to see her parents every month. They sighed a lot because she hadn't married. They sighed over the fact that she was working among the poor and ruffians instead of bettering herself.

They sighed a great deal.

After her mother died, her visits became less frequent. Now she would go back just once or twice a year to the ramshackle farmhouse she had once called home.

She wished that her block of flats had a garden but the other residents had all voted for more car parking, so it was just yards of concrete outside. Still, democracy ruled, she thought, and made do with window boxes that were the envy of her neighbors. She liked her work, but it was rarely, if ever, straightforward.

Noel Lynch was someone who puzzled her. It appeared he had known nothing of the child he had fathered until a few short weeks before the baby arrived. He had lost touch with the mother. And then, suddenly, he had almost overnight changed his lifestyle totally, joined a twelve-step program, taken up lectures and approached his job in Hall's seriously. Any one of these things would have been life-changing, but to take them all on while looking after an infant seemed to be ludicrous.

Moira had read too many concerned and outraged articles about social workers who didn't do their jobs properly to feel any way at ease. She knew what they would write. They would say that all the signs were staring everyone in the face. This was a dangerous situation. What were the social workers *doing*? She didn't know why she was so certain about this, but it was a feeling that wouldn't go away. Every box had been ticked, all the relevant authorities had been contacted, yet she was completely convinced that there was something out of place here.

This Noel Lynch was an accident waiting to happen. A bomb about to explode.

Lisa Kelly was thinking about Noel at the same time.

She had said to Katie that if she were a betting woman she would give him one week before he went back on the drink and two weeks before he gave up his lectures. And as regards minding an infant—the social workers would be in before you could say "foster home!"

Just as well she hadn't found a betting shop.

Lisa had done a job for a garden center but her heart wasn't in it. All the time that she toyed with images of floral baskets, watering cans and sunflowers in full bloom she thought of Anton's restaurant. She found herself drawing a bride throwing a bouquet—and then the thought came to her.

Anton could specialize in weddings.

Real society weddings. People would have to fight to get a date there. They had an underused courtyard where people often escaped for a furtive cigarette. It could be transformed into a permanent, mirror-lined marquee for weddings.

He didn't open for Saturday lunch so that was the time to do it; the guests would have to leave by six o'clock. There was a singing pub called Irish Eyes nearby and they could make an arrangement with the pub that there would be a welcoming pint or cocktail and the scene would move seamlessly onward. The bride's father would be relieved that he wasn't paying for champagne all night and the restaurant could get straight into "serving dinner" mode. There would be only fifty "Anton Brides" a year, so there would be huge competition to know who they would be.

It was too good an idea to keep to herself.

Anton had sounded fretful in his recent texts. Of course he couldn't fix a date for their trip to Normandy. Not now, not in the middle of a recession. Business was so up and down. No groups of estate agents and auctioneers celebrating another sale, like they had every day during the property boom. No leisurely business lunches. Times were tough.

So Lisa knew that he would love this idea. But when to tell him?

If only she had her own place. It would have been totally different: Anton could have popped around in the afternoon or the early evening. Or better, he could have come to visit late in the evening, when he could unwind and stay the night. When she did spend time with Anton it was always at a conference hotel or on a visit to a specialty restaurant where they would stay overnight at a nearby inn. This hope of Honfleur was what had kept her going for weeks and now it looked as if it wasn't definite, but when he saw all the work she had done on the concept of Anton Brides, he would pay attention. Yet again she would have rescued him and he would be so grateful.

She just couldn't wait any longer. She would tell him tonight. She would go to his restaurant tonight, straight after her lectures. She would go home and change first. She wanted to look her very best when she told him about this news that would turn his fortunes around and change their lives.

At home, Lisa went to her room and held two dresses up to the light, the first a black and red dress with black lace trimming, the other a light wool rose-colored dress with a wide belt. The black-and-red was sexy, the pink more elegant. The black-and-red was a little tarty but the pink would attract every stain going and would need to be dry-cleaned.

She had a quick shower and put on the black and red dress and a lot of makeup.

Teddy the maître d' was surprised to see her when she arrived at Anton's.

"You're a stranger round here, Lisa," he said with his professional smile.

"Too busy thinking up marvelous ideas for this place, that's why," she laughed. In her own ears her laughter sounded brittle and false; she didn't much care for Teddy. Tonight, though, she was going to establish her place in this restaurant. Anton would see how brilliant her scheme was; she wasn't even remotely nervous about meeting him and explaining her new plan.

"And are you dining here, Lisa?" Teddy was unfailingly polite but very focused. There was no room for vagueness in Teddy's life.

"Yes. I hoped you could squeeze me in. I need to talk to him about something."

"Alas, full tonight." Teddy smiled regretfully. "Not a table left in the place." They were having a special event, he explained, a four-for-the-price-of-two night in order to get the word out about Anton's. Of course it had been April's idea.

"The place is packed out tonight," Teddy said. "There's a wait list for cancellations."

This was not what she had come to hear. She had

come here to give Anton news about how to change the downward spiral.

"But I really need to talk to him," she insisted. "I've got a great idea for bringing in new business. Look, Teddy," she continued, becoming aware that the shrillness in her voice was attracting attention, "he's really going to want to hear my ideas—he's going to be very angry if you don't let me see him."

"I'm sorry, Lisa," he said firmly. "That's just not going to be possible. You see how busy we are."

"I'll just go back into the kitchen and see what Anton has to say about that . . . ," Lisa began.

"I think not," said Teddy firmly, stepping smoothly to one side and gripping her elbow. "Why don't you telephone tomorrow and make an appointment? Or better still, make a reservation. We'd love to see you here again, and I will certainly tell Anton you called in." As he spoke, he was guiding her firmly towards the door.

Before she knew what had happened, Lisa found herself outside on the street, looking back at the diners, who were staring at her as if hypnotized.

She needed to get away quickly; turning on her heels, she fled as quickly as her too-tight skirt would allow her.

When she was able to draw breath, she pulled out her cell phone to call a taxi and found, to her annoyance, that she had let the battery run down. The night was going from bad to worse.

And then it started to rain.

The house was quiet when she let herself in but that didn't make it any different than usual. Here there was no conversation, unless Katie had come on one of her infrequent visits. Lisa hoped that no one was going to be there tonight. She was in luck. As she reached the bottom of the stairs, there was just silence about the house, as if it were holding its breath.

And that's when it happened. Lisa saw what the newspapers would have called "a partially clothed woman" come out of the bathroom at the top of the stairs holding a mobile phone to her ear. She had long, damp hair and was wearing a green satin slip and nothing much else by the look of her.

"Who are *you*?" Lisa asked in shock.

"I might ask you the same," the woman said. She didn't seem annoyed, put out or even embarrassed. "Are you here for him? I'm just ringing a taxi."

"Well, why are you ringing it here?" Lisa asked childishly. Who could she be? You often heard of burglars coming into a house and just brazening it out with the householders. Maybe she was part of a gang?

Then she heard her father's voice. "What is it, Bella? Who are you talking to?" And her father appeared at his bedroom door in a dressing gown. He looked shocked to see Lisa. "I didn't know *you* were at home," he said, nonplussed.

"Obviously," Lisa said, her hand shaking as she reached for the front door.

"Who *is* she?" the girl in the green satin slip asked.

"It doesn't matter," he said.

And Lisa realized that it didn't. It had never mattered to him who she was or Katie either.

"Well, who am I to say what you should do with your own money. . . ." The woman called Bella shrugged in her green satin underwear and went back into the bedroom.

Lisa and her father looked at each other for a long minute; then he followed Bella back into the bedroom as, unsteadily, Lisa left the house again.

Noel allowed himself to think that Stella would have been pleased with how he was coping with their daughter. He had been without an alcoholic drink for almost two months. He attended an AA meeting at least five times a week and telephoned his friend Malachy on the days he couldn't make it.

He had brought Frankie to Chestnut Court and was making a home for her. True, he was walking round like a zombie from tiredness, but he had kept her alive, and what's more, the visiting nurses seemed to think she was doing well. She slept in a small crib beside him and when she cried he woke and walked around the room with her. He sterilized all the bottles and nipples, made up her formula and changed her. He bathed her and burped her and rocked her to sleep.

He sang songs to her as he paced up and down the bedroom every night, every song he could think of, even if some of them were mad and inappropriate. "Sittin' on the Dock of the Bay" . . . "I Don't Like Mondays" . . . "Let Me Entertain You" . . . "Fairytale of New York" . . . Any snippet of any song he could remember. Why didn't he know the words to proper lullabies?

He had conducted three satisfactory meetings with the social worker Moira Tierney and five with Imelda, the visiting nurse.

His leave was over and he was about to go back to work at Hall's; he wasn't looking forward to it, but babies were expensive and he really needed the money. He would wait a while and then ask for a bit of a raise in salary. He was catching up with his lectures from the college—Lisa had been as good as her word—and was back on track again there.

He was tired all the time, but then so was every young mother whom he passed on the street or at the supermarket. He was certainly too tired to pause and wonder was he happy with it all himself. The little baby needed him and he would be there. That's all there was to it. And his life was certainly much better than it had been eight weeks ago.

He put his books away in the silent apartment. His cousin Emily was asleep in her room, little Frankie was sleeping in the crib beside his own bed. He looked out of his window in Chestnut Court. It was late, dark, drizzly and very quiet.

He saw a taxi draw up and a young woman get out. What strange lives people led! Then, two seconds later, he heard his doorbell ring. Whoever it was was coming to see him—Noel Lynch—at this time of night!

"Lisa?!" Noel was puzzled to see her on the entry-phone screen at this time of night.

"Can I come in for a moment, Noel? I want to ask you something."

"Yes . . . well . . . I mean . . . the baby's asleep . . . but, sure, come in." He pressed the buzzer to release the door.

She looked very woebegone. "I don't suppose you have a drink? No, sorry, of course you don't. I'm sorry. Forgive me." She had forgotten with that casual, uncaring, shruggy attitude of someone who had never been addicted to drink.

Malachy had told Noel that it was this laid-back attitude that really got to him. His friends saying they could take it or leave it, bypassing the terrible urgency that the addicted felt all the time.

"I can offer tea or chocolate," he said, forcing back his annoyance. She didn't know. She would never know what it felt like. He would not lose his temper, but what was she doing here at this time of night?

"Tea would be lovely," she said.

He put on the kettle and waited.

"I can't go home, Noel."

"No?"

"No."

"So what do you want to do, Lisa?"

"Can I sleep on your sofa here, please? *Please*, Noel. Just for tonight. Tomorrow I'll sort something out."

"Did you have a row at home?"

"No."

"And what about your friend Anton, whom you talk so much about?"

"I've been there. He doesn't want to see me."

"And I'm your last hope—is that it?"

"That's it," she said bleakly.

"All right," he said.

"What?"

"I said all right. You can stay. I don't have any women's clothes to lend you. I can't give you my bed—Frankie's crib is in there and she's due a feed in a couple of hours. We'll all be up pretty early in the morning. It's no picnic being here."

"I'd be very grateful, Noel."

"Sure, then have your tea and go to bed. There's a folded blanket over there and use one of the cushions as a pillow."

"Do you not want to know what it is about?" she asked.

"No, Lisa, I don't. I haven't got the energy for it. Oh, and if you're up before I am, Emily, that's my cousin, will be getting Frankie ready to take her to the health center."

"Well, I'll sort of explain to her then."

"No need."

"What a wonderful way to be," Lisa said in genuine admiration.

She didn't think she would sleep at all, but she did, stirring slightly a couple of times when she thought she heard a baby crying. Through a half-opened eye she saw Noel moving about with an infant in his arms. She didn't even have time to think about what kind of mind games Anton was playing with her or whether her father was even remotely embarrassed by the incident in their home. She was fast asleep again and didn't wake until she heard someone leave a mug of tea beside her.

Cousin Emily, of course. The wonder woman who had stepped in just when needed. She in turn didn't seem remotely surprised to see a woman in a black and red lace-trimmed dress waking up on the sofa.

"Do you have to be anywhere for work or anything?" the woman asked.

"No. No, I don't. I'll just wait until my parents have left home, then I'll go back and pick up my things and . . . find myself somewhere else to stay. I'm Lisa, by the way."

Emily looked at her.

"I know. We met at Stella's funeral. And I'm Emily. What time will your parents be gone?" she asked.

"By nine—on a normal morning, anyway."

"But this might not be a normal morning?" Emily guessed.

"No, it might not. You see . . ."

"Noel left half an hour ago. It's eight o'clock now. I have to go to the clinic with Frankie via the charity shop fairly soon . . . and I'm not quite sure what's the best thing to do."

"I'm a friend of Noel's, from college . . ." Lisa began.

"Oh, I know that too."

"So you wouldn't have to worry about leaving me here when you go out, but then you might not want to. . . ."

Emily shook her head as if to get rid of any evidence of such deep thinking on her part. "No, I was thinking of breakfast, actually. Noel made a banana sandwich for himself and then he'll have coffee on his way to work. I'm going to open up the thrift shop when I've given Frankie her bottle; I'll have some fruit and cereal there. I thought you might like to come with me. Would that suit?"

"That would be great, Emily. I'll just go and give myself a quick wash."

Lisa hopped up and ran to the bathroom. She looked quite terrible. All her makeup was smeared across her face. She looked like a tart down on her luck.

No wonder the woman didn't want to leave her in charge of the apartment. Nobody would let anyone who looked like Lisa did be in charge of anything at all. Maybe Lisa would be able to buy something at the thrift shop to take away the wild look of her. She cleaned her face and gave herself a splash wash, then put on over her dress a sweater Emily had given her.

Emily was ready to leave: she was dressed in a fitted green wool dress and she carried a huge tote bag. The baby in the pram was tiny—barely a month old—looking up trustfully at the two women.

Lisa felt a great wave of warmth towards the small, defenseless baby relying on what were after all two strangers, Emily and Lisa, to get her through this day. She wondered if anyone had looked out for her like this when she was tiny and defenseless. Possibly not, she thought bleakly.

It was the most unreal day Lisa had ever lived through. Emily asked nothing of Lisa's circumstances. Instead she talked admiringly of Noel and the great efforts he was making on every front. She told Lisa how she and Noel had known nothing about how to raise a child but between the Internet and the health clinics they were doing fine.

Emily found a dark-brown trouser suit in the thrift shop and asked Lisa to try it on. It fit her well enough.

"I have only forty euros to see me through today," Lisa said apologetically, "and I may need a taxi to take my things out of my parents' home."

"That's all right. You can pay for it by working, can't you?" Emily saw few problems.

"Working?" Lisa asked, bemused.

"Well, you could help me out today. For now, we need to feed Frankie and change her and take her to the clinic. Then you could come with me while I pop into the medical center and later we could walk down St. Jarlath's Crescent, where I look after the gardens, and you could walk the pram around if baby Frankie gets bored. That would be a good day's work and would well cover the cost of that trouser suit."

"But I have to collect my things," Lisa pleaded. "And find somewhere to live."

"We have all day to think about that," Emily said calmly.

And the day began.

Lisa had never met so many people in one working day. She, who worked alone at her desk tinkering with drawings and designs for Anton, often these days spent hours without talking to another human being. Emily Lynch lived a different life.

When Frankie was fed and changed, they moved to the health clinic, where Frankie was weighed and pronounced very satisfactory. There had been an appointment to see Moira, but when they arrived they heard that she had been called away on an emergency.

"That poor woman's life must be one long emergency." Emily was sympathetic instead of being annoyed that she had just made a totally unnecessary visit to the social worker's office. Then it was up to the doctors' practice, where Emily collected a sheaf of papers and spoke pleasantly to the doctors.

"This is Lisa. She's helping me today." They all nodded at her acceptingly. No other explanations. It was very restful indeed.

Frankie was a pretty baby, Lisa thought. Hard work, of course, but babies were, weren't they? Or at least they were supposed to be. She didn't suppose she or Katie had ever got half the attention this one was getting.

Emily had left a parcel for Dr. Hat, who was expected in shortly. He did a day's locum work at the doctor's offices each week. Emily had discovered that he couldn't cook and didn't seem anxious to learn, so she always left a portion of whatever she and Noel had cooked the night before. Today it was a smoked cod, egg and spinach pie, plus instructions on how to reheat it.

"Only meal that Hat eats in the week, apparently," Emily said disapprovingly.

"Hat?"

"Yes, that's his name."

"What's it short for?" Lisa was curious.

"Never asked. I think it's because he seems to wear a hat day and night," Emily said.

"Night?" Lisa asked, with a sort of a laugh.

"Well, I have no way of knowing that." Emily looked at her with interest and Lisa realized that this was the first time today she had allowed herself to relax enough to smile, let alone laugh. She had been like a clenched fist, unable to think about the only family she had known and the only man she had ever loved.

"Right. Where to now?" Lisa was determined to keep cheerful.

"The market and then St. Jarlath's Crescent. We'll give Frankie to her grandmother for a couple of hours, then I can make a start on this paperwork. I'll ask Dingo Duggan to drive you up to collect your things. He can use the thrift shop van."

"Hey, wait a minute, Emily, not so fast. I haven't found anywhere to go yet."

"Oh, you'll find somewhere." Emily was very confident of this. "You don't want to delay once you make a decision like this."

"But you don't know how bad things are," Lisa said.

"I do," Emily said.

"How do you know? I didn't even tell Noel."

"It must have been something very bad for you to come to Chestnut Court in the middle of the night," Emily said, and then seemed to lose interest in it. "Why don't we see if they have any chicken livers down in the market. We could get some mushrooms and rice. Tonight's one of Noel's lectures. He'll need a good meal to see him through. Well, of course, you know that, and you'll need all *your* papers and files and everything."

"Oh, no, I can't go tonight. The world is falling to bits on me. I have no time at all to go to classes!" Lisa cried.

"Always the very time we *must* go—when the world is falling to bits," Emily said, as if it were totally obvious. "Now, would you like a baked potato with cheese for lunch? I find it gives you lots of energy, and you'll need that over the next couple of days."

"Baked potato is just fine," Lisa gasped.

"Good. Then off we go. And after the market we'll go on garden patrol. Could you have a paper and pencil ready and write down what we need for the various gardens in St. Jarlath's Crescent?"

Lisa wondered what it would be like to have a life like this—where everyone sort of depended on you, but nobody actually loved you.

Dingo Duggan said that of course he'd drive Lisa to collect her things. Where would he bring them?

"We will be discussing that over lunch, Dingo," Emily explained. "We'll let you know when we see you."

Lisa was almost dizzy with the speed with which it was all happening. This small, busy woman with the frizzy hair had involved her effortlessly in a series of activities and at no stage had suggested she explain the situation at home and why she had to flee from it. Instead she had been to market and bargained at every stall. Emily seemed to know everyone. Then they had pushed the pram down St. Jarlath's Crescent, where Lisa made lists of plants needed, weeds dug up, paint required for touch-ups. Some gardens were expertly kept, some were neglected, but Emily's regular patrol gave the street a comfortable, established air of being well cared for. Lisa had only begun to take it all in when they arrived at Noel's family home. Again, Lisa marveled at Emily's speed.

The introductions to his parents were made briskly and briefly.

"Charles and Josie are very good people, Lisa. They do good works all day and are busy setting up a fund to have a statue erected to St. Jarlath. We won't detain them from their good work for too long. This is Lisa. She's a good friend of Noel's from his college lectures and has been a great help today in looking after Frankie. And here is your beautiful granddaughter, Josie. She has been longing to see you."

"Poor little thing." Josie took the baby in her arms and Charles beamed up from his unappetizing-looking sandwich.

In Emily's room on the ground floor a bottle of wine was produced.

"Normally I don't have a drink anywhere around Noel, but today is special," Emily explained. "We'll wait until you've collected your things and then we'll have lunch."

"Yes, you must be worn out." Lisa thought that Emily was referring to the hectic pace of the morning.

"Oh, no, that's nothing." Emily dismissed it. "I meant that today is a day of decision for all of us. A glass of wine might be badly needed."

At his restaurant, Anton was planning menus and talking about Lisa. "I'd better call her," he said gloomily.

"You'll know exactly what to say, Anton. You always do." Teddy was admiring and diplomatic.

"Not as easy as it sounds," said Anton, reaching for his phone.

Lisa's phone was switched off. He tried the number of the house where she lived with her parents. Her mother answered.

"No, we haven't seen her since yesterday." The voice was distant, not at all concerned. "She didn't come home last night. So . . ."

"So . . . what?" Anton was impatient with the woman.

"Well . . . nothing, really . . ." Her voice trailed away. "Lisa is, as you must know, an adult. It would be fruitless, to say the least, to worry about her. Shall I give her a message for you?" Lisa's mother had a voice that managed to be indifferent and courteous at the same time in a way that irritated him hugely.

"Don't bother!" he said and hung up.

Lisa's mother shrugged. She was about to go upstairs when her husband let himself in the front door.

"Has Lisa been talking to you?" he began.

"No, I haven't seen her. Why?"

"She will," he said.

"Will what?"

"Will talk to you. There was an incident last night. I didn't realize she was at home and I had a young woman with me."

"How lovely." His wife's scorn was written all over her face.

"She seemed upset."

"I can't imagine why."

"She doesn't have your sense of detachment—that's why."

"She hasn't gone for good. I see her door is open. She's left all her things here." Lisa's mother spoke as if she were talking about a casual acquaintance.

"Of course she hasn't gone for good. Where would she go?"

Lisa's mother shrugged her shoulders again. "She'll end up doing what she wants to do. Like everyone . . . ," she said and walked out the door that her husband had just come in.

"Where will we take your things?" Dingo asked Lisa.

"We're just going to leave them in the van, if that's all right?" Lisa said. She was feeling slightly dizzy from the many encounters that the morning had brought.

"Where are you going to live?" Dingo persisted.

"It hasn't been decided yet." Lisa knew that she sounded as if she were avoiding his questions, but she was actually telling the truth.

"So where do you plan to lay your head tonight, then?" Dingo was determined to get all the answers.

Lisa felt very weary indeed. "Why do they call you Dingo?" she asked in despair.

"Because I spent seven weeks in Australia," he said proudly.

"And why did you come back?" She *must* keep the conversation going about him and avoid cosmic questions about herself.

"Because I got lonely," Dingo said, as if this were the most natural thing in the world. "You will too, mark my words. When you're living with Josie and Charles and saying ten Rosaries a day, you'll look back on your own home and there'll be an ache in you."

"Living with Charles and Josie Lynch? No, that was never on the cards," Lisa said, horrified.

"Well, where am I to bring you when we've collected your things? Oh, look, here's your house."

"I'll be ten minutes, Dingo." She got out of the van.

"Emily said I was to go in with you and carry out your things."

"Does she think she runs the whole world?" Lisa grumbled.

"There's others who'd make a worse job of it," Dingo said cheerfully.

It didn't take Dingo long to pack the van. He already had a dress rail installed in there, so he just hung up Lisa's clothes on that. He had cardboard boxes in which he expertly packed her computer and files, and more boxes for her personal possessions. It wasn't much to show after a lifetime, Lisa thought.

The house was quiet, but she knew her father was at home. She had seen the curtain of his room shift slightly. He made no move to come out to stop her. No attempt to explain what she had seen last night. In a way she was relieved, yet it did show how little he cared about whether she stayed or left.

As she and Dingo got into the van, she saw the curtains move again. However much of a failure her own life had been, it was nothing compared to his and her mother's.

She wrote a note and left it on the hall table.

> *I am leaving the house key. You will realise now that I have left permanently. I wish you both well and certainly I wish you more happiness than you have now. I have not discussed my plans with Katie. I will wait until I am settled, then I will let you have a forwarding address.*
> *Lisa*

No love, no thanks, no explanation, no good-byes. She looked around the house as if she had never seen it before. She realized it was the way her mother looked at things.

Not long ago Katie had said Lisa was turning into her parents and that she should leave home as soon as possible. She longed to tell Katie that she had finally taken her advice but she would wait until she had found somewhere to stay. It would not be in St. Jarlath's Crescent with Charles and Josie, no matter what Dingo thought, and no matter how Emily might try to persuade her.

Back at the Lynches' house, Emily wanted to know how it had all gone. She was relieved that there had been no confrontation. She had feared that Lisa would say more than she meant to.

"I'm never going to say anything to them again," Lisa said.

"Never is a long time. Now let's get these potatoes into the microwave."

Lisa sat down weakly and watched Emily moving expertly around this little place, which she had made completely her home, and suddenly it was easy to talk, to explain the shock of seeing her father with a prostitute last night, the realization that Anton did not see her as the center of his life, the fact that she had no money, nowhere to live, no career to speak of. Lisa spoke on in measured tones. She did not allow herself to get upset. There was something about Emily that made confiding easy—she nodded and murmured agreement. She asked the right questions and avoided the awkward ones. Lisa had never been able to talk like this before. Eventually she came to a full stop.

"I'm so sorry, Emily. I've been going on about myself all afternoon. You must have plans of your own."

"I've telephoned Noel. He'll be here around five. I'll take Frankie back to Chestnut Court and Dingo can spring into action then."

Lisa looked at her blankly.

"What action exactly, Emily? I'm a bit confused here. Are you suggesting that I live with Charles and Josie, because I honestly don't think . . ."

"No, no, no. I'm going to live here again for a little bit, then who knows what will happen?" Emily looked as if it should have been obvious to anyone that this was going to happen.

"Yes, well . . . but, Emily, all my things are outside in Dingo's car. Where am I going to live?"

"I thought you could go to live with Noel in Chestnut Court," Emily said. "It would sort out everything. . . ."

Chapter Six

Moira Tierney was good at her job. She had a reputation for following up the smallest detail. With its faultless filing system, her office was a model for young social workers. Nobody ever heard Moira moan and groan about her caseload or the lack of backup services. It was a job and she did it.

Social work was never going to be nine-to-five; Moira expected to be called by problem families after working hours. In fact, this was often when she was most needed. She was never away from her cell phone, and her colleagues had become used to Moira getting up and leaving in the middle of a meeting because there was an emergency call. She was easy about it. It went with the territory.

Moira spent days and nights picking up the pieces for people where love had gone wrong: where marriages had broken down, where children were abandoned, where domestic violence was too regular. These had once been people filled with romance and hope, but Moira had not known them then. They wouldn't have been in her casebook. It didn't make her deliberately cynical about love and marriage; it was more a matter of time and opportunity.

At the end of a day Moira had little energy left to go to a nightclub. Anyway, even if she had she might well have had to take a call while on the dance floor—a call meaning that she would have to go deal with somebody else's problems.

Yes, of course she would like to meet somebody. Who wouldn't?

She wasn't a beauty—a little squarish, with curly brown hair—but she wasn't ugly either. Much plainer women than Moira had found boyfriends, lovers, husbands. There must be someone out there, someone relaxed and calm and undemanding. Someone much more peaceful than those she had left behind her at home.

When Moira visited Liscuan, she took the Saturday train across the country and the bus to the end of their road. She spent most of her time there cleaning up the house and trying to find out what benefits her father could claim. She came back the following day.

Nothing ever changed; in all the years since she had left to study in Dublin, things had been like this. Nothing altered.

People didn't much like coming to the house anymore, and her father took to going to Mrs. Kennedy's house, where she would give him a meal in return for his cutting logs for her. Apparently Mr. Kennedy had gone to England looking for a job. He may or may not have found one, but he had never come back to report.

Moira's brother, Pat, was left to his own devices. He

worked around the place, milking the two cows and feeding the hens. He went for a couple of pints in Liscuan village on a Saturday night, so Moira had very little conversation with him. It made her sad to see him dress himself up in a clean shirt and put on hair oil for his weekly outing. Any more than in her own, there was no sign of a love in Pat's life.

Pat said little about it all, just burned the bottom of one frying pan after another as he cooked bacon and eggs for supper every night. This cramped little farmhouse would never know the laughter of grandchildren.

It was lonely going home to Liscuan but Moira did it with a good grace. She could tell them nothing about her life in Dublin. They would be shocked if they knew she had dealt with an eleven-year-old girl constantly raped by her father and now pregnant, or a battered wife, or a drunken mother who locked her three children in a room while she went to the pub. Nothing like this happened in Liscuan, or so the Tierneys thought.

So Moira kept her thoughts to herself. This particular weekend she was glad of the time. She needed to think something through. Moira Tierney believed that you often had a nose for a situation that wasn't right, and this was your role in the whole thing. After all that, what those years of training and further years on the job taught you was to recognize when something wasn't right.

And Moira was worried about Frankie Lynch.

It seemed entirely wrong that Noel Lynch should be given custody of the child. Moira had read the file carefully. He hadn't even lived with Stella, the baby's mother. It was only when she was approaching her death and the baby's birth that she had got in touch with Noel.

It was all highly unsatisfactory.

Admittedly, Noel had managed to build up a support system that looked pretty good on paper. The place was clean and warm and adequately stocked with what was necessary for the baby. The sterilizing for bottles was set up, the baby bath in position. Moira couldn't fault any of that.

His cousin, a middle-aged, settled person called Emily, had stayed with him for a time, and she still took the baby with her wherever she went. And sometimes the baby stayed with a nurse who had a new baby of her own and was married to a doctor. Very safe environment. And there was an older couple called Signora and Aidan who already looked after their grandchild.

There were other people too. Noel's parents, who were religious maniacs and were busy drumming up a petition to erect a statue for some saint who died thousands of years ago; then there was a couple called Scarlet: Muttie and Lizzie and Simon and Maud—they were part of the team. And there was a retired doctor who seemed to be called Dr. Hat, of all things, who was supposed to be particularly soothing to infants, apparently. All reliable people, but still . . .

It was all too bitty, Moira thought: a flimsy daisy chain of people, like the cast of a musical. If one link blew away, everything could crash to the ground. But could she get anyone to support her instinct? Nobody at all. Her immediate superior, who was head of the team, said that she was fussing about nothing—everything seemed to be in place.

She had tried to enlist the American cousin on her side, but to no avail. Emily appeared to have a blind spot about Noel. She said he had made amazing strides in turning his life around so that he could look after his daughter. He was persevering at his job. He was even studying at night to improve his work chances. He had given up alcohol, which he found very hard to do, but he was resolute. It would be a poor reward for all this if the social workers were going to take his child away. He had promised the baby's mother that the child would not be raised in care.

"Care might be a lot better than he can offer," Moira had muttered.

"It might, but then again it might not." Emily was not to be convinced.

Moira had to hold back. But she was watching with very sharp eyes for anything to go out of step.

And now it had.

Noel had brought a woman in to live in the flat.

He had done up the spare room for her to sleep in.

She was young, this woman—young and restless. One of those tall, rangy women with hair down to her waist. She knew nothing about babies and seemed defensive and resentful when asked about any parenting skills.

"I'm not here permanently," she had said over and over. "I'm in a relationship elsewhere. With Anton Moran. The chef. Noel is just giving me somewhere to stay, and in return I'm helping him with Frankie." She shrugged as if it were simple and clear to the meanest intelligence.

Moira didn't like her at all. There were too many of these bimbos around the place, leggy, airheaded young women with nothing in their minds except clothes. You should *see* the dress that this Lisa had hanging on her wall! A red and blue designer outfit probably costing the earth.

Whatever doubts Moira had had about Noel's judgment, they had been increased a hundred-fold by the arrival of Lisa Kelly on the scene.

There were great plans afoot for a double christening. Frankie Lynch and Johnny Carroll, born the same day, minded by all the same people, were to be baptized together. No one but Emily saw the irony in their names. Frankie and Johnny were as famous as apple pie at home. She started to hum the familiar lyrics *"Frankie and Johnny were lovers . . ."* then shuddered when she remembered the line *"He was her man, he done her wrong."* Well, that wasn't going to happen with this Frankie and Johnny! She decided to keep it to herself, but she had to write to Betsy about it:

Betsy, everyone here is so intent that the two babies should be best friends; I just hope that these namesakes never live up to the originals. And if I have anything to do with it, and I intend to, they won't. You should see them together in their carriages with all the love around them. It makes me feel so warm inside.

Moira was surprised to be invited. Noel had said that there would be a baptism in Father Flynn's church down by the Liffey, and a little reception in the hall afterwards. Moira was very welcome to join them.

She tried to put the right amount of gratitude onto

her face. They didn't need to do this, but perhaps they were trying to underline the stability of their situation.

"What kind of christening gift would you like?" she said suddenly.

Noel looked at her in surprise.

"There's no question of that, Moira. Everyone is giving a card to both Frankie and Johnny; we're going to put them in albums for them with the photographs so that they will know what this day was like."

Moira felt very reproved and put down. "Oh, yes, of course, certainly," she said.

Noel couldn't help being pleased to see her wrong-footed for once. "I'm sure everyone will be delighted to see you there, Moira," he said with no conviction whatsoever.

There was a much larger congregation than Moira had expected at Father Flynn's church. How did they know all these people? Most of them must be friends of Dr. Carroll and his wife. Surely Noel Lynch wouldn't know half the church?

The two godmothers were there, Emily holding Frankie, and Fiona's friend Barbara, who was also a nurse in the heart clinic, carrying Johnny. The babies, freshly fed and changed, were beautifully behaved and for the most part slept through the ceremony. Father Flynn kept it brief and to the point. The water was poured over their little foreheads—that of course woke them up, but they were quickly soothed and calmed—vows were made for them by the godparents and they were now part of God's Church and His family. Father Flynn hoped that they would both find happiness and strength in this knowledge.

Nothing too pious, nothing that anyone could object to. The babies took it all in their stride. Then everyone moved to the hall next door, where there was a buffet and a huge cake with the names Frankie and Johnny iced on it.

Maud and Simon Mitchell were in charge of the catering, Moira remembered the names being listed among Noel's babysitters for Frankie. They seemed out of place in her vision of Frankie's life. But then, so did this whole christening party.

Moira stood on the outside watching the people mingle and talk and come up to gurgle at the babies. It was a pleasant gathering, certainly, but she didn't feel involved.

There was music in the background and Noel moved around easily, drinking orange juice and talking to everyone. Moira watched Lisa, who was there looking very glamorous, her honey-colored hair coiled up under a little red hat.

Maud noticed Moira standing alone and came over to her, offering her the serving tray. "Can I get you another piece of cake?" she offered.

"No, thank you. I'm Moira, Frankie's social worker," she said.

"Yes, I know you are. I'm Maud Mitchell, one of Frankie's babysitters. She's doing very well, isn't she?"

Moira leaped on this. "Didn't you expect her to do well?" she asked.

"Oh, no, the reverse. Noel has to be both mother and father to her, and he's doing a really great job."

More solidarity in the community, Moira thought. It

was as if there were an army ranked against her. She could still see in her mind the newspaper headlines: SOCIAL SERVICES TO BLAME. THERE WERE MANY WARNINGS. EVERYTHING WAS IGNORED . . . "How exactly are you and your brother friends of Noel?" she asked.

"We live on the same street as he used to live, where his parents live now. But we're hoping to go to New Jersey soon—we have the offer of a job." Her face lit up.

"No work here?"

"Not for freelance caterers, no. People have less money these days, they're not giving big parties like they used to."

"And your parents—will they be sorry to see you go . . . ?"

"No, our parents sort of went ages ago, we live with Muttie and Lizzie Scarlet, and it will be hard saying good-bye to them. Honestly it's too long a story, and I'm meant to be collecting plates. That's Muttie over there, the one in the middle telling stories." She pointed out a small man with a wheeze that didn't deter any of his tales.

Why had he brought up these two young people? It was a mystery, and Moira hated a mystery.

At the weekly meeting, Moira's team leader asked for a report on any areas that were giving cause for alarm.

As she always did, she brought up the subject of Noel and his baby daughter. The team leader shuffled the papers in front of her.

"We have the nurse's report here. She says the child is fine."

"She sees only what she wants to see." Moira knew that she sounded petty and mulish.

"Well, the weight gain is normal, the hygiene is fine—he hasn't fallen down on anything so far."

"He's brought a flashy girl in to live there."

"We are not nuns, Moira. This isn't the nineteen fifties. It's no business of ours what he does in his private life as long as he looks after that child properly. His girlfriends are neither here nor there."

"But she says she's *not* a girlfriend, and that's what he says."

"Really, Moira, it's impossible to please you. If she *is* a girlfriend you're annoyed and if she's not you're even *more* annoyed. Would anything please you?"

"For that child to be put into care," Moira said.

"The mother was adamant and the father hasn't put a foot wrong. Next business."

Moira felt a dull, red flush rise around her neck. They thought she was obsessing about this. Oh, let them wait until something happened. The social workers were always blamed and they would be again.

But not Moira. She had made very sure of this.

The next morning, Moira decided to go and examine this St. Jarlath's Thrift Shop, where the baby spent a couple of hours a day.

The place was clean and well ventilated. No complaints there. Emily and a neighbor, Molly Carroll, were busy hanging up dresses that had just come in.

"Ah, Moira," Emily said, welcoming her. "Do you want a nice knitted suit? It would look very well on you. It's fully lined, see, with satin. Some lady said she was tired of looking at it in her wardrobe and sent it over this morning. It's a lovely heather color."

It was a nice suit, and ordinarily Moira might have been interested. But this was a work visit, not a social shopping outing.

"I really called to know whether you are satisfied with the situation in Chestnut Court, Ms. Lynch?"

"The situation?" Emily looked startled.

"The new 'tenant,' for want of a better word."

"Oh, Lisa! Yes, isn't it great? Noel would be quite lonely there on his own at night, and now they go over their college notes together and she wheels Frankie down here in the mornings. It's a huge help."

Moira was not convinced. "But her own relationship. She says she's involved with someone else?"

"Oh, yes, she's very keen on this young man who runs a restaurant."

"And where is this 'relationship' going?"

"Do you know, Moira, the French—who are very wise about love, cynical but wise—say, 'There is always one who kisses and one who turns the cheek to be kissed.' I think that's what we have here: Lisa kissing and Anton offering his cheek to be kissed."

This silenced Moira completely. How had this middle-aged American woman understood everything so quickly and so well? Moira wondered would she buy the heather knitted suit. But she didn't want them to think that somehow she was in their debt. She might ask a colleague to go in and buy it later.

There was a notice on the corridor wall just outside Moira's office. The heart clinic in St. Brigid's wanted the services of a social worker for a couple of weeks.

Dr. Clara Casey said they needed a report done that she could show to the hospital management to prove that the part-time help of a social worker might contribute to the well-being of the patients who attended the clinic. The staff, though eager and helpful, were not aware of all the benefits and entitlements that existed, nor did they have the expertise to advise patients about how best to get on with their lives.

Moira looked at it vaguely. It wasn't of any interest to her. It was just politics. Office politics. This woman, Dr. Casey, wanted to enlarge her empire, that's all. Moira couldn't have cared less.

She was surprised and very annoyed, therefore, when the team leader dropped in to see her about it. As usual, she admired the streamlined office and sighed, wishing that all the social workers could be equally organized.

"You see that job in St. Brigid's—it's only for two weeks. I'd like you to do it, Moira."

"It's not my kind of thing," Moira began.

"Oh, but it is! No one would do it better or more thoroughly. Clara Casey will be delighted with you."

"And my own caseload?"

"Will be divided between us all while you are away."

Moira didn't have to ask was it an order. She knew it was.

Moira had tidied up all the loose ends about Noel before her two weeks at St. Brigid's. But she had one more stop to make. She called on Declan Carroll, who opened the door with his own son in his arms.

"Come on in," he said. "The place is like a tenement. Fiona is going back to work tomorrow."

"And how will you cope?" Moira was interested.

"Oh, there's a baby mafia on this street, you know—we all keep an eye out for Frankie; well, they'll do the same for Johnny. My parents are dying to get their hands on him, turn him into a master butcher like my dad! Emily Lynch, Noel's parents, Muttie and Lizzie, the twins, Dr. Hat, Signora and Aidan. They're all there for the children. The list is as long as my arm."

"Your wife works in a heart clinic?" Moira had checked her notes.

"Yes, up in St. Brigid's."

"I'm going there for two weeks tomorrow, as it happens," Moira said glumly.

"Best place you'll ever work. There's a great atmosphere in the place," Declan Carroll said effortlessly, shifting the baby round in his arms.

"Do you think Noel is fit to raise a child?" Moira asked suddenly. If she had hoped to shock him into a direct answer, she had hoped in vain.

Declan looked at her, perplexed. "I beg your pardon?" he said slowly.

Nervously, she repeated the question.

"I can't believe that you are asking me to give you a value judgment about a neighbor."

"Well, you'd know the setup. I thought I'd ask you."

"I think it's best if I assume you didn't just say that."

Moira felt the slow, red flush come up her neck again. Why did she think that she was good at working with people? It was obvious that she alienated everyone everywhere she went.

"That social worker is a real pain in the arse," Declan said that evening.

"I suppose she's just doing her job," Fiona said.

"Yeah, but we all do our jobs without getting people's backs up," he grumbled.

"Mostly," Fiona said.

"What did she expect me to say? That Noel was a screaming alcoholic and the child should be taken away? The poor fellow is killing himself trying to make a life for Frankie."

"They're pretty black-and-white, social workers," Fiona said.

"Then they should join the world and be gray like the rest of us," Declan said.

"I love you, Declan Carroll!" Fiona said.

"And I you. I bet nobody loves Miss Prissy Moira, though."

"Declan! That's so unlike you. Maybe she has a steaming sex life that we know nothing about."

Moira had sent her colleague Dolores in to buy the knitted suit. Dolores was a foot smaller than Moira and two feet wider. Emily knew exactly what had happened.

"Wear it in happiness," she said to Dolores.

"Oh . . . um . . . thank you," said Dolores, who would never have got a job in the Secret Service.

Moira wore the heather-colored suit for her first day at the heart clinic. Clara Casey admired it at once.

"I love nice clothes. They are my little weakness. That's a great outfit."

"I'm not very interested in clothes myself." Moira wanted to establish her credentials as a hands-on worker. "I've seen too many people get distracted by them over the years."

"Quite." Clara was crisp in response and yet again Moira felt that she had somehow let herself down. That she had turned away the warmth of this heart specialist by a glib, smart remark. She wished, as she wished so many times, that she had paused to think before she spoke.

Was it too late to rescue things?

"Dr. Casey, I am anxious to do a good job here. Can you outline to me what you hope I will report to you?"

"Well, I am sure that you won't hand my own words back to me, Ms. Tierney. You don't seem that sort of person."

"Please call me Moira."

"Later, maybe. At the moment Ms. Tierney is fine. I have listed the areas where you can investigate. I do urge, however, some sensitivity when talking to both staff and patients. People are often tense when they are confronted with heart problems. We are heavily into the reassurance business and we emphasize the positive."

Not since she was a student had Moira received such an obvious ticking-off. She would love to be able to rewind the meeting to the moment where she had come in; at the point when Clara had admired her outfit, she would thank her enthusiastically—even show her the satin lining. Someday she would learn, but would it be too late?

The head of the team had not said she must stay away from her caseload. Moira went home by way of Chestnut Court. She rang Noel's doorbell. He let her in immediately.

They looked like a normal family. Lisa was giving the baby a bottle and Noel was making spaghetti Bolognese.

"I thought you were going to work somewhere else for two weeks?" Lisa said.

"I never take my eye off the ball," Moira said. She looked at Lisa, who was now holding the infant closely and supporting the baby's head as she had been taught to do. She was rocking to and fro and the baby slept peacefully. The girl had obviously bonded with this child. Moira could find nothing to criticize; on the contrary, there was something very safe and solid about it all. Anyone looking in might think they were a normal family instead of what they were: unpredictable.

"Must be dull for you here, Lisa," she said. "And I thought *you* had a relationship."

"He's away at the moment. Anton went to a trade fair," Lisa said cheerfully.

"Bit lonely for you, I imagine." Moira couldn't resist it.

"Not at all. It's a great chance for Noel and myself to catch up on our studies. Do you want a bowl of spaghetti, by the way?"

"No, thank you. It's very nice of you, but I have to get on."

"Plenty of it . . . ," Lisa said.

"No . . . thanks again." And she left.

Moira was going back to her own flat. Why had she not sat down and eaten a bowl of spaghetti? It smelled very good. She had hardly any food at home: a little cheese, a couple of rolls. It wasn't compromising her whole stance to have stayed and eaten some of their supper.

But as she walked home, Moira was glad she hadn't stayed. This was all going to end in tears, and when it did she didn't want to be anyone who had stayed and had dinner in their house.

As she walked along the canal, Moira saw a small man surrounded by dogs walking towards her. It was Noel's father, Charles Lynch, marching along with dogs of different sizes and shapes: a spaniel, a poodle and a miniature schnauzer trit-trotting on their leads on one side and a huge Great Dane padding along on the other. Two elderly Labradors, unleashed, circled the group, barking joyously. Charles Lynch should have looked ridiculous. Instead he looked blissfully happy. In fact, Charles took his dog walking very seriously. Clients paid good money to have their pets exercised, and he never shortchanged them.

He recognized the stony-faced social worker who had been dealing with his son and granddaughter.

"Miss Tierney," he said respectfully.

"Good evening, Mr. Lynch. Glad to see someone else apart from myself in this city is actually working."

"But what easy work I have compared to yours, Miss Tierney. These dogs are a delight. I have been minding them all day, and now I am taking them home to their owners—except Caesar, here, who lives with us now."

"There are two other dogs not on leads—whose are they?" Moira asked.

"Ah, those are just our local dogs, Hooves and Dimples, from St. Jarlath's Crescent. They came along for the fun of it." And he nodded in the direction of the old dogs that had just come along to share the excitement.

Moira wished that life was as simple for her. Charles Lynch didn't have to fear a series of articles in the newspapers saying that yet again the dog walkers had been found wanting and that all the signs had been there ready for anyone to see.

Next day, Moira began to understand the nature of her job. She was helped in this by Hilary, the office manager, and a Polish girl, Ania, who had recently had a miscarriage and had only just returned to work. She seemed devoted to the place and totally loyal to Clara Casey.

There was, apparently, a bad man called Frank Ennis who was on the hospital board and was the hospital manager, who tried to resist spending one cent on the heart clinic. He said there was absolutely no need for any social services whatsoever in the clinic.

"Why can't Clara Casey speak to him herself?" Moira asked.

"She can and does, but he's a very determined man."

"Suppose she just took him out to lunch one day?" Moira was anxious for this matter to be tied up so she could get back to her real work.

"Oh, she does much more than that," Ania explained. "She sleeps with him. But it's no use—he keeps his life in different compartments."

Hilary tried to gloss over what had been said. "Ania is just giving you the background," she said hastily.

"I'm sorry. I thought she was on our side." Ania was repentant.

"And I am, indeed," Moira said.

"Oh, that's all right then," Ania said happily.

The whole atmosphere in the clinic was a combination of professionalism and reassurance. Moira noticed that the patients all understood the functions of the various medications they received and they had little booklets where their weight and blood pressure were recorded at every visit. They were all very adept at entering information and retrieving it from the computer.

"You wouldn't *believe* the trouble we had getting a training course organized. Frank Ennis managed to make it sound like devil worship. Clara practically had to go to the United Nations to get the instructors in."

"He sounds like a dinosaur, this man," Moira said disapprovingly.

"That's what he is, all right," Hilary agreed.

"But you say that Dr. Casey sees him . . . um . . . socially?" Moira probed.

"No. Ania was saying that, not me—but indeed it is true. Clara has humanized him a lot but there's a long way to go still."

"Does Frank Ennis know that *I'm* here?"

"I don't think so, Moira. No point in troubling him, really, or adding to his worries."

"I like playing things by the book," Moira said primly.

"There are books and *books*," Hilary said enigmatically.

"If I am to write a report, I'll need to know his side of things as well."

"Leave him until you've nearly finished," Hilary advised.

And as she so often did these days, Moira felt she wasn't handling things as well as she might have. It was as if Hilary and the clinic were drawing away from her. She had meant to be there as their savior but somehow playing it by the book had meant that she had stepped outside her brief and that they were all withdrawing their support and enthusiasm.

The story of her life.

Moira worked on diligently.

She saw that there was a case for having a social worker attend one day a week. She looked through her notes. There was Kitty Reilly, possibly in the early stages of dementia, conducting long conversations with saints. There was Judy, who definitely needed home help but had no idea where to turn to find it. There was Lar Kelly, who gave the appearance of being an extroverted, cheerful man but who was obviously as lonely as anything, which was why he kept dropping into the clinic "just to be sure," as he put it.

A social worker would be able to point Kitty Reilly in the direction of care a few days a week, find an aide for Judy and arrange for Lar to go to a social center for lunch and entertainment.

It was time to approach the great Frank Ennis.

She made an appointment to see him on her last day in the clinic. He was courteous and gracious—not at all the monster she had been told about.

"Ms. Tierney!" he said, with every sign of pleasure at meeting her.

"Moira," she corrected him.

"No, no, Clara says you are a 'Ms.' person for sure."

"Really? And did she say anything else about me?" Moira was incensed that Clara had somehow got in ahead of her.

"Yes. She said you were probably extremely good at your job, that you were high in practicality and doing things by the book and low in sentimentality. All the hall-marks of a good social worker, it would appear."

It didn't sound that way to Moira. It sounded as if Clara had said she was a hard-faced workaholic. Still, on with the job.

"Why do you think they *shouldn't* have the part-time services of a social worker?" she asked.

"Because Clara thinks the hospital is made of money and that there are unlimited funds that should be at her disposal."

"I thought you and she were good friends . . . ," Moira said.

"I like to think we are indeed friends, and more, but we will never see eye-to-eye about this bottomless-pit business," he said.

"You really do need someone part-time, you know," Moira said. "It would round it all off perfectly; then St. Brigid's can really be said to be looking after patients' welfare."

"All the social workers and people in pastoral care are run off their feet in the hospital already. They don't want to be sent over to that clinic, coping with imaginary problems from perfectly well people."

"Get someone new in for two or three days a week." Moira was firm.

"One day a week."

"One and a half," she bargained.

"Clara is right, Ms. Tierney: you have all the skills of a negotiator. A day and a half a week and not a minute more."

"I feel sure that will be fine, Mr. Ennis."

"And will you do it yourself, Ms. Tierney?"

Moira was horrified even at the thought of it. "Oh, no! No way, Mr. Ennis. I am a senior social worker. I have a serious caseload. I couldn't make the time."

"That's a pity. I thought you could be my friend in court: my eyes and ears, curb them from playing fast and loose with expenses and taxis." He seemed genuinely disappointed not to have her around the place, which was rare these days. Most people seemed to be veering away from her.

But of course it was totally impossible. She could barely keep up with her own work, let alone take on something new. And yet she would be sorry to leave the place.

Ania had brought in some shortbread for their afternoon tea to mark the fact that Moira was leaving. Clara joined them and made a little speech.

"We were lucky that they sent us Moira Tierney. She has done a superb report and has even braved the lion's den itself. Frank Ennis has just telephoned to say that the board have agreed to us having the services of a social worker for one and a half days a week."

"So you'll be coming back!" Ania seemed pleased.

"No, Ms. Tierney made it clear that she has much more important work to do elsewhere. We are very grateful to her for putting it on hold for the two weeks that she was here."

Frank Ennis had obviously briefed his girlfriend very adequately on the situation so far. Moira wished she had not stressed so heavily to Frank Ennis how important her own work was compared to the work here in the clinic. In ways, it would be pleasant to come here on a regular basis. Apart from Clara Casey, they were all welcoming and enthusiastic. And to be fair, Clara had been enthusiastic about the work Moira had done.

Hilary was always practical. "Maybe Ms. Tierney knows someone who might be suitable?" she said.

As if from miles away Moira heard her own voice saying, "I can easily reorganize my schedule, and if you thought I would be all right, then I would be honored to come here."

They all looked at Clara, who was silent for a moment. Then she said, "I feel that we would all love Moira to join us here, but she will have to sign in under the Official Secrets Act. Frank will expect her to be his eyes and ears, but Moira will know that this can never happen."

Moira smiled. "I get the message, Clara," she said.

And to her great surprise she got a round of applause.

The head of the social-work team was not impressed.

"I asked you to write a report, not to get yourself yet another job, Moira. You work too hard already. You should lighten up a little."

"I did there. I lightened up a lot. I know the setup in the clinic now. It makes sense that I do it rather than train someone in."

"Right. You know what you *can* do and what you *can't*, and no more behaving like some kind of private eye."

"I'm just watchful, that's all," Moira said.

She went to Chestnut Court with her briefcase and clipboard. Noel was out, but Lisa was there. Moira went through the routine that had been agreed upon.

"Who bathed her today?" she asked.

"I did," Lisa said proudly. "It's quite hard on your own—they get so slippery, but she enjoyed it and she clapped her hands a lot."

The baby was clean and dry and powdered. Nothing to complain about there.

"When is her next feed?" Moira asked.

"In an hour's time. I have the formula there and the bottles are sterilized."

Again, Moira could find no fault. She checked the number of nappies and whether the baby's clothes had been aired.

"Would you like a coffee?" Lisa suggested.

Last time Moira had been rather swift and ungracious, so she decided she would say yes.

"Or, actually, I'm exhausted. You don't have a proper drink or anything? I could do with a glass of wine."

Lisa looked at her with a very level glance.

"Oh, no, Moira. We don't have any alcohol here. As you know, Noel has had a problem with it in the past so there's nothing at all. You *must* know that—you were always asking about it before, hunting for bottles stacked away and everything."

Moira felt humbled. She had been so obvious. She

was, indeed, like some kind of a private eye, except an inefficient one.

"I forgot," she lied.

"No, you didn't, but have a coffee anyway," Lisa said, getting up from a table covered with papers and drawings to go to the kitchen.

"Did I interrupt you?"

"No, I was glad of the interruption. I was getting stale."

"Where's Noel tonight?"

"I have no idea."

"Didn't he say?"

"No. We're not married or anything. I think he went back to his parents' house."

"And left you literally holding the baby?"

"He's given me a place to live. I'm very pleased to hold the baby for him. Very pleased indeed," Lisa said.

"And why exactly did you leave home?" Moira fell easily into interrogation mode.

"We've been over this a lot, Moira. I told you then and I tell you now, it was for personal reasons. I am not a runaway teenager. I am a quarter of a century old. I don't ask you why you left home, do I?"

"This is different . . . ," Moira began.

"It's not remotely different and honestly it's got nothing to do with the case. I know you have to look out for Frankie, and you do it very well, but I'm just the lodger helping out. My circumstances have nothing to do with anything." She went into the kitchen and banged around for a while.

Moira sought subjects that wouldn't cause any further controversy. They were hard to find.

"I met Fiona Carroll. You know . . . Johnny's mother."

"Oh, yes?" Lisa said.

"She said that you and Noel were doing a great job minding Frankie."

"Yes . . . well . . . good."

"Most impressed, she was."

"And were you surprised?" Lisa asked suddenly.

"No, of course not."

"Good, because I tell you I have *such* admiration for Noel. All this came out of a clear blue sky at him. He's been very strong. I wouldn't have anyone bad-mouthing him, not anyone at all." She looked like a tiger defending her cub.

Moira made a few bleating noises intended to suggest support and enthusiasm. She hoped she was giving the desired impression.

Her next visit was to a family where they were trying to make an elderly father a ward of the court. To Moira, Gerald, the old man, was perfectly sane. Lonely and frail, certainly, but mad? No.

His daughter and her husband were very anxious to have him defined as being incapable and sign his house over to them and then have him committed to a secure nursing home facility.

Moira was having none of it. Gerald wanted to stay in his home and she was his champion. She picked up a stray remark from the son-in-law, something that made her think that the man had gambling debts. It would suit him nicely if his father-in-law were put away. They might even sell the house and buy a smaller place.

It wouldn't happen on Moira's watch. Her clipboard was filled with notes for letters she would send to the relevant people. The son-in-law collapsed like a house of cards.

The old man looked at Moira affectionately.

"You're better than having a bodyguard," he said to her.

Moira was very proud of this. This was exactly what she saw herself as being. She patted the old man's hand.

"I'll get you a regular carer to come in and look after you. You can tell her if anyone steps out of line or anything. I'll liaise with your doctor also. Let me see . . . that's Dr. Carroll, isn't it?"

"It used to be Dr. Hat," Gerald said. "Dr. Carroll is a very nice lad, certainly, but he could be my grandson, if you see what I mean. Dr. Hat was nearer to my own generation."

"And where is he?" Moira asked.

"He comes in to their practice from time to time when they're short-staffed," the old man said sadly. "I always seem to miss him, though."

"I'll find him for you," Moira promised and went straightaway to the doctors' group practice at the end of St. Jarlath's Crescent.

Dr. Carroll was there and happy to talk about Gerald.

"I think he's totally on the ball and playing with the full deck."

"His family think otherwise." Moira was terse.

"Well, they would, wouldn't they? That son-in-law would do anything to get his hands on the family checkbook."

"That's my view too," Moira said. "Can I ask you—does Dr. Hat do house calls?"

"No, not really. He's retired, but he does the odd locum for us. Why do you ask?"

Moira chose her words carefully for once.

"He thinks very highly of you, Doctor. He said that several times, but I think he finds Dr. . . . er . . . Hat more in his age group."

"Lord, he must be fifteen years older than Hat!"

"Yes, but he's fifty years older than you, Doctor."

"Hat's a very decent man. He might well go round and see your Gerald as a social visit from time to time. I'll tell him."

"Could I tell him, do you think?" Moira had a history of people promising to do things that they fully intended to do but that never got done.

"Of course. I'll give you his address."

For Declan Carroll it was just one less thing to do. She was efficient, this Moira Tierney, and dedicated to her job. Such a pity that she had taken so against poor Noel, who was breaking his back trying to keep the show on the road.

Dr. Hat was indeed wearing headgear: a smart navy cap with a peak. He welcomed Moira in warmly and offered her a cup of hot chocolate.

"You don't know what I'm here about yet," she said cautiously. Maybe he would find this intrusive. She didn't want to accept a hot chocolate under false pretenses.

"Yes, I do. Declan called me so that I could be prepared."

"That was courteous of him," Moira said, though she would have preferred to handle this on her own.

"I like Gerald. I have no problem going to see him. In fact, we could play chess. I'd like that."

Moira's shoulders relaxed. She would have the hot chocolate now. Sometimes things worked out well at work. Not always, but sometimes. Like now.

Just after she got back to her flat there was a phone call from home. Her brother, Pat, never called her usually: she was alarmed. She knew from experience that there was no point in hurrying him. He would take his time. "It's Dad," he said eventually. "He's selling everything—the house, the land, the livestock. He's moved out."

"Moved out where?"

"He's up with Mrs. Kennedy. He's not coming back."

"Well, can't you bring him back?"

"I did once and he wasn't best pleased," Pat said. "Couldn't you do something, Moira?"

"God Almighty, Pat, I'm two hundred miles away. You and Da have to sort this out between you. Go on up to Mrs. Kennedy. Find out what he's up to. I'll come down next weekend and see what's going on."

"But," Pat asked, "what am I to do? I'll have nowhere to go."

"Why would he want to sell the farm?" Moira was impatient.

"You don't know the half of it," said Pat.

Moira sat in her chair for a while thinking about what to do. She knew how to run everyone else's lives but not her own. Eventually she pulled herself together and got on the phone. She had kept Mrs. Kennedy's number in her huge address book in case she ever needed to contact her father when he was chopping wood up there. She asked could she speak to her father and, to use Pat's phrase, he certainly was not best pleased with the call.

"Why are you bothering me here?" he asked querulously.

"I'll be down next weekend. I need to see you, Dad. We need to talk about all this. . . ." And she hung up before she could learn exactly how displeased her father was with this call.

Clara Casey turned out to be a friend rather than a foe. In fact, she even suggested that Moira come to lunch with her one day. This was not the norm at work. Her team leader would never have suggested a social lunch.

Moira was surprised, but very pleased. She was even more pleased when the restaurant turned out to be Quentins. Moira had thought they would go somewhere in the shopping precinct.

Clara was obviously known in the place. Moira had never been there before.

It was amazingly elegant, and Brenda Brennan, the proprietor, recommended the monkfish: it was beautifully prepared in a saffron sauce.

"I don't suppose this restaurant is feeling any bad effects of the recession," Clara said to Brenda.

"Don't you believe it. They're all drawing in their horns. Plus we have a rival now. Anton Moran is getting a lot of business for his place."

"I read about it in the papers. Is he good?" Clara asked.

"Very. Huge flair and a great manner."

"Do you know him?"

"Yes, he worked here once and came back to do the odd shift. A real heartbreaker—he has half the women in Dublin at his beck and call."

Moira was thoughtful. Surely this was the name of the young man whom Lisa Kelly had a relationship with? She had mentioned his name more than once. Moira smiled to herself. For once, it looked as if Lisa might not find the world going entirely her way.

Clara was easy company. She asked questions and was helpful about Moira's brother.

"You might want to stay there Monday morning and catch people at work," Clara said. "We can change your days around—no problem."

Moira wished they didn't have to go back to the clinic. It would have been lovely to have had a bottle of wine and a real conversation where Clara could tell her about the other people who worked in the clinic and maybe even about this friendship she had with Frank Ennis, which seemed entirely improbable. But it was an ordinary working day. They each had one drink, a mixture of wine and mineral water, and they didn't linger over the meal.

Moira had learned little about Clara, except that she was long divorced from her husband and she had two married daughters: one working on an ecology project in South America and the other running a big CD and DVD store. She had originally taken on the heart clinic for one year, but it was now her baby and she would let nobody, particularly anyone like Frank Ennis, take away one single vestige of its power or authority.

Clara was particularly sympathetic about Moira's mother having died. She said her own mother was straight out of hell, but she knew that this was not the case with everyone. Hilary, back at the clinic, had been heartbroken when her own mother had died.

Moira was to take the time she needed to sort out her family problems. It was as simple as that.

Of course it wasn't simple when she got back home to Liscuan. Moira had known that it wouldn't be. Pat had completely broken down. He hadn't milked the cows, he hadn't fed the hens, he babbled about his father's plan to sell the family home from under him and move in with Mrs. Kennedy. This did indeed appear to be the case.

Moira asked her father straight out. "Pat has probably got this all wrong, Da, but he thinks that you have plans to move in permanently with Mrs. Kennedy and sell this place."

"That's right," her father said. "I intend to go and live with Mrs. Kennedy."

"And what about Pat?"

"I'm selling up." He shrugged, gazing around at the shabby kitchen. "Look around you, Moira. I can't do it anymore. I've dealt with this all my life while you were having a fine time up in Dublin. I deserve a bit of happiness now."

With every single client in her caseload, Moira knew what to do. She had known how to set things in order for Kitty Reilly, Judy and Lar at the heart clinic. Why was her own situation so totally impossible?

She spent the Monday helping Pat to look for accommodation. Then she wished her father well with Mrs. Kennedy and took the train back to Dublin.

In Chestnut Court, Frankie was crying again. Noel was beginning to think that he would never know what the crying meant. Some nights she didn't sleep for more than ten minutes at a time. There was one level for food, but she'd just been fed and burped. Perhaps it was more wind. Carefully, he picked up his daughter and laid her against his shoulder, patting her back gently. She cried on. He sat down and laid her chest across his arm while he rubbed her little back to soothe her.

"Frankie, Frankie, please don't cry, little one, hush now, hush now . . ." Nothing. Noel was aware that his voice was sounding increasingly anxious as Frankie cried on piteously. Perhaps for a nappy that needed changing? Could it be a changing job?

He was right. The nappy was indeed damp. Carefully he placed the baby on a towel spread over the table where they changed her. As soon as he removed her wet nappy, the crying stopped and he was rewarded with a sunny smile and a coo.

"You, my pet," he said, smiling back at her, "are going to have to learn how to communicate. It's no good just wailing. I'm no good at understanding what you want."

Frankie blew bubbles and reached up towards the paper birds flying from the mobile above her head. As Noel stretched out his hand to reach for the cleaning wipes, to his horror she twisted away from him and began to slip off the table.

Quick as he was, he was not in time.

It felt as though everything were happening in slow motion as the baby began to fall from the table. As Noel froze in horror, she hit the chair beside, then fell to the floor. There was blood around her head as she started to scream.

"Frankie, *please, Frankie,*" he wept incoherently as he picked her up and clutched her to him. He couldn't tell if she was hurt or where she was hurt or how badly. Panic overwhelmed him. "No, please, *dear God, no,* don't take her away from me, make her be all right. Frankie, little Frankie, please, please . . ."

It was a few moments before he pulled himself together and called an ambulance.

Just as the train was pulling into Dublin, Moira got a text message on her cell phone.

There had been an accident. Frankie had cut her head. Noel had taken her to the A&E of St. Brigid's Hospital, and he thought he should let Moira know.

She took the bus straight from the railway station to St. Brigid's. She had *known* that this would happen, but she felt no satisfaction at being proved right. Just anger, a great anger that everyone else's bleeding-heart philosophy said that a drunk and a flighty young girl could be left responsible for raising a child.

It had been an accident waiting to happen.

She found a white-faced Noel at the hospital. He was almost babbling with relief.

"They say it's just a deep graze and she'll have a bruise. Thank God! There was so much blood I couldn't imagine what it was."

"How did it happen?" Moira's voice was like a knife cutting across his words.

"She rolled over when I was changing her and fell off the table," he said.

"You let her fall from the table?" Moira managed to sound taken aback and full of blame at the same time.

"She hit the chair. . . . It sort of broke her fall." Noel was aware of how desperate this sounded.

"This is intolerable, Noel."

"Don't I know that, Moira? I did the best I could. I called an ambulance straightaway and brought her here."

"Why didn't you get Dr. Carroll? He was nearer."

"I saw all the blood. I thought it was an emergency and that he'd probably have to send her here anyway."

"And where was your partner while all this was going on?"

"Partner?"

"Lisa Kelly."

"Oh, she had to go out. She wasn't there."

"And why did you let the child fall?"

"I didn't *let* her fall. She twisted away from me. I told you. . . ." Noel looked frightened and almost faint from the stress of it all.

"God, Noel, we're talking about a defenseless baby here."

"I know that. Why do you think I'm so worried?"

"So, what caused you to let her fall? That's what it was—*you* let her fall. Was your mind distracted?"

"No, no, it wasn't."

"Did you have a little drink, maybe?"

"*No,* I did *not* have a little drink or a big drink, though by God I could do with one now. It put the heart across me and of course I feel guilty but now I have you yapping at me as if I threw the child on the floor."

"I'm *not* suggesting that. I realize that it was an accident. I am just trying to work out how it happened."

"It won't happen again," Noel said.

"How do we know this?" Moira spoke gently, as if she were talking to someone of low intelligence.

"We know because we are going to move the table up against the wall," Noel said.

"And we didn't think of this sooner?"

"No, we didn't."

"Can I have a word with Lisa when we get back to Chestnut Court? I'd like to go over some of the routines with her once more."

"I told you, she's gone away."

"But she'll be back, won't she?"

"Not for a couple of days. Anton has been asked to take part in a celebrity chef thing in London and it's going to be televised. He's taking Lisa with him."

"Is this Anton happy about his girlfriend living with you, do you think, Noel?"

"I never thought about it one way or the other. It suits her. He knows we aren't a couple in *that* sense. Why do you ask?"

"It's my business to make sure Frankie grows up in a stable household," Moira said righteously.

"Yes, sure. Well, now that you're here, will you help me get her to the bus stop?"

"How do you mean?"

"You know, open doors for me and things. I didn't

bring her pram, you see. I was afraid I wouldn't get it into the taxi."

Moira went ahead of him, opening doors and assisting him through the maze of corridors. He *did* seem concerned and worried about the child. Maybe this was the wake-up shock he needed. But she must be very firm with him. Moira had found over the years that firmness always paid off in the end.

Noel didn't want to let the baby out of his grasp. He lay back in his chair with Frankie clutched to his chest.

"You're going to be just fine, Frankie," he said over and over as he rocked her in his arms. If only he could have a drink to steady his nerves. He contemplated calling Malachy, but he was all right. The child was more important than the drink. He would manage.

"Here, Frankie, I'm going to stop talking to myself, I'm going to read you a story," he said. He put all the concentration in the world into reading her a story about a bird that had fallen out of its nest. It all ended very happily. It worked for Noel: it drove all thought of a large whiskey way out of his mind.

It worked for Frankie too, as she fell into a deep sleep.

Three days later Lisa Kelly phoned her.

"Oh, Moira, Noel asked me to call you. He said you want to go over some of Frankie's routines with me."

"Did you have a good time in London?" Moira asked.

"So-so. What routines did you want to discuss?"

"The usual: bath time, feeding, changing. You know she had an accident while you were away?"

"Yes. Poor Noel is like a hen on a hot griddle about it all. No harm done, I gather."

"Not this time, but it's not good for a baby to fall on its head."

"Well, I know that, but Declan has been round and he says she's fine."

Moira was pleased she had obviously scared Noel enough to make him aware of the gravity of it all.

"And did your friend do well in the celebrity chef thing?"

"No, not as well as he should have. But then I'm sure you read that in the papers."

"I thought I saw something, yes."

"It was all totally slanted the wrong way. You see, this woman April turned up out of the blue there, talking about column inches and potential. She knows nothing really, except how to get her own name into the papers."

"Yes, I saw she was mentioned. I was a little surprised. Noel told me that *you* had gone to assist him, but it made it seem as if she did all the work."

"If drinking cocktails and handing people her business card is work then she did a lot of that, all right," Lisa said. Then she pulled herself together. "But about this routine you wanted?"

"I'll call round this evening," Moira said.

Not for the first time Lisa told Noel that Moira's social life must be the most empty and dull canvas in the whole world.

"Let's ask Emily to be here. She can take some of the heat away from us," Noel suggested.

"Good idea," Lisa agreed. "I was going to ask Katie to come to supper. The more lines of defense we can draw up, the easier it will be for us coping with Generalissimo Moira."

Moira was surprised to see the little flat full of people. She wished that she had not been wearing the heather-colored suit she had bought from St. Jarlath's Thrift Shop. Now they would know that she had sent her friend Dolores to make the purchase!

Noel showed her the new positioning of the table. He stood obediently while she measured the formula out, even though he had been doing these bottles perfectly for months. Frankie went off to sleep obediently like a text-book baby.

"Please join us for some supper *this* time, Moira," Lisa suggested. "I put two extra drumsticks in for you."

"No, really, thank you."

"Oh, do, for God's sake, Moira. Otherwise we'll all fight over the extra bits," Lisa's sister, Katie, said.

They sat down and Lisa produced a very tasty supper. Moira decided that for a brainless blonde she *did* have some skills. But then, of course, she was a chef's girlfriend.

Katie was practical and down-to-earth. She showed them pictures of her trip to Istanbul and talked affectionately of her husband, Garry.

Neither she nor Lisa talked about their home life. But then, to be fair, Moira told herself, she didn't talk about her home life much either.

Instead they talked about Noel and Lisa's lectures, and when Katie mentioned that Father Flynn was away visiting his mother in Rossmore, Noel mentioned that he'd first met the priest when he used to bring Stella cigarettes in hospital.

"Hardly a helpful thing to do under the circumstances." Moira was very disapproving.

"Stella's view was that it was already way too late and she just wanted to enjoy the last bit," Noel said.

"Why don't the clergy provide the priest with a place to live? They do have these flats, I believe. . . ." Moira needed to know the answer to everything.

"He doesn't want that. Says it's like living in a religious community and he's more of a lone bird, really."

"And why didn't you go and stay in Katie's flat, Lisa, rather than here?" Moira asked.

Lisa looked at her impatiently. "Are you *ever* off the job, Moira?" she asked, annoyed.

Emily stepped in to make peace. "Moira has all the best qualities of a social worker, Lisa. She is very interested in people." And then she turned to Moira. "Father Flynn was installed before Lisa needed to move. That's right, isn't it?" She looked around her good-naturedly.

"That's it." Lisa was brief.

"Exactly." Katie was even briefer.

It would have been churlish to ask any more, like why Lisa had needed to move, so very reluctantly Moira decided to leave it there. Instead she said that the chicken was delicious.

"Just olives, garlic and tomatoes," Lisa said, pleased. "I learned it from Emily, actually."

They *seemed* a normal enough group and there was no sign of alcohol anywhere during the meal. Moira sometimes wished she didn't have such a strong instinct for when things were going to go wrong. And she had felt this about Noel from the very beginning.

Anton's restaurant was advertising Saturday lunches. Moira decided to invite Dr. Casey, to return the hospitality at Quentins.

"There's no need, Moira," Clara had said.

"No, of course not, but I'd enjoy it. Please say yes."

It didn't suit Clara at all. Normally she had an easy lunch with Frank Ennis on a Saturday and then they went to the cinema or a matinee at the theater. Sometimes they went to an art exhibit. It had become a relaxed and undemanding routine. But what the hell, she could meet him later.

"That would be delightful, Moira," she said.

Moira booked the table. She would like to have that easy confidence that Clara had. She would like it if they knew her in Anton's and made a fuss of her, as had happened with Clara in Quentins. But that would never happen.

When she went to make the table reservation she was greeted by Anton himself. He was indeed very charming. Small and handsome in a boyish way, he pointed around the room.

"Where would you like to sit, Ms. Tierney? I'd love to give you the nicest table in the room," he said.

She pointed out a table.

"Excellent choice. You can see and be seen there. Are you inviting a friend?"

"Well, my boss, actually. She's a doctor in a heart clinic."

"Well, we'll make sure you both have a good time," he said.

Moira left feeling ten years younger and much more attractive. No wonder this girl Lisa was so besotted with the boy. Anton was truly something special.

And he had not forgotten that they were to be well looked after. As soon as she entered the restaurant, she was greeted as though she were a regular and valued customer.

"Ah, Ms. Tierney!" Teddy said, as she gave him her name. "Anton said to look out for you and to offer you and your guest a house cocktail."

"Lord, I don't think so," Clara said.

"Why not? It's free." Moira giggled.

And they sipped a colored glass of something that had fresh mint and ice and soda, some exotic liqueur and probably a triple serving of vodka.

"Thank God it's Saturday," Clara said. "Nobody could have gone back to work after one of these house cocktails."

It was a very pleasant lunch. Clara talked about her daughter Linda, who was very anxious to have a child and had been having fertility treatment for eighteen months without success.

"Any babies coming up for adoption in your line of business?" Clara asked.

Moira gave the question serious attention. "There might be," she said, "a little girl, a few months old now."

"Well, I mean is she available for adoption or not?" Clara was a cut-and-dried person.

"Not at the moment, but I don't think she's going to last long in the present setup," Moira explained.

"Why? Are they cruel to her?"

"No, not at all. They are just not able to manage properly."

"But do they love her? I mean they'll never give her up if they are mad about her."

"They might have no choice in it," Moira said.

"I won't tell Linda anything about it in case. No point in raising her hopes," Clara said.

"No. If and when it does come up, I'll let you know immediately."

Then they chatted about the various patients who came to the heart clinic. Moira asked about Clara's friend Frank Ennis and learned that he was a very decent man in most ways, but had a blind spot about saving St. Brigid's money.

Clara asked did Moira have anyone in her life and Moira said no because she had always been too busy. They touched briefly on Clara's ex-husband, Alan, who was the lowest of the low, and on Moira's father, now happily settled in with Mrs. Kennedy, who had asked only for one more crack at happiness and seemed to have found it.

Just as Moira was paying the bill, Anton came in accompanied by a very pretty girl who looked about twenty. He came over to their table.

"Ms. Tierney, I hope everything was all right for you?" he said.

"Lovely," Moira said. "This is Dr. Casey. . . . Clara, this is Anton Moran."

"It was all delicious," Clara said. "I will certainly tell people about it."

"That's what we need." Anton had an easy charm.

Moira looked at the young woman expectantly.

Eventually Anton broke and introduced her. "This is April Monaghan," he said.

"Oh, I read about you in the papers. You were in London recently," Moira said, gushing slightly.

"That's right," April agreed.

"It's just that I know a great friend of yours. A *great* friend, Lisa Kelly, and she was there too at the same time."

"Yeah, she was," April agreed.

Anton's smile never faltered.

"How exactly do you know Lisa, Ms. Tierney?"

"Through work. I'm a social worker," Moira said, surprised at herself for answering so readily.

"I thought social workers didn't discuss their cases in public." His smile was still there, but not in his eyes.

"No, no, Lisa isn't a client. I just know her sort of through something else. . . ." Moira was flustered now. She could sense Clara's disapproval. Why had she brought up this matter, anyway? It was in order to fill in the missing parts of the jigsaw in Chestnut Court. The unaccustomed house cocktail and the bottle of wine had loosened her tongue. Now she had somehow managed to spoil the whole day.

Everything settled into a routine at the heart clinic. Clara Casey seemed pleased by Moira's input and could not fault her in terms of diligence and following up everything that needed to be checked. But the warmth had gone. Moira did not feel as included as she had thought herself to be.

The others were all welcoming, but Clara seemed to

have lost respect for her. Moira had seen some forms on Hilary's desk asking whether the part-time social worker was to be a permanent position. Clara had attached a note.

"Tell them not yet. Position is still under review."

So Clara Casey didn't really trust her just because of a stupid, tactless slip in the restaurant. Moira redoubled her efforts on all fronts.

She got Gerald full-time care in his home, to the great annoyance of his daughter and son-in-law. She had saved him from going to the old people's home, which he had dreaded, and he told everyone she was a knight in shining armor. She managed to get children of a drug addict mother fostered in a happy home where they had warmth and toys and regular meals for the first time in their lives. She found a teenage runaway sleeping rough under a bridge by the river and invited her home for soup and a good talking-to. The girl slept for seventeen hours on Moira's sofa and then went back like an obedient lamb to her family home.

She managed to frighten a couple who were signing on for unemployment benefits at the same time as making a very reasonable living from a sandwich bar and to terrify a factory owner who was paying much less than the minimum rate with threats of major publicity. She had even managed to get her brother, Pat, into not only sheltered housing but a sheltered workshop doing woodwork as well.

Her father had agreed to sell his house and divide the money among himself and his two children. Mrs. Kennedy had apparently thought this was highly satisfactory and was busy planning a new kitchen. So there were *some* areas of Moira's life that were a great success.

But not all. Maybe she was just too ambitious about her success rate.

Her father's house did not fetch a big price at the auction. It was a small holding and this was the wrong time to sell. But it did mean that she had the deposit for a house. She must look around for somewhere to live.

"Make sure you get a place with a small garden," Emily advised.

"Have it be somewhere near a tram or a bus," said Hilary, who managed the heart clinic with the same practical sense.

"Buy a dilapidated sort of house and do it up," said Johnny, who did the exercise routines at the heart clinic.

"Get a nice, modern place that isn't falling to bits," said Gerald, who seemed to have a new lease on life and whose brain cells seemed to be working at full power.

She called at Noel's family home in St. Jarlath's Crescent, as she did from time to time. It was easier than facing Noel and Lisa in Chestnut Court, where they both seemed very resentful of her role in anything. At least Emily and Noel's parents could have a civilized conversation.

"This is exactly the kind of street I would like to live in," Moira said. "Do you know of any houses coming up for sale in the area?"

Emily knew that Noel wouldn't like Moira, who was regarded as "the enemy," moving closer to him and being a neighbor of his parents.

"I've heard nothing of anyone moving," Emily said, and, as they did so often, Josie and Charles took their lead from her.

"It's nice to think that people would want to come to live here," Josie said, heading off down memory lane. "When Charles and I were young it was regarded as the last place on earth."

"Maybe Declan would know of someone thinking about moving . . . ," Emily said.

She knew very well that Declan and Fiona had no great love for Moira, and thought her unnecessarily interfering in Noel's efforts to make a reliable home for himself and Frankie. Even if Declan knew that half the street was for sale, he wouldn't give the news to Moira.

Moira asked politely about the campaign for the statue to St. Jarlath and Josie and Charles showed her some quotes they had from sculptors. Bronze was very expensive, but they hoped they might be able to afford it.

"Do you have a particular devotion to St. Jarlath, by any chance?" Josie was always hopeful of recruiting others to the cause.

"Admiration, certainly," Moira murmured, "but *devotion* might be putting it a bit strongly."

Emily hid her smile. When Moira was being diplomatic you could see she'd be good at her job. What a pity she couldn't see what huge strides Noel was making. Why did she have to behave like a policeman with him rather than an encourager and someone he could turn to if there were any problems? As usual, Emily wrote it all to her friend Betsy back in New York. Somehow, typing it on her laptop made it seem clearer.

Honestly, Bets, you just have to get yourself over here.
When you and Eric get married, as you will, sooner
rather than later, I hope, you will need a honeymoon.
Find a good airfare and I'll find you somewhere to stay.
But you have to meet this cast. Noel and his little girl. A
changed man, he hasn't had a drink in months and
he's working his butt off in this dreary company *and* he
is keeping up with his lectures too.

He and a slightly kooky girl named Lisa live like an old
married couple in their apartment, taking care of the
child and studying for their diploma. There's no sex
because she is involved with some society guy—
a celebrity chef, no less! They are being stalked by this
social worker, Moira. She *is* doing her job, but she sort
of hides in their garden and pounces on them, hoping to
catch them at something.

And the campaign for the statue is going great guns. We
are thinking of having it cast in bronze at this stage. And
the whole business of the thrift shop has given Josie a new
lease on life. She works away there happily with Molly
Carroll and me. A lovely fedora came in last week and
Josie took it to this man Dr. Hat to add to his collection.

My uncle Charles has a very satisfactory dog-walking
business now—even the hotel where he used to work
has employed him to come and walk their customers'
dogs.

He has even become a babysitter for his granddaughter
on the evenings when Noel and Lisa go to their lectures.

When I'm not helping out at the doctors' clinic I'm busy doing gardens and window boxes—the whole crescent looks just great. We might even win a prize in a competition for Most Attractive Street. In fact, I'm so busy that I haven't read a book or been to a play. And as for an art exhibit—it's been months!

Tell me about yourself and life back there. I have forgotten I ever lived in New York!

Love,
Emily

She got a reply in minutes:

Emily,

You must be psychic.

Eric asked me to marry him last night. I said I would if, and only if, you came back to New York to be my maid of honor. Considering our great age, I thought a small wedding would be best, but nobody said anything about keeping the honeymoon low-key.

Ireland, here we come!

Love,
Betsy

"I hear your aunt is going back to America for a vacation," Moira said to Noel.

"She's actually my cousin, but you're right—she *is* going to New York. How did you know?" Noel asked, surprised.

"Someone mentioned it," Moira, who made it her business to know everything, said vaguely.

"Yes, she's going to be in her friend's wedding," Noel said. "But then she's coming back again. My parents are very relieved, I tell you. They'd be lost without Emily."

"And you would too, Noel, wouldn't you?" Moira said.

"Well, I would miss her certainly, but as far as my mother is concerned, the thrift shop would close down without Emily, and my father thinks the world of her too."

"But surely you are the one she has helped most, Noel?" Moira was persistent.

"How do you mean?"

"Well, didn't she pay your tuition fees at the college? Get you this apartment, arrange a babysitting roster for you and probably a lot more. . . ."

There was a dull red flush on Noel's face and neck. He had never been so annoyed in his whole life. Had Emily blabbed to this awful woman? She had gone over to the enemy and told Moira all about things that were meant to be private between them. *Nobody* was ever going to know about the fees—that was their secret. He felt betrayed, like he had never felt before. There was no way he could know that Moira was only guessing.

She was looking at him politely, waiting for a reply, but he didn't trust himself to speak.

"You must have thought about who would take over her duties when she was away?"

"I thought maybe Dingo might help," Noel said eventually in a strangled voice.

"Dingo?" Moira said the name with distaste.

"You know, he does some deliveries to the thrift shop. Dingo Duggan."

"I don't know him, no."

"He only helps out the odd time when no one else is available."

"And you never thought to tell me about this Dingo Duggan?" Moira asked, horrified.

"Listen to me, Moira, you give me a pain right in the arse," Noel said suddenly.

"I beg your pardon?" She looked at him in disbelief.

"You heard me. I'm breaking my back to do this right. I'm nearly dead on my feet sometimes, but do you ever see any of this? Oh, no, it's constantly moving the goalposts and complaining and behaving like the secret police."

"Really, Noel. Control yourself."

"No, I will *not* control myself. You come here investigating me as if I were some sort of criminal. Repeating poor Dingo's name as if he were a mass murderer instead of a decent poor eejit, which is what he is."

"*A decent poor eejit.* I see." She started to write something down, but Noel pushed her clipboard away and it fell to the ground.

"And then you go and pry and question people. And try to get them to say bad things about me, pretending to look out for Frankie's good."

Moira remained very still during this outburst. Eventually she said, "I'll leave now, Noel, and come back tomorrow. You will hopefully have calmed down by then."

And she turned and left the apartment.

————

Noel sat and stared ahead of him. That woman was bound to bring in some reinforcements and get Frankie taken away from him. His eyes filled with tears. He and Lisa had been planning her first Christmas, but now Noel wasn't certain that Frankie would still be with them by next week.

Noel picked up his phone and called Dingo. "Mate, can you do me a great favor and come and hold the fort for a couple of hours?"

Dingo was always agreeable.

"Sure, Noel. Can I bring a DVD or is the child asleep?"

"She'll sleep through it if it's not too loud."

Noel waited until Dingo was installed. "I'm off now," he said briefly.

Dingo looked at him. "Are you okay, Noel? You look a bit, I don't know, a bit funny."

"I'm fine," Noel said.

"And will you have your phone on?"

"Maybe not, Dingo, but the emergency numbers are all in the kitchen, you know: Lisa, my parents, Emily, the hospital or anything. They're all there on the wall." And then he was gone. He took a bus to the other side of Dublin, and in the anonymity of a cavernous bar Noel Lynch drank pints for the first time in months.

They felt great . . . bloody great. . . .

Chapter Seven

It was Declan who had to pick up the pieces. Dingo phoned him a half an hour after midnight, sounding very upset.

"I'm sorry for waking you, Declan, but I didn't know what to do—she's roaring like a bull."

"Who is roaring like a bull?" Declan was struggling to wake up.

"Frankie. Can't you hear her?"

"Is she all right? When did you last feed her? Does she need changing?"

"I don't do changing and feeding. I was just holding the fort. That's what he asked me to do."

"And where is he? Where's Noel?"

"Well, I don't know, do I? Fine bloody fort-holding it turned out to be. I've been here six hours now!"

"His phone?"

"Turned off. God, Declan, what am I to do? She's bright red in the face."

"I'll be there in ten minutes," Declan said, getting out of bed.

"*No*, Declan, you don't have to go out. You're not on call!" Fiona protested.

"Noel's gone off somewhere," Declan told her. "He left the baby with Dingo. I have to go over there."

"God, Noel would never do that!" Fiona was shocked.

"I know, that's why I'm going over there."

"And where's Lisa?"

"Not there, obviously. Go back to sleep, Fiona. No use the whole family being unable to go to work tomorrow."

He was dressed and out of the house in minutes.

He was worried about Noel—very worried indeed.

"God bless you, Declan," Dingo said with huge relief when Declan came into Chestnut Court. He watched, mystified, as Declan expertly changed a nappy, washed and powdered the baby's bottom, made up the formula and heated the milk, all in seamless movements.

"I'd never be able to do that," Dingo said admiringly.

"Of course you would. You will when you have one of your own."

"I was going to leave it all to the woman, whoever she might be . . . ," Dingo admitted.

"I wouldn't rely on it, Dingo, me old mate. Not these days. It's shared everything, believe me. And quite right too."

Frankie was perfectly peaceful. All they had to do now was to find her father.

"He didn't say where he was going, but I sort of thought it was for an hour or two. I thought he was going home to his parents for something."

"Was he upset about anything before he went out?"

"I thought he was a bit distracted. He showed me all the numbers on the wall. . . ."

"As if he were planning to stay out, do you think?"

"God, I don't know, Declan. Maybe the poor lad was hit by a bus and we're all misjudging him. He could be in an A&E somewhere with his phone broken."

"He could." Declan didn't know why he felt so certain that Noel had gone back on the drink. The man had been heroic for months. *What* could have changed him? And, more important, how would they ever find him?

"Go home, Dingo," Declan sighed. "You've held the fort for long enough. I'll do it until Noel gets back."

"Should we ring anyone on this list, do you think?" Dingo didn't want to abandon everything.

"It's one in the morning. No point in worrying everyone."

"No, I suppose not." Dingo was still reluctant.

"I'll call you, Dingo, when he's found, and I'll tell him you didn't want to leave but I forced you to." He had hit the right note. Dingo hadn't wanted to leave his post without permission. Now he could go back home without guilt.

Declan sat down beside Frankie's crib. The baby slept on as peacefully as his own son slept back at home. But little Johnny Carroll had a much more secure future ahead of him than poor baby Frankie here. Declan sighed heavily as he settled himself into an armchair.

Where could Noel be until this hour?

Noel was asleep in a shed on the other side of Dublin.

He had no idea how he had got there. The last thing

he could remember was some kind of argument in a bar and people refusing him further drink. He had left in annoyance and then found, to his rage, that he couldn't get back in again, and there were no other public houses in the area. He had walked for what seemed a very long time and then it got cold, so he decided to have a rest before he went home.

Home?

He would have to be careful letting himself in to 23 St. Jarlath's Crescent—then he remembered with a shock that he didn't live there anymore.

He lived in Chestnut Court with Frankie and Lisa.

He would have to be even more careful going back there. Lisa would be shocked at him and Frankie might even be frightened. But Lisa was away. He remembered that now. His heart gave a sudden jump. What about the baby? He would never have left Frankie alone in the apartment, would he?

No, of course he hadn't. He remembered Dingo had come in. Noel looked at his watch. That was hours ago. Hours. Was Dingo still there? He wouldn't have contacted Moira, would he? Oh, please, God, please, St. Jarlath, please, anyone up there, let Dingo not have rung Moira.

He felt physically ill at the thought and realized that he was indeed going to be sick. As a courtesy to whoever owned this garden shed, Noel went out to the road. Then his legs felt weak and wouldn't support him. He went back into the shed and passed out.

In spite of the discomfort, Declan slept for several hours in the chair. When the light came in the window he realized that Noel hadn't come home. He went to make himself a cup of tea and decide what to do. He rang Fiona.

"Is today one of Moira's days up in your clinic?"

"Yes, she'll be there for the morning. Are you coming home?"

"Not immediately. Remember, don't say a word to her about any of this. We'll try to cover for him, but she can't know. Not until we've found him."

"Where is he, Declan?" Fiona sounded frightened.

"Out on the tear somewhere, I imagine. . . ."

"Listen, Signora and Aidan will be here soon. They're collecting Johnny and will be going to pick up Frankie then and take them to their daughter's place. . . ."

"I'll wait until they're here. I'll have her ready for them."

"You really are a saint, Declan," Fiona said.

"What else can we do? And remember, Moira knows nothing."

"Not a word to the Kamp Kommandant," Fiona promised.

The clinic was in a state of fuss because Frank Ennis was paying one of his unexpected visits.

"You were out with him last night—did he not give you *any* idea he was coming in today?" Hilary asked Clara Casey.

"*Me?*" asked Clara in disbelief. "I'm the very last person on earth that he'd tell. He's always hoping to catch me out in something. It's driving him mad that he hasn't been able to do it so far."

"Look, he's talking to Moira very intently about something," Hilary whispered.

"Well, we marked her card for her about Frank," Clara said, "and if Ms. Tierney says a word out of order she's out of here."

"I'll get nearer and see what they're talking about," Hilary offered.

"Really, Hilary, I *am* surprised at you," Clara said in mock horror.

"You go away and I'll hover," said Hilary. "I'm a great hoverer. That's why I know so much."

Clara made for her desk, which was in the center of the clinic; there was a phone call from Declan.

"Don't say my name," he said immediately.

"Sure, right. What can I do for you?"

"Is Moira near you?"

"Quite, yes."

"Could you find out what she's doing after she leaves you today? I'll make myself clear. We share baby-minding arrangements with a friend and his baby. It's just that they're clients of Moira's and she's been a bit tough on him. He's gone off on a batter. I have to drag him back here and sort things out. We want to keep Moira out of the place until tomorrow, at any rate. If she discovers the setup, then things will really hit the fan."

"I see . . ."

"So, if there was any other direction you could head her towards . . . ?"

"Leave it with me," Clara said, "and cheer up—maybe your worst scenario won't turn out to be right."

"No, I'm afraid it's only too right. His AA buddy has just called in. He's getting him back here in about half an hour."

Hilary came over to Clara with a report.

"He's pumping her for information. Like 'Do you see any areas of conspicuous waste,' and 'Do the healthy cookery classes work or are they just a distraction.' You know, the usual kind of thing he goes on about."

"And what's she singing in response?"

"Nothing yet, but that may be because she's here under our eye. If he got her on his own, Lord knows what he'd get out of her."

"Be more confident, Hilary. We're not doing anything wrong here. But you've given me an idea."

Clara approached Frank Ennis and Moira.

"Seeing you two together reminded me that Moira hasn't seen the social-work setup in the main hospital. Frank, maybe you could introduce her to some of the team over there—today, possibly?"

"Oh, I have a lot of calls to make on my caseload."

Clara gave a tinkling laugh. "Oh, really, Moira, you're so much on top of everything, I imagine your caseload is run like clockwork."

Moira seemed pleased with the praise.

"You know the way it is. You've got to be watchful," she said.

"I agree," Frank boomed unexpectedly. "Everyone should be much more watchful than they are."

"I *was* hoping, Moira, that you could link up with the whole system, but of course if you feel it's too much for you . . . then . . ."

Clara had judged it exactly right. Moira made an arrangement to meet Frank at lunchtime.

Clara had managed to give Noel, Declan and the man from Alcoholics Anonymous a bit of a head start.

————

Aidan and Signora Dunne had arrived with little Johnny Carroll and taken Frankie with them. They would wheel the two baby buggies along the canal to Aidan's daughter's house. There Signora would look after all three children—their grandson, Joseph Edward, along with Frankie and Johnny, while Aidan gave private Latin lessons to students who hoped to go to university.

It was a peaceful and undemanding morning. If they had wondered what Dr. Carroll was doing in Noel Lynch's place and why there was no sign of a normally devoted father, they had said nothing. They minded their own business, the Dunnes. Declan was glad of them many times, but never more so than today. The fewer people who knew about this, the better.

Malachy arrived, more or less supporting Noel in the doorway. Noel was shaking and shivering. His clothes were filthy and stained. He seemed totally disoriented.

"Is he still drunk?" Declan asked Malachy.

"Hard to say. Possibly." Malachy was a man of few words.

"I'll turn on the shower. Can you get him into it?"

"Sure."

Malachy was as good as his word. He propelled Noel into the water, letting it get cooler all the time until it was almost cold. Meanwhile, Declan picked up all the dirty clothes and put them into the washing machine. He laid out clean clothes from Noel's room and made them all a pot of tea.

Noel's eyes were more focused now, but still he said nothing.

Malachy was not speaking either.

Declan poured another mug of tea and allowed the silence to become uncomfortable. He would *not* make things easy for Noel. The man would have to come up with something. Answers, or even questions.

Eventually Noel asked, "Where's Frankie?"

"With Aidan and Signora."

"And where's Dingo?"

"Gone to work," Declan said tersely. Noel was going to have to speak again.

"And did he phone *you*?" He nodded towards Declan.

"Yes, that's why I'm here," Declan said.

"And are you the only one he phoned?" Noel's voice was a whisper.

Declan shrugged. "I've no idea," he said. Let Noel sweat a bit. Let him think that Moira was on the case.

"Oh, my God . . . ," Noel said. His face had almost dissolved in grief.

Declan took pity on him. "Well, no one else turned up, so I suppose I was the only one," he said.

"I'm so sorry," Noel began.

"Why?" Declan cut across him.

"I can't remember. I really can't. I felt a bit uptight and I thought one or two drinks might help and wouldn't matter. I didn't know it was going to end like this. . . ."

Declan said nothing and Malachy was silent too. Noel couldn't bear it.

"Malachy, why didn't you stop me?" he asked.

"Because I was at home doing a jigsaw with my ten-year-old son. I didn't hear from you that you were going out—that's why." Malachy hadn't spoken such a long sentence before.

"But, Malachy, I thought you were meant to . . ."

"I am *meant* to come when there's a danger that you might be about to go back to drinking. I am *not* meant to be inspired by the Holy Ghost as to when you decide this kind of activity all on your own," Malachy said.

"I didn't know it was going to turn out like this," Noel said piteously.

"No, you thought it would be lovely and easy like the movies. And I bet you wondered what we were all doing at those meetings."

Noel's face showed that this is exactly what he had wondered.

Declan Carroll suddenly felt very tired. "Where do we go from here?" he asked both men.

"It's up to Noel," Malachy said.

"Why is it up to me?" Noel cried.

"If you want to try to kick it again, I'll try to help you. But it's going to be hell on earth."

"Of course I want to," Noel said.

"It's no use if you are just waiting for me to get out of your hair so that you can sneak off and stick your face into it again."

"I won't do that," Noel wailed. "From tomorrow on it will be back just the same as it was up to now."

"What do you mean *tomorrow*? What's wrong with *today*?" Malachy asked.

"Well, tomorrow, fresh start and everything."

"Today, fresh start and everything," Malachy said.

"But just a couple of vodkas to straighten me up and then we can start with a clean slate?" Noel was almost begging now.

"Grow up, Noel," Malachy said.

Declan spoke. "I can't let you look after our son anymore, Noel. Johnny won't come here again unless we know you're off the sauce," he said slowly and deliberately.

"Ah, Declan, don't hit me when I'm down. I wouldn't hurt a hair of that child's head." Noel had tears in his eyes.

"You left your own daughter with Dingo Duggan for hour after hour. No, Noel, I wouldn't risk it. And even if I did, Fiona wouldn't."

"Does she have to know?"

"I think so, yes." Declan hated doing it, but it was the truth. They couldn't trust Noel anymore. And if he felt like that, what would Moira feel?

It didn't bear thinking about.

"We have to tell Aidan and Signora," Declan said.

"Why?" Noel asked, worried. "I'm over it now. I hate them knowing I'm so weak."

"You're *not* weak, Noel—you're very strong. It's not easy for you doing what you do. I know. Believe me."

"No, I don't believe you, Declan. You were always a social drinker, a pint in the evening and no more. That's balance and moderation—two things I was never any good at."

"You took on more than most men would have done. I admire you a lot," Declan said simply.

"I don't admire myself. I disgust myself," Noel said.

"And what help will that be to Frankie as she grows up? Come on, Noel—it's her first Christmas coming up. The whole street is going to celebrate. You've got to get yourself into good form for it. No self-pity."

"But Signora and Aidan?"

"They know *something* is wrong. We mustn't play games with them. They can cope with it, Noel. They've coped with a lot in their lives."

"Anyone else I should tell?" Noel looked defensive and hurt by it all.

"Yes, Lisa, of course, and Emily." Declan was very definite.

"No, please. Please, not Emily."

"No need to tell your parents or my parents or anyone like that, but Emily and Lisa need to know."

"I thought it was over," Noel said sadly.

Declan forced himself to be cheerful. "It will be over soon and meanwhile the more help you can get, the better."

"Go back to the real world and heal the sick, Declan. Don't bother with me and my addictions."

"What could be more real than the man whose daughter is going to be best friends with our son—remember? We arranged it with Stella."

"Thank God she doesn't know how it all turned out," Noel said fervently.

"It turned out very well until now and it will again. Anyway, according to people like your parents and mine, Stella *does* know, and she understands it all perfectly."

"You don't believe any of that claptrap, Declan, do you?"

"Not exactly, but you know . . ." Declan ended it vaguely.

"No, I don't know, I don't know at all. But if I have to tell Aidan and Signora then I will. Is that okay?"

"Thanks, Noel."

Declan had, of course, already told Fiona all about Noel. She had been, as usual, practical and optimistic.

"He sounds shocked by what he did," she said.

"Yes, but I wish I knew *why* he did it," Declan said, worried.

"You said yourself he was in bad form."

"But he must have been in bad form a hundred times during the last few months and he never went out on the town. He loves that child. You should see him with her. He's as good as any mother."

"I know, I *have* seen him . . . everyone has. That child has a dozen families round here who'll all do a bit more at the moment."

"Noel's very sensitive about not letting people know, but he has to tell them. Until he does, don't say anything."

"Quiet as the grave," Fiona said.

Declan Carroll took his morning surgery. He had been two hours late, so Dr. Hat had been called in to help.

"Muttie Scarlet rang a couple of times. He said you'd have some results for him today."

"And I do," Declan said glumly.

"I thought you might." Dr. Hat was sympathetic.

"Isn't it a shit life, Hat?" Declan said.

"It is indeed, but I'm usually the one who says that and you always say it's not so bad."

"I'm not saying that today. I'm off out to Muttie's house. Can you stay a bit longer?"

"I'll stay as long as you like. They don't want me, though; they'll ask when the *real* doctor will be back," Dr. Hat said.

"I bet they do! They still ask me was I born when they got their first twinge of whatever they have and the answer is always that I wasn't."

"Ah, Declan, any news yet?" Muttie answered the door. He spoke in a low voice. He didn't want his wife, Lizzie, to hear the conversation.

"You know how they are," Declan said. "They're so laid-back up there in the hospital they give a new urgency to the word *mañana*. . . ."

"So?" Muttie asked.

"So I was wondering would we go and have a pint?" Declan said.

"I'll go and get Hooves," Muttie suggested.

"No, let's go to Casey's instead of Dad's and your pub—too many Associates there . . . we'd get nothing said."

Declan saw from Muttie's face that he realized immediately that the news wasn't good.

Old Man Casey served them and, since there was no response to his conversation about the weather, the neighborhood and the recession, he left them alone.

"Give it to me straight, Declan," Muttie said.

"It's only early days yet, Muttie."

"It's bad enough for a drink in the middle of the day, lad. Will you tell me or do I have to beat it out of you?"

"They saw a shadow on the X-ray; the scan showed a small tumor."

"Tumor?"

"You know . . . a lump. I've made an appointment for you with a specialist next month."

"Next *month*?"

"The sooner we deal with it, the better, Muttie."

"But how in the name of God did you get an appointment so soon? I thought there was a waiting list as long as your arm?"

"I went private," Declan said.

"But I'm a workingman, Declan, I can't afford these fancy fees. . . ."

"You won a fortune a few years back on some horse. You've got money in the bank—you *told* me."

"But that's for emergencies and rainy days. . . ."

"This is a rainy day, Muttie." Declan blew his nose very loudly. This was more than he could bear at the moment. He heard himself lying as he felt he had been lying all day.

"The thing is, Muttie, once this appointment is made you can't cancel it. You have to pay for it anyway."

"Isn't that disgraceful!" Muttie was outraged. "Aren't they very greedy, these people?"

"It's the system," Declan said wearily.

"It shouldn't be allowed." Muttie shook his head in disapproval.

"But you'll go, won't you? Tell me you'll go?"

"I'll go because you can't get me out of it. But it's very high-handed of you, Declan. But if he suggests some mad, expensive treatment, he's not getting another cent out of me!" Muttie vowed.

"No, it's just to know the treatment that he would advise. One visit . . ."

"All right then," Muttie grumbled.

"You never asked me one single thing about the whole business," Declan said. "I mean, there are a lot of options: chemotherapy, radiotherapy, surgery . . ."

Muttie looked at him with the air of a man who has seen it all and heard it all. "Won't I hear all about it from the fellow whose Rolls-Royce *I'm* paying for? No point in thinking about it until I have to. Okay?"

"Okay," agreed Declan, who was beginning to wonder would this day ever end.

By the time that Moira called at Chestnut Court, things had settled down a lot.

Noel had agreed not to drink today. Malachy had taken him to an AA meeting, where nobody had blamed him but everyone had congratulated him on turning up that day.

Halfway through the meeting, Noel remembered that he had not let them know in Hall's that he wouldn't be in today.

"Declan did that ages ago," Malachy said.

"What did he say?"

"That he was your doctor and you weren't able to go in. That he was telephoning from your flat."

"I wonder how Mr. Hall took that?" Noel was full of anxiety.

"Oh, Declan would have reassured him. You'd believe anything he said. Anyway, it was all true. You weren't able to go in and he *was* at your flat."

"He looked very put out about everything," Noel said. "I hope he won't turn against me."

"No, I think he was put out about something else."

Malachy knew when there was a time to be very firm and a time to be more generous.

Moira viewed the presence of Malachy in the house with no great pleasure.

"Are you a babysitter?" she asked.

"No, Ms. Tierney, I am from Alcoholics Anonymous. That's how I know Noel."

"Oh, really . . ." Her eyes narrowed slightly. "Any reason for the visit?"

"We were at a meeting together up the road and I came back for some tea with Noel. That's permitted, isn't it?"

"Of course—you mustn't make me into some kind of a monster. I'm merely here for Frankie's sake. It's just that we had a full and frank exchange of views yesterday and I suppose, well, when I saw you here, I thought that you might . . . that Noel could possibly . . . that all was not well."

"And so now you are reassured?" Malachy asked silkily.

"Frankie will be coming back shortly. We want to get things ready for her . . . unless there's anything else?" Noel spoke politely.

Moira left.

Malachy turned to Noel. "One ball-breaker," he said, and for the first time that day Noel smiled.

Everyone had been planning a Christmas party for Frankie and Johnny. Balloons and paper decorations had been discussed at length and in detail. It was going to be held in

Chestnut Court: the apartment block had a big communal room that could be rented for such occasions. Lisa and Noel had reserved it weeks back. Was it to go ahead or was Noel too frail to be part of it?

"We've got to go for it," Lisa encouraged him. "Otherwise when she looks back on her album she'll wonder why there was no celebration for her first Christmas."

"She won't be looking back on any album with us," Noel said grimly.

"What do you mean?"

"They'll take her from me, and rightly so. Who would leave a child with me?"

"Well, thank you very much from the rest of us who are doing our best to make a home for her," Lisa said tartly. "We are not going to give up so easily. Get her into the pram, Noel, and we'll head off and look at this room."

Just then the phone rang.

"Noel, it's Declan. Can we leave Johnny with you for an hour or so—it would be a great help." This was the first time since Noel's drinking incident that Johnny had been offered.

Noel knew it was a peace offering and an olive branch. But he also knew it was a vote of confidence. He stood a bit taller now.

"Sure, Declan, we'll take him off to see the room where he's having his first Christmas party," he said. And he felt that Declan was pleased too, glad to know the party was going ahead.

Having a party for the children three days before Christmas was a great opportunity for the families to get together. Most of them celebrated the actual day quietly, eating too much of their own turkeys and sitting with family in front of the television. But this was an excuse to get together and wear paper hats and pretend that it was all for the children, two small babies who would sleep through most of it.

Lisa was in charge of decorating the hall, and she did it in scarlet and silver. Emily helped her to drape huge red curtains borrowed from the church hall, Dingo Duggan had brought a van full of holly from what he described vaguely as the countryside, Aidan and Signora had decorated a tree that would be left in the big room over the Christmas season. They were going to bring their own grandson, Joseph Edward, to the party as a guest, and Thomas Muttance Feather, Muttie's grandson, was coming on the assurance that he wouldn't have to talk to babies or sit at a children's table.

Josie and Charles were wondering if a picture of St. Jarlath would be appropriate in the decorations, and tactfully, Lisa found a place for it. Somewhere it wouldn't look utterly ludicrous.

Simon and Maud had a job doing a house party, so they couldn't do the catering, but Emily had arranged a supper where all the women would bring a chicken or vegetable dish of some sort, and all the men would bring wine and beer or soft drinks and a dessert. The desserts had of course turned out to be an immense number of chocolate ones bought in supermarkets. They were arranged artistically on paper plates on a separate table to be wheeled in after the main course was finished.

Noel showed Frankie all the Christmas decorations and smiled at her adoringly as she squealed with pleasure and sucked her fingers. Dressed in a red Babygro and with a little red pixie hat keeping her head warm, she was passed around from one doting adult to another, and featured in a hundred photographs along with Johnny. Even Thomas was persuaded to join in and posed for pictures with the three youngsters and a plate of mince pies.

Father Flynn had brought a Czech trio to play. They had been lonely in Dublin and missed their homeland, so he arranged a number of outings like this, which they enjoyed doing while they got a good meal and their bus money, and an audience cheering them on.

They sang Christmas songs and carols in Czech and in English. And when it came to

> *Away in a manger*
> *No crib for His bed*
> *The little Lord Jesus*
> *Laid down His sweet head*

a hush fell on family and friends as they looked at the two sleeping babies. Then they all joined in the singing for the next bit:

> *The stars in the bright sky*
> *Looked down where He lay*
> *The little Lord Jesus*
> *Asleep on the hay*

and everyone in the room, believers or nonbelievers, felt some sense of Christmas that they had not felt before.

"You're very good giving Muttie a lift," Lizzie said when Declan called at the Scarlet house on a cold, gray January morning. "He hates going to the bank—it makes him feel uneasy. He's dressed himself up likes a dog's dinner, but he's been like a caged lion all morning."

"Oh, don't worry, Lizzie—I'm going there anyway and I'd enjoy the company."

Declan realized that Muttie had told Lizzie nothing whatsoever about his appointment with the specialist. He looked at Muttie, dressed in his best suit and tie, and couldn't help noticing how thin the older man had become. It was a wonder Lizzie hadn't seen it.

They drove in silence while Muttie drummed his fingers and Declan rehearsed what he was going to say when Dr. Harris delivered the news that was staring at Declan from X-rays, scans and reports. They called first at the bank, where Declan cashed a check just to prove that he had business there. Muttie withdrew 500 euros from his savings.

"Even Scrooge Harris can't charge that much," he said, nervously putting it in his wallet. Muttie Scarlet wasn't happy about carrying huge sums of money like this, but he was even less happy still about handing it over it to this greedy man.

As it turned out, Dr. Harris turned out to be a kindly man. He was more than pleased to have Declan join them for the consultation.

"If I start talking medical jargon, Dr. Carroll can turn it into ordinary English," he said with a smile.

"Declan is the first person who grew up on our street who became a professional man," Muttie said proudly.

"That so? I was the first in my family to get a degree

too. I bet they have a great graduation picture of you at home." Dr. Harris seemed genuinely interested.

"It replaces the Sacred Heart lamp." Declan grinned.

"Right, Mr. Scarlet, let's not waste your time here while we go down memory lane." Dr. Harris came back to the main point. "You've been to St. Brigid's and they've given me a very clear picture of your lungs. There are no gray areas—it's black-and-white. You have a large and growing tumor in your left lung and secondary tumors in your liver."

Declan noted that there was a carafe of water on the desk and a glass. Dr. Harris poured one for Muttie, who was uncharacteristically silent.

"So, now, Mr. Scarlet, we have to see how best to manage this."

Muttie was still wordless.

"Will an operation be an option?" Declan asked.

"No, not at this stage. It's a choice between radiotherapy and chemotherapy at the moment and arranging palliative care at home or in a hospice."

"What's palliative care?" Muttie spoke for the first time.

"It's nurses who are trained to deal with diseases like yours. They are marvelous, very understanding people who know all about it."

"Have they got it themselves?" Muttie asked.

"No, but they have been well trained and they know a lot about it from nursing other people—what patients want and how to give you the best quality of life."

Muttie thought about this for a moment. "The quality of life I want is to live for a long, *long* time with Lizzie, to see all my children again, to see the twins well settled in a business or good jobs and to watch my grandson Thomas Muttance Feather grow up into a fine young man. I'd like to walk my dog, Hooves, for years to the pub, where I meet my Associates, and go to the races about three times a year. That would be a great quality of life."

Declan saw Dr. Harris remove his glasses for a moment and concentrate on cleaning them. When he trusted himself to speak again he said, "And you *will* be able to do a good deal of that for a time. So let's look forward to that."

"Not live for a long, long time, though?"

"Not for a long, long time, Mr. Scarlet, no. So the important thing is how we use what time is left."

"How long?"

"It's difficult to say exactly. . . ."

"*How long?*"

"Months. Six months? Maybe longer, if we're lucky. . . ."

"Well, thank you, Dr. Harris. I must say you've been very clear. Not worth hundreds of euros, but you were straight and you were kind as well. How much exactly do I owe you?" Muttie took his wallet from his pocket and laid it on the desk.

Dr. Harris didn't even look at it. "No, no, Mr. Scarlet, you were brought here by Dr. Carroll, a fellow doctor. There's a tradition that we never charge fellow doctors for a consultation."

"But there's nothing wrong with Declan," Muttie said, confused.

"You're his friend. He brought you here. He could have gone to other specialists. Please accept this for what it is, normal procedure, and put that away. I will write my report and recommendations to Dr. Carroll, who will look after you very well."

Dr. Harris saw them to the lift. Declan noticed him shake his head at the receptionist as she was about to present the bill and Declan breathed a little more easily. Now all he had to do was to keep Noel on the wagon and, more immediately, go home with Muttie and help him tell Lizzie.

Thank God Hat was able to keeps things going until he got back to his surgery.

Fiona knew there was something wrong the moment he came in the door.

"Declan, you're white as a sheet! What happened? Was it Noel?"

"I love you, Fiona, and I love Johnny," he said, head in his hands.

"Ah, God, Declan, what *is* it?"

"It's Muttie."

"What's happened to him? Declan, tell me in the name of God. . . ."

"He has just a few months," Declan said.

"Never!" She was so shocked she had to sit down.

"Yes. I was at the specialist this morning with him."

"I thought you were taking him to the bank."

"I did, so that he could get the money for a specialist."

"Muttie went private? God, he *must* have been worried," Fiona said.

"I hijacked him into it, but the specialist waived the fee."

"Why on earth did he do that?"

"Because Muttie is Muttie," Declan said.

"He'll have to tell Lizzie," Fiona said.

"It's done. I was there." Declan looked stricken.

"And?"

"It was as bad as you'd think. Worse. Lizzie said she still had so many things to do with Muttie. She had been planning to take him to the Grand National in Liverpool. You know, Fiona, Muttie's never going to make it to Aintree."

And then he sobbed like a child.

Maud and Simon, who had grown up with Muttie and Lizzie and hardly remembered any former life, were heartbroken.

"It's not as if he were really old," Maud said.

"Sixty is meant to be only middle-aged nowadays," Simon agreed.

"Remember the cake we made for his birthday?"

" 'Sixty Glorious Years.' "

"We'll have to put off going to America," Maud said.

"We can't do that. What if they won't keep the job for us?" Simon was very anxious.

"There will be other jobs. Later, you know, afterwards." Maud didn't want them to go.

But Simon wasn't willing to let it go easily. "It's such a chance, Maud. He'd want us to have it. We'll be earning a big salary. We could send him money."

"When was Muttie ever interested in money?"

"I know . . . you're right. I was just trying to think of excuses, really," Simon admitted.

"So let's try to get shifts in good Dublin restaurants."

"They'd never take us on. We don't have enough experience."

"Oh, come on, Simon, don't be such a defeatist. We have terrific recommendations and references from all the people we did catering for. I bet they'll take us on."

"Where will we start?"

"I think we should invest a little money first, have dinner somewhere like Quentins, Colm's or Anton's. You know, top places. And we'd regard it as research, keep our eyes open and *then* go back and ask for a job."

"It seems a heartless sort of thing to be doing when poor Muttie is in such bad shape."

"It's better than going to the other side of the earth," Maud said.

They would start with Colm's up in Tara Road. They chose the cheapest items on the menu, but took notes on everything: the way the waiters served, how they offered the wine for tasting, the way the cheeses were brought to the table and how they were sliced according to the customers' wishes, with some advice from the waiter.

"We had better learn our cheeses before trying here," Maud whispered.

"That's the head guy there." Simon pointed out Colm, the owner.

He came to their table. "Nice to see a younger set coming in," he said, welcoming them.

"We're in the catering business ourselves," Maud said suddenly.

"Really?"

Simon was annoyed. They hadn't planned to blurt it out so quickly. Now they had exposed themselves as spies and not real diners.

"We have terrific recommendations and I was wondering if we could leave you our business card. Just in case you were short-staffed."

"Thank you. Of course I'll keep it. Here, are you any relation of Cathy Mitchell of Scarlet Feather?"

"Yes, she trained us," Maud said proudly.

"She was married to a cousin of ours, Neil Mitchell." Simon saw no need to explain the situation any further.

"Well, well, if Cathy trained you, you must be great! But I won't have anything just for the moment. My partner's daughter Annie— that's her over there—she's just started here, so we're fairly well covered at the moment. Still, I'll put your names in the book." Then he retired to the kitchen.

"He was nice," Maud whispered.

"Yeah, I hope he won't go checking up with Cathy on us just now. She's very upset about Muttie and it would look a bit heartless."

They decided on chemotherapy for Muttie, and by this stage everyone in St. Jarlath's Crescent knew about him and had a variety of cures. Josie and Charles Lynch said that in recognition for Muttie's interest in the campaign for his statue, St. Jarlath would put in a word for him. Dr. Hat said that he would be happy to drive Muttie to the pub any evening he wanted to go. Hat wouldn't stay, but he'd come back and pick him up later. Emily Lynch managed to distract Muttie by planting winter-color shrubs in his garden.

"But will I be still here to see them, Emily?" he asked one day.

"Oh, come on, Muttie. The great gardeners of history always knew that someone would see them. That's what it's all about."

"That makes sense," Muttie said, and put aside any thought of self-pity.

Declan's own parents saw that there was a half leg of lamb left over at the end of the day or four fillet steaks.

Cathy came by every day, often with something to eat.

"We made far too many of these little salmon tarts, Dad. Mam, you'd be helping me out if you were to take them."

Often she brought her son, Thomas, with her. He was a lively lad and kept Muttie well entertained.

In fact, it was all going better than Declan could have hoped. He had thought that the normally cheerful Muttie would fall into a serious depression. But it was far from being the case. Declan's father said that Muttie was still the life and soul up at the pub and he had the same number of pints as ever on the grounds that there wasn't much damage they could do to him now.

Declan wrote to the specialist, Dr. Harris.

> *You were so kind and gracious when I brought Muttie Scarlet to a consultation. Your gesture about the fees was so appreciated that I thought you would like to know he is making very good progress, keeping his spirits up and generally living each day to the full.*
>
> *You and your positive attitude have contributed greatly to this, and I thank you most sincerely.*
> *Declan Carroll*

Mr. Harris responded by return.

Dr. Carroll,

I was glad to hear from you. I have friends who run a general practice and they are looking for a new partner. They asked me could I recommend anyone and I immediately thought of you. It's in a very attractive part of Dublin and would come with accommodation, which would be available for purchase, if required. I have attached some details for your interest.

These are very good, concerned people and just because their neighbourhood is affluent does not mean that their patients are rich people with hypochondria. They are sick and worried like people everywhere.

Let me know if it interests you, and send me your CV, and it can be arranged. Sooner rather than later, they tell me.

I will never forget your friend Muttie Scarlet. Only occasionally in life do you come across a genuinely good person like that. Someone with no disguises whatsoever.

I look forward to hearing from you.

Sincerely,

James Harris

Declan had to read the letter three times before it sank in. He was being offered a place in one of the most prestigious practices in the whole of Dublin. A house with a big garden and a posh school for Johnny. It was the kind of post he might have tried for in ten years' time. But *now*! Before he was thirty! It was too much to take onboard. Fiona had gone to work when the letter arrived so he couldn't share the news. Emily had come to pick up Johnny and wheel him up to Noel's to collect Frankie. Today the children were going to the thrift shop for the morning and back here to his parents' in the afternoon. The system ran like clockwork and Noel seemed to be back on track also.

Declan's surgery began at ten so he would have time to call in to Muttie and discuss the palliative-care nurse who was arriving for the first time today. Declan knew the nurse. She was an experienced, gentle woman called Jessica, trained in making the abnormal seem reasonable and quick to anticipate anything that might be needed.

"He's his own man, Jessica," Declan had warned her. "He might tell you there's nothing wrong with him at all."

"I know, Declan, relax. We'll get on fine together." And Declan knew that they would.

Moira was bustling down St. Jarlath's Crescent when Declan went out. She seemed surgically attached to her clipboard of notes. Declan had never seen her without them. He waved and kept walking, but she stopped him. She clearly had something on her mind.

"Where are you heading?" he asked easily.

"I heard there was a house for sale in this street," Moira said. "I've always wanted a little garden. Do you know anything about it? It's Number Twenty-two."

Declan thought quickly; it belonged to an old lady who was going into an old people's home, but it was exactly next door to Noel's parents. Noel would not welcome that.

"Might be in poor condition," Declan said. "She was a bit of a recluse."

"Well, that might make it cheaper," Moira said cheerfully. She looked nice when she smiled.

"Noel still okay?" she asked.

"Well, you actually see him more than I do, Moira," Declan said.

"Yes, well, it's my job. But he can be a little touchy at times, don't you find?"

"Touchy? No, I never found that."

"Just one day there recently, he actually pushed my notes out of my hands and shouted at me."

"What was all that about?"

"About someone called Dingo Duggan who had been appointed as an extra babysitter. I asked about him and Noel shouted at me that he was a *'decent poor eejit'* and used most abusive language. It was quite intolerable."

Declan looked at her steadily. So *that* was what had tilted Noel that night. He hardly trusted himself to speak.

"Is anything wrong, Declan?" she asked. "I get the feeling that I am not being told everything."

Declan swallowed. Soon he would be far away from Moira and Noel and St. Jarlath's Crescent. He reminded himself he must not explode and leave behind him a trail of confusion and bad feeling.

"I'm sure you were able to handle it very well, Moira," he said insincerely. "You must be used to the ups and downs of clients, as we are with patients."

"It's good when you're told the full story," Moira said. "But at the moment I think something is being kept from me."

"Well, when you discover what it is, you'll let me know, won't you?" Declan managed to fix a smile on his face and moved on.

———

He called in at the Laundromat where his mother worked, and kissed his son, who was sitting with his friend Frankie. The children were both like advertisements for Bonny Babies; they seemed to be endlessly fascinated with their hands.

"Who is his daddy's little boy, then," Declan said.

His voice sounded different. Molly Carroll looked at her son, concerned.

"Did you come in for anything, Declan?" she asked.

"Just to say hello to my son and heir and to thank my saintly mother and my friend Emily for making life so easy for us both." He smiled. A real smile this time.

"Well, isn't it the least I could do?" Molly was pleased. "Haven't I got what every mother dreams of? Her son and now her grandson living at home! When I think of all the people who hardly ever see their grandchildren, I feel blessed every single day."

Not for much longer, Declan thought to himself grimly. He went on to see Muttie and Lizzie. They were having a good-natured argument about how to welcome Jessica, who was going to arrive on her first call that day.

"I've made some scones, but Muttie thinks she'd like a good dinner. What do you think, Declan?"

"I think the scones would be fine and you can suggest lunch to her another time," Declan said.

"Is she a married person or a single lady?" Muttie asked.

"She's a widow, as it happens. Her husband died about three years ago."

"The Lord have mercy on him—it must be very hard on her," said Lizzie, without any apparent acknowledgment that she too would soon be a widow.

"Yes, but Jessica has great heart. She puts everything into her family and her work."

"That's very wise," said Lizzie. "And I hope she had a great doctor at the time like we do." She looked at Declan fondly.

"You can say that again," said Muttie.

"Stop that, Muttie, you're making my head swell!" he said.

"It deserves to swell. I've told everyone about that Dr. Harris and how he wouldn't charge me because you were a professional colleague of his and I was your Associate."

Declan felt a slight stinging behind his eyes. By the time that Muttie died, Declan and Fiona would be in a totally different part of Dublin. Not only would Muttie and Lizzie have lost their trusted doctor, but his own parents would have lost their son and grandson.

Before he got to work, he met Josie and Charles Lynch.

"I believe the house next door to you is up for sale?" he said.

"Yes, the notice is going up tomorrow. How do you know already?"

"Moira," he said simply.

"Lord, that woman can hear the grass grow," Josie said.

"She's been round to the house checking that there are no dog hairs. What kind of a world does she live in thinking that dogs don't shed hairs?"

"She's thinking of buying the house," Declan said.

"*Never!*" Josie was shocked. "Lord, she'll be practically *living* in our house!"

Charles shook his head. "Noel won't like this . . . not one little bit."

"Well, we always have Declan to stand up to her for us all." Josie was good at looking on the bright side.

Not for long, Declan thought to himself.

In the surgery that morning all the patients seemed to need to tell him some story or recall some instance where he had helped them. If Declan were to believe a quarter of the praise he got that morning, he would have been a very vain man. He just wished they had not chosen today to tell him all this. Today, of all days, when he was just about to change his life and leave them all.

He booked a table at Anton's restaurant for dinner. He wanted to tell Fiona in good surroundings, not in the house they shared with his parents, where everything could be heard in some degree anyway.

"How did you hear of us, sir?" the maître d' asked.

Declan was about to say that Lisa Kelly talked of little else, but something made him keep this information to himself.

"We read about it in the papers," he said vaguely.

"I hope we will live up to your expectations, sir," said Teddy.

"Looking forward to it," said Declan.

It seemed a long day until Dingo would come to pick them up at seven.

A couple of weeks before, Dingo had been to a party in a Greek restaurant and danced unwisely on some broken plates. Declan had tweezed the worst bits out of the soles of Dingo's feet. Money had not changed hands. It didn't, usually, in Dingo's case, but an offer of four trips in his van was agreed to be a fair exchange. This meant they could have a bottle of champagne when he told Fiona the great news.

Just before he left the surgery, Noel came by.

"Just three minutes of your time, Declan, please."

"Sure, come on in."

"You're always so good-natured, Declan. Is it real or is it an act?"

"Sometimes it's an act, but sometimes, like now, it's real." Declan smiled encouragingly.

"I'll come straight to the point then. I'm a bit worried about Lisa. I don't know what to do. . . ."

"What's wrong?" Declan was gentle.

"She's lost complete touch with reality when it comes to this Anton. I mean, she doesn't know what's real and what's not. Listen, I should know. I know what denial is. She's right in the center of it."

"Is she drinking or anything?" Declan wondered whether Noel might have developed an alcoholic's sudden lack of tolerance for any kind of drinking.

"No, no, nothing like that, just an obsession. She's deluding herself all the time. There's no future there."

"It's tough, all right."

"She needs help, Declan. She's ruining her life. You're going to have to refer her to someone."

"I'm not her doctor and she hasn't *asked* anyone to refer her anywhere."

"Oh, you were never one to play it by the book, Declan. Get somebody . . . some sort of psychiatrist to throw an eye over her."

"I *can't,* Noel. It doesn't work that way. I can't go in

off the side of the road and say: Lisa, Noel thinks you are heading in the wrong direction, so let's go and have a nice soothing visit to a shrink."

"It *should* be the way things work, and anyway, you'd know how to say it." Noel was pleading with him.

"But she hasn't done anything out of line. Your feelings about all this do you credit, but honestly there's no way that outside interference is going to help. Can't *you* get her to see sense? You live with her—you're flatmates."

"Sure, who would listen to a word I say?" Noel asked. "*You* always did, to give you your due. You used to make me feel I was a normal sort of a person and not a madman."

"And you *are*, Noel." Declan wondered was there anyone left who hadn't told him how important he was to them.

Fiona was in great form. She said she had starved herself at lunchtime. Barbara had wanted them to go for lunch together for a long chat about the complexity of men, but Fiona had said that she was going to Anton's that evening, so Barbara said there was no point in talking about the complexity of men to her anyway, that she had got a jewel of a husband and there weren't enough of them to go round.

She was all dressed up in her new outfit: a pink dress with a black jacket. Declan looked at her proudly as they were settled in at the restaurant. She looked so beautiful. She had a style equal to any of the other guests. He took her face in his hands and kissed her for a long time.

"Declan, really! What will people think?" she asked.

"They'll think we are alive and that we are happy," he said simply, and suddenly he made the second biggest decision of his life. The first had been to pursue Fiona to the end of the world. This one was different. It was about what he was not going to do.

He wouldn't tell her now about the letter from Dr. Harris. In fact, he might never tell her. It suddenly seemed so clear to him.

"I was thinking . . . I was wondering should we buy Number Twenty-two in the Crescent? It would be a home of our own, and we'd still be beside everyone."

Chapter Eight

"I have a bit of a problem," Frank Ennis said to Clara Casey as he picked her up at the heart clinic.

"Let me guess," she said, laughing. "We used one can of air freshener too many in the cloakroom last month?"

"No, nothing like that," he said impatiently, as he negotiated the traffic.

"No, don't tell me. I'll work it out. It's the brass plates on the door. We got a new tin of brass-cleaning stuff and I forgot to ask you? That's it, isn't it?"

"Truly, Clara, I don't know why you persist in painting me as this penny-pinching sort of clerk instead of the hospital manager. My worry has nothing to do with you and your extraordinary and lavish expenditure on your clinic."

"On *our* clinic, Frank. It's part of St. Brigid's."

"I'd say it's an independent republic—always was from day one."

"How petty and childish of you," she said disapprovingly.

"Clara, are you wedded to this concert tonight?" he asked suddenly.

"Is anything wrong?" She looked at him sharply. Frank never canceled arrangements.

"No, nothing is *wrong,* exactly, but I do need to talk to you," he said.

"Will you promise that it's not about boxes of tissues and packets of paper clips and huge areas of wastefulness that are bleeding your hospital dry?" Clara asked.

He actually smiled. "No, nothing like that."

"All right, then. Sure, we'll cancel the concert. Will we go out to a meal somewhere?"

"Come home with me."

"We have to eat somewhere, Frank, and you don't cook."

"I asked a caterer to leave in a dinner for us," he said, embarrassed.

"You were so sure I'd say yes?"

"Well, in a lot of areas of life you are quite reasonable—normal, even." He was struggling to be fair.

"Caterers. I see . . ."

"Well, they're quite young. Semi-professional, I'd say. Haven't learned to charge fancy prices yet."

"Slave labor? Ripe for exploitation, yes?" Clara wondered.

"Oh, Clara, will you give over just for one night?" Frank Ennis begged.

Maud and Simon were in Frank's apartment. They had set a table and brought their own paper napkins and a rose.

"Is that over the top?" Simon worried.

"No, he's going to propose to her. I know he is," Maud said.

"Did he tell you?"

"Of course he didn't, but why else is he making a meal for a woman in his flat?" To Maud it was obvious.

They had laid out the smoked salmon with the avocado mousse and a little rosette carved from a Sicilian lemon. The chicken-and-mustard dish was in the oven. An apple tart and cream were on the sideboard.

"I hope to God she says yes," Simon said. "It's a heavy outlay for that man, all this food and the cost of us and everything."

"She must be fairly old. . . ." Maud was thoughtful. "I mean, Mr. Ennis is as old as the hills. It's amazing that he still has the energy to propose, let's not even mention anything else!"

"No, let's not," said Simon, with relief. They let themselves out of the house and posted the keys back through the door.

Clara had always thought Frank's apartment rather bleak and soulless. Tonight, though, it looked different. There was subdued lighting and a lovely dinner table prepared.

And she noticed the red rose. This wasn't Frank's speed. She wondered whether the young caterers had dreamed it up. Suddenly she felt a great thudlike shock. He couldn't possibly be about to propose to her. Could he?

Surely not. Frank and she had been very clear about where they were going, which was a commitment-free re-

lationship. They were both able to go out with other people. Sometimes when they went away for a weekend, such
as the time they had that holiday in the Scottish High-
lands, they stayed in the same room and had what Clara
might have described as a limited, but pleasant, sex life.
That was if she were to tell anyone about it. But she told
nobody. Not her great friend Hilary in the clinic, nor her
oldest friend, Dervla.

Certainly not Clara's mother, who made occasional inquiries about her new escort. Not her daughters, who were
inclined to think that their poor old mother was long past
that sort of thing. Not her ex-husband, Alan, who was always hovering in the background, waiting for her to come
running back to him.

No. Frank could not have got the wires so hopelessly
crossed? Definitely not!

He went into his study and came out with some papers.

"This all looks very nice." Clara admired the place.

"Well, good. Good. And thank you for agreeing to
change the plans so readily."

"Not at all. It must be important. . . ." Clare wondered
what she would say if he really *had* lost the run of himself
and proposed. It would obviously be no, but how to put
it without hurting him or making him look ridiculous.
That was the problem.

Frank poured her a glass of wine and then passed the
papers over to her.

"This is my problem, Clara. I've had a letter from a
boy in Australia. He says he's my son."

———

Simon and Maud had asked Muttie to test out a recipe they had for koulibiac for them that evening. In fact, they both knew the dish worked perfectly well. They just wanted to give themselves an excuse for going to the trouble for him and to give him a role to play. They showed Muttie carefully how they had folded the pastry leaves and prepared the cooked salmon, rice and hard-boiled eggs.

He watched with interest. "When I was young, if we ever got a bit of salmon we'd be so delighted that we'd never wrap it up in rice and eggs and all manner of things!" He shook his head in wonder.

"Ah, well, nowadays, Muttie, they like things complicated," Maud explained.

"Is that why you're always talking about making your own pasta instead of buying it in the shops like everyone else?"

"Not a bit," Simon butted in with a laugh. "She's interested in pasta because she's interested in Marco!"

"I hardly know him," said Maud unconvincingly.

"But you'd like to know him more," Simon responded definitely.

"Who's Marco, anyway?" asked Muttie.

"His father is Ennio Romano—you know, Ennio's restaurant, the place we were telling you about," Simon added.

"We were hoping to get work there," said Maud.

"Some of us were *praying* we get work there," Simon added, laughing at his sister's blushes.

Maud tried to look businesslike. "It's an Italian restaurant; it makes sense for us to know how to make our own pasta. And even if we don't get work there, it would be useful for our home catering. The clients would be very impressed."

"And thinking they're knocking people's eyes out with envy," Simon said.

"But what's the point of asking people to your house and then upsetting them?" For Muttie this was a real problem.

The twins sighed.

"I wonder, has he asked her yet?" Maud said.

"If he doesn't want his dinner burned to a crisp, I'd say he has."

"Who's this?" Muttie asked with interest.

"A desperately old man called Frank Ennis is proposing to some very old woman."

"Frank Ennis? Does he work up in St. Brigid's?"

"Yes, he does. Do you know him, Muttie?"

"Not personally, but I know all about him from Fiona. Apparently, he is their natural enemy in the clinic where she works. Declan knows him too. He says your man is not a bad old skin, just obsessed with work."

"That will all end if he marries the old lady," Simon said thoughtfully.

"It will change for the old lady too, remember," Maud reminded them.

"Has he paid you?" Muttie asked suddenly.

"Yes. He left an envelope for us," Simon confirmed.

"Good. That's fine, then. I hear from Fiona that he's a total Scrooge and won't pay his bills until the last moment."

"He did mention thirty days' grace," Simon said.

"You didn't tell me!" Maud said.

"I didn't need to. I said to him we operated a money-up-front, no-credit business. He totally understood."

Simon was immensely proud of his negotiating skills and his command of the language of commerce.

Clara Casey was looking at the letter that Frank had handed to her.

"Are you sure you want me to read it?" she asked. "He didn't write it to me. . . ."

"He didn't *know* about you," Frank explained.

"But the question is what does he know about *you*?" Clara asked gently.

"Read it, Clara."

So she began to read a letter from a young man:

> You will be surprised to hear from me. My name is Des Raven and I believe that I am actually your son. This will probably strike terror into your heart and you will expect someone searching for a fortune turning up on your doorstep. Let me say at once that this is not at all the case.
>
> I live very happily here in New South Wales, where I'm a teacher and—just to reassure you—where I will go on living!
>
> If my presence in Dublin will cause embarrassment to you and your family, I will quite understand. I just hoped it might be possible for us to meet at least once when I am in Ireland. My mother, Rita Raven, died last year. She got a heavy pneumonia and didn't have it properly treated.
>
> I have not lived at home for the past six years while I went to teachers' training college, but I always came home once a week and cooked her a meal. Sure, she put the

washing through the machine for me, but she liked to do that. Truly she did.

Funny thing, I never asked her any questions about where I came from and what kind of a guy was my father. I didn't ask because she didn't seem very easy about the whole thing. She would say she had been very young and very foolish at the time and hadn't it all worked out so well. She said she never regretted one day of having me, which was good. And Australia had been good to her. She arrived here pregnant and penniless when she had me and then she trained as a hotel receptionist.

She had a couple of romances: one fellow lasted six years. I didn't much like him but he made her happy . . . and then I think something marginally more interesting for him turned up. She had a lot of good friends and kept in touch with her married sister, who lives in England. She was forty-two when she died, although she claimed to be thirty-nine and I'd say, all in all, she had a good and happy life.

Of you, Frank Ennis, I know nothing except your name on my birth certificate. I found you on the Internet and called the hospital from here and asked were you still working there and they said yes.

So here goes with the letter!

You only have my assurance that I will not make trouble for you and your present wife and family. I also know that you didn't know anything about where I lived. Mum was very adamant about that. She told me that every single birthday so that I wouldn't expect a gift.

I truly hope that we will meet.

Until then . . .

Des Raven

Clara put the letter down and looked over at Frank. His eyes were too bright and there was a tear on his face. She got up and went across to him with her arms out.

"Isn't this *wonderful*, Frank!" she cried. "You've got a son! Isn't that the best news in the world?"

"Well, yes, but we've got to be cautious," Frank began.

"What do we have to be cautious about? There was a woman called Rita Raven, wasn't there?"

"Yes, but . . ."

"And she disappeared off the scene?"

"She went to some cousins in the U.S.A.," he said.

"Or to some non-cousins in Australia . . . ," Clara corrected him.

"But it will all have to be checked out . . . ," he began to bluster.

She deliberately misunderstood him. "Of course the airlines and everything, but let him do that, Frank—the young are much better at getting flights online than we are. The main thing is what time is it in Australia? You can ring him straightaway." She busied herself removing the plastic wrap from the smoked salmon.

He hadn't moved. He couldn't bring himself to tell her he had had the letter for two weeks and hadn't been able to decide what to do.

"Come on, Frank, it's surely morning there and if you leave it any longer he'll have gone out to school. Call him now, will you?"

"But we'll have to talk about it?"

"Like what do we have to talk about?"

"But don't you mind?"

"*Mind*, Frank? I'm delighted. The only thing I mind is

you, after all these years, having to talk to an answering machine."

He looked at her, bewildered. There were so many things that he would never understand.

"How was Frank last night?" Hilary asked Clara the next day at the clinic. Only Hilary was ever given any information, and she was the only one who dared to ask.

"Amazing," Clara said and left it there.

"And did you enjoy the opera?" Hilary persisted.

"We didn't go. He arranged a catered meal in his apartment."

"My God, this sounds serious!" Hilary was delighted. She always said that they were made for each other. Something Clara continued to deny.

"Frank is as he always was and always will be: cautious and watchful, never spontaneous. Stop trying to matchmake, will you, Hilary?"

Frank had dithered so long last night that the telephone rang unanswered in Des Raven's home on the other side of the world. Frank had managed to miss talking to the son he hadn't known he had, just because he was anxious to talk it over and check it out. All this had led to nothing, but Clara told none of this to Hilary. It was still Frank's secret. She wasn't going to blurt it out.

"Where is Moira? Today's one of her days, isn't it?"

"She's just taken Kitty Reilly on a tour of residential homes. She has a checklist as long as her arm about what Kitty needs—you know, easy access to church, vegetarian food . . . that sort of thing." Hilary sounded half impressed, half annoyed.

"She's very thorough, I'll say that for her," Clara said grudgingly.

"I know what you mean. If she smiled more, maybe?" Hilary wondered. "Anyway, Linda rang you earlier. You were with somebody, so I took the call."

Hilary's son was married to Clara's daughter. The two women had schemed to introduce their children to each other and it had worked spectacularly well. Apart from not producing a grandchild. Despite a lot of intervention, there was no success. Both her son, Nick, and Clara's Linda were very despondent.

"She said no luck again."

"If she's so het up, she will *never* conceive. She has a list of three dozen people she phones every month. You, me and about thirty more."

"Clara!" Hilary was shocked. "She's your daughter and she thinks you are as excited as she is at the thought of you becoming a granny, and of me becoming one at the same time!"

"You're right—I'd forgotten. Pass me the phone." Hilary watched as Clara soothed Linda and patted her down.

Linda was obviously crying at the other end. Hilary moved away. She would have loved Nick and Linda to have given them good news. She could hear Clara saying, "Of *course* you're normal, Linda. Please stop crying, sweetheart. You'll have horrible, piggy, red eyes. I *know* you don't care, but you will later on when you're getting dressed to go out. . . . Well, to Hilary's, of course—that's where we're all going tonight. Don't even consider canceling, Linda. Hilary has bought *the* most gorgeous dessert."

"Oh, I have, have I?" Hilary said when Clara hung up.

"I had to say something. She was about to go home to a darkened room."

"All right, then. I had been going to serve cheese and grapes, but you've raised my game," Hilary said. "What did Frank Ennis serve last night as a dessert?"

"Apple tart," Clara said.

"Are you *sure* he didn't ask you some question? Something you've forgotten to tell me. . . ."

"Oh, shut up, Hilary. Look, here comes Moira. Let's pretend to be doing *some* work here."

Moira was triumphant. The fifth place they had looked at was perfect for Kitty Reilly—full of retired nuns and retired priests and a vegetarian option at every meal. All you could ask for, in fact.

"Lord, I hope I'll ask for a lot more than that when the time comes," Clara said piously.

"What would you like, exactly?" Moira asked.

An innocent enough question, but Moira's tone seemed to suggest that for Clara the time probably had come already.

"I don't know: a library, a casino, a gym, oh, and a grandchild!" Clara said. "What about you, Moira, when the time comes?"

"I'd like to be with friends. You know, people I have known for a long time so that we could do a lot of remembering together."

"And will you do that, do you think? Get a group of friends and set up your own place?" Clara was interested. She and her friend Dervla had often discussed doing just that.

"Probably not. I don't have many friends. I never had

time to make friends along the way," Moira said unexpectedly.

Clara looked at her sharply. For a moment the veil had been lifted and she saw a very lonely woman indeed. Then the veil fell again and it was as before.

"Will you come round this evening and we'll call him? Earlier than we did last night . . ." Frank was full of plans.

"No, Frank, I can't tonight. Hilary's cooking dinner," Clara said.

"But you *have* to come!" He was outraged.

"I can't, Frank. I told you . . ."

"You're very doctrinaire," he said crossly.

"And so are you. If you had called immediately you would have caught him."

"Please, Clara."

"No. I'm not saying it again. Wait until the next night if you need me to be there and hold your hand for you." She hung up.

Frank sat listening to the empty line. What a fool he had been not to have telephoned the boy immediately! Clara was right. He *had* dithered, and the only result of his delay was the boy would think he was having a door closed in his face. Of course he remembered Rita Raven. Who wouldn't have remembered her? His mother and father had been most disapproving.

Rita was from entirely the wrong kind of family. The Ennises hadn't worked hard and risen to this degree of respectability just to be dragged down by their son. Frank Ennis had had parents who acted swiftly. Rita Raven had disappeared from everyone's life. Frank had thought of her from time to time slightly wistfully, and now she had died. So young. He still saw her as the pretty seventeen-year-old she had been then. Imagine, she had gone all the way to Australia and had her child without ever letting him know. He had had simply no idea of this.

If he had known, what would he have done? He was uneasy thinking about it. Back then, on the edge of a career, back then, in a more disapproving climate, he might not have acted well. His parents had been so hostile about his relationship with Rita and so open in their relief that she had left the country. They couldn't possibly have known more than they said, could they? His stomach churned at the possibility of it. But they *couldn't*. Not paid a sum of money to buy her off. That was impossible. They were careful with money. No, he mustn't go down that avenue of suspicion.

Damn Clara and her hen parties! He really needed to have her at his side.

Hilary served them an elegant meal. When she had gone to the gourmet shop to buy a deluxe dessert, she saw some unusual salads and bought those too.

The conversation was tense and stilted, as it always was on the days after Linda had discovered that, yet again, she wasn't pregnant. Clara and Hilary looked at each other. Years ago it had been so different. There were orphanages full of children yearning for happy homes. Today, there were allowances and grants for single mothers.

Clara wondered if Moira had any further news about the child she said would shortly be going into care. She'd said the little girl was a few months, exactly the same age as Declan and Fiona's baby. Lucky little girl if she got Linda and Nick as parents. No child would find a more welcoming home, not to mention two besotted grannies. She must ask Moira about it tomorrow.

Clara let her mind wander to Frank's apartment. She hoped he was being tactful and diplomatic with Des Raven. Had she stressed enough that he must *sound* delighted and welcoming? The first impression was crucial. This boy had waited for over a quarter of a century to talk to his father. Let Frank make it a good experience for him. *Please.*

Yet again the call went to the answering machine.

Frank was unreasonably annoyed. Did this guy spend *any* time at home? It must be about six-thirty in the morning. Where *was* he? Absently, later in the evening he dialed again, and to his surprise the phone was answered by a girl with what seemed a very strong Australian accent. Frank realized that Des Raven probably spoke like that too.

"I was looking for Des Raven . . . ," he began.

"You missed him, mate," she said cheerfully.

"And who am I talking to?" Frank asked.

"I'm Eva. I'm housesitting."

"And when will he be back?"

"Three months. I'm walking his dog and looking after his garden."

"Oh, and are you his girlfriend?"

"Who are *you*?" she asked with spirit.

"Sorry, I'm just a . . . friend . . . from Ireland."

"Well, he's on his way to you, then." Eva was pleased

to have it all settled so easily. "Probably there now. No, wait, he's going to England first because that's where he lands. It's near you, right?"

"Yes, under an hour's plane journey." Frank felt the entire conversation was very unreal.

"Right, then, he knows where to find you?"

"He does?"

"Well, he left here with a briefcase full of papers and notes and letters. He showed a big batch to me. I think they were all from people he had written to who had written back."

"Yes, yes, indeed . . ." Frank was miserable.

"So, will I say who called him? I'm keeping a list beside the phone."

"Have many people called?" he asked out of interest.

"Nope, you're the first. What will I put down?"

"As you say, he'll be here in a day or two. . . ." Frank Ennis had no wish to muddy these waters any further.

He contemplated telling Clara, but she was at this confounded dinner and might not value an interruption about his private life. It was *impossible* to know how women would react to anything. Look at Rita Raven, heading to the ends of the earth to have a child by herself! Look at how childishly pleased Clara had been to hear that Frank had fathered a child outside marriage!

He thought morosely about the women after Rita and before Clara. A line, not a long line, but they all had one thing in common: they were incredibly hard to understand.

The boy would have to get in touch through the hospital. He didn't know Frank's home address. He wasn't going to blurt out the whole story to whoever he met first.

Frank had no fears on that score. The boy, Des, as he must learn to think of him, had written that he understood the moral climate might not have changed or moved on in Ireland as much as it had in Australia. He wished Des had sent a picture of himself. Then he realized that the boy . . . all right, Des . . . didn't know what his father looked like either.

Quite possibly there was a picture of Frank from many years ago. He hoped not. He hated being seen twenty-five years later, hair beginning to thin, stomach beginning to expand. What would Des Raven think of the father he had waited so long to meet? The days seemed to be crawling by.

When it happened it was curiously flat.

Miss Gorman, who had been hired by Frank ten years previously because she was not flighty, came in to see him. The years had resulted in Miss Gorman becoming even less flighty, if this was possible. She had a disapproval rating about almost everything. A man with an Australian accent had been on the phone wishing to talk to Mr. Ennis on a personal matter. He had been condemned because of his accent, his persistence and his defining anything to Miss Gorman as being personal. It was surprising, then, that Frank seemed to take it all so seriously.

"Where was he calling from?" he asked crisply.

"Somewhere in Dublin. He didn't really know *where* he was, Mr. Ennis." Miss Gorman's sniff was unmerciful.

"When he calls again, make sure that you put him right through."

"Well, I am sorry if I did the wrong thing, Mr. Ennis. It's just that you never *ever* talk to anyone you don't know."

"Miss Gorman, you didn't do the wrong thing. You are *incapable* of doing the wrong thing."

"I hope that I have been able to make this clear over the years." She was mollified and withdrew to await the call.

"I'm putting you through, Mr. Ennis," she said eventually.

"Thank you, Miss Gorman." He waited until she was off the line, then in a shaky voice he asked, "Des? Is that you?"

"So you *did* get my letter?" Very Australian but not very warm, not excited like his letter had been.

"Yes, I tried to call you but first it was the answering machine and then it was Eva. I talked to her and she told me that you had set out. I've been waiting for your call."

"I nearly didn't ring. . . ."

"Why was that? Was it nerves?" Frank asked.

"No, I thought why bother. You don't want to be involved with me. You've made that clear."

"That's *so* wrong," Frank cried out, stung by the unfairness of this. "I do indeed want to be involved with you. Why else would I have called you in Australia and talked to Eva?" He could almost hear the shrug of shoulders at the other end of the phone. "Why would I do that?"

Frank felt hollow. Somehow Clara had been right. He had paused when he should have gone enthusiastically forward. But that wasn't his nature. His nature was to examine everything minutely, and when he was sure, and not a moment before, then he would pronounce.

"You probably thought I was coming to claim my inheritance," Des said.

"It never crossed my mind. You said you wanted to get in touch. That's what I thought it was. I was as astonished as you. You know I only just heard of your existence, and I'm delighted!"

"Delighted?" Des sounded unconvinced.

"Yes, sure, I was delighted," Frank was stammering now. "Des, what *is* all this? You got in touch with me, I called you back. Will you come and have lunch with me today?"

"Where do you suggest?" Des asked.

Frank breathed out in relief. Then he realized he had to think quickly. Where to take the boy? "Depends what you'd like. . . . Quentins is very good and this new place, Anton's, is talked about a lot."

"Are these jacket-and-tie jobs?"

Frank realized that it had been years since he had gone anywhere that a jacket and tie was *not* necessary. There would be a lot of adapting ahead.

"Sort of traditional but not stuffy."

"I'll take that as a yes. Which place?"

"Anton's. I've never been there. Will we say one o'clock?"

"Why *don't* we say one o'clock?" Des sounded faintly mocking as if he were sending Frank up.

"I'll tell you how to get there . . . ," Frank began.

"I'll find it," Des said and hung up.

Frank buzzed through to Miss Gorman. Could she kindly find him the number for Anton's restaurant? No, he would make the reservation himself. Yes, he was quite sure. Perhaps she would cancel all appointments for the afternoon. She called back with the number and then added that she had spoken to Dr. Casey from the heart clinic, who said that there was no way the four p.m. meeting could be canceled. Too many people were setting too much store on the outcome. To have the meeting without Frank Ennis would be *Hamlet* without the prince. He would *have* to be back by four. What kind of a lunch would last three hours?

Chastened, Frank rang the restaurant.

"Can I speak to Anton Moran, please? . . . Mr. Moran? I have never begged before and I never will again, Mr. Moran, but today I arranged to meet for the first time a son I never knew I had and I picked your restaurant. Now I am hoping you will be able to find me a table. I don't know where to contact the young man . . . my son. . . . It will be such a messy start to our relationship if I have to tell him we couldn't get a booking."

The man at the other end was courteous. "This is far too important a matter to mess up," he said gracefully. "Of course you can have a table. Service today isn't full," he added, "but your story sounds so dramatic and so obviously true that I would have found a table for you even if I had to kneel down on all fours and pretend to be one."

Frank smiled, and suddenly he remembered Clara saying that he should be more immediate, more up-front with people. Nothing worked as well as the truth, she had advised him.

Another round to Clara. Was the woman going to be right about *everything*?

———

Frank was in the restaurant early. He looked around at the other diners, not a man without a collar, tie and smart jacket. *Why* had he chosen this place? But then again, if he had brought them to a burger place, it would hardly look festive. Or celebratory. It would look as if he were hiding this new member of his family. He watched the door and every time some man came in who might be about twenty-five his heart gave a lurch.

Then he saw him. He was so like Rita Raven that it almost hurt. Same little freckles on the nose, same thick, fair hair and same huge, dark eyes. Frank swallowed. The boy was talking to the maître d' at the door and making signs around his neck. Seamlessly, Teddy produced a necktie, and Des tied it quickly. Then Teddy was leading him over to the table.

"Your guest, Mr. Ennis," he said and slipped away.

Frank thought this man should have been an ambassador somewhere rather than working in what he realized was an outrageously expensive restaurant.

"Des!" he said and held out his hand.

The boy looked at him appraisingly.

"Well, well, well . . . ," he said. He ignored the hand that had been offered to him.

Frank wondered should he attempt the kind of bear hug men did nowadays.

He was bound to get it wrong, of course, and knock half the things off the table. And maybe the boy, used to more rugged Australian ways, might pull away, revolted.

"You found the place," Frank said foolishly.

He shrugged and looked so dismissive.

"I didn't know where you were, you see. Where you would be starting out from . . ." Frank's voice trailed away. This was going to be much harder than he had thought.

Near the kitchen door Teddy spoke to Anton.

"I've had Lisa on the phone."

"Not again," he sighed.

"She wants to come in for a meal sometime when we are not too busy."

"Try to head her off, will you, Teddy?"

"Not easy . . . ," Teddy said.

"Just buy me a week, then. Tell her Wednesday of next week."

"Lunch or dinner?"

"Oh, God, lunch."

"She has her eyes on dinner," Teddy said.

"An early-bird dinner, then." Anton was resigned.

"She does work her butt off for this place. I don't think we ever pay her anything."

"Nobody asked her to slave." Anton strained to hear what the newly united father and son were saying to each other. The conversation seemed to be limping along.

"Wouldn't families make you sick, Teddy?" Anton said unexpectedly.

Teddy paused before answering. Anton's family had not troubled him very much. Teddy didn't understand what was wrong with families from Anton's viewpoint, but he knew enough to agree with him.

"You're so right, Anton, but think of all the business we get out of the guilt that families create! Half the people here today are here from some kind of family guilt.

Anniversaries, birthdays, engagements, graduations. We'd be bankrupt without it." Teddy always saw the bright side.

"Good man, Teddy." Anton was slightly distracted. That man, Mr. Ennis, was making heavy weather over his meeting with his son. Even from across the room you could cut the atmosphere with a knife.

Clara always said that when in doubt, you should speak your mind. Ask the question that is bothering you. Don't play games.

"What's wrong, Des? What has changed? In your letter you were eager to meet. . . . Why are you so different?"

"I didn't know the whole story. I didn't know what your family did."

"What did they do?" Frank cried.

"As if you didn't know."

"I don't know," Frank protested.

"You don't fool me. I've got documents, receipts, forms signed—I know the whole story now."

"You know more than I do," Frank said. "Who was writing these documents and filling in these forms?"

"My mother was a frightened girl of seventeen. Your father gave her a choice. She could leave Ireland forever and she would get a thousand pounds. One thousand pounds! That's how much my life was worth. A miserable grand. And for this she was to sign an undertaking that she would never approach the Ennis family claiming any responsibility for her pregnancy."

"This can't be true!" Frank's voice was weak with shock.

"Why did you think she had gone away?"

"Her mother told me she had gone to America to stay with cousins," Frank said.

"Yes, that's the story they all put out."

"But why shouldn't I have believed them?"

"Because you weren't a fool. If you played according to their rules you were in a win-win situation. Troublesome girl irritatingly pregnant, out of your hair, out of the country. Everything sorted. You leapt at the chance."

"No, I didn't. I didn't know there was anything *to* sort out. I never knew until I got your letter that I had a child."

"Try another story, Frank."

"Where did you hear all this about my parents asking Rita to sign documents?"

"From Nora. Her sister. My aunt Nora. I went to see her in London and she told me everything."

"She told you wrong, Des. Nothing like that ever happened."

"Give me credit for some brains. You're not going to admit it now if you didn't then."

"There was nothing to admit. You don't understand. All this came to me out of a clear blue sky."

"You never got in touch with her. You never wrote to her once."

"I wrote to her for three months every day. I put proper stamps for America on them, but got no reply."

"Didn't that ring any alarm bells?"

"No, it didn't. I asked her mother if she was forwarding the letters and her mother said she was."

"And eventually you gave up?"

"Well, I was getting no response. And her mother said . . ." He stopped as if remembering something.

"Yes?"

"She said I should leave Rita alone. That she had moved on in life. She said there had been a lot of fuss made, but the Ravens had done everything according to the letter of the law."

"And you didn't know what she meant?" Des was not convinced.

"I hadn't an idea what she meant, but now I see . . . no, it couldn't be . . ."

"What couldn't be?"

"My parents—if you had known them, Des! Sex was never mentioned in our house. They would be incapable of any discussion about paying Rita off."

"Did they like her?"

"Not particularly. They didn't like anyone who was distracting me from my studies and exams."

"And her folks, did they like you?"

"Not really, same sort of reasons. Rita was skipping her classes to be with me."

"They thought you were a pig," Des said.

"Surely not!" Frank was surprised at his calmness in the face of insult.

"That's what Nora says. She says you ruined everyone's life. You and your so-grand family. You broke them all up. Rita never came back from Australia because she had to swear not to. A perfectly decent family, minding its own business, ruined because of you and your snobbish family." He looked very upset and very angry.

Frank knew he had to walk carefully. This boy had been so excited and enthusiastic about meeting him; now he was hostile and barely able to sit at the same table as the father he had crossed the world to meet.

"Rita's sister in London—Nora, is it? She must be very upset."

"Which is more than you are," Des said mulishly.

"I *am* sorry. I tried to tell you that, but we got bogged down in a silly argument."

"Silly argument is what you call it? A row that destroyed my mother's family!"

"I didn't know *any* of it, Des. Not until I heard from you."

"Do you believe me?"

"I believe that's what Nora said to you, certainly."

"So you think *she* was lying?"

"No, I think she believes what she was told. My parents are dead now. Your mother is dead. We have no one to ask." He knew that he sounded weak and defeated.

But oddly Des Raven seemed to recognize the honesty in his tone. "You're right," he said, almost grudgingly. "It's up to us now."

Frank Ennis had seen the waiter hover near them and leave several times. Soon they must order.

"Would you like something to eat, Des? I ordered an Australian wine to make you feel at home."

"I'm sorry—I like to know who I am eating and drinking with." Des was taking no prisoners.

"Well, I don't know how well you'll get to know me. . . . They say that I'm difficult and that I make a mess of things," Frank said. "That's what I'm told, anyway."

"Who tells you that? Your wife?"

"No. I never married."

Des was surprised. "So no children, then?"

"Apart from you, no."

"I must have been a shock."

Frank paused. He must not say the wrong thing here. It was a time to be honest and speak from the heart. But how could he admit to this boy that his instincts and first reactions had been doubt and confusion and a wish to check it all out? He knew that if he were wholly truthful he could alienate Des Raven forever and lose the son he had only just met.

"It may sound cold to you, Des, but my first reaction was shock. I couldn't believe that I had a child—my own flesh and blood—without my having an idea about it. I am a tidy, meticulous sort of person. This was like having my whole neat world turned upside down. I had to think about it. That's what I do, Des, I think about things slowly and carefully."

"Really?" Des sounded slightly scornful.

"Yes, really. So when it had got clear in my mind, I called you."

"And what had you to get clear, exactly?"

"I had to get my head around the fact that I had fathered a son. And if you think that's something that can be accepted as natural and normal in two minutes then you are an amazing person. It takes someone like me a bit of time to get used to a new concept, and as soon as I did I called you and you had already gone."

"But you must have been afraid that people would find out." Des was still taunting him.

"No, I wasn't afraid of that. Not at all." He had to think what Clara might have said, and it came to him. "I was proud to have a son. I would want people to know."

"I don't think so. . . . Big Catholic hospital manager

having illegitimate child. No, I can't see you wanting people to know."

"There is no such word, no concept of an illegitimate child nowadays. The law has changed and society has changed too. People are proud of their children, born in wedlock or outside." Frank spoke with spirit.

Des shook his head. "All very fine, very noble, but you haven't told anyone about me yet."

"You are *so* wrong, Des. I have indeed talked about you and said how excited I was to be going to meet you. . . ."

"*Who* did you tell? Not Miss Frosty in your office, that's for sure. Did you tell your mates at the golf club or the racetrack or wherever you go? Did you say, 'I have a boy too. I'm like you, a family man'? No way. You told nobody."

Frank sat there, miserable. If he started to tell him about Clara it made it all the more pitiable. There was only one person to whom he had told the secret. At that moment Anton Moran appeared at their side.

"Mr. Ennis," he said, as if Frank had been a regular customer since the place had opened.

"Ah, Mr. Moran." Frank had the feeling of being rescued. It was as if this man were throwing him some sort of a lifeline.

"Mr. Ennis, I was wondering would you and your son like to try our lobster? It is this morning's catch, done very simply, with butter and a couple of sauces on the side."

Anton looked from one to the other. A sudden silence had fallen between the two men. They were looking at each other, dumbfounded.

"I'm sorry," the younger man said.

"No, I'm sorry, Des," said Frank. "I'm sorry for all those years. . . ."

Anton murmured that he would come back in a few moments to take their order. He would never know what was going on there, but they seemed to have turned a corner. At least they were talking, and soon they were ordering food. He looked over again and they were raising a glass of Hunter Valley Chardonnay to each other. That was a relief. As soon as he had mentioned the boy being the man's son, Anton had felt a twinge of anxiety.

Possibly he had been indiscreet? But no, it seemed to be working fine. Anton breathed deeply and went back into the kitchen. Imagine—there were some people who believed that running a restaurant was all to do with serving food!

That was only a very small part of it, Anton thought.

Chapter Nine

Moira had an appointment with Frank Ennis. It was her quarterly report. She had to show the manager her case list and explain the work she had done that was costing the hospital a day and a half's wages.

Miss Gorman, his fearsome secretary, asked Moira to take a seat and wait. Today she was, if possible, more fearsome still.

"Is Mr. Ennis very busy?" Moira inquired politely.

"They never leave him alone, pulling him this way and that." Miss Gorman looked protective and angry. Maybe she fancied him and was annoyed that he had taken up with Dr. Casey.

"He always seems so much in control," Moira murmured.

"Oh, no, he's at their beck and call all day. It's totally disrupting his schedule."

"Who is doing this disrupting?" Moira was interested. She liked stories of confrontation.

Miss Gorman was vague. "Oh, people, you know.

Fussing people saying it's a personal matter. It's so distracting for poor Mr. Ennis."

She *definitely* fancied him, Moira thought, sighing over the way people wasted their lives over love. Look at that Lisa Kelly, who thought she was the girlfriend of Anton Moran despite all the women that he paraded around the place. Look at that silly girl in her own social worker team who had refused promotion because her plodding boyfriend might have felt inadequate.

Look at poor Miss Gorman, sitting here fuming because these people, whoever they were, were actually daring to ring Frank Ennis saying that it was personal. She sighed again and settled down to wait.

Frank Ennis was much more cheerful than on earlier visits. He checked her figures and report carefully.

"You certainly seem to be taking a load off the main hospital . . . the *real* hospital," he said.

"I think you'll find that the heart clinic thinks of itself very much as the *real* hospital," Moira corrected him.

"Which is why I wouldn't use such an expression in front of them. Credit me with *some* intelligence, Ms. Tierney."

"It's very well run, I must say."

"Well, yes, they do deliver a service. I give them that much, but it's like a mothers' meeting in there—this one is having a baby, that one is getting engaged, the other one is getting married. It's like a gossip column in a cheap newspaper."

"I couldn't agree with you less." Moira was cold. "These are professional women; they know their subject and they do their job well. They reassure the patients and teach them to manage their own condition. I don't see that as being in *any* way like a gossip column or a mothers' meeting."

"But I thought I could talk to you about it. I thought you were my eyes and ears. My spy in there . . ."

"You suggested that, certainly, but I never accepted the role."

"That's true, you didn't. I suppose you've been sucked into it like everyone else."

"I doubt it, Mr. Ennis. I'm not easily sucked into things. Shall I leave this report with you?"

"Have I annoyed you in any way, Ms. Tierney?" Frank Ennis asked.

"No, not at all, Mr. Ennis. You have your job to do, I have mine. It's a matter of mutual respect. Why do you think you might have annoyed me?"

"Because apparently that's what I *do,* Ms. Tierney, annoy people, *and* you look disapproving, as if you didn't like what you saw."

Several people had said that to Moira, but usually in the heat of the moment when they were objecting to something she had to do in the line of work. Nobody had ever said it in a matter-of-fact way and an even tone like Frank Ennis.

"It must be the way my face is set, Mr. Ennis. I assure you, I'm not disapproving of anything you do."

"Good, good." He seemed satisfied. "So you'll smile a bit from now on, will you?"

"I can't smile to order. It would only be a grimace," Moira said. "You know . . . twisting my features into a smile . . . it wouldn't be real or sincere."

Frank Ennis looked at her for a moment.

"You're quite right, Ms. Tierney, and I hope we will meet under some circumstances that do call for a real or sincere smile."

"I hope so," Moira said. She thought that he was looking at her with some sympathy and concern. Imagine, this man pitied *her*!

How ridiculous.

It was a long weekend and everyone was going somewhere.

Noel and his parents were taking baby Frankie to the country for two nights. They had booked a bed-and-breakfast place outside Rossmore. There was a statue of St. Ann and a holy well there; Josie and Charles were very interested in it. Noel said he would probably give the holy well a miss, but he would take the baby for walks in the wood for the fresh air. He had shown Moira the case he had packed for the journey. Everything was there.

Lisa was going to London. Anton was going to look at a few restaurants there and she was going to take notes. It would be wonderful. Moira had sniffed, but said nothing.

Frank Ennis said that he was going to take a bus tour. It would take in some of Ireland's greatest tourist attractions. It seemed a very unusual thing for him to do. He had someone he wanted to show Ireland to and this seemed to be the best way. It was certainly going to be interesting, he told Moira.

Emily said that she was going to see the west of Ireland for the first time. Dingo Duggan was going to drive the van, taking Emily and Declan's parents, Molly and Paddy Carroll. They would have a great time.

Simon and Maud were going with friends to North Wales. They were bringing sleeping bags and a sort of makeshift tent. They would take the boat to Holyhead and then might find a hostel, but if not, they could sleep anywhere with all their gear. There would be six of them altogether. It would be terrific fun.

Dr. Declan Carroll and his wife, Fiona, were taking Johnny to a seaside hotel. Fiona said that she was going to sleep until lunchtime both days. They had baby minders there to look after young children. It would be magical.

Dr. Hat was going to go fishing with three friends. It was an all-in weekend with no hidden extras. Dr. Hat said he was a poor old pensioner now and had to be careful with his money—Moira never knew whether he was joking or not. It certainly wasn't the time to bring out one of those rare smiles.

Most of her colleagues were going away or else they were having parties or doing their gardens.

Moira suddenly felt very much out of it, as if she were on the side of things looking on. Why wasn't she going somewhere, like sitting in Dingo's van heading west or going to see some statue in Rossmore or setting out for the lakes in the Midlands with Dr. Hat and his mates?

The answer was only too clear.

She had no real friends.

She had never needed them in life—the job was too absorbing—and to do it right you needed to be on duty all hours of the day. Friends would find it very tedious to go out to supper with someone who might well have to disappear in the middle of the main course.

But it was lonely and restless to see everyone else with plans for the long weekend.

Moira announced that she was going home to Liscuan. She talked so little about her private life, people assumed that there must be a big family waiting for her.

"That will be nice for you, to go home and meet everyone," Ania said. "You will have a great welcome, yes?"

"That's right," Moira lied.

Ania lived in a world where everyone was good and happy. She was pregnant again and taking things easy. The doctor had said that she needed bed rest, and so she lay at home contemplating a great future with their child. This time it would happen, and if lying around in bed would ensure it, then Ania was willing to do it.

Once a week, Carl drove her in to the clinic so that she could see everyone and keep up to date on what was happening. She was pleased that Moira was going to the country place for the weekend. It might cheer her up. . . .

Moira looked out of the train as she crossed Ireland towards her home. She had packed her little case and had no idea where she would stay. Perhaps her father and Mrs. Kennedy might offer her a bed?

Mrs. Kennedy was fairly frosty when Moira telephoned to speak to her father. "He's having a lie-down. He always takes a siesta from five till six," she said, as if Moira should somehow have known this.

"I'm in the area," Moira said. "I was wondering if I could call in and see him?"

"Would that be before or after supper?" Mrs. Kennedy inquired.

Moira drew a deep breath.

"Or even *during* supper?" she suggested.

Mrs. Kennedy was more practical than welcoming. "We only have two lamb chops," she said.

"Oh, don't mind about me. I'm happy with vegetables," she said.

"Will you arrange that with your father when he wakes up? We don't know what he would want."

"Yes, I'll call again at six," Moira said through her teeth. She had eased her father's passage to live openly with Mrs. Kennedy and this was the thanks she got. Life was certainly unfair.

But then Moira knew that already from her work. Men laid off from work with no warning and poor compensation; women drawn into the drugs business because it's the only way to get a bit of ready money; girls running away from home and refusing to go back because what was there was somehow worse than sleeping under a bridge. Moira had seen babies born and go home from the hospital to totally unsatisfactory setups while hundreds of infertile couples ached to adopt them.

Moira sat in a café waiting for the time to pass until her father woke from his siesta. Siesta! There would have been little of that in the old days. Father would come in tired from his work on the farm. Sometimes Mother had cooked a meal—most times not. Moira and Pat used to peel the potatoes so that that much was done anyway. Pat was not considered a reliable farmhand, so Dad would ensure that all the hens had been returned to their coop. He would call out until the sheepdog came home. Then he would pat the dog's head. "Good man, Shep." Every dog they had over the years was called Shep.

Only then would he have his supper. Often he had had to get the supper ready—a big pot of potatoes and a couple of slices of ham, the potatoes often eaten straight from the saucepan and the salt spooned from the packet.

Life had changed for the better in her father's case. She should be glad that he had that wordless Mrs. Kennedy looking after him and cooking him a lamb chop of an evening. Why was the woman so unwelcoming? She had no fear of Moira and she should know that. But then she had always been stern and forbidding. She seldom smiled.

With a shock she realized that this is what people actually said about *her.* Even Mr. Ennis had mentioned that Moira was very unsmiling and seemed highly disapproving of things.

When Moira rang back, her father sounded lively and happy. She knew that he spent a lot of time wood carving nowadays and had built an extra room for his work. He did most of the talking and finally said, "So are you coming for supper tonight?" as if there was never any question.

She took a bus out to Mrs. Kennedy's and knocked on the door timidly.

"Oh, Moira." Mrs. Kennedy showed just enough recognition and acknowledgment that she had arrived, but no real pleasure.

"I'm not disturbing you or my father?"

"No, please come in. Your father is freshening himself up for supper."

That was a personal first, Moira thought to herself. Her poor father would sit down for whatever meal there might be with muddy boots and a sweaty shirt, ready to spoon out the potatoes to Pat and herself and her mother, if she ever sat down. Things were very different now.

Moira saw a table set for three. There were folded table napkins and a small vase of flowers. There were gleaming saltcellars and shining glass. It was far from suppers like this that he had spent his former life.

"You have the house very nice." Moira looked around her as if she were a housing inspector looking for flaws or damp.

"Glad it passes the test," Mrs. Kennedy said.

Just then her father came out. Moira gasped—he looked ten years younger than the last time she had seen him. He wore a smart jacket and he had a collar and tie.

"You look the real part, Dad," she said admiringly. "Are you going out somewhere?"

"I'm having supper in my own home. Isn't that worth dressing up for?" he asked. Then, softening up a little, he said, "How are you, Moira? It's really good to see you."

"I'm fine, Dad."

"And where are you staying?"

So no bed here, Moira thought. She waved it away. "I'll find somewhere . . . don't worry about me." As if he worried! If he did, then he would ask his fancy woman to get a bed ready for her.

"That's grand, then. Come and sit down."

"Yes, indeed," Mrs. Kennedy said. "Have a glass of sherry with your father. I'll serve the meal in about ten minutes."

"Isn't she great?" Her father looked admiringly at the retreating Mrs. Kennedy.

"Great, altogether," Moira said unenthusiastically.

"Is there anything wrong, Moira?" He looked at her, concerned.

"No. Why? Should there be?"

"You look as if something's wrong."

Moira exploded. "God Almighty, Dad, I came across the country to see you. You never write . . . you never phone . . . and now you criticize the way I look!"

"I was just concerned for you, in case you'd lost your job or something," he said.

Moira looked at him. He meant it. She must have looked sad or angry or disapproving—all these things that people said.

"No, it's just it's the long weekend. I came back to see my family. Is that so very unusual? The train was full of people doing just that."

"I thought it was kind of sad for you: your home gone, sold to other people, Pat all tied up in his romance."

"Pat has a romance?"

"You haven't seen him yet, then?"

"No, I came straight here. Who is it? What's she like?"

"Remember the O'Learys who ran the garage?"

"Yes, but those girls are far too young. They'd only be fourteen or fifteen," Moira said, shocked.

"It's the mother. It's Mrs. O'Leary—Erin O'Leary."

"And what happened to Mr. O'Leary?" Moira couldn't take it in.

"Gone off somewhere, apparently."

"Merciful hour!" Moira said. It was an expression of her mother's. She hadn't said it in years.

"Well, exactly. You never know what's around the next corner," her father agreed.

He was in an awkward position, Moira realized. He

couldn't really remonstrate with Pat for moving in with a married lady. Hadn't he done the very same thing himself? Mrs. Kennedy came in just then to ask would Moira like to freshen up before supper. Her father was nodding. Moira decided that she did want to freshen up. She took a clean blouse out of her suitcase and went to the bathroom.

It was an amazing room. The wallpaper had lots of blue mermaids and blue sea horses on it. There were blue and white china ornaments on the windowsill and a blue shell held the soap. A crinoline lady dressed in blue covered the next roll of lavatory paper in case people might know what it was and be affronted. There were blue gingham curtains on the window and a blue patterned shower curtain.

Moira washed her face and shoulders and under her arms. She put on her clean blouse and returned to the table.

"Lovely bathroom," she said to Mrs. Kennedy.

"We do our best," Mrs. Kennedy said, serving melon slices with a little cherry on top of each. Then she brought in the main course.

"Remember, vegetables are fine for me," Moira said.

Her father waved her protest aside. "I walked into town and got an extra lamb chop," he said.

Mrs. Kennedy looked as if Moira's father had given her a priceless jewel.

Moira showed huge gratitude. She didn't feel that she could easily discuss Pat's new situation, so she ate her supper mainly in silence. Her father and Mrs. Kennedy talked animatedly about this and that—his wood carving of an owl, a festival that was going to exhibit some local art.

Mrs. Kennedy said that of course he should offer some of his work to be put on show. This was also news to Moira.

They spoke about Mrs. Kennedy's involvement in a local women's group. They all felt that farming was finished and that there was no living to be made from the land. A lot of them were training to go into the bed-and-breakfast business. Mrs. Kennedy was thinking she might join in. After all, they had three rooms more or less ready; all they'd need to buy was new beds. That would be six people, and they would make a tidy living.

Moira realized that she didn't know Mrs. Kennedy's first name.

If she had, she might say suddenly, "Maura" or "Janet"—or whatever she was called—"can I sleep the night in one of those three rooms, please?" But she had never known her name and Dad referred to her as "herself" and, when he was talking to her, as "dear" or "love." No help there.

When she had finished the meal, Moira stood up and picked up her suitcase.

"Well, that was all lovely, but if I am to find a place to stay, I'd better go now. The bus still goes by at half past the hour, right?"

"Leave it to the next half hour," her father said. "You'll easily get into Stella Maris. They'll give you a grand room."

"I was thinking of calling on Pat," Moira said.

"He won't be there. He'll be up at the garage. Leave him till the morning, I'd say."

"Right, I'll do that, but I'll go now, as I'm standing. Thank you again for the nice meal."

"You're very welcome," Mrs. Kennedy said.

"It's good to see you, Moira. Don't work too hard up there in Dublin."

"Do you know what kind of work I do, Dad?"

"Don't you work for the government in an office?"

"That's it, more or less," Moira said glumly.

She set out on the road. She wanted to go past her old home before the next bus came. She walked down the old familiar lane, a lane that her father must have walked many a time before he had officially left his home to live with Mrs. Kennedy. And why would he *not* want to live with her? A bright, clean house where he got a welcome and a warm meal and maybe a bit of a cuddle as well. Wasn't it much better than what he had had at home?

She arrived at her old house. Straightaway she could see that the new owners had given it a coat of paint; they had planted a garden. The stables, byres and outhouses had all been changed, cleaned and modernized, and this was where they made their cheese. They had a successful business, and it all centered around the house where Moira had grown up.

She went into the old farmyard and looked around her, bewildered. She must now see the house. If they came out, she would tell them that she had once lived here. She could see through the windows that there was a big fire in the grate and a table with a wine bottle and two glasses on it.

It made her very sad.

Why couldn't her parents have provided a home like this for Pat and herself? Why were there no social workers then who would have taken them away to be placed in better, happier homes?

Her mother and father were not functioning as parents over those years. Her mother was in deep need of help, and her father struggled ineffectually to cope. Moira and Pat should have grown up in a household where they could have known the language of childhood. A family where, if Pat ran round pretending to be a horse, they would have laughed with him and encouraged him and not cuffed him around the ears, as would have happened in this house.

Moira never had a doll of her own, not to mention a doll's house. There were no birthday celebrations that she could remember. She could never invite her school friends home, and that was how she had learned to be aloof. She had feared friendship and closeness as a child because sooner or later that friend would have expected to be invited to Moira's home and then the chaos would be revealed.

There were tears in her eyes as she saw what the house could have been like when she was young. It could have been a home.

Moira caught the bus to town and booked two nights at the Stella Maris. The room was fine and the cost reasonable, but Moira burned with injustice. She had a father who had a home with spare bedrooms, and yet she was forced to pay for a bed and breakfast in her own hometown.

She would go to see how Pat was faring the next morning. It was ludicrous to think of him with Mrs. O'Leary—she was so much older. It was nonsense. Mr. O'Leary couldn't have left because of Pat.

She would find out tomorrow.

———

Next morning, she went to the garage. Pat was there on the forecourt, filling cars with petrol or diesel. He seemed genuinely pleased to see her.

"Have you got a car at long last, Moira?" he called.

"I have, but it's up in Dublin," she said.

"Well, we can't fill it up for you from here then." He laughed amiably. He was totally suited to this work, easy-going and natural with the customers, good-tempered and cheerful in what some might have found a tedious and repetitive job.

"I came to see *you*, actually, Pat. Do you have a break or anything coming up?"

"Sure, I can go anytime. I'll just tell Erin."

Moira followed him towards the pay desk and the new shop that had been built in a once-falling-down garage.

"Erin, my sister, Moira, is here. Okay if I take a break and go and have a coffee with her?"

"Oh, Pat, of course it is. Don't you work all the hours God sends? Go for as long as you like. How are you, Moira? Long time no see."

Moira looked at her. Erin O'Leary—about ten years older than Moira—a mother of two girls and wife of Harry, who was a traveler and often traveled rather longer and farther than his job required. He had now traveled out of the country, it was said at the Stella Maris, where Moira had brought up the subject at breakfast.

Erin was wearing a smart yellow shop coat with a navy trim. Her loose, rather floppy hair was tied back neatly with a navy and yellow ribbon. She was slim and fit and looked much younger than the forty-four or -five she must have been. She looked at Pat with undeniable affection.

"I hear you've been very good to my brother," Moira said.

"It's mutual, I tell you. I couldn't do half the work I do without him."

Pat had come back wearing his jacket and heard her say that. He was childishly pleased.

"I'm glad. He was a great brother," Moira said, trying to put a lot of sincerity into her voice. In fact, he had been a worry and given her huge concern over the years—but no point in sharing that with Mrs. O'Leary.

"I don't doubt it," Erin O'Leary said, putting her arm affectionately around Pat's shoulders.

"And is all this a permanent sort of thing?" Moira asked, trying desperately to smile at the same time so that they would realize it was a good-natured, cheery kind of inquiry.

"I certainly hope so," Erin said. "I'd be lost without Pat, and so would the girls."

"I'm not going anywhere," Pat said proudly.

Would she have encouraged this setup herself as a social worker? She might have examined Erin O'Leary's circumstances more carefully, checked that her husband would not return and evict Pat Tierney from his home and business. She would always have put the best needs of her client forward, but was there a possibility that by challenging the living arrangements at Mrs. O'Leary's, she might have deprived Pat of the loving home and workplace that he now seemed to have?

They went for coffee to a nearby place where everyone knew Pat. He was his own man, with plenty to say.

People asked him about Erin and he told them how

she had made a cake with his name on it for his birthday last week and they had all given him a present. And Erin must have told some of the regular customers too, because there wasn't room on the mantelpiece for all his cards.

With a heart like stone, Moira remembered that she had not sent him a card.

She had, she said, been to see their father. "He seems happy with Mrs. Kennedy," she said grudgingly.

"Well, why wouldn't he be? Isn't Maureen the best in the world?"

"Maureen?" Moira was at a loss.

"Maureen Kennedy," he said, as if everyone knew her as that.

"And how did you find out her name?"

"I asked her," Pat said simply, looking at his watch.

"Are you anxious to be back there?" Moira asked him.

"Well, she's on her own—there's only a young girl in the shop and she's a bit of an eejit with the till."

Moira looked at him and bit her lip. She hoped that there were not tears in her eyes. Pat reached over and took her hand.

"I know, Moira, it's hard for you having no one of your own and seeing Dad all settled with Maureen and me with Erin, but it will happen, I'm sure."

She nodded wordlessly.

"Come back to the garage with me. Come in and talk to Erin."

"I will." Moira paid for their coffee and walked like an automaton back to the garage.

Erin was pleased to see them. "There was no hurry, Pat. You could have stayed longer."

"I didn't want to leave you on your own too long."

"Well, there, Moira! Isn't that music to the ears?" Pat had gone to put on his working gear again.

Moira looked at Erin. "It's great that he's here with you. He has had so little warmth and affection. He was never in a loving family. You won't . . . you wouldn't . . ."

Erin interrupted her. "He's found a loving family now and here he will stay. Rest assured of that."

"Thank you, I will," Moira said.

"And come back and see us again and when you do, stay in our house—don't be paying fancy prices up in Stella Maris."

"How did you know I was there?"

"One of my friends works there. She rang and told me you were asking questions about me. Harry's long gone, Moira. He's not coming back. Pat is staying. He is exactly what we all need. He's cheerful and happy and reliable and always there. I didn't have that before, and for me it's lovely too."

Moira gave her an awkward hug and went back to Stella Maris.

"I wonder if it will be an inconvenience if I cancel tonight's booking? I find I have to go back to Dublin on the afternoon train."

"No problem, Ms. Tierney. I'll just prepare your bill for one night. Will you be coming back to us again?"

Moira remembered that Erin had a friend here who reported things.

"Well, I may stay with Erin O'Leary next time. She very kindly invited me. I was so pleased."

"Very nice," the receptionist said. "Always nice to stay in a family home. . . ."

Moira looked out the window at the rain-covered countryside. Cows standing wet and bewildered, horses sheltering under trees, sheep oblivious to the weather, farmers in rain gear going along narrow lanes.

Most people on the train were going to Dublin for some outing or activity. Or else they were going back to a family. Moira was going home to an empty flat halfway through the long weekend. She could not bear to stay in the place where her brother and her father had found such happiness and where she had found nothing but resentment and sadness.

It was still early enough to go somewhere. But where? She was hungry, but she didn't feel like going to a café or a restaurant on her own. She went into a shop to buy a bar of chocolate.

"Gorgeous day, isn't it? The rain's gone," said a woman about her own age behind the counter.

"Yes, it is," Moira said, surprised she hadn't noticed that the weather had improved.

"I've only another hour here and then I'm off," the shop assistant confided. She had stringy hair and a big smile.

"And where will you go to?" Moira asked. She wasn't being polite; she was interested. Possibly this woman, like everyone else in the universe, had a huge, loving family dying for her shift to finish.

"I'll go out to the sea by train," she said. "Don't know where yet, but maybe Blackrock, Dun Laoghaire, Dalkey or even Bray. Anywhere I can walk beside the sea, have a bag of chips and an ice cream. Maybe I'll have a swim, maybe I'll meet a fellow. But I wouldn't be standing in-doors here all day with the sun shining outside and every-one else free as a bird."

"And you'd do all this by yourself?" Moira was curi-ous.

"Isn't that the best part? No one else to please, and all my options open."

Moira walked out thoughtfully. She had never taken the train out to the seaside. Not in all her years in Dublin. If work brought her that way, she would go. Not other-wise. She didn't know that people *did* that—just went out to the sea, like children in storybooks.

That's what she would do now. She would walk on be-side the River Liffey until she caught the little train south. She would sit beside the sea, go for a paddle, maybe. It would calm her, soothe her. Oh, yes, there would certainly be crowds of people playing at Happy Families or Being in Love with each other, but maybe Moira would be like the woman in the shop who was aching to have the sun-shine on her shoulders and arms and watch the sea lapping gently towards the shore.

That's what she would do. She would spend some of the long weekend by the sea.

Of course it wasn't magic.

And it didn't really work.

Moira did not become calm and mellow. The sun did shine on her arms and shoulders but there was a breeze coming in from the sea at the same time and it felt too chilly. There were too many people who had decided their families must go to the seaside.

Moira studied them.

In her whole childhood she never remembered once being brought to the seaside and yet it seemed that every child in Dublin had a God-given right to go to the seashore as soon as the sun came out. Her sense of resentment was enormous and she frowned with concentration as she sat silently amid all the families who were calling out to one another on the beach.

To her surprise, a big man with a red face and an open-necked red shirt stopped beside her.

"Moira Tierney as I live and breathe!"

She hadn't an idea who he was. "Um, hello," she said cautiously.

He sat down beside her.

"God, isn't this beautiful to be out in the open air? We're blessed to live in a capital city that's so near the sea," he said.

She still looked at him, confused.

"I'm Brian Flynn. We met when Stella was in hospital and then again at the funeral and the christening."

"Oh, *Father* Flynn. Yes, of course I remember. I just didn't recognize you in the . . . I mean without the . . ."

"A Roman collar wouldn't be very suitable for this weather." Brian Flynn was cheerful and dismissive. He was a man who rarely wore clerical garb at all, except when officiating at a ceremony.

"Did your parents take you to the sea when you were young?" Moira asked him unexpectedly.

"My father died when we were young, but my mother brought us for a week to the seaside every summer. We stayed in a guesthouse called St. Anthony's and we all had a bucket and spade. Yes, it was nice," he said.

"You were lucky," Moira said glumly.

"You didn't get to the sea when you were young?"

"No. We never got anywhere. We should never have been left in our home. We should have been placed somewhere . . . anywhere, really."

Brian Flynn saw where the conversation was leading. This woman seemed to have an obsession about taking children away from parents and into care. Or that's what Noel said, in any case. Noel was terrified of Moira, and Katie said that Lisa felt just the same way.

"Well, I suppose things have changed a bit . . . moved on," Brian Flynn said vaguely. He began to wish that he hadn't approached Moira but she had looked so lonely and out of place in her jacket and skirt, right in the middle of all the seaside people.

"Do you ever feel your work is hopeless, Father?"

"I wish you'd call me Brian. No, I don't feel it's hopeless. I think we get things wrong from time to time. I mean the Church does. It doesn't adapt properly. And I get things wrong myself, quite apart from the Church. I keep battering away to get people a Catholic wedding and, just when I succeed, it turns out that they got tired of waiting and got the job done in a register office and I'm left like a fool. But, to answer your question, no, I don't think it's all hopeless. I think we do *something* to help and I certainly see a lot that inspires me. I expect you do too?" He ended on a rising note, but if he was expecting some reciprocal statement of job satisfaction he was wrong.

"I don't think I do, Father Flynn, truly I don't. I have a caseload of unhappy people, most of them blaming their unhappiness on me."

"I'm sure that's not true." Brian Flynn wished himself a million miles from here.

"It *is* true, Father. I got a woman into exactly the kind of facility she was looking for—a place with vegetarian cookery and, if you'll excuse the expression, with religion seeping from the walls. It's coming down with saintliness, and she's still not happy."

"I expect she's old and frightened," Brian Flynn said.

"Yes, but she's only one of them. I have a very nice old man called Gerald. I kept him *out* of a home and stopped a lot of nonsense with his children, built up all the support systems for him, but now he says he's lonely all day. He'd like to go to a place where they play indoor bowls."

"He's probably old and frightened too," Brian Flynn suggested.

"But what about the ones who are *not* old? They don't want any help either. I have a thirteen-year-old girl who slept rough. I got her back to her family. There was a row over something—black lipstick and black nail polish, I think. Anyway, she's gone again. The Garda are looking for her. It needn't have got this far. All that talking, sitting under a bridge way into the night, and it meant nothing."

"You never know . . . ," Brian Flynn began again.

"Oh, but I *do* know. And I know how there's an army of people lined up against me over that unfortunate child who is being raised by an alcoholic. . . ."

Brian Flynn's voice was a lot more steely now.

"Noel adds up to much more than being just an alcoholic, Moira. He has turned his life around to make a home for that child."

"And that child will thank us all later for leaving her with a drunken, resentful father?"

"He loves his daughter very much. He's *not* a drunk. He's given it up." Brian Flynn was fiercely loyal.

"Are you telling me, hand on heart, that Noel never strayed, never went back on the drink since he got Frankie?"

Brian Flynn couldn't lie. "It was only the once and it didn't last long," he said. Immediately he realized that Moira hadn't known. He saw that in her face. As usual he had managed to make things worse. In future he would walk about with a paper bag over his head and slits cut for his eyes. He would talk to nobody. Ever again.

"I hope you don't think I'm rude, Moira, but I have to um . . . meet someone . . . um . . . farther along here . . ."

"No, of course." Moira realized that there was less warmth in his face now. But then that was often the case in her conversations.

Father Flynn had moved on. She felt conspicuous on this beach. It wasn't her place. Slowly Moira gathered her things together and headed towards the station, where a little train would take her back into the city.

Most people liked the train journey. Moira didn't even see the view from the window. She thought instead of how she had been duped. They had even told that priest, who had nothing to do with the setup. But they hadn't seen fit to tell the social worker assigned to the case.

Moira could not call to Chestnut Court armed with her new information, since she knew that Noel and his parents had taken the baby off to some small town that she had never heard of—a place with a magic statue, apparently. Or, to put it another way, Charlie and Josie would be investigating the statue. Noel could well have the child in some pub by now.

She would deal with Emily when she came back from her sojourn in the west with Dingo Duggan, with Lisa when she and Anton came back from London, and eventually she would deal with Noel, who had lied to her. There were so many places where she could put Frankie, where the child would grow up safely, with love all around her. Look at that couple—Clara Casey's daughter Linda and her husband, Nick, who was the son of Hilary in the heart clinic—they were just aching for a baby girl. Think of the stability of a home like that: two grandmothers to idolize the child and a big, extended family.

Moira sighed again. If only there had been a magical social worker who could have placed Pat and herself in a home like that. A place where they would have been loved, where there would have been children's books on a shelf, maybe a story read to them at night, people who would be interested in a child's homework, who would take her to the seaside on a hot day with a bucket and spade to make sandcastles.

Coming fresh as she did from visiting the wreckage that was her own childhood, Moira was now determined that she would ease Frankie Lynch's path into a secure home.

It would be the only thing that might make any sense of Moira's own loss—if she could make it right for someone else. All she had to do was to get through this endless weekend until all the cast eventually came back from their travels and reassembled and she could get things going.

Lisa was actually back in Dublin, even though Moira didn't know it. There had been some crossed wires in London. Lisa had thought that it was a matter of visiting restaurants and talking to various patrons. April had thought it was a PR exercise and had arranged several interviews for Anton.

"They don't have a bank holiday in England this weekend, so it will be work as usual," April had chirruped to them.

"Not much work at a weekend, though." Lisa had tried hard to be casual.

"No, but Monday is an ordinary day in London and we can rehearse on Sunday." April's face was glowing with achievement and success. It would have been churlish and petty for Lisa not to enthuse. So she had appeared delighted with it all; she decided to get out with her pride.

She had loads to see to back in Dublin, she said casually, and saw, to her pleasure, that Anton seemed genuinely sorry to see her go. And now she was back in Dublin with nothing to do and nobody to meet.

As she let herself in to Chestnut Court she thought she saw Moira in the courtyard talking to some of the neighbors. But it couldn't be. Noel and the baby were off in this place Rossmore; Moira, herself, was meant to have gone to the country to see her family. Lisa decided she was imagining things.

But she looked over the wall on the corridor leading to their apartment and saw that it was indeed Moira. She couldn't hear the conversation, but she didn't like the look of it. Moira knew nobody in this apartment block except them. She was here to spy.

Lisa turned and crossed the courtyard.

"Well, *hello*, Moira," she said, showing great surprise. The two middle-aged women whom Moira had been interrogating shuffled with embarrassment. Lisa knew them both by sight. She nodded at them briefly.

"Oh, Lisa . . . I thought you were away?"

"Well, yes, I was," Lisa agreed, "but I came back. And you? You were going away too?"

"I came back too," Moira said. "And did Noel and Frankie come back as well?"

"I don't think so. I haven't been in to the apartment yet. Why don't you come up and see with me?" The women neighbors were busy making their excuses and looking to escape.

"No, no, it wouldn't be appropriate," Moira said. "You've only just got back from London."

"Moira is our social worker," Lisa explained to the fast-retreating neighbors. "She's absolutely great. She drops in at the least expected times in case Noel and I are battering Frankie to death or starving her in a cage or something. So far she hasn't caught us out in anything, but of course time will tell."

"You completely misunderstand my role, Lisa. I am there for Frankie."

"We're all bloody there for Frankie," Lisa said, "which is something you'd realize if you saw us walking her up and down at night when she can't sleep. If you saw us changing her nappy, trying to spoon food into her when she keeps turning her head away."

"Exactly," Moira cried. "It's too hard for you both. It's my role to see whether she would be better placed with a more conventional family . . . people with the maturity to look after a child."

"But she's Noel's daughter!" Lisa said, unaware that the other women who had been about to leave were standing there, open-mouthed. "I thought you people were all meant to be keeping the family together and that sort of thing."

"Yes, but you are not family, Lisa. You're just a room-mate, and Noel, as a father, is unreliable. We have to admit that."

"I do *not* have to admit that!" Lisa knew she looked like a fishwife with her hands on her hips, but really this was too much. She began to list all that Noel had done and was doing. Moira cut across her like a knife.

"Can we move somewhere that we can have more privacy, please?" She glared at the two neighbors, who were still hovering at the corner, and they vanished quickly.

"I don't want any more time with you," Lisa said. She knew she sounded pettish but she didn't care.

Moira was calm but furious at the same time. "In all this hymn of praise about Noel," she said, "you managed to forget that he went off the rails and was back on the drink. That was a situation where the baby was at risk and not one of you alerted me."

"It was over before it began," Lisa said. "No point in alerting you and starting World War Three!"

Moira looked at her steadily for a moment. "We are all on the same side," she said eventually.

"No, we're not," Lisa said. "You want to take Frankie away. We want to keep her. How's that the same side?"

"We all want what is *best* for her." Moira spoke as if to a slow learner.

"It's best for all of us if she stays with Noel, Moira." Lisa sounded weary suddenly. "She keeps him off the drink and keeps his head down at his studies so that he'll be a good, educated father for her when the time comes for her to know such things. And she keeps me sane too. I have a lot of worries and considerations in my life, but minding Frankie sort of grounds me. It gives it all some purpose, if you know what I mean."

Moira sighed. "I *do* know what you mean. You see, in a way, she does exactly the same for me. Minding Frankie is important to *me* too. I never had a chance as a child. I want her to have a start of some kind, not to get bogged down by a confused childhood like I did."

Lisa was stunned. Moira had never admitted anything personal before. "Don't talk to me about childhood! I bet mine could leave yours in the ha'penny place!" Lisa said in a chirpy voice. Moira didn't know what to say, then she surprised herself as much as she did Lisa.

"You don't feel like having supper tonight, do you? It's just that I'm a bit beaten. I was down in my old home and it was all a bit upsetting and there seems to be nobody in town . . ."

Lisa ignored the gracelessness of the invitation. She didn't want to go back to the flat alone. There was nothing in—well, there might be a tin of something in the kitchen cupboard or a pack of pasta in sauce in the freezer. But it would be lonely. It might be better to hear what Moira had to say, but would it only be more of the same?

"Will we agree that Frankie is not on the agenda?" Lisa asked.

"Frankie who?" Moira said, with a strange kind of lopsided look on her face. Lisa realized that it was meant to be a smile.

They chose to go to Ennio's trattoria. It was a family restaurant: Ennio himself cooked and greeted; his son waited on the tables. Ennio had lived in Dublin for rather more than twenty years and was married to an Irishwoman; he knew that having an Italian accent added to the atmosphere. Anton, on the other hand, had said to Lisa that Ennio was a fool of the first order and that he would never get anywhere. He never advertised, you never saw celebrities going in and out, he never got any reviews or press attention. It seemed like an act of independence to go there.

Moira had often passed the place and wondered who would pay seven euros for a spaghetti Bolognese when you could make it at home for three or four euros. For her it was an act of defiance to go there, defying her natural thrift and caution.

Ennio welcomed them with a delight that made it appear as if he had been waiting for their visit for weeks. He gave them huge red and white napkins, a drink on the house and the news that the cannelloni was like the food of angels—they would love it with an almighty love. He had opened his restaurant two decades ago and his simple, fresh food had proved instantly popular. Since then, word of mouth had kept the place full to bursting almost every night. Lisa thought to herself that Anton might be wrong about Ennio. The place was almost full already, everyone was happy, there were hardly any overheads. No client was attracted here by style or decor or lighting—nor, indeed, publicity interviews. Maybe Ennio was far from being a fool.

Moira was beginning to realize why people actually paid seven euros for a plate of pasta. They were paying for a bright, checked tablecloth, a warm welcome and the feeling of ease and relaxation. She could have put together a cannelloni dish, but it wouldn't be the same as this if eaten in her small, empty flat. It would not be the food of angels.

She relaxed for the first time in a long time and raised her glass. "Here's to us," she said. "We may have had a bad start, but, boy, we're survivors!"

"Here's to surviving," Lisa said. "Can I begin?"

"Let's order his cannelloni first and then you can begin," Moira agreed.

She was a good listener. Lisa had to hand her that. Moira listened well and remembered what you said and went back and asked relevant questions, like how old was Lisa when she realized that her parents disliked each other, and irrelevant questions, like did they ever take the girls to the seaside? She was sympathetic when she needed to be, shocked at the right times, curious about *why* Lisa's mother stayed in such a loveless home. She asked about Lisa's friends and seemed to understand exactly why she never had any.

How could anyone bring a friend home to a house like that?

And Lisa told her about working as a graphic designer for Kevin and how she met Anton and everything had changed. She had left the safe harbor of Kevin's office and set up on her own. No, she didn't really have any other clients, but Anton had needed her to give him that boost and he always said he would be lost without her. Even this time in London, this very morning, he had begged her not to leave, not to abandon him to April.

"Oh, April," Moira said, breezily, recalling her lunch with Clara at Anton's. "A very *vapid* sort of person."

"*Vapid!*" Lisa seized on the word with delight. "That's exactly what she is! Vapid!" She said it again with pleasure.

Moira gently moved the conversation away, towards Noel, in fact. "And wasn't it great that you found somewhere to stay so easily?" she hinted.

"Oh, yes, if it hadn't been for Noel, I don't know what I would have done that night, the night when I realized my father, my own father, in our own house . . ." She paused, upset at the memory.

"But Noel welcomed you?" Moira continued.

"Well, I suppose 'welcomed' might be putting it a bit strongly . . . but he gave me a place to stay, which, considering he hardly knew me, was very generous of him, and then we worked out with Emily that it might be best if I could stay; it would share the whole business of looking after Frankie and I could have a place to stay for free."

"Free? You mean Noel has to pay for you as well as all his other expenses?" Moira's eyes were beginning to glint. More and more information was coming her way without her even having to ask for it.

Lisa seemed to recognize that she had spoken too freely. "Well, not exactly *free*. I mean, we each contribute to the food. We have our own phones and we share the work with the baby." Lisa didn't say she was overdrawn on her bank account.

"But he could have let that room to a real tenant for real money."

"I doubt it," Lisa said, with spirit. "You wouldn't get anyone paying real money to live in a house with a baby. Believe me, Moira, it's like 'Macbeth shall sleep no more.' It can be total bedlam at three a.m. with the two of us trying to soothe her down."

Moira just nodded sympathetically. She was getting more and more ammunition by the second.

But, oddly, it did not delight her as much as she had once thought it would. In a twisted way, she would prefer if these two awkward, lonely people—Lisa and Noel—should find happiness to beat their demons through this child. If it were Hollywood, they would also find great happiness in each other.

Lisa knew nothing of her thoughts.

"Now you," she said to Moira. "Tell me what was so terrible."

So Moira began. Every detail from the early days when she came home from school and there was nothing to eat, to her tired father coming in later and finding only a few potatoes peeled. She told it all without self-pity or complaint. Moira, who had kept her private life so very, very private for years, was able to speak to this girl because Lisa was even more damaged than she was.

She told the story right up to the present, when she had left Liscuan and come back because the sight of her father and brother having made something of the shambles of their lives was too much to bear.

Lisa listened and wished that someone—anyone—had ever said to Moira that there was a way of dealing with all this, that she should be glad for other people instead of appearing to triumph over their downfall. She might have to pretend at first, but soon it would become natural. Lisa had managed to make herself glad that Katie had a happy marriage and a successful career. She was pleased that Kevin's agency was doing well. Of course, when people were enemies like her father was, and April was, then it would be superhuman to wish them well. . . .

As Lisa's mind began to drift, she realized that the woman at the next table was beginning to choke seriously. A piece of amaretto had become lodged in her throat; the young waiter stared, goggle-eyed, as she changed from scarlet to white.

"What is it, Marco?" asked the young blond waitress—was that Maud Mitchell? What was she doing working here? Lisa wondered—who then, taking in the situation at a glance, called over her shoulder, "Simon, we need you here *now*!"

Immediately her brother arrived, and he too was dressed in a waiter's uniform.

"She's getting no air in . . . ," Maud said.

"It's a Heimlich . . . ," Simon agreed.

"Can you get her to cough once more?" asked Maud, in total control.

"She's trying to cough—something's stuck there. . . ." The woman's daughter was nearly hysterical at this point.

"Madam, I'm going to ask you to stand up now and then my brother is going to squeeze you very hard. Please stay calm, it's a perfectly normal maneuver," said Maud in a voice both firm and reassuring.

"We've been trained to do this," Simon confirmed. Standing behind the woman and putting his arms around the diner's diaphragm, he pushed hard inwards and up-wards. The first time there was no response but the second time he squeezed her abdomen, a small piece of biscuit shot out of her mouth.

Instantly she was breathing again. Tears of gratitude

followed, then sips of water and a demand to know the names of the young people who had saved her life.

Lisa had been mesmerized by the entire scene and suddenly realized she hadn't been listening to a word Moira had been saying for the last few minutes. The entire episode had happened so quickly it looked as though few other people had noticed anything amiss. Really, those twins were something else. Out of the corner of her eye, she saw the waiter they'd called Marco shake Simon enthusiastically by the hand and then give Maud a hug that looked more than just grateful. . . .

Lisa and Moira divided the bill and got up to leave, well pleased with their evening.

Ennio, in his carefully maintained broken English, wished them good-bye.

"Eet is always so good to meet the good friends who 'ave a happy dinner together," he said cheerfully, as he escorted them to the door. They were not good friends but he didn't know this. If they had been real friends, they would not have gone home with such unfinished business between them. Instead they just touched the levels of each other's loneliness but had made no effort each to find an escape route for the other or a bridge between them for the future. It was one night made less bleak by a series of circumstances and the warmth of Ennio's welcome, but it was no more than that.

It would have saddened him to know this as he locked the doors after them—they had been the last to leave. Ennio was a cheerful man. He would have much preferred to think he had been serving a pair of very good friends.

Chapter Ten

Emily had a wonderful weekend in the west with Paddy and Molly Carroll. Dingo Duggan had been an enthusiastic, if somewhat adventurous, driver. He seemed entirely unable and unwilling to read a map and waved away Emily's attempts to find roads with numbers on them.

"Nobody can understand those numbers, Emily," he had said firmly. "They'll do your head in. The main thing is to point west and head for the ocean." And they did indeed see beautiful places like the Sky Road, and drove through hills where big mountain goats came down and looked hopefully at the car and its occupants as if they were new playmates come to entertain them. They spent evenings in pubs singing songs, and they all said it had been one of the best outings they had ever taken.

Emily had told them about her plans to go to America for Betsy's wedding. The Carrolls thought this was marvelous: a late marriage, a chance for Emily to dress up and be part of the ceremony, two kindred souls finding each other.

Dingo Duggan was less sure. "At her age marriage might all be too much for her," he said helpfully.

Emily steered the conversation into safer channels.

"How exactly did you get your name, Dingo?" she inquired.

"Oh, it was that time I went to Australia to earn my fortune," Dingo said simply, as if it should have been evident to everyone, and it wasn't asked by one and all. Dingo's fortune, if represented by the very battered van he drove, did not seem to have been considerable, but Emily Lynch always saw the positive side of things.

"And was it a great experience?" she asked.

"It was, really. I often look back on it and think about all I saw: kangaroos and emus and wombats and gorgeous birds. I mean *real* birds with gorgeous feathers looking as if they had all escaped from a zoo, flying round the place picking at things. You never saw such a sight." He was settled happily, remembering it all with a beatific smile.

"How long did you stay there?" Emily was curious about the life he must have led thousands of miles away.

"Seven weeks." Dingo sighed with pleasure. "Seven beautiful weeks and I talked a lot about it, you see, when I got back, so they gave me the nickname Dingo. It's a kind of wild dog out there, you see. . . ."

"I see." Emily was stunned at the briefness of his visit. "And, er . . . why did you come back?"

"Oh, I had spent all my money by then and couldn't get a job . . . too many Irish illegals out there snapping them all up. So I thought, Head for home."

Emily had little time to speculate about Dingo's mindset and how he seriously thought he was an expert on all things Australian after a visit of less than two months, ten years ago. She had a lot of e-mailing to cope with to and from New York.

Betsy was having pre-wedding nerves. She hadn't liked Eric's mother, she was disappointed with the gray silk outfit she had bought, her shoes were too tight, her brother was being stingy about the arrangements. She needed Emily badly.

Could Emily please come a few days earlier, she asked, or there might well be no wedding for her to attend. Emily soothed by e-mail, but also examined the possibility of getting an earlier flight. Noel helped her sort through the claims and offers of airlines, and they found one.

"I don't know why I am helping you to go back to America," Noel grumbled. "We're all going to miss you like mad, Emily. Lisa and I have been working out a schedule for Frankie and it's looking like a nightmare."

"You should involve Dr. Hat more," Emily said unexpectedly. "Frankie likes Dr. Hat, he's marvelous with her."

"Do I tell Moira?" Noel was fearful.

"Most certainly."

Emily was already busy e-mailing the good news to her friend Betsy; she would be there in three days. She would sort out the dull gray dress, the tight shoes, the miserly brother, Eric's difficult mother. All would be well.

"Moira will be worse than ever when you're gone," Noel said, full of foreboding.

"Just take Frankie to Hat's place in the afternoon. He plays chess online with a boy in Boston—some student, I gather. Hat gets great fun out of it. He even asked me if I could go to visit him when I was in the States and give the boy a chess set, but I told him that I'd never have time to get all that way in such a short time."

"Hat playing chess online! How did he ever learn how to use the computer?"

"I taught him," Emily said simply. "He taught me chess in exchange."

"I don't know the half of what's going on round here," Noel said.

"Don't be afraid of Moira. She's not the enemy, you know."

"She's so suspicious, Emily. When she comes into the flat she shakes a cushion suddenly in case she might find a bottle of whiskey hidden behind it and looks in the bread bin for no reason, just hoping to unearth a half a bottle of gin."

"I'll be back, Noel, and Frankie will have grown, so she'll need a couple of new dresses from New York. Just you wait until she's old enough for me to teach her painting. We can start booking the galleries for twenty years ahead because she'll be exhibiting all over the world."

"She might too." Noel's face lit up at the thought of his daughter being a famous artist. Maybe he'd take out his art supplies box from the closet. He had made sure before he moved it that there were no bottles hidden, but he hadn't had time to draw. Wouldn't it be a good influence on Frankie if he started drawing again?

"If she wants it enough it will happen." Emily nodded as if this were a certainty.

"What about you? What did you want for yourself, Emily?"

"I wanted to teach art and I got that and then eventually, when they thought I wasn't modern enough for them, I wanted to travel and I've started that. I like it very much."

"I hope you won't want to move on again from here," Noel said.

"I'll wait until Frankie's raised and you've found yourself a nice wife." She smiled at him.

"I'll hold you to that," Noel said.

He was very pleased. Emily didn't make promises lightly, but if she had to wait for him to find a nice wife . . . Emily might well be here forever!

They would all miss Emily. Down at the charity shop there was already confusion. Molly said that Emily was able to judge someone's size and taste the moment that she walked in the door. Remember that beautiful heather suit that Moira had bought and pretended she hadn't? People whose window boxes she had planted and tended were beginning to panic that their flowers would wilt during Emily's three-week absence.

Charles Lynch was wondering how he could keep his dog-walking business in credit. Emily was always finding him new clients and remembering to segregate dogs of different sexes in case they might do something to annoy their owners greatly. Emily did his books for him so that nobody from the income tax could say that he was anything other than meticulous.

At the doctors' practice they would miss her too. Nobody seemed to know exactly where to find this document or that. Emily was a reassuring presence. Everyone who worked there had her mobile number, but they had been told that she couldn't be called for three weeks. As Declan Carroll said, it was unnerving, just like going out on a high diving board, facing all this time without Emily.

Who else would know all the things that Emily knew? The best bus route to the hospital, the address of the chiropodist whom all the patients liked, the name of the pastoral care adviser in St. Brigid's?

"Perhaps you could get all this wedding business over within a week?" Declan suggested.

"Dream on, Declan. I don't want to 'get it over with.' I'm longing for it. I want it to go on for at least two months! My very best friend getting married to a man who has adored her for years! I have to sort out shoes that turned out to be too tight, brothers, mothers-in-law, a dress that turned out to be dull. I can't be dealing with you, Declan, and where you put your dry-cleaning ticket."

"I suppose we'll have to muddle through without you," Declan grumbled. "But don't stay away too long."

Lisa was just the same. "We can't phone you if Frankie starts to cough."

"Well, you don't normally," Emily said mildly.

"No, but we *feel* that we could," Lisa confessed. "Listen, while I have you, Emily, I may have slightly ballsed things up with Moira. We had a meal together and I sort of said or let drop that it was fairly exhausting cleaning Frankie, feeding her, burping her and taking her from place to place. I meant it to be a compliment to

Noel, you know, and how well we are managing things, but it came out sounding like a whine or a moan, and of course Moira picked up on it and wondered were we capable of minding Frankie and all that, which was the *last* thing . . ."

"Don't worry about it," Emily advised. "I'll have a talk with Moira."

"I wish you'd stay and have a talk with her every day," Lisa grumbled.

"You can always e-mail me, but, for the Lord's sake, don't tell everyone else that."

"Just about Frankie," Lisa promised.

"That's a deal, then—just about Frankie," said Emily, knowing that no law was so strict that it couldn't be bent for an emergency.

Eventually Emily got away.

She could hardly believe that it was just a matter of months since she had arrived here knowing nobody and now she seemed to be making seismic gaps in their lives by leaving for three weeks. It was amazing how much she had been absorbed into this small community.

She hoped she wasn't going to speak with an Irish brogue when she got back to the United States. She hoped too that she wouldn't use any Irishisms such as saying "Jaysus!" like they did in Dublin with no apparent blasphemy or disrespect. It had startled her at first, but then it had become second nature.

As she got nearer to New York she became excited at all that lay ahead. She tried to force the Irish cast of characters away from the main stage of her mind. She had to concentrate on Eric's mother and Betsy's brother, but images kept coming back to her.

Noel and Lisa in Chestnut Court soothing the baby as they prepared for a college degree that might or might not be any help to either of them. Josie and Charles kneeling down saying the Rosary in their kitchen, remembering to add three Hail Marys for St. Jarlath and a reminder that the statue campaign was going well. Dr. Hat playing chess with the boy in Boston who had something wrong with his foot and was out of school for a week. Molly in the thrift shop wondering how much to charge for a pleated linen skirt that had never been worn. Paddy Carroll bringing round, big wrapped parcels that contained juicy bones for the dogs that passed through. Aidan and Signora singing Italian songs to three children: their own grandchild, as well as Frankie and little Johnny Carroll. She thought about Muttie, wheezing happily to his dog, Hooves, or solving the world's problems with his Associates. She thought about the decent priest Father Brian Flynn, and how he tried to hide his true feelings about the statue of a sixth-century saint being erected in a Dublin working-class street.

There were so many images that Emily dropped off to sleep thinking about them all. And there she was in Kennedy Airport, and, after collecting her luggage and clearing customs, she could see Eric and Betsy jumping up and down with excitement. They even had a banner. In uneven writing it said WELCOME HOME, EMILY! How very odd that it didn't seem like home anymore.

But home or not, it was wonderful.

————

Emily talked to Eric's mother in a woman-of-the-world manner. She managed to convey the impression that Eric was very near his sell-by date and that he was very, *very* lucky that Betsy had been persuaded to consider him. Betsy had, apparently, written over to Ireland that there were some "obstacles" in the way of the marriage. Emily couldn't think what they might be. She looked Eric's mother in the eye and asked if *she* knew of any. Betsy's future mother-in-law, who was just a bit of a fusspot, started to babble a bit. Emily felt the point had been made. Betsy needed huge enthusiasm and support for her big day; otherwise she might pull out at the last moment and poor Eric would be left bereft.

Emily sorted out the shoes simply by insisting Betsy buy a pair in the correct size; she sorted out the dull dress problem by taking the very plain gray dress to an accessories store and asking everyone's advice. Together, they chose a rose-pink-and-cream-colored stole, which transformed it.

She went to Betsy's brother and explained that since Betsy had waited this long to get married, it had better be a classy celebration; this way she managed to upgrade the menu considerably and arranged sparkling wine.

And, of course, the wedding was splendid. Emily was pleased to see her friend in comfortable shoes wearing a newly adorned dress. Betsy's brother had put on a very elegant spread, and her mother-in-law had been like charm personified.

Betsy cried with happiness; Eric cried and said that

this was the best day of his whole life; Emily cried because it was all so marvelous; and the best man cried because his own marriage was on the rocks and he envied people just starting out.

When all the relations went home and the best man had gone to make one more ineffectual stab at repairing his own marriage, the bride and groom set off with the maid of honor for Chinatown and had a feast. There would be no honeymoon, but a holiday in Ireland would certainly be in the cards before the end of the year.

Emily told them about some of the people they would meet. Eric and Betsy said they could hardly wait. It all sounded so intriguing. They wanted to go right out to Kennedy Airport and fly to Ireland at once.

To: Emily
From: Lisa

I know we agreed only to e-mail about Frankie and there's no crisis—I just felt like talking to you. She is very well and sleeping much better.

Moira didn't seem to pick up on what I had said about Frankie being a lot of work, so with any luck that's all been forgotten.

Frankie seems to enjoy going to Dr. Hat. He sings little sea shanties to her. He got her some jars of apple puree and spoons them into her all the time—she can't get enough of them!

Maud and Marco from Ennio's restaurant are a definite
number— they've been seen at the cinema together.
Nice for Maud because things are sad in that house,
but I think Simon is feeling a bit left out.

Noel went out on a date last week. I set him up with a
friend of Katie's called Sophie, but it just didn't take.
When he told her about Frankie, she asked, "And when
do you give her back to her mother?" Noel told her
that Stella was dead and suddenly this girl Sophie
wanted to be miles away. A man with a child! Beware!
Beware!

Poor Muttie looks awful. Declan doesn't say anything,
but I think it's not sounding too good.

Life is very good otherwise.

Everything going well. Anton's picture was in the paper
today and April has blotted her copybook, I am
delighted to say.

How was the wedding?

Love,
Lisa

There were a lot of questions when Emily read the e-
mails to Betsy and Eric, so Emily explained who was who.
Moira was considered the enemy and April was considered a love rival of Lisa's; the twins were teenagers in the
catering business; Muttie was their grandfather or uncle or

guardian, no one quite knew. And Anton? The nonavailable object of Lisa's adoration . . .

From: Emily
To: Lisa

Thanks for the news. The wedding was fabulous—will show you pictures.

What did April do? How did she make a mess of things?

Love,
Emily

To: Emily
From: Lisa

April told everyone that a group of food critics were coming to Anton's on Tuesday last, and amazingly they never turned up: someone had told them it had been canceled. Anton was SO furious with her. He and I had a dinner together in the restaurant to cheer him up. . . .

Eric and Betsy, by now an established married couple, saw Emily off at the airport. They waved long after she had disappeared in the crush of people heading into Terminal 4. They would miss her, but they knew that soon she would be sitting on that Aer Lingus flight, resetting her mind and orienting herself towards Dublin again.

It sounded like an insane place and it had certainly changed Emily. Normally so reserved and quiet, she seemed to have been entirely seduced by a cast of characters who sounded as if they should be on an old Broadway variety show. . . .

Emily didn't sleep, like so many of the other passengers did. She sat making comparisons between this journey and the one she had made across the Atlantic when coming to Ireland for the very first time. Then she had been looking for roots, trying to work out what kind of life her father had lived back then in Dublin and how it had shaped him. She had learned next to nothing about this, but had become deeply involved in a series of dramas, ranging from helping to raise a motherless child who was living with a functioning alcoholic to working in a thrift shop trying to help her aunt to raise money to build a statue to an unknown saint who, if he had ever existed, had died back in the sixth century, to organizing a dog-walking business for her uncle.

It seemed quite mad, and yet she felt like she was going home.

It was early morning in Dublin when the transatlantic flights came in, and the crowds stood around the luggage carousels. Emily reached for her smart new suitcases—a gift from Eric to thank her for being maid of honor.

As they moved out through customs, she thought it would be nice if someone had come to meet her, but then who would have been able to?

Josie and Charles didn't have a car. Neither did Noel or Lisa. Dingo Duggan, with his van, would have been nice, but that was hardly likely. She would get the bus as before. Except this time she would know what she was getting into.

Just as she came out into the open air, she saw a familiar figure; Dr. Hat was standing there waving at her.

"I thought I'd come to meet you," he said, taking one of her cases.

In the midst of all the crowds of people embracing each other, Emily was thrilled to see him.

"I'm in the short-term car park," he said proudly and led the way. He must have gotten up very early to be there in time.

"It's so good to see you, Hat," she said as she settled into his small car.

"I brought you a flask of coffee and an egg sandwich. Is that as good as America?" he asked.

"Oh, Hat, how wonderful to be home!" Emily said.

"We were all afraid that you would stay out there and get married yourself." Hat seemed very relieved this was not the case.

"I wouldn't do that," Emily said, flattered that they had wanted her back here. "Now you can tell me all the news before I get back to St. Jarlath's Crescent."

"There's a lot of news," Hat said.

"We've a lot of time." Emily settled happily back in his car.

It was mixed news.

The bad news was that Muttie had got a great deal

worse. His prognosis, though not discussed or admitted in public, was no more than a few months now. Lizzie seemed to find it difficult to take this onboard and was busy planning a trip to the sunshine. She was even urging the twins to speed up their plans to go to New Jersey—somewhere that she and Muttie could come and visit.

Simon and Maud realized that there would be no such journey; they were very down. Young Declan Carroll had been marvelous with them, giving them extra babysitting to keep their minds off things.

Hat's good news was that baby Frankie was going from strength to strength. Emily didn't dare to ask, but Hat knew what she wanted to know.

"And Noel has been a brick. Lisa has been away a bit, but he manages fine."

"Which means that you help him too." Emily looked at him gratefully.

"I love the child. She's no trouble." Hat negotiated the traffic.

"Any more news?" Emily inquired.

"Well, Molly Carroll said you wouldn't believe how many garments she got from some madwoman."

" 'Mad'? Angry or crazy? I never know which you mean."

"Oh, crazed is what she was. She discovered her husband had been buying clothes for another lady and she took them all and brought them to the thrift shop!" He seemed amused.

"But are we entitled to them? Were they the crazy lady's to give?"

"Apparently so. The husband was singing dumb over it all, saying that he had bought them for his wife, but they were entirely the wrong size and the wrong color! Amazing things, I heard, like black and red corsets!"

"Heavens! I can't wait to get back," Emily said.

"And you know the old lady who gave Charles the dog?"

"Mrs. Monty, yes? Don't tell me she took Caesar away. . . ."

"No. The poor lady died—rest in peace—but didn't she leave all her money to Charles!"

"Did she have any money?"

"We think, amazingly, that she did."

"Isn't that wonderful!" Emily cried.

"It is until you think how it's going to be spent," Dr. Hat said, drawing a halo around his head with his finger.

Charles and Josie were waiting for her at Number 23; they were fussing over Frankie, who had a bit of a cold and was very fretful, not her usual sunny self. Emily was delighted to see her and lifted her up to examine her. Immediately, the child stopped grizzling.

"She's definitely grown, so much in three weeks. Isn't she wonderful?" She gave the baby a hug and was rewarded with a very chatty babble. Emily realized how much she had missed her. This was the child none of them had expected or, to be honest, really wanted, at the start— and look at her now! She was the center of their world.

Dr. Hat had been invited in for a cup of tea and was enjoying a game of picking up Frankie's teddy bear in order for her to drop it again, and Molly Carroll stopped in to welcome Emily back. Noel rang from work to make sure she really *had* returned and hadn't decided to relocate to New York.

Frankie was fine, he said, a runny nose, but otherwise fine. The nurse had said she was thriving. Lisa was away again. She had missed three lectures now and it would be so hard for her to catch up. Oh, yes, he had plenty of help. There was this woman called Faith at his lectures who had five younger brothers at home and had no place to study, so she had come to help Noel three evenings a week.

Faith was delighted with Frankie. She had a lot of experience bringing up younger brothers herself but had never been close to a little girl.

The evening slipped into an easy routine: bath time, bottle, Frankie off to sleep, then revision papers and the Internet notes to help them study. Faith sympathized deeply with Noel having to work in a place like Hall's: she was in a fairly dead-end office job but had great hopes that the diploma they were working for would make a difference. People in her office respected such things greatly.

She was a cheerful and optimistic woman of twenty-nine; she had dark curly hair, green eyes, a mobile face and a wide smile and she loved walking. She showed Noel a great many places he had never known in his own city. She said she needed to walk a lot because it concentrated her mind. She had suffered a great blow: six years ago, her fiancé had been killed in a car accident just weeks before the wedding day. She had coped by walking alone and being very quiet, but recently she had felt the need to get involved with the world about her. That was one of the reasons she had joined the course at the college, and it was one of the reasons she had adapted so easily to Noel's demanding life.

She had bought a baby album for Frankie and put in

little wisps of the child's hair, her first baby sock and dozens of photographs.

"Have you any pictures of Stella?" she asked Noel.

"No—none at all."

Faith didn't inquire further.

"I could do a drawing of her, maybe," he said after a while.

"That would be great. Frankie will love that when she gets older."

Noel looked at her gratefully. She was very good company to have around the place. Perhaps later he might try to sketch her face too.

Lisa and Anton were at a Celtic food celebration in Scotland. They were looking into the possibility of pairing with some similar-type Scottish restaurant where they could do a deal: anyone who spent over a certain sum in Anton's could get a voucher for half this amount in the Scottish restaurant and vice versa. It would work because it was tapping into an entirely new market, mainly American.

It was Lisa's idea. She had special cards printed to show how it would work. The Scottish restaurant's name was a blank at the moment until the deal was done.

Several times Lisa felt rather than saw Anton's glance of approval, but she knew better now than to look at him for praise. Instead, she concentrated entirely on getting the work done. There would be time later over meals together.

At one of the hotels they had visited the receptionist asked them if they'd like the honeymoon suite. Lisa deliberately said nothing. Anton asked, with apparent interest, if they looked like a honeymoon couple.

"Not really, but you *do* look happy," the girl said.

Lisa decided to let Anton speak again. "Well, we are, I hope. I mean, who wouldn't be happy in this lovely place and if there was a complimentary upgrade to the honeymoon suite, that would be the icing on the cake." He smiled his heartbreaking smile and Lisa noticed the receptionist join the long line of women who fancied Anton.

It was so cheering to be here with him and to know that April was out in the wilderness, not posturing and putting her small bottom in her skintight jeans on Anton's desk or the arm of his chair. April was miles and miles away. . . .

But then the trip was over and it was back to reality. Back to lectures in the college three nights a week, back to Frankie waking up all hours of the night, back to April, who was inching her way again into Anton's life.

Lisa noted that a lot of free events had been arranged in Anton's, occasions that would be written up in the papers, perhaps, but that did not put paying customers in seats, which was what they needed. She worried that too much was being spent on appearance rather than reality. The bottom line was the numbers of people you got in to pay for the meals and tell their friends, who would also come in and hand over money. Not just another charity press conference with minor celebrities who would be photographed for gossip columns. This was April's world.

Lisa was not so sure it was right. But when Lisa was alone with Anton, she kept quiet about her misgivings. Anton hated being nagged. To tell him he was high on publicity and low on paying punters could well have been considered nagging.

Lisa was not happy to be home.

Emily was walking towards Muttie and Lizzie's house when she saw Lisa, and she could judge Lisa's mood from a long way off. She wondered was it going to be her only role in life from now on cheering people up and stressing the positive.

"How are things, Lisa? Noel told me you've been on a great trip to Scotland," Emily said, without giving Lisa a chance to ask her about Betsy's wedding.

"It was magic, Emily. Were you ever somewhere and wished that it would never end?"

Emily thought for a moment. "Not really. I suppose there has been a day here and there that I never wanted to end. My friend Betsy's wedding day was one, and driving around Connemara was another. I suppose there were good days when I was teaching art too."

"I had days which were all like that in Scotland," Lisa said, her face radiant at the thought of it all.

"Great—you'll have the memory of that to keep you going when you get back to your studies." Emily knew she sounded brisk.

"Noel's been marvelous; he has all his notes photocopied for me and he's arranged for Molly Carroll to take Frankie for a walk in the park and he had to make sure that Bossy Boots knows all our plans. I'm just coming down here to make sure that Mrs. Carroll has cover for the thrift shop."

"You can't stand in the thrift shop all day—you have your studies to catch up on."

"I have some of my notes here. It won't be that busy," Lisa said.

"I'll look in after I've seen Muttie and Lizzie."

"Not much good news there," Lisa said, shaking her head. "Muttie's chemo has stopped and Lizzie keeps making impossible plans for the future. Hey, you have enough to do getting over jet lag and visiting Muttie. I'll survive in the thrift shop for a bit."

"We'll see," Emily said.

Muttie looked much frailer even after three weeks. His color was poor and his face seemed to have hollows in it; his clothes hung off him. His good humor was clearly not affected, though.

"Well . . . show us pictures of how the Americans do a wedding," he said, putting on his spectacles.

"It's not very typical," Emily explained. "Fairly mature bride and maid of honor, for one thing."

"The groom is no spring chicken either," Muttie agreed.

"Look at the lovely clothes!" Lizzie was delighted with it all. "And what are all these Chinese signs?"

"Oh, we went to Chinatown for dinner," Emily said. "Dozens of Chinese restaurants, Chinese shops and little pagodas and decorations everywhere."

"That's where we'll go when we go to New York later on in the year. Emily will mark our card."

"That's if I can ever get myself on the plane." Muttie shook his head. "I seem to have run out of puff, Emily.

Hooves here wants me to take him up to have a drink with my Associates, but I find the walk exhausts me."

"Do you get to see them at all?" Emily knew how much Muttie loved talking horses to the men in the bar while Hooves sat with his head on Muttie's knee and his eyes full of adoration.

"Oh, Dr. Hat is very good. And sometimes young Declan Carroll gets a fierce thirst on him and he drives me up there for a few pints."

Emily knew very well that Declan would often pretend a fierce thirst and get himself a pint or two of lemonade shandy while he drove his elderly neighbor up to the pub.

"And how are all the family?" Emily inquired.

As she had expected, they all seemed to be making sudden visits to Ireland from Chicago. Muttie was shaking his head at the coincidence of it all.

"I don't know where they get the money, Emily, I really don't. I mean, there's a recession out in those places as well as here."

"And the twins? Busy as ever?"

"Oh, Maud and Simon are wonderful. There's less chat about their going to New Jersey, but then again Maud has an Italian boyfriend—a really polite, respectful young man called Marco. They're all setting up this phone for us where you can see the person at the other end. It's called Skype and this weekend we'll be calling my daughter Marian in Chicago and we'll see her and all her family. It doesn't sound right to me."

"Amazing thing, technology," Emily agreed.

"Yes, but it's almost going too quickly. Fancy our children getting on planes and coming from the ends of the earth over here to see us and then this magic phone. I don't understand it at all. . . ."

Emily went to the thrift shop and found the twins working there. Lisa was in a corner sighing over her notes. There were no customers.

"We don't all have to be here," Emily said, taking off her coat.

"Maud and I were just wondering . . ."

"We don't want to put anyone out . . ."

"It's just there's this Italian cookery demonstration . . ."

"At Ennio's restaurant on the quays . . ."

"And Maud fancies the son of the house there rotten . . ." Simon wanted everything to be clear.

"Not true. We've been out a few times . . ."

"But it's starting in half an hour, you see . . ."

"And if it was possible for us to work here some other time . . ."

Emily cut across this double act. "Go now. This minute," she said.

"If you're sure . . ."

"If it's not putting you out . . ."

"Is that the pasta house where I saw you?" Lisa asked suddenly.

"You were there with Moira. Traitor!" Maud took no prisoners.

"You saw her socially?" Simon sounded disgusted.

"It was different. She was lonely."

"I wonder why. . . ." Maud was unforgiving.

"Are you still here?" Emily asked, opening the door of

the thrift shop. As they left, she turned to Lisa. "Go back to Chestnut Court and study properly, Lisa, and I'll do the pricing on the new clothes that have come in. Otherwise you and I will waste the morning and not a penny will be raised for St. Jarlath."

Lisa looked at her in surprise. "But you don't believe any of this St. Jarlath nonsense, do you, Emily?"

"I suppose we're just keeping our options open." Emily was slightly apologetic.

"But think about it, Emily. If there were a God, then I would be engaged to Anton, Stella wouldn't have died in childbirth and Frankie would have a mother. Noel would be recognized for what he could do at Hall's, Muttie wouldn't be dying of cancer, you would be running the world or the civil service or something, with a nice, undemanding husband to cook you a meal when you got home every night."

"What makes you think that's what I'd want a God to get for me?" Emily asked.

"What else would you want? Except to run things . . ."

"I'd want something totally different: a home of my own, the chance to take up painting to see if I was any good at it, a small office from which I could run Emily's Window Boxes . . . I don't want the undemanding husband or the great power of running the country. No way!"

"So you say." Lisa knew it all.

"Is it going to be as hard to get rid of you as the twins?" Emily asked.

"Right. I'm going. Thanks, Emily. You're amazing. If I'd just come back from America, I'd be on all fours rather than going straight in to work. I'm nearly a basket case and I was only in Scotland!"

"Well, you were probably much more active on your holiday than I was on mine," Emily said.

Rather than work out what Emily might have in mind, Lisa left. As she walked up the road she thought about Scotland. They had stayed in five different hotels and in every one of them Anton and she had made love. Twice in the place where they had the honeymoon suite. Why did Anton not miss this and want her to stay with him every night? He had kissed her good-bye when they got to Dublin Airport and said it had been great. Why did he use the past tense? It could all have continued when they were back home.

It was meant to continue.

He had said he loved her—four times he had said it— two of them were sort of jokey when she had got things right about various hotels and restaurants, but twice when they were making love. And so he must have meant it, because who would say something like that at such an intense time and not mean it?

In the thrift shop there was a beautiful green and black silk blouse. An "unwanted gift," said the lady who had brought in. It was still in its box with tissue paper. Emily hung it up on a clothes hanger and tried to price it.

When it was new it had probably cost a hundred euros, but nobody who came here would pay anything remotely like that. The lady who had donated it wouldn't be back to see how it was priced, but in any event Emily didn't want to price it too low. It was beautiful. If it were in her own size she would happily have paid fifty euros for it. She was still holding it when Moira came in.

"Just checking where Frankie is," she said abruptly.

"Good morning, Moira," Emily said, with pointed politeness. "Frankie has gone to the park with Mrs. Carroll, Dr. Declan's mother."

"Oh, I know Mrs. Carroll, yes. I was just making sure nobody had put Frankie in a 'File and Forget' file." Moira smiled to take the harm out of her words. It was not entirely successful.

Emily had a touch of frost in her voice. "That would never happen to Frankie Lynch."

"You mean well, certainly, Emily, but she's not *your* responsibility."

"She's family." Emily's eyes glinted. "She is the daughter of my first cousin. That makes her my first cousin once removed."

"Imagine!" Moira wasn't impressed.

"Can I do anything else for you, Moira?" Emily was managing to hold on to her manners, but only just.

"Well, I'm going out to the heart clinic and the woman who runs it is like a clotheshorse. She's interested in nothing but clothes."

"I believe she's a good heart specialist also," Emily said.

"Oh, yes, well, I'm sure she is, but she's always commenting on what you wear. . . . I was just wondering if you had anything . . . well, you know . . ."

"This is your lucky day. I have this beautiful green and black blouse. It would look so good with your black skirt there. Do try it on."

Moira looked very well in it. "How much?" she asked, in her usual charmless way.

"Would be over a hundred in the shops. I was going to put fifty on it, but you're a good customer, so shall we say forty-five?" It was more than Moira had intended to spend, but they agreed on forty-five and Moira headed off towards the heart clinic in her finery. The shabby gray blouse she had been wearing was wrapped up in the bottom of her briefcase.

As soon as she was gone, Emily telephoned Fiona at the clinic.

"I know this is a bit sneaky . . . ," she began.

"I *love* sneaky," said Fiona.

"Moira Tierney is on her way to you wearing a smashing new blouse she bought here. She may start to regret her buy and grizzle about the price, so build her up to the skies."

"Will do," Fiona said enthusiastically.

By the time Moira reached the clinic, there were quite a lot of people there. Frank Ennis had come in for one of his unexpected and disliked visits. They were having tea when he arrived.

"Oh, nice biscuits," he said, with a look of utter disapproval.

"Paid for by ourselves, Frank," Clara said cheerfully. "Every week someone gets to choose the biscuits and pay for them. Lord forbid that the whole of St. Brigid's would have to come to a halt because the heart clinic charged the central fund for biscuits. Do have another while you're here. . . ."

Moira came in just then.

"You bring a touch of class to this place," Frank Ennis said.

Barbara took offense. "She doesn't have to wear a uniform," she whispered to her friend Fiona, nodding her head at Moira. To her bewilderment, Fiona didn't seem to agree.

"That's a beautiful blouse, Moira." Fiona played her part perfectly.

Clara was looking at it too.

"You have a great eye for clothes, Moira. That's top-class silk."

In a million years Moira would never tell them where she'd bought it. She murmured a bit, refused tea and biscuits and went straight to her room. She had three new patients to see today.

The first man came into her small room. He was large, with a lined face and shaggy hair, and was fairly wordless. Moira flashed him one of her very brief smiles and took out a piece of paper.

"Well, now, Mr. . . . er . . . Kennedy. Your address first, please."

"St. Patrick's Hostel."

"Yes, I see you've been there since you left hospital. And before that . . . ?"

"In England."

"Addresses?"

"Ah, well, I was here and there, you know . . ."

Moira did know. Only too well. Irishmen who had lost years of their lives working on the buildings, using a different name every month, paying no tax, having no insurance, no record of years spent and wages passed over in cash in a pub of a Friday evening.

"Before that, then," she said wearily. One way or another, she needed some kind of paperwork for this man.

"Oh, long ago I lived in Liscuan," he said.

She looked up sharply. She had thought he looked somehow familiar.

It was Maureen Kennedy's long-gone husband. She was planning the future of the man whose wife now lived with her father.

Noel came back from Hall's tired.

He let himself in to Chestnut Court and found Lisa asleep at the kitchen table with his college notes all around her. He had been hoping that she might have made supper and even gone down to the Carrolls' to collect Frankie.

But what the hell, she was probably worn out after her time in Scotland and was sorry to be home. He would go to collect Frankie. He might even bring home fish and chips. Thank God there were no lectures tonight. He might even drop in to see Muttie. Poor guy was looking desperate these days. . . .

Muttie welcomed him with a big smile. It made his skull-like face look worse than ever.

"Lizzie, it's Noel. Have you a slice of cake for the lad?"

"No, thanks, Muttie. I'm collecting Frankie from Molly and Paddy. I only came to say hello. I have to get her home and put to bed."

Maud and Simon were there, blond heads bent over a computer.

"We've put Skype on for Muttie," Maud said proudly.

"So he can talk to people face-to-face," added Simon, equally pleased.

"Well, when the two of you get settled in New Jersey,

I can talk to you every week!" Muttie was bright and cheerful about it.

"Yeah, but we're not going to New Jersey," Maud said.

"Too much to keep us here," Simon added darkly.

"The cookery demonstration in Ennio's restaurant was brilliant today," Maud said.

"He's a very nice lad, that Marco. You'd walk many a mile before you'd meet as nice a fellow," Muttie said. "Hurry up now, Simon, and find yourself a girl before it's too late for us all."

They looked at him sharply, but he didn't mean anything sinister.

"It's too early to settle down," Simon said carelessly.

"Who said anything about settling down?" Maud asked.

There was a knock on the door. It was a young man with black curly hair who came in carrying a huge saucepan of something bubbling in a tomato sauce.

"This is for the grandfather of lovely Maud," he said.

"Well, thank you, Marco," Muttie said, pleased. "Lizzie, come in and see what's arrived."

Lizzie came running in from the kitchen.

"Marco! Imagine, I was just about to get the supper."

"So that was good timing, then?" Marco beamed around the little group.

"Well, I have to go." Noel stood up. "I'm Noel, by the way. I'd love to join you, but I have to pick up my daughter. *Buon appetito.*"

Noel wished he could stay. It was heartening to see such happiness in a house that was about to go through so much sadness soon.

———

In Chestnut Court Lisa woke with a stiff neck. She saw Noel's coat hanging on the back of the door. He must have come in and left again. She should have made him some kind of supper or gone to pick Frankie up from Molly Carroll's. Too late now. He had scrawled a note saying he would come back with a fish supper. He was so kind. Wouldn't it have been so easy if only she could have loved Noel rather than Anton. But then life didn't work like that and maybe there would be even more obstacles in the way. She got up, stretched and set the table.

She would really love a glass of wine with the cod and French fries, but that was something that would never be brought into this house. She thought back to the lovely wine they had drunk in Scotland. She had paid for the meals on alternate nights, but she had maxed out on her credit cards and was seriously broke now. But Anton never realized that. She hoped things would change soon; she would have to get a job if Anton didn't make a commitment.

Noel would be home shortly and she mustn't be full of gloomy thoughts.

At 23 St. Jarlath's Crescent, Josie and Charles Lynch sat in stunned silence. They had just closed the door behind a very serious lawyer in a striped suit. He had come to tell them just how much they had inherited from the late Meriel Monty. When all the assets were liquidated, the estate would come, the lawyer said very slowly, to a total of approximately 289,000 euros.

Chapter Eleven

It was good that Eddie Kennedy didn't recognize her, Moira thought. This way she could continue to be professional.

The hostel where he was living was only a short-stay place; soon he would need something long-term. If things had been different, she might have inquired more about the setup in Liscuan, wondered whether he might even at this late stage be able to patch things up with his wife. After all, he didn't drink now. But the very thought of destroying the great content that her father had finally found late in a troubled life was one she could not bear to let into her mind.

Wherever Eddie Kennedy was to find his salvation, it must not be in Liscuan.

Moira sighed deeply and tried to remember what she would have done for this man if things had been different, if she hadn't known for certain that his long-abandoned wife was living with her own father. Wearily she continued with fruitless questions about any possible benefits that might be due to him after a lifetime of working in England. This man had never signed on anywhere or joined any system. It would be a progression of hostels from now on.

It would have been the same if he had come across any other social worker, wouldn't it? Maybe one of them would have made inquiries back in Liscuan. And if inquiries *had* been made? Perhaps Mrs. Kennedy and her father would have sung low, in which case there would have been nothing different to the way it was now. . . .

Yet Moira felt guilty. This man shouldn't have his options restricted just because his social worker wanted her own father to continue undisturbed in what should have been this man's home. Moira wished, not for the first time, that she had a friend, a soul mate whom she could discuss it with.

She remembered that meal with Lisa in Ennio's: it had been pleasant and it was surprisingly easy to talk to Lisa. But of course the girl would think she was quite insane if she were to suggest it.

Worse—both insane and pathetic.

Muttie told Lizzie that something was worrying him.

"Tell me, Muttie."

Lizzie had listened to Muttie for years. Listened to stories of horses that were going to win, backs that ached, beer that had been watered and, more recently, of some poor unfortunates he had met up with at the hospital. Muttie had discovered there was a desperate lot of illness about—you just didn't come across it when you were in the whole of your health.

She wondered what she would hear now.

"I'm worried that the twins are putting off their trip to America because of my having to have those treatments." He said it defiantly, as if waiting, hoping, for her to deny it.

If that was what he wanted, then that was what he got. Lizzie's face split in two with a great laugh.

"Well, if that's all that's bothering you, Muttie Scarlet, aren't you a lucky man? Have you eyes in your head at all? They didn't want to go because Maud is crazy about Mario. The *last* thing she wants to do is to go away and let some Dublin dolly get her claws into Mario. It has nothing to do with you whatsoever!"

He was vastly relieved. "I suppose I was making myself the big man," he said.

Noel Lynch and Lisa Kelly were shopping for fruit and vegetables in a market where Emily had pointed them. Moira had complained that they did very little home cooking and Frankie's diet might be lacking in all kinds of nutrients.

"She always moves the bloody goalposts," Lisa said in fury.

"Why are home purees better than the ones we buy?" Noel said crossly. "What *are* all these additives she talks about? And why do the makers put them in?"

"I bet they don't. It's just Moira making life more difficult. Right, show me the list Emily made. Apples, bananas. No honey—that can poison her. Vegetables, but no broccoli. We have stock, and it's low-salt and organic— I checked."

"Have we?" Noel was surprised. "What does it look like?"

"Like a sort of toffee wrapped up. We have it, Noel. Come on, let's pay for this lot and we'll go home and puree it and while it's cooking we'll go over the notes for that lecture we both missed. Thank God for Faith!"

"Yes, indeed."

Lisa looked at him sharply. It was obvious to everyone except Noel that Faith fancied him. Lisa didn't feel at all drawn to Noel except as a housemate and friend, but she didn't want the situation complicated.

In some strange, odd way Anton felt slightly more on his toes because Lisa lived with a man. It was more racy somehow. Once or twice Anton had asked if there was any frisson between the two of them. That was a very Anton type of word and he asked it casually, as if he didn't care very much anyway.

But that was his way. He wouldn't have asked if he hadn't cared.

Lisa was comfortable in Chestnut Court. Noel made sure she went to her lectures when she wasn't running off with Anton at a moment's notice. And even though she wouldn't admit it to anyone, she had become amazingly fond of that little girl. Life without Frankie was going to be hard when it happened. As soon as Anton realized that commitment did not mean a life sentence, it meant the opening of doors.

Emily Lynch was also in the vegetable market; she had promised Dr. Hat she would teach him how to make a vegetarian curry for his friend Michael, who was coming to visit.

"Could you not just . . . er . . . make it for me?" Dr. Hat begged.

"No way! I want you to be able to tell Michael how you made it." She was very firm.

"Emily, *please*. Cooking is women's business."

"Then why are the great chefs mainly male?" she asked mildly.

"Show-offs," said Dr. Hat mutinously. "It won't work, Emily. I'll burn everything."

"Don't be ridiculous—we'll have a great time chopping everything up; you'll be making this recipe every week."

"I doubt it," said Dr. Hat. "I seriously doubt it."

The whole encounter with Eddie Kennedy had made Moira restless. Her own small apartment felt like a prison, with the walls enclosing her more and more. Perhaps she was a kindred soul to him and would end up beached, with no friends, being looked after by some social worker who was still at school now.

It was her birthday on Friday. It was a sad person who had nobody to celebrate with. Nobody at all. Yet again her thoughts went back to that pleasant evening at Ennio's restaurant. She had felt normal for once.

What would Lisa say if Moira asked her to have a meal with her—except that she wasn't free? Nothing would be lost. She would go around to Chestnut Court now.

"God Almighty, it's Moira *again*!" Lisa said when she had put down the entry phone and buzzed her in.

"What can she want now?" Noel looked around the flat nervously in case there was something that could be discovered, something that would be a black mark against them. Frankie's clothes were drying on the radiators— but that was good, wasn't it? They were making sure that the little garments were properly aired.

He continued spooning the puree into Frankie, who enjoyed it mainly as a face-painting activity and some-thing to rub into her hair.

Moira arrived in a gray pantsuit and sensible shoes. She looked businesslike, but then she was always busi-nesslike.

Noel saw her properly for the first time. There was a sort of shield around her, as if it were keeping people away. She had good, clear skin. Her hair was curly in a color that suited her. It was just that it didn't add up to much.

"Will you have a cup of tea?" he asked her wearily.

Moira had taken in the domestic scene at a glance: the child was being well cared for. Anyone could see that. They had even listened to her about getting fresh vegeta-bles and making purees.

She saw the books and note files out for their studies. These were her so-called hopeless clients, a family at risk, not fit to be minding Frankie, and yet they seemed to have got their act together much better than Moira had.

"I had a tiring day today," she said unexpectedly.

If the roof had blown off the apartment block, Noel and Lisa could not have been more surprised. Even Frankie looked up, startled, with her food-stained face.

Moira never complained about her workload. She was tireless in her efforts to impose some kind of order on a mad world. This was the very first time she had even given a hint that she might be human.

"What kind of things were most tiring?" Lisa asked politely.

"Frustration, mainly. I know this couple who are desperate for a baby. They would provide a great home, but can they get one? Oh, no, they can't. People can ignore babies, harm them, take drugs all round them, and that's perfectly fine as long as they are kept with the natural parent. We are meant to be proud of this because we have kept the family unit intact. . . ."

Noel found himself involuntarily holding Frankie closer to him.

"Not you, Noel," Moira said wearily. "You and Lisa are doing your best."

This was astounding praise. Lisa and Noel looked at each other in shock.

"I mean it's a hopeless situation, but at least you're keeping to the rules," Moira admitted grudgingly.

Noel and Lisa smiled at each other in relief.

"But the rest of it's exhausting and I ask myself, Is it getting anyone anywhere?"

Lisa wondered whether Moira might be having a nervous breakdown.

"It must be very stressful, your job. I suppose you have to try to compensate for it in your private life," Lisa babbled, in an attempt to restore normality.

"Yes, indeed, if all I had to think about was Hall's, I'd be locked up by now," Noel agreed. "If I didn't have Frankie to come home to, I'd be a right mess."

"I'm the same." Lisa thought of Anton's. "Honestly,

the comings and goings, the highs and lows, the dramas. I'm glad I have another life outside it all."

Moira listened to all this without much sign of agreement or pleasure. Then she delivered the final shock.

"It was actually about my social life that I called," Moira said. "I'm going to be thirty-five on Friday and I was hoping, Lisa, you might join me for supper at Ennio's. . . ."

"Me? Friday? Oh, heavens. Well, thank you, Moira, thank you indeed. I'm free on Friday, aren't I, Noel?"

Was she looking at him beseechingly, begging him to find some kind of excuse? Or was she eager to go? Noel couldn't work it out. Honesty seemed safest.

"Friday is my day on—you're free Friday evening," he said.

Lisa's face showed nothing. "Well, that's very kind of you, Moira. Will there be many people there?"

"In Ennio's? I don't know. I suppose there will be a fair number."

"No, I mean to celebrate your birthday?"

"Oh, just the two of us," Moira said, and she gathered herself up and left.

Noel and Lisa didn't dare to speak until she had left the building.

"We should have said she didn't look thirty-five," Lisa said.

"What does she look?" Noel asked.

"She could be a hundred. She could be any age. Why did she ask me to dinner?"

"Maybe she fancies you," Noel said, and then, "Sorry, sorry. I'm just making a joke."

"Right, you can afford to make jokes. You're not the one having dinner with her on Friday."

"She may be going mad," Noel said thoughtfully.

Lisa had been wondering exactly the same thing.

"Why do you say that?"

"Well . . ." Noel spoke slowly and deliberately. "It's a very odd thing to do. No one normal would invite you to dinner. You of all people."

She looked up at him and saw he was smiling.

"Yes, you're right, Noel. The woman's lonely and she has no friends. That's all."

"I was wondering . . ." Noel paused. "I was thinking of inviting Faith to dinner. A proper dinner, not just a bowl of soup or something on toast. You know, to thank her for the notes and everything."

"Oh, yes?" Lisa said.

"I wonder, would Friday be a good night? You'll probably be out late, hitting the clubs with Moira. I'd feel safer having a meal here. It's such a temptation to order a bottle of wine or have a cocktail in a restaurant." Noel rarely spoke of his alcoholism at home. He went to meetings and there was no drink in the flat. It was unusual for him to bring the subject up.

He must be interested in Faith after all. Lisa's mind leapt ahead again. Suppose Faith really did move in with Noel? Where would that leave Lisa? But she mustn't start to fuss. That was her least attractive quality. Anton had told her when they were in Scotland that she was an absolute angel when she didn't fuss. And Noel deserved some happiness in his life.

"That's a great idea. I'll do a salad for you before I go

out and maybe you could cook that chicken in ginger you do sometimes. It's very impressive. And we'll make sure to iron the tablecloth and napkins."

"It's only Faith. It's not a competition," Noel protested.

"But you want her to know you've gone to some trouble to entertain her, don't you?"

Noel realized with a shock that this was the first date he had planned in years.

"And in return you have to help me think of a present for Moira. Not too dear. I'm broke!"

"Ask Emily to look out for something from the thrift shop for you. She finds great things—new things, even."

"That's an idea." Lisa brightened. "Well, Frankie, social life around here is getting very lively. You're going to be hard pushed to keep up with us. . . ."

Frankie stretched her arms out to Lisa.

"*Mama,*" she said.

"Nearly there, Frankie, but it's Lee-Za, much posher." But from this child, "mama" was perfectly fine.

Faith was surprised and pleased to be invited.

"Will there be many people there?" she asked nervously.

"Just the two of us," Noel said. "Will that be all right?"

"Oh, fine!" Faith seemed very relieved. She smiled at him. "Thanks, Noel, I'm looking forward to dinner."

"Me too," said Noel. He wondered suddenly was she expecting that they would go to bed together. He realized he had never made love in his life while sober. He had heard some terrible stories on this topic at AA. It was apparently fraught with difficulties and had disastrous effects on performance. Many people had told his AA group that they had taken a quick shot of vodka just to see them right and were back on full-time drinking within a week.

But he would face that if and when it occurred. No point in destroying Wednesday thinking about Friday. This one-day-at-a-time thing really worked.

Friday eventually came.

Emily had found a small mother-of-pearl brooch as a gift for Lisa to give Moira. She even produced a little box and some black velvet. Moira couldn't help but like that.

Anton had laughed when Lisa had said she was going to Ennio's with Moira.

"That should be a bundle of fun," he had said dismissively.

"It will be fine," she said, suddenly feeling defensive.

"If you want cheapo pasta, a bottle of plonk and a couple of Italians bunching up their fingers to kiss them and say *'bella signora'*..."

"They're nice there." Why she was being protective towards this little trattoria, she didn't know.

"Yeah and we're nice in Anton's too, so why didn't you and the social worker choose us?"

"Be real, Anton. A Friday night! And anyway, it was her shout. She chose Ennio's."

He looked like a small boy who had been crossed. "I'd have given you early-bird rates all night."

"I know that, she didn't. See you."

"Are you coming round later? It's Teddy's birthday too and we're having a few drinks after closing time."

"Oh, no, we'll be hitting the clubs by then." She remembered Noel's expression. It was worth it to see the look of surprise and irritation on Anton's face.

Noel set the table at Chestnut Court. Lisa had left the salad in the fridge covered in cling wrap and his chicken-and-ginger dish was under foil and ready to put in the oven for twenty-five minutes. The potatoes were in a saucepan.

Frankie had been delivered to Declan and Fiona's: she was going to have a sleepover.

"Dada," she said as he waved her good-bye, and his heart turned over as it always did when she smiled at him. Now he was in the apartment waiting for a woman to come to supper, like someone normal would do.

Lisa had looked very well as she set out to the birthday celebration. It was so comforting to know that Anton was jealous, that he really thought she would go to a nightclub.

At Ennio's the host was waiting for them.

"*Che belle signore!*" he said, giving them each a small bunch of violets. Exactly as Anton had said he would. "Marco, *vieni qui, una tavola per queste due bellissime signore.*"

The son of the house bustled towards them and dusted chairs. Moira and Lisa thanked him profusely.

Lisa spotted that Maud was working there that night, and Marco saw Lisa recognize her.

"I think you know my friend and colleague Maud," he said proudly.

"Yes, indeed I do. Lovely girl," Lisa said. "And this is Moira Tierney, who chose the restaurant for her birthday celebration."

"Moira Tierney . . . ," Marco repeated the words fearfully. "Maud has mentioned your name to me." Written all over his face was the fact that the mention had perhaps not been the most cordial, but he struggled to remember his job of welcoming guests and handed them the menus.

They began choosing their food. If Moira said once that the markup on the food was enormous, she must have said it a dozen times.

"Imagine charging that for garlic bread!" she gasped, as if astonished.

"We don't have to have garlic bread," Lisa said.

"No, no, we'll have everything we want. It's a celebration," Moira said in a sepulchral voice.

"Indeed it is." Lisa was bright and positive. This looked like it would be a long night.

Emily went to Dr. Hat's house to check that he had his curry ready for his friend Michael. She wanted to show him that he should have a dish of sliced bananas and a little bowl of coconut as well.

To her surprise the table was set for three.

"Will his wife be with him?" Emily asked, surprised. Only Michael had been mentioned up to now.

"No, Michael never married. Another crusty old bachelor," Dr. Hat said.

"So who is the third person?"

"I was rather hoping that *you* would join us," he said hesitantly.

———

Paddy Carroll and his wife, Molly, were going to a butchers' dinner. It took place every year; the wives dressed up and it was held in a smart hotel. It was an occasion where Paddy Carroll had been known to over-imbibe, so Declan would drive them there and a taxi would be ordered to take them home.

Fiona waved them off as they left in a flurry, then she sat down with a big mug of tea to watch over the two little ones crawling around the floor before she had to settle them in their cribs. They were both a bit restless this evening and she was going to have to separate them if they were going to go to sleep. She was wondering if she might possibly be pregnant again. If she was, it would be great and Declan would be so pleased, but it would mean that they would have to stir themselves and make sure the house was ready for them to move into before the baby was born. They couldn't put Paddy and Molly through all that business of a crying baby again.

Finally, along with the second bottle of wine, Moira broached the subject of Eddie Kennedy. Lisa thought she understood the situation, but she didn't really see the problem.

"Of course you don't have to do anything for him," she said. "It was the luck of the draw that he got you as a social worker. You don't have to tell him about the cozy little homestead down there."

"But he bought that house before he got addled with drink. He's entitled to live there."

"Nonsense. He gave up all rights and entitlements when he went off to England. He chose to opt out of this life. He can't expect you to turf your father out and get his wife to take him back. She probably wouldn't want him anyway. . . ."

"But is he to die in a hostel because I don't want to disturb things?"

"He chose that route." Lisa was firm.

"If it was your father . . . ," Moira began.

"I hate my father. I wouldn't spit on him if he was on fire!"

"I feel guilty. I've always given my clients the best. I'm not doing this with Eddie Kennedy," Moira said bleakly.

"Suppose you made it up to him in other ways? You know, went to see him in the hostel, took him out for the odd afternoon."

Moira looked at her in disbelief. How could this be doing her duty? It would be crossing the thin line that divided professionalism from friendship. Entirely unsuitable.

Lisa shrugged. "Well, that's what I'd do, anyway." She caught Marco's eye, and in thirty seconds a little cake with one candle came from the kitchen. The waiters sang "Happy Birthday" and everyone in the restaurant clapped.

Moira was pink and flustered. She tried to cut the cake and all the filling oozed out of one side. Lisa took the knife from her.

"Happy birthday, Moira," she said, putting as much warmth into it as she could. To her amazement she saw the tears falling down Moira's face.

Thirty-five and this was probably the only birthday party she had ever had.

———

Up in Chestnut Court the dinner was going very well.

"Aren't you a dark horse, being able to cook like this!" Faith said appreciatively. She was easy to talk to—not garrulous, but she talked engagingly of her background.

She spoke briefly about the accident that had killed her fiancé, but she didn't dwell on it. Terrible things happened to a lot of people. They had to pick themselves up.

"Do you still love him?" Noel asked as he spooned out another helping of chicken.

"No. In fact I can barely remember him. And you, Noel, do you miss Frankie's mother a lot?" Faith asked.

"No, I'm a bit like you. I hardly remembered Stella, but then that was in my drinking days. I don't remember anything much from those times." He smiled nervously. "But I love to have Frankie around the place."

"Where is she now? I brought her a funny little book of animals. It's made of cloth, so it doesn't matter if she eats it!"

"Lisa dropped her in to Fiona and Declan's. Lisa's gone out to supper."

"With Anton?"

"No, with Moira, actually."

"A different kind of outing, certainly." Faith knew the cast of characters.

"You could say that." Noel beamed at her. This was all going so well.

———

Fiona had just brought Declan a mug of coffee when she heard running feet outside the door and there was Lizzie, disheveled and distraught.

"Can Declan come quickly? I'm so sorry to interrupt you, but Muttie's been sick and it's all blood!"

Declan was already out of his chair and grabbing his doctor's bag.

"I'll come in a minute—I'll have to sort out the kids," Fiona shouted.

"Fine." In seconds Declan was through the Scarlets' front door. Muttie was ashen-faced, and he had been vomiting into a bowl. Declan took in the scene at a glance. "A thing of nothing, Muttie. They'll have you as right as rain in the hospital."

"Couldn't you deal with it, Declan?"

"No, you need to be where they can take care of you properly."

"But it will take forever to get an ambulance," Muttie objected.

"We're going in my car. Get in there right now," Declan said firmly.

Lizzie wanted to go with them, but Declan persuaded her to wait for Fiona. He took her back inside the house and whispered that as the hospital might need to keep Muttie in overnight, the best thing was for her to go and pack a small bag for him. Fiona would bring Lizzie up to the hospital in a taxi when she was ready, and not to worry, he would make sure that Muttie was in safe hands. He knew that having something useful to do would calm her.

By now, Fiona had arrived and they quickly realized

that they had to find somewhere for Johnny and Frankie to spend the evening and do it fast or there would be total confusion. Noel was having the first date of his life; his parents were away. Lisa had gone out with Moira—which at least would keep the social worker out of their hair; Emily would be the one to call on. Leaving Fiona to make the arrangements, Declan sped off with Muttie beside him, looking pale and frightened.

Emily had insisted that Dr. Hat serve the meal himself. After all, he had made it.

Michael proved to be a quiet, thoughtful man. He asked her gentle questions about her past life. It was as if he were checking her out for his old friend Hat. She hoped that she was giving a good account of herself. Hat was such a good and pleasant companion, she would hate to lose his friendship.

She was surprised when her phone rang in the pocket of her jacket as they were at the dining table. She wasn't expecting any calls.

"Emily, big crisis. Can you do baby patrol?" Fiona sounded frightened.

Emily didn't hesitate. "Certainly. I'm on my way!" She quickly excused herself and hastened down the road.

Outside the Carrolls' house all was confusion. Lizzie was there crying and clutching a small suitcase; Fiona was hovering between the Scarlets' front door and her own. Hooves was barking madly. Dimples was answering from the Carrolls' back garden. Declan had taken Muttie to hospital. The taxi was on its way for Fiona and Lizzie.

"I'm going up to the hospital with Lizzie to be with

her while we wait for news of him," Fiona said as soon as Emily arrived.

"Can I move baby patrol up to Dr. Hat's house? I'm sort of in the middle of a meal there."

"Of course, Emily. I'm so sorry. I didn't mean to interrupt. . . ."

"No, it's fine, don't worry. Two old bachelors and myself. This will lower the age level greatly. Good luck—and let us know . . ."

"Right," Fiona said, as the taxi pulled up outside the house. She grabbed Lizzie and the suitcase and bundled her into the back of the car. "Emily, you are amazing. Key under the usual flowerpot."

"Go now," Emily ordered. She ran to the Carrolls' house and picked Johnny up out of his crib in the front room and fastened him into his buggy.

"We're going for a visit to Uncle Hat and Auntie Emily," she said. She pushed the baby buggy out the door, locked it behind her and then put the key carefully under the flowerpot.

Dr. Hat and Michael were suitably impressed with little Johnny. The boy, exhausted from the journey, fell asleep on Dr. Hat's sofa and was covered with a blanket. The meal continued seamlessly.

Hat admitted, when he produced dessert, that he had not made the meringues himself but had bought them in a local confectionery shop.

"I think he'd have gotten away with saying he made them himself, don't you, Michael?" said Emily.

Michael was flushed with wine and good humor. "I'd have believed anything Hat were to tell me tonight." He beamed at them. "Never saw such a change in a person. If that's what retirement did for you, Hat, then lead on, I say. And I do admire the way you all look after these children. It was never like that in our day—people were stressed and fussed and never believed that anyone else could look after a child for more than two minutes."

"Ah, they have it down to a fine art," Dr. Hat said proudly. "Whenever Johnny and Frankie need a minder, they're all here on tap."

"Frankie?" Michael asked.

"She's my cousin Noel's daughter. He's bringing her up as a single father and doing a great job of it too. Actually Noel has a date tonight. All of us chattering spinsters have great hopes for this girl Faith. He's entertaining her in his own apartment."

"And so Faith is meeting the baby tonight?" Michael asked.

"No, she knows the child already; she goes in to study there, you see. But the baby is out for the night to give them a bit of space, I think."

"So who's minding Frankie tonight?" Michael asked. His question was innocent—he was fascinated by this toy town atmosphere, with good Samaritans coming out of every house in the street.

Emily stopped to think.

"It can't be Lisa. She's going out with the dreaded Moira. The twins are out on the town. The Carrolls have gone to a butchers' dinner. Noel's parents, my uncle Charles and aunt Josie, are in the west . . . who *is* minding Frankie?" Emily felt the first constriction of alarm in her chest.

If Noel had been going to bring in someone from outside the circle he would have told them. Moira had been behaving like a Rottweiler at the thought of any new face on the horizon.

"If you'll excuse me, I'll call Noel," she said, "just to set my mind at rest."

"You'd interrupt the boy's first proper date with Faith?" Dr. Hat shook his head. "Think, Emily, she must be somewhere."

"I have run out of options, Hat—let me call Noel."

"I only want to say you'll be annoyed with yourself when it's all perfectly all right."

"No. I'll be able to sleep easy," she said.

"Noel, I'm so sorry," she began.

"Is anything wrong, Emily?" He was alert to her tone immediately.

"No, nothing. I was just checking something. Where is Frankie tonight?"

"Lisa took her down to Fiona and Declan's earlier. I'm having a friend to dinner."

"To the Carrolls' house?"

"Is everything all right, Emily?" he asked again.

"Everything's fine, Noel," she said and hung up immediately. "You two mind Johnny here. I must have left Frankie in the Carrolls' house. There was only one baby in the crib." She was out the door before they could ask any more.

Emily ran down St. Jarlath's Crescent at a greater speed than she had known to be possible. What had Fiona said? She hadn't said "babies." She had said "baby patrol." Her hand shook as she reached under the flowerpot for the key and opened the door.

"Frankie?" she called as she ran into the house.

There was no sound.

In the kitchen there was a second crib with some of Frankie's toys in it. Frankie's buggy was parked beside it. There was no sign of the child. The strength left Emily's legs, and she sat down on a kitchen chair to support herself.

Someone had let themselves in and taken Frankie.

How could this have happened?

Then the thought struck her.

Of course! Fiona had come back home to check on things. Yes, that must be it.

She ran to Muttie and Lizzie's house. It was dark and closed. She knew before she started hammering on the door that there was no one there. Now she was really frightened. Fingers starting to shake, she dialed Fiona's mobile number. As the number connected, she heard a phone start to ring from inside the Scarlet house. It was Fiona's ring tone—she recognized it. After a few seconds the ringing stopped and she heard the voice-mail message start.

Declan. She had to call Declan.

"Emily?" He answered straightaway. "Is everything all right? Is it the children?"

"Johnny's fine," she said straightaway. "He's asleep on Dr. Hat's sofa."

"And Frankie?" Declan suddenly sounded alarmed. "What about Frankie?"

But Emily had already started running.

Chapter Twelve

They tried to be methodical about it but panic overwhelmed them; the list was checked over and over. Signora and Aidan knew nothing about where Frankie was, but would join in any searches. No point in trying to contact Charles and Josie: they were miles away and couldn't do anything; they'd just go mad with worry. It would be ages before Paddy and Molly would be home from the butchers' dance. Paddy would be fueled with brandy and good cheer; Molly's shoes would be too tight. Who could have come into the Carrolls' house and spirited Frankie away? She couldn't have got out herself and Emily had been back into the house and searched the place from top to bottom. Anywhere, any small space a child might be able to crawl into—she must be here somewhere.

She wasn't.

Could somebody have been watching the house? It seemed less than possible and there was no sign of a break-in. There must be a rational explanation. Should the police be called?

Having left Faith in the flat to answer any calls and white-faced with anxiety, Noel ran in and out of all the houses in St. Jarlath's Crescent. Had anyone seen anything? Anything at all?

He had sent Lisa a text and asked her to call him from the ladies', out of Moira's earshot. Lisa was shocked at how frightened she felt when he told her the news. For the time being, she was *not* to come home. It didn't matter where she went, as long as she kept Moira occupied. She felt sure that Moira must be able to tell something was wrong; nailing a smile onto her face, she went back to the table.

Up at the hospital, Lizzie wandered up and down the corridors asking plaintively when she was going to be able to see how Muttie was getting on. Fiona persuaded her to come back into the waiting room and sit down. They would wait for Declan to come.

He arrived twenty minutes later. "Well, he's stable now but they're going to keep him in for a while." His voice was grim. "They've made him comfortable and he's sleeping," he said to Lizzie. "You'll probably not be able to speak to him until tomorrow but he should feel better after a good night's rest. We should all go home."

Lizzie was pleased with the news. "I'm glad he's getting a good rest. I'll leave his suitcase in for him for tomorrow."

"Do that, Lizzie," Fiona said, realizing that there was something Declan hadn't told her. Could this night get any worse?

———————

It was a time of frantic comings and goings. Michael stayed with Johnny as Hat and Emily went through the whole thing over and over. At least a hundred times Emily must have said that she should never have gone along with the silly phrase "baby patrol." She should have asked what it meant and how many babies were involved.

Hat, in her defense, said that it was all Fiona's fault. Imagine having two babies in different rooms and not mentioning it! It was unheard-of.

Noel was almost out of his mind with grief and worry and rage—what were those idiotic women doing, risking his daughter's safety like that? How could they be so stupid as to abandon her in that house, leaving her prey to—who knew what? And as for him, it was all his own fault. Stella had trusted him with their daughter and he'd let her down, all because he'd wanted to spend some time with a woman. Now some monster, some pervert, had taken his little girl, and he might never see her again. He might never hold her in his arms and see her smile. He might never hear her voice calling him "Dada." If anyone had hurt her, if anyone had touched a hair of his Frankie's head . . . And in the middle of St. Jarlath's Crescent, Noel knelt down on the pavement and wept for his little girl.

Lisa managed to escape Moira on two occasions by going back to the ladies' room, but she couldn't go on doing this all night. She decided to persuade Moira to go to Teddy's birthday party at Anton's.

"But I won't know anyone," Moira had wailed.

"Neither will I. Most of them will be strangers to me, friends of silly April, but come on, Moira, it's free drink and it's your birthday too. Why not?" And as Moira agreed, Lisa dragged herself together. She wished that she was at home with Noel helping to coordinate the search. There *must* be an explanation. Lisa had heard very little except a trembling hysteria from Noel about what could have happened.

"Noel, don't hate me for saying this, but in the name of God, don't go back on the drink."

"No, Lisa, I won't." His voice was clipped.

"I know you're cross with me, but I *had* to say it."

"Yes, I realize you did."

"Go back to where we were before I said it. She's fine. There's been a misunderstanding. It will be sorted."

"Sure it will, Lisa," he said.

Sergeant Sean O'Meara had seen it all and done it all and, if he was honest, he would say that most of it was fairly depressing, but this occasion was just bizarre.

An extremely drunk man called Paddy Carroll was explaining over and over that he had been at a butchers' dinner and someone had spiked his drinks. He had started to behave foolishly and so he agreed that his wife should take him home in a taxi. The wife, a Mrs. Molly Carroll, said that she was not a serious partaker of alcohol herself and had been delighted when her husband agreed to come home with her, as her feet were killing her. But when they got home, they were bemused to find Frankie asleep in the crib and their own family—son, daughter-in-law and grandson—nowhere to be found.

They had tried to contact several people, but hadn't been able to speak to anyone who might know what was going on. They'd tried to find the child's father but had arrived at his apartment block not knowing which flat he lived in. What sort of people don't put their names on doorbells, asked Paddy Carroll, looking around him accusingly. What sort of people don't want people to know where they lived? So what were they to do?

"So, you want us to find this Noel Lynch. Is that it?" Sergeant O'Meara asked. "Had you ever thought of ringing him?" And he handed the phone to Paddy Carroll, who suddenly looked even more confused.

Faith was pacing up and down at Chestnut Court. She had a sheet of paper beside the phone and she perched nervously beside it, trying not to jump when it rang. Anyone who phoned in was asked for their telephone number, but she had little information to give out. Yes, Frankie was still missing; no, Noel wasn't there, he was out looking. No, they hadn't called the police yet, but the time was fast approaching when they would have to do so. They had agreed that if Frankie were not found within the hour, Faith would call the guards. There wasn't long to go.

Noel had phoned her eight times already, knowing as he did that she would call him the moment there was any news.

She checked her watch again. It was time. She had to call the police. Hand shaking, she reached for the phone, and as she did so, it rang. Her stomach lurched. Anxiously she answered.

At first, she thought it was a crank call. The man's voice on the other end of the phone sounded muffled, incoherent, angry, she thought at first, but soon she realized he might be drunk. No, Noel wasn't there, he was . . . No, he had been at home earlier in the evening but . . . No, his daughter was missing and the police were about to be called. . . .

"But that's what I'm telling you," the voice said. "I've got his daughter here. She's with us now. . . ." And suddenly Faith heard the unmistakable sound of Frankie crying.

"She's *found*, Noel! Not a hair of her head touched," she said. "She's great. She's asking for her daddy."

"Have you seen her? Is she there with you?"

"No. They brought her to the Garda station. It was the Carrolls. It was Paddy and Molly Carroll. It was *all* a misunderstanding. They were looking for *you*."

"What the hell did they mean by that? What do you mean, *looking for me*? We were in all night!" Noel was torn between overpowering relief and fury.

"No, it's all right—don't get angry. They got enough of a shock already."

"They got a shock! What about the rest of us? What happened?"

"They came home early from their do and they found her in the crib alone in the house. They must have arrived just after Fiona and Lizzie set off for the hospital. They called on all the neighbors, but there was no one around—

Declan and Fiona were at the hospital with the Scarlets, Emily had been at Dr. Hat's but they didn't know that and, of course, Charles and Josie weren't there. They tried to call Fiona, but she'd left her phone at Lizzie's. Declan's phone was busy, so they came to Chestnut Court to see you. Only by the sound of it they'd got the wrong flat number and were pressing the wrong doorbell. By the time we knew Frankie was missing they were on their way to the Garda. They thought something was terribly wrong and quite rightly didn't want to put the child at further risk. But she's fine and we need to get over there to pick her up."

But Noel was still distraught. "Frankie's in a police station. What chance will I have of keeping her once bloody Moira gets to hear of this?"

"Don't worry—I'll call Lisa as soon as I put the phone down and let her know Frankie is found. Then I'll put together some things for Frankie—why don't you collect me here and we'll go up together? Let's get her home before Moira ever knows she was missing. . . ."

Sergeant O'Meara had no idea what they were all doing in a police station, and he wished someone, anyone, would shut the screaming child up. Mrs. Carroll kept bouncing the baby up and down, but the decibel level was getting higher. It was all starting to grate on him.

"Why *exactly* did you bring the child here? If you know who she is and all belonging to her?"

Paddy Carroll tried to explain. "It seemed like the right thing to do at the time. Be on the safe side," he said.

"The safe side of what?" Sergeant O'Meara asked, raising his voice above the din.

Paddy wished that his mind was less fuzzy and his speech more clear. "Could I have a cup of tea?" he asked plaintively.

"It's a pity you didn't think of having tea earlier in the evening," Mrs. Molly Carroll said sharply.

Sergeant O'Meara went to get tea, glad to get away from the screaming baby for a moment. "So this Noel Lynch is on his way here now," he said wearily, when he came back with the tea.

"There he is!" Paddy Carroll cried out, pointing at the glass door out in the front office. "There he is! Noel! Noel! Come in here! We've got Frankie for you!"

And Sergeant O'Meara rescued Paddy Carroll's teacup just before it pitched onto the child as Noel threw himself at his baby girl.

"Frankie! Are you all right?" he cried, his voice muffled with emotion. "Darling little Frankie. I'm so sorry, really I am. I'll never leave you again. . . ." Frantically, he checked that she was all right, uninjured in any way; then he wiped her face and her nose, and dried her eyes.

Behind him, meanwhile, stood a small, slim woman with green eyes and a big smile. She was carrying one of Frankie's coats and a woolly scarf; more important, she was carrying a jar of baby food, which she handed to Noel straightaway.

As Noel fed his daughter, almost magically, the crying stopped, the baby calmed down and peace was restored.

Sergeant O'Meara was profoundly grateful that the situation seemed to be sorting itself out.

More and more people were arriving: a stressed-out middle-aged woman with frizzy hair and an older man, wearing a hat like something from a black-and-white movie.

"Oh, Frankie! I'm so sorry . . ." The woman bent down to kiss the baby girl. "I didn't know you were there. I'll never forgive myself. *Never.*"

The man in the hat introduced himself as Dr. Hat; he looked like the only person with any degree of control. "If ever there was a case of all's well that ends well . . . it's here." He beamed at everyone. "And well done, Mr. and Mrs. Carroll. You did exactly the right thing in the circumstances. Noel, we'll all get out of here, don't you think, and leave Detective O'Meara to his business. No need to write a report at all—wouldn't you agree?"

The sergeant looked at Dr. Hat gratefully. The writing of a report about this was going to be Gothic. "If everyone's satisfied . . ." he began.

"I'm so sorry about this," Dr. Hat said to him quietly. "It's a terrible waste of your time, but I assure you that it was well meant. We're sorry to have disturbed you—but no harm done. . . ."

And as they all shuffled out of the police station, Sergeant O'Meara heard them saying to one another in tones of relief that Moira need never know a thing about any of it. He wondered vaguely who Moira might be, but it was late and he could now go home to his wife, Ita, who always had a hundred stories of her day's work on the wards in St. Brigid's. He would tell her this one, if he had the energy to unpick who was who.

Muttie was asleep when Lizzie arrived at his bedside. They told her that he would need a scan in the morning but that he was comfortable now; far better for her to be at home and get a good night's sleep. She left the suitcase for him beside his bed.

"Can I leave him a note?" she asked, fearful of strange places and unfamiliar surroundings. A nurse brought her pen and paper.

Lizzie pinned a note to the suitcase.

> *Muttie, my darling, I've gone home but I'll be back tomorrow. You're going to be fine. The next time we use this suitcase will be when we go to New York and have dinner in Chinatown.*
>
> *Love from Lizzie*

She felt better, she told Declan, now that she had written a letter.

Declan's relief at the safe return of Frankie was tempered by what he had just discovered: he had spoken to the medical team that had examined Muttie. The cancer had spread all over his body.

It would not be long now.

Lisa thought that the night would never end. Teddy's birthday party at Anton's was in full swing when they got there. They had just put on music and were beginning to dance. Straightaway she noticed April dancing around Anton.

"Hey, that's not dancing! That's lap dancing!" she called in a very loud voice. A few people laughed. Anton looked annoyed.

April went on weaving and squirming.

"Suit yourself," she said to Lisa. "You dance your way—I dance mine."

Lisa, her rage fueled by alcohol and jealousy, was about to engage in further conversation, but Moira interrupted quickly.

"I need a glass of water, Lisa. Can you come and get one with me?"

"You don't need water," Lisa said.

"Oh, but I do," Moira countered, pushing her towards the ladies' room. There she took a glass of water and offered it to Lisa.

"You're not expecting me to drink this, are you?"

"I think you should, then we'll go home."

Lisa was only just holding herself together. Moira must never know Frankie was missing.

"I'll think about it," she said.

Moira spoke firmly. "I think it would be wise. Yes, then I'll phone us a taxi."

"No, we can't go home. Wherever we go, we can't go home!" Lisa said in fright.

Moira asked mildly, "Well, where *do* you want to go, then?"

"I'll think," Lisa promised. Just then her own phone buzzed with a text message. Trembling, she read it.

ALL CLEAR. COME HOME ANYTIME. F SAFE AND SOUND.

"They *found* her!" Lisa cried.

"Who?" Moira paused in the middle of talking to the taxi firm.

Lisa stopped herself in time. "My friend Mary! She was lost and now she's found!" she shouted, with a very unfocused look on her face.

"But you were talking to her earlier, weren't you?" Moira was perplexed.

"Yes and she got lost. And then found since then," Lisa said foolishly.

Moira completed her call to the taxi and began to support Lisa towards the exit. On the way, they passed Teddy, the birthday boy, who whispered in Moira's ear.

"Well done. Anton will owe you for this. We have an unexploded bomb here," he said, nodding towards Lisa.

"Well, it's a pity he wasn't able to do something about it!" Moira retorted.

"Not his problem." Teddy shrugged.

"Good enough to sleep with, but not important enough to be nice to, right?"

"I just said he'd be grateful to you. She was about to make a scene."

Moira pushed past him, supporting Lisa into the taxi. Her dismal outlook on men seemed to have been confirmed tonight.

Lisa sang a little in the taxi. Sad songs about loss and infidelity, and then they were in Chestnut Court.

"Lisa's home, slightly the worse for wear," Moira said into the entry phone.

"Can you help her in, please, Moira?"

"Certainly."

Noel put Frankie down for the first time since she had been found. He realized he had been clinging to her since they came back to the flat.

Faith had washed the dishes and tidied up the place.

Moira brought Lisa in the door and settled her into a chair.

"Partly my fault. We had a lot of wine at Ennio's and then we went to this party at Anton's."

"Oh, I see," Noel said.

"You'll be fine, Lisa," Faith said, holding Lisa's trailing hand.

"Oh, Moira, I'm Faith, by the way. A friend of Noel and Lisa's from the college."

"How do you do?" Moira was gruff. She felt an unreasoning jealousy of Lisa. Nobody was blaming her for having become drunk. There was a household of people welcoming her. Even the child had stretched out her little arms towards Lisa as she lay slumped in her chair. If it had happened to Moira, she would have had to go home to an empty apartment. It seemed that almost everyone else in the world had sorted out his or her relationships while she, Moira, still was alone.

She left abruptly. Lisa let out a deep breath.

"I didn't tell her," she said.

"I know you didn't," Noel said.

"You did a great job," Faith said soothingly.

"Good. Glad it's sorted," Lisa said, her voice slurring. She began to slide off the chair, but they caught her before she reached the ground.

"When I think," she said intensely, "when I remember what I said to you, Noel, that it would be terrible if you were to fall into drink . . . and then I went and did it myself . . ."

"It doesn't matter, Lisa. You'll be fine tomorrow," Noel said. "And you did great work keeping Moira distracted. You did brilliantly."

"Why don't we give Lisa a hand to get into bed?" Faith

made it all sound as if it had been a completely normal evening, what everyone did every night all over the place. . . .

When she got home, Lizzie was surprised to see so many people in her house. Her sister Geraldine was there, her daughter Cathy and Cathy's husband, Tom Feather. The twins and Marco were there, and there were constant phone calls coming in from Chicago and Australia. Everyone seemed to be making tea and Marco had provided a tray of cakes.

"Won't Muttie be disappointed to have missed all this," Lizzie said, and people looked away before she could see the pain in their faces.

Eventually they persuaded her to go to bed. The sitting room was still full of people. Cathy went upstairs with her mother and tried to reassure her.

"They're terrific in St. Brigid's, Mam—don't be worrying about him. Geraldine's just been saying how good they are. All the best consultants and everything. They'll have Da right in no time."

"I think he's very sick," Lizzie said.

"But he's in the right place," Cathy said for the twentieth time.

"He'd prefer to be in his own home," Lizzie said for the thirtieth time.

"And he will be, Mam, so you're to get to sleep so that you'll be up and ready for him when he *does* come home. You're asleep on your feet."

That worked. Lizzie made a slight movement towards the bed and Cathy had her nightdress ready. Her mother looked so small and frail; Cathy wondered would she be able to bear all that lay ahead.

Maud said that Marco had texted to say that he and Dingo Duggan would be available night and day with Dingo's van if anyone needed to be driven anywhere.

Marco had said, "I am so sorry about your grandfather. Please God, he will get better."

"Please God, indeed," Simon said, when Maud read him the text message.

"I think he just says that automatically."

"Like Lizzie says 'DV,' " Simon agreed.

"Yes. I remember Mother used to say that too, except that she started to say 'VD' instead," Maud said. "Dad would explain it over and over. DV meant *Deo volente*, God willing, but Mother always nodded and said 'VD.' " Simon and Maud talked very little about the parents who had abandoned them when they were young. This was their home. Muttie was the man they loved, rather than the elegant father who had gone away on his travels. Lizzie was the mother they never really had. Their own mother had always been frail, with a light grip on reality. If they had heard that either of their biological parents had died, there would be a minor sense of regret. The news about Muttie was as if somebody had stuck a knife right into their bodies.

Nurse Ita O'Meara looked down at the man in the bed. He was in very poor shape. All she could do for him was to keep him under observation and make him comfortable.

"What's your name?" he asked her.

"I'm Ita, Mr. Scarlet."

"Then I'm Muttie," he said.

"Well, Muttie, what can I do for you? A cup of tea?"

"Yes, I'd love some tea. Could you sit down and talk to me for a bit?"

"I could indeed, and would be glad to. We're not busy tonight."

"Ita, you see, you don't know me from a hole in the ground."

"That's true, but I'll get to know you," she reassured him.

"No, that's not what I meant. I *want* someone who doesn't know me."

"Oh, yes?"

"It's easier to talk to a stranger. Will you tell me—am I for the chop?"

Ita had been asked this question before. It was never easy to answer. "Well, you know your illness is serious and that we're at the stage where all we can do is make you comfortable. But you're not on the way out tonight."

"Good. But some night soon, do you think?"

"It won't be long, Muttie, but I'd say you've time to sort things out." Ita was reassuring. "Is there anyone you want me to call for you?"

"How do you know I want to sort things out?" he asked.

"Everyone does at night, especially their first night in hospital. They want to make speeches and talk to lawyers and they want to talk to all kinds of people. Then, when they're leaving here, they've forgotten it all."

Muttie's eyes beseeched her. "And do you think I'll get out of here?"

Ita looked him in the eye. "I tell you, as sure as I know my own name, you'll go home from here and then you'll forget all about us. You won't remember me and my cups of tea anymore."

"I will indeed remember you and how kind you are. I'll tell everyone about you. And you're right, I do want to make speeches and talk to lawyers and tell people things. I hope to do it all from home."

"Good man, yourself, Muttie," Ita said, as she took his empty teacup away. She knew he didn't have long, but she'd do her best to make his mind easy. She sighed. He was such a warm little man. Why was he being taken when so many grumpy and sour-faced people were left for years with nobody involved in their lives? It was beyond understanding. She and Sean sometimes said it was very hard to believe in a kind, all-knowing God when you saw the random way fate worked. A decent man with a huge family and group of friends was about to die.

Sean would have similar stories from being a policeman. A kid who had joined a gang and had been caught on his first outing, faced with a criminal record; a mother who had no access to money of any kind, shoplifting to get food for her baby and ending up in court.

Life was many things, but it certainly wasn't fair.

It was clear that Muttie wanted to go home, so they contacted the palliative-care team. Two nurses would visit him each day. After three days, Ita handed him over to a small crowd of people, all of them delighted to see him coming home. Two of Muttie's children, Mike and Marian, together with Marian's husband, Harry, had arrived from Chicago, which shocked him.

"You must be made of money that you fly all that way just to see me. Aren't I grand? I'm going home today and Ita's going to come to see me," Muttie added.

"Oh, trust him to find someone else the moment I leave him out of my sight!" Lizzie said, with a laugh of pride in the notion of Muttie the Lothario.

Muttie's Associates from the pub were anxious to see him when he returned. Lizzie wanted to keep them at bay, but her daughter Cathy wasn't so sure.

"He relaxes when he's talking to them," Cathy said.

"But is it sensible to have six big men in the sitting room when he's so tired all the time?" Lizzie wasn't sure how much relaxation that would involve. Cathy knew that she was trying to restore order to the home; her brother and sister were, she knew, going to be staying for some time. They all realized their father only had a very short time to live.

Much as Lizzie and Cathy wanted to keep Muttie to themselves, with only the family around him, he did seem to blossom when friends, neighbors and Associates visited. He had always been a man who loved talking with others. None of that side of him had disappeared. It was only his little thin body that showed any sign of the disease that was killing him.

Hooves sat at his feet most of the day. He stopped eating and lay in his basket listlessly.

"Hooves and I," said Muttie, "we're not able to get up and about much at the moment. Maybe tomorrow . . ."

Cathy and Lizzie provided endless cups of tea as a file of people passed through each day. The Associates all came together in a group and the women would hear bursts of laughter as they planned a great new world—a world without the present government, the previous governments, the banks and the law.

The Associates were mild men who talked big, and Muttie had always been at their center. They were jovial and blustering when they were with him, but Cathy could see their faces fall when they were out of his presence.

"It won't be long now, God save us all," said one of them, a man not usually known to respect the Almighty and ask for divine help.

But mainly people came in one by one, monitored by Lizzie and Cathy. They were given fifteen minutes at the most. The kind Ita O'Meara came. She spoke about everything except illness. They talked horses and greyhounds. "Very sound woman," Muttie remarked approvingly when she left. And they came in their droves, first asking Lizzie what would be a good time. She kept a notebook on the hall table.

Fiona and Declan came and brought little Johnny with them. They told their secret to Muttie: that they were expecting another baby. He said it would remain a secret right up to the end of his life.

Dr. Hat came and brought some scones that he had made himself. Emily Lynch had been teaching him to cook, and it wasn't bad at all if you put your mind to it.

Muttie promised that when he got stronger he would think about it.

Josie and Charles came and talked about how a devotion to St. Jarlath could help in almost any situation. Muttie thanked them and said he was as interested in St. Jarlath as the next man and that if ever he needed him he would certainly try to get in touch with the saint. However, fortunately, he was getting better now and would be back to full strength before long.

Like everyone else, Charles and Josie Lynch were mystified. They so wanted to talk to Muttie about their inheritance from Mrs. Monty and how it should be spent or invested. Up to now they hadn't told anyone how much money was involved, not even Noel. But it seemed insensitive to talk about such things to a man who was so near death. Could Muttie really not know that he was dying?

Molly and Paddy Carroll felt the same. "He's talking of going to New York in a couple of months' time." Molly was genuinely puzzled. "Muttie won't go as far as the River Liffey, for heaven's sake—doesn't he know that?"

It was a mystery.

Noel came and brought Frankie. As Frankie sat on Muttie's knee and offered him her sippy cup, Noel talked more openly than he did to anyone. He told Muttie about the terrible fright when Frankie had been lost and how he had felt a pain in his chest as bad as if someone had put a great spade into him and lifted out his insides.

"You've made a grand job of this little girl," Muttie said approvingly.

"I sometimes dream that she's not my little girl at all and that someone comes to take her away," Noel confessed.

"That will never happen, Noel."

"Wasn't I lucky that Stella contacted me? Suppose she hadn't—then Frankie would be growing up in a different place and she'd never know any of you."

"And wasn't she lucky that she got you, even though you work too hard," Muttie said begrudgingly.

"I have to work hard. I want to have some kind of a job that I'd be proud of by the time she's old enough to know what I'm doing."

"And you gave up the gargle for her. That wasn't easy."

"It's not too bad most of the time. I'm so busy, you see, but there are days when I could murder six pints. Those are bad days."

"What do you do?" Muttie wanted to know.

"I ring my buddy in AA, and he comes over or meets me for coffee."

"Marvelous bloody organization. Never needed them myself, fortunately, but they do the job." Muttie was full of approval.

"You're a great fellow, Muttie," Noel said unexpectedly.

"I'm not the worst," Muttie agreed, "but haven't I a great family around me. I'm luckier than anyone I ever heard of. There's nothing they wouldn't do for us, traveling like millionaires back from Chicago because I had a bit of a turn back there. And as for the twins . . . ! If I lived in a high-class hotel, I couldn't get better food served to me. They're always coming up with something new for me." Muttie's smile was broad at the thought of it all.

Noel held Frankie tight and she, with her interest in sharing the sippy cup now complete, returned her father's hug. Noel wondered why he dreamed that she would be taken away. She was his daughter. His flesh and blood.

Marco came to see Muttie. He was dressed in a collar and tie as if he were going somewhere very formal. Lizzie said that of course he must go in to see Muttie, but to go very gently. Hooves had died during the night, and even though they had tried to keep it from Muttie he had known there was something wrong. Eventually, they had had to tell him.

"Hooves was a great dog—we won't demean him by crying over him," he said.

"Right," Lizzie agreed. "I'll tell the others."

When Marco was ushered in he came and stood beside the bed.

"I am so sorry about your dog, Mr. Scarlet."

"I never thought he'd go before me, Marco. But it's all for the best—he'd have been very lonely without me."

"Mr. Scarlet, I know you're not well and it's probably the wrong time to ask you this, but there is a question I would love to ask you."

"And what would that be, Marco?" Muttie smiled at the boy. The good suit, the anxious face, the sweaty palms. It was written all over him what question he was going to ask.

"I would like to ask you to give me the honor of your granddaughter's hand in marriage," Marco said stiffly.

"You want to marry Maud? She's very young, Marco— she hasn't grown up properly and seen the world or anything."

"But *I* would show her the world, Mr. Scarlet. I would look after her so well, see that she wanted for nothing."

"I know you would, lad, and have you asked her your-self?"

"Not yet—it's important I ask the father or grandfa-ther first."

"I'm not her grandfather—you know that."

"She thinks of you as her grandfather, she loves you as if you were."

Muttie blew his nose. "Well, that's good, because that's the way Lizzie and I feel about her and Simon. But how can Maud marry you if she's going to New Jersey with Simon?"

"She's not going now, they've put that off," Marco said.

"That's only because I have been sick. They'll go . . . you know . . . afterwards."

"You will be here for a long time, Mr. Scarlet."

"No, son, I won't, but I'm sure you and Maud have it all worked out between you."

"I couldn't tell her I wanted to marry her until I asked you first. . . ." The boy's handsome face was beseeching him to give his blessing.

"And would she work with you in your father's restau-rant?"

"Yes, for the moment, if she liked to do that, then we would both like to open a restaurant of our own. It may be many years ahead but my father says he will give me some money. You must have no fears about her—she will be treasured by our family."

Muttie looked at him. "If Maud says she would like to marry you, then I would be delighted."

"Thank you, dear Mr. Scarlet," said Marco, hardly daring to believe his good luck.

———

Lisa came to see Muttie also.

"I don't know you well, Mr. Scarlet, but you're a great character. I heard you'd been ill and I was wondering if there was anything I could do for you?"

Muttie looked around to make sure there was no one in the room with them.

"If I gave you fifty euro, could you put it on the nose of Not the Villain for me?"

"Oh, Mr. Scarlet, really . . ."

"It's my money, Lisa. Can't you do that for me? You *did* say you wanted to help me."

"Sure. I'll do it. What odds do you expect?"

"Ten to one. Don't take less."

"But then you'd win five hundred," she said, stunned.

"And you will get an enabler's fee," Muttie said, laughing heartily as Lizzie bustled in to clear the teacups and arrange a little rest time before the next visitor.

Lisa didn't know where there were any local betting shops, but Dingo Duggan was able to come up with the name of a nearby place.

"I'll drive you there," he said helpfully.

Dingo rather fancied Lisa and he liked to be seen with a good-looking girl sitting up front in his van.

"Got a good tip, then?" he asked.

"Someone asked me to put fifty euro on a horse at ten to one."

"God, that must be a great horse," Dingo said wistfully. "Wouldn't it be wonderful if you were to drop the name to me. I mean it won't shorten the price or anything.

I have only ten euro, but it would be great to have a hundred. Great altogether."

Lisa told him the name of the horse but warned him, "The source is not entirely reliable, Dingo. I'd hate to see you lose your money."

"Don't worry," Dingo reassured her. "I have a very sharp mind."

Lisa felt out of place in the betting shop, and the presence of Dingo made it worse.

"Where are you off to now?" Dingo asked when the transaction was over.

"I'm going to see Anton," Lisa said.

"I'll drive you there," Dingo offered.

"No, thank you—I need a walk to clear my head and I've got to get my hair done too."

These were perfectly ordinary things to do, but Dingo noticed that Lisa announced them as if they were matters of huge importance. He shrugged.

Women were very hard to understand.

Katie sighed when Lisa came in. Yet another demand for a quick fix. The salon was already full. Had she ever heard of the appointment system?

"I need something, Katie," Lisa said.

"It will be half an hour at least," Katie said.

"I'll wait." Lisa was unexpectedly calm and patient.

Katie glanced at her from time to time. Lisa had magazines in her lap, but she never looked at them. Her eyes and mind were far away.

Then Katie was ready. "Big date?" she asked.

"No. Big conversation, actually."

"With Anton?"

"Who else?"

"You'd want to be careful, Lisa." Katie was concerned.

"I've been careful for years and where has it got me?" Lisa looked, without pleasure, at her reflection in the mirror. Her pale face and wet hair showed up the dark circles under her eyes.

"We'll make you lovely," said Katie, who seemed to have read her thoughts.

"It would help if I looked a bit lovelier, all right." Lisa smiled very weakly. "Listen, I want you to cut it all off. I want very short hair, cropped short all over."

"You're out of your mind—you've always had long hair. Don't do anything reckless."

"I want it short, choppy, a really edgy style. Will you do it or do I have to go to a rival?"

"I'll do it, but you're going to wake up tomorrow and wish you hadn't done it."

"Not if you give me a good cut, I won't."

"But you said he liked you with long hair," Katie persisted.

"Then he'll have to like me with short hair," Lisa countered.

It was achieved in two hours: a full makeup, a manicure and a new hairdo. Lisa felt a lot better. She offered to pay, but Katie waved it away.

"Don't say anything to Anton in a temper. Say nothing that you don't want to stand over. Be very careful."

"Why are you telling me this? You don't like Anton. You don't think he's right for me," Lisa asked in confusion.

"I know. But you like him and I like you a lot, so I want you to be happy."

Lisa kissed her sister. It was a rare thing to happen.

Katie felt it was unreal. Lisa, always so prickly and distracted, had actually put her arms around her, hugged her and kissed her on the cheek.

What next?

Lisa walked purposefully towards Anton's. This was a good time to catch him. The afternoons were easier and less fussed. All she would have to do was get rid of Teddy and hunt April off the premises if she was there, then she would talk to Anton properly.

Teddy saw her coming in but didn't recognize her at first.

"Fasten your seat belt," he hissed at Anton.

"Oh, God, not today, not on top of everything else . . ." Anton groaned.

When Lisa came in, she looked well and she knew it. She walked confidently and had a big smile on her face. She knew they were looking at her, Anton and Teddy, registering shock at the difference in her. The short hair gave her confidence; it was much lighter than before, still golden and silky. She smiled from one to the other, turning her head so that they could get a good view of her and her changed look.

"Teddy, will you forgive me—I have to talk to Anton

about something for a short while?" She spoke on a rising note as if she were asking a question to which there was only one answer.

Teddy looked at Anton, who shrugged. So then he left.

"Well, Lisa, what is it? You look terrific, by the way."

"Thank you so much, Anton. How terrific do I look?"

"Well, you look very different, shiny, sort of. Your hair is gone!"

"I had it cut this morning."

"So I see. Your beautiful long golden hair . . ." He sounded bemused.

"It just covered the floor of the salon. In the olden days they used to sell their hair for wigs—did you know that?"

"No, I didn't," Anton said weakly.

"Oh, they did. Anyway, there we are."

"I liked your hair—in fact, I *loved* your long hair," he said regretfully.

"Did you, Anton? You *loved* my long hair?"

"You look different now, changed somehow, still gorgeous but different somehow."

"Good, so you like what you see?"

"This is silly, Lisa. Of course I like it. I like you."

"That's it? You like me?"

"Is this Twenty Questions or what? Of course I like you. You're my friend."

"Friend—not *love*?"

"Oh, well, love. Whatever . . ." He was annoyed now already.

"Good, because I love you. A lot," she said agreeably.

"Aw, come on, Lisa. Are you drunk again?" he asked.

"No, Anton. Stone cold, and the one time I ever did

get drunk, you weren't very kind to me. You more or less ordered Teddy to throw me out of here."

"You were making a fool of yourself. You should thank me."

"I don't see it that way."

"Well, I was the one who was sober on that occasion—believe me, you were better out of here before even more people saw you."

"What do you think of when you think of me? Do you love me a lot or only a little?"

"Lisa, these are only words. Will you stop this thirteen-year-old chat?"

"You say you love me when we make love."

"Everyone says that," Anton said defensively.

"I don't think so."

"Well, I don't know. I haven't conducted a survey on it." He was really annoyed now.

"Calm down, Anton."

"I'm totally calm . . ."

"It would make this discussion easier if you didn't fly into a temper. Just tell me how important I am in your life."

"I don't know . . . very important—you do all the designs; you have lots of good ideas; you're very glamorous and I fancy you a lot. Now will that do?"

"And do you see me as part of your future?" She was still unruffled.

There was a silence.

Lisa remembered Katie's advice not to be reckless, not to say anything she couldn't stand over. Maybe he would say no, that she wasn't part of the future for him. This would leave her like an empty, hollow shell, but she didn't think he would say it.

Anton looked uncomfortable. "Don't talk to me about the future. None of us knows where we will be in the great future."

"We're old enough to know," Lisa said.

"Do you know what Teddy and I were talking about now when you came in and turfed him out?"

"No. What?"

"The future of this restaurant. The takings are appalling, we're losing money hand over fist. The suppliers are beginning to scream. The bank isn't being helpful. Some days we're almost empty for lunch. Today we had only three tables. We'd be better giving everyone who booked fifty euro and telling them to go away. Tonight we will be only half full. Investors notice these things. It needs some kind of a lift. It's going stale. You want to talk about the future—I don't think there is one."

"Do you see *me* in your future?" Lisa asked again.

"Oh, God Almighty, Lisa, I do if you could come up with some ideas rather than bleating like a teenager. That is if we *have* a future here at all . . ."

"Ideas—is that what you want?" Her voice was now, if anything, dangerously composed.

Anton looked at her nervously. "You're a great ideas woman."

"Okay. Light lunches—low-calorie healthy lunches in one part of the dining room, where they can't see roast beef or tiramisu going past. And even that fool April could get you some publicity for this. Oh, and you could organize a weekly section on a radio show where people could send in their recipes for things that are under two hundred and fifty calories and you could judge them. Are those good ideas?"

"As usual, you're right on the button. Will we call in the others to discuss this?"

"And what ideas do you have about me?" she asked.

"Are you still on this thing?"

"Just tell me.. Tell me now—answer me and I'll stop asking you," she promised.

"Okay. I admire you a lot. I'm your friend. . . ."

"And lover . . . ," she added.

"Well, yes, from time to time. I thought you felt the same about it all."

"Like what, exactly?"

"That it was something nice we shared—but not the meaning of life or anything. Not a steady road to the altar."

"So why did you continue to have me around?"

"As I've said, you're bright, very bright, you're lovely and you're fun. And also I think a little lonely."

As she heard the words, something changed in Lisa's head. It was like a car moving into another gear. It was almost as if she were coming out of a dream. She could take his indifference, his infidelity, his careless ways.

She could not take his pity.

"And you might be a little lonely too, Anton, when this place fails. When Teddy has bailed out and gone to another trendy place, when little Miss April has flown off to something that's successful. There's nowhere in her little life for failure. When people say, 'Anton? Isn't he the one who used to own some restaurant . . . popular for a while but it disappeared without trace,' you might well be lonely then too. So let's hope someone will take pity on you and you'll see how it feels."

"Lisa, please . . ."

"Good-bye, Anton."

"You'll come back when you're more yourself."

"I think not." She was still composed.

"Why are you so angry with me, Lisa?" His head was on one side—his persuasive position.

But it didn't change her mind. "I'm angry with myself, Anton. I had a perfectly good job and I left it because of you. I meant to get other clients, but there was always something to be done here. I'm broke to the world. I'm depending on a horse called Not the Villain to win a race today because if he does I get something called an enabling fee and I'll be able to buy my share of the groceries for the flat where I have a room."

"*Not the Villain,*" Anton said slowly. "That's how I see myself—I didn't think you were serious. I really am actually like that horse you've put money on. I'm not the villain here, you know."

"I know. That's why I'm angry. I got it so wrong. . . ."

Teddy heard the door bang closed and came in.

"Okay?" he asked.

"Teddy, if this place looked seriously like going under, would you go somewhere else?"

"Little bitch—she told you," Teddy said.

"Told me what?"

"She must have seen me or heard somehow. I went to the new hotel on the river to know if there might be a vacancy and they said they'd see. This city is worse than a small village. Lisa must have heard it from them."

"No, she didn't even know about it." Anton suddenly

felt very tired. There had been something very final about the way Lisa had left the restaurant. But it was all nonsense, wasn't it? She hadn't been serious about any of it. Probably some of her girlfriends were settling down and getting pregnant and she felt broody. And that idea about the light lunches wasn't a bad one at all. They could get little cards designed with some kind of logo on them. Lisa would be great at that when she stopped all this other nonsense. . . .

Lisa walked out of the restaurant jauntily, and as she moved through the crowded streets she was aware that people glanced at her with what she thought was admiration. She wouldn't think about what she had just said and done. She would compartmentalize things. Park this side of her life here and leave it until it was needed again. Concentrate on another side of life. This was a city full of promise, potential friends and even possible loves. She would tidy Anton away and hold her head high.

Then, quite unexpectedly, she met Emily, who was wheeling Frankie in her buggy.

"I'm getting her used to shopping—she's going to spend years of her life doing it so she might as well know what it's all about."

"Emily, you are funny. What have you bought today?"

"A bedspread, a teapot, a shower curtain. Really exciting things," Emily said.

Frankie gurgled happily.

"She sounds happy now, but you should have heard her half an hour ago. I wonder if she's starting to teethe, poor thing. She was red-faced and howling and her gums look a little swollen. We're in for a bumpy ride if that's it," Emily explained.

"Sure we are," said Lisa. "I think I'd better move out for the next few months!" and, with a smile and a hug for Frankie, she was gone.

When Emily and Frankie got back to Number 23 it was obvious that Josie had something important to say.

"Things aren't great down the road," she said, her face grim.

That could have meant almost anything. That the takings were down at the thrift shop or Dr. Hat had put out some washing that had blown away in the wind or that Fiona and Declan were moving house. Then, with a lurch, Emily realized that Josie might be talking about Muttie.

"It's not . . . ?"

"Yes. Things are much worse." Josie seemed unsure whether she should call on the household or not.

Emily thought not. They would only be in the way. Muttie and Lizzie would have lots of family already. Josie accepted this.

"I saw Father Brian going in there earlier," she said.

Frankie chuckled, reaching out for Emily to be picked up.

"Good girl." Both women spoke slightly distractedly, then each of them sighed.

Josie was wondering whether saying another Rosary would help. Emily was wondering what would be of most practical help. A big shepherd's pie, she thought, something they could keep warm in the oven or whenever anyone needed food. She would make one straightaway.

Muttie was annoyed that he felt so weak. Day and night seemed to merge, and there was always someone in the room, usually telling him to rest. Hadn't he been resting since he came back from that hospital?

There were so many things still to sort out. The lawyer would drive you insane with the way he talked, but he did seem clear about one thing. The tiny amount of money the Mitchell family had paid towards the upkeep of the twins years ago and that had stopped promptly on their seventeenth birthday had all been kept in a deposit account, and with it there was a percentage of Muttie's Great Win, the time he won a fortune and they all nearly went into heart failure.

The rest of the will was simple: everything to Lizzie and their children. But Muttie was very agitated in case the twins were not properly provided for.

"They will be well set up when they inherit all this," the lawyer said.

"Well, so should they be. You see, when they came to us they gave up any chance of being in society. They were born to be with classier people than us, you see. They must be compensated properly."

The lawyer turned away so that Muttie wouldn't see his face and watch him swallowing the lump in his throat.

Father Flynn came to see him.

"God, Muttie, and you grand and peaceful here compared to the world outside."

"Tell me all about what's going on outside." Muttie's curiosity was undimmed, despite his illness.

"Well, down at the center where I work, there's all hell to pay over a Muslim wedding. This couple want one and I directed them towards the mosque. Anyway, some of the family don't want to go to it and some do. I said we would do the catering—your grandchildren could cook for anyone—and then there's a wing that says the center is a Catholic place and run with money from the Church. I tell you, you'd be demented by it all, Muttie."

"I wouldn't mind being out in it for a bit, though." Muttie sounded wistful.

"Ah, you will, you will." Brian Flynn hoped that he sounded convincing.

"But if I don't see it all again and I'm for the high jump, do you really think there's anything, you know . . . up there?"

"I'm going to tell you the truth, Muttie. I don't know, but I think there is. That's the glue that has held me together for all these years. I will be one disappointed man if there isn't anything up there."

Muttie was perfectly pleased with this as an answer. "You couldn't say fairer than that," he said approvingly.

And as Brian Flynn left the house, he wondered had any other priest of God delivered such a banal and bland description of the faith to a dying man.

Lisa Kelly came to call again. The family weren't sure Muttie was up to seeing her.

"I have a secret I want to tell him," she said.

"Go in then with your secret—but only ten minutes," Lizzie said.

Lisa put on her biggest smile.

"I have five hundred euro for you, Muttie. Not the Villain won by three lengths."

"Lower your voice, Lisa. I don't want any of them knowing I'm gambling," he said.

"No, I told them I had a secret to discuss with you."

"They'll think we are having an affair," Muttie said, "but Lizzie would prefer that than the gambling."

"So where will I put the money, Muttie?"

"Back in your handbag. It was only the thrill of winning I wanted."

"But, Muttie, I can't take five hundred euro. I was hoping for an enabler's fee of about fifty, that's all."

"Spend it well, child," Muttie said, and then his head drooped back on the pillow and Lisa tiptoed out of the room.

Immediately, Maud went in to see him.

Muttie opened his eyes. "Do you love this Marco, Maud?" he asked.

"Very much. I know I haven't had a series of people to compare him to, like you should."

"Says who?" Muttie asked.

"Says everyone, but I don't care. I'll never meet anyone better than Marco. They couldn't exist."

He put out his hand and held hers. "Then hold on to him, Maud, and find a nice girl for Simon too. Maybe at the wedding."

Maud held the thin hand and sat with him as he fell asleep. Tears came to her eyes and trickled down, but she didn't raise a hand to brush them away. Sleep was good.

Sleep was painless. Maud wanted Muttie to have as much of this as he could get.

Muttie's children knew it would be today or tomorrow. They kept their voices low as they moved around the house. They reminded one another of days in their childhood when Muttie and Lizzie had made a picnic with jam sandwiches and taken them on a train to the sea in Bray.

They remembered the time of a small win, which Muttie had spent on two roast chickens and plates full of chips. And how they had always been dressed up for First Communion and Confirmation like the other children, though this might have meant a lot of visiting the pawnshop. Muttie at weddings; the dog, Hooves; Muttie carrying the shopping for Lizzie.

They had to share all these thoughts when they were out of Lizzie's hearing. Lizzie still thought he was getting better.

Ita, the nurse, came that day with an herbal pillow for Muttie. She looked at him and he didn't recognize her.

"He'll go into a coma shortly," she said gently to Maud. "You might ask Dr. Carroll to look in, and the care nurses will do all that has to be done."

For the first time it hit Maud really hard. She cried on Simon's shoulder. Soon there would be no more Muttie, and her last conversation with him had been about Marco.

She remembered what Muttie had said when their beloved Hooves had died: "We all have to be strong in honor of Hooves. He wasn't the kind of spirit that people go bawling and crying about. In his honor, be strong."

And they were strong as they buried Hooves.

They would be strong for Muttie as well.

"It's going to be hardest knowing that he doesn't exist anymore," Simon said.

Brian Flynn was having a cup of tea with them. "There is a thought that if we remember someone, then we keep them alive," he said.

There was a silence. He wished he hadn't spoken.

But they were all nodding their heads.

If keeping people in your memory meant that they still lived, then Muttie would live forever.

Lizzie said she was going to go in and sit with him.

"He's in a very deep sleep, Mam," Cathy said.

"I know. It's a coma. The nurses said it would happen."

"Mam, it's just . . ."

"Cathy, I know it's the end. I know it's tonight. I just want to be alone with him for a little bit."

Cathy looked at her, openmouthed.

"I knew for ages, but I just didn't let myself believe it until today, so look at all the happy days I had when the rest of you were worrying yourselves sick. . . ."

Cathy brought her mother into the room, and the nurse left. She closed the door firmly.

Lizzie wanted to say good-bye.

"I don't know if you can hear me or not, Muttie," Lizzie said. "But I wanted to tell you that you were great fun. I've had a laugh or a dozen laughs every day since I met you and I've been cheerful and thought we were as good as anyone else. I used to think we were lower, somehow. You made me think that even if we were poor, we were fine. I hope you have a great time until . . . well, until I'm there too. I know you're half a pagan, Muttie, but you'll find out that it's all there—waiting for you. Now won't that be a surprise? I love you, Muttie, and we'll manage somehow, I promise you."

Then she kissed his forehead and called the family back in for a short visit.

Twenty minutes later the palliative-care nurse came out and asked if Dr. Declan Carroll was there.

Fiona phoned his mobile.

"I'll be there in fifteen minutes," he said, and somehow they sat there for a quarter of an hour until Declan arrived and went into the bedroom.

He came out quickly. "Muttie is at peace . . . at rest," he confirmed.

They cried in disbelief, holding on to one another.

Marco had arrived, and he was considered family for this. Some of Muttie's Associates, who seemed to fill the house with their presence, took out handkerchiefs and blew their noses very loudly.

And suddenly Lizzie, frail Lizzie, who had until today held on to the belief that she was going to go to Chinatown in New York with Muttie, took control.

"Simon, will you go and pull down all the blinds, please. The neighbors will know then. Maud, can you phone the undertaker. His number is beside the phone, and tell him that Muttie has gone. He'll know what to do. Marco, can you arrange some food for us. People will call and we must have something to give them. Geraldine, could you see how many cups, mugs and plates we have?

And could you all stop crying. If Muttie knew you were crying he would deal with the lot of you."

Somehow they managed a few watery smiles.

Muttie's funeral had begun.

The whole of St. Jarlath's Crescent stood as a guard of honor when the coffin was carried down the road.

Lisa and Noel stood with Frankie in her carriage and they were joined by Faith, who had heard so much about this man, she felt part of it all. Emily stood beside her uncle and aunt with Dr. Hat and Dingo Duggan. Declan and Fiona, holding Johnny close to her, stood with Molly and Paddy. Friends and neighbors watched as Simon and Marco carried the coffin. They walked in measured steps.

The Associates stood in a little line, still stunned that Muttie wasn't there, urging them all to have a pint and a look at the 3:30 at Wincanton.

Somewhere far away a church bell was ringing. It had nothing to do with them but it seemed as if it were ringing in sympathy. The curtains, blinds or shutters of every house in the street were closed. People placed flowers from their gardens on the coffin as it passed by.

Then there was a hearse and funeral cars waiting to take the funeral party to Father Brian Flynn's church in the immigrant center.

Muttie had left very definite instructions.

> *If I die, which is definitely on the cards, I want my funeral service to be done by Father Brian Flynn in his center, after a very brief sort of speech and one or two prayers. And then I'd like to give my bits to science in*

case they're any use to anyone and the rest cremated
without fuss.
    Signed in the whole of my wits,
    Muttance Scarlet

Marco worked in Muttie and Lizzie's kitchen, producing platters of antipasti and bowls of fresh pasta. Lizzie
had said he was not to hold back. He had brought forks
and plates from his father's restaurant.

Though Muttie had given Marco permission to ask
Maud to marry him, he wouldn't—not until she had
stopped crying for her grandfather. Then he would ask
her. Properly. He wondered would he and Maud be as
happy as Muttie and Lizzie. Was he enough for her—she
was so bright and quick.

There was a picture of Muttie on the wall. He was
smiling as usual. Marco could almost hear him saying,
"Go on there, Marco Romano. You're as good as any of
them and better than most."

It was true what they had been saying: if people remember you, then you're not dead. It was very comforting.

At the church, Father Flynn kept the ceremony very
short. One Our Father, one Hail Mary and one Glory Be
to the Father. A Moroccan boy played "Amazing Grace"
on a clarinet. And a girl from Poland played "Hail, Queen
of Heaven" on an accordion. Then it was over.

People stood around in the sunshine and talked about
Muttie. Then they made way back to his home to say
good-bye.

Properly.

Chapter Thirteen

Everyone in St. Jarlath's Crescent was the poorer after Muttie's death, and people tried to avoid looking at the lonely figure of Lizzie standing by her gate, as she always had. It was as if she were still waiting for him. Of course, everyone rallied round to make sure that she wasn't alone, but one by one her children went back to their lives in Chicago and Australia; Cathy went back to her catering company. The twins were busy working at Ennio's and deciding on their future.

Everyone was slowly getting back to life, but with the knowledge that Lizzie had no life to get on with.

One night she might be invited to Charles and Josie's, but her eyes were far away as they talked of the campaign for the statue. Sometimes she went to sit with Paddy and Molly Carroll for an evening, but there was a limit to what she could listen to about Molly's work at the thrift shop or Paddy's confrontations at the meat counter. She had no tales of her own to tell anymore.

Emily Lynch was sympathetic company; she would ask

questions about Lizzie's childhood and her early working days. She took Lizzie back to a time before Muttie, to places where Muttie had never walked. But then she couldn't expect Emily to be there all the time. She seemed to be very friendly with Dr. Hat these days. Lizzie was glad for her but at the same time she mourned Muttie.

There were so many things she wanted to tell him. Every day she thought of something new: how Cathy's first husband, Neil, had come to the funeral and said that Muttie was a hero; how Father Flynn had blown his nose so much they thought he might have perforated an eardrum and how he had said the kindest things about Muttie and Lizzie's wonderful extended family.

Lizzie wanted to tell Muttie that Maud would be getting engaged to Marco and that Simon was happy about it and was still thinking of going to New Jersey. She wanted to discuss with him whether she would stay on in the house or get a smaller place. Everyone advised her that she must make no decisions for at least a year. She wondered would Muttie think that was wise.

Lizzie sighed a lot these days but she tried to smile at the same time. People had always found good humor and smiles in this house, and it must not change now. It was when she was left alone in their little house that the smiles faded and she grieved for Muttie. She often heard his voice coming from another room, just not quite loud enough for her to hear what he said. When she made tea in the morning, she automatically made a cup for him; she set a place for him at mealtimes, and the sadness of it filled her with desolation.

Her bed felt huge and empty now, and when she slept, she did so with her arm around a pillow. She dreamed of him almost every night, sometimes good dreams of happy days and joyful times; often they were terrible dreams of abandonment, loss and sorrow. She didn't know which was worse: every morning she woke afresh to the knowledge that he was gone and he would never come back. It would never be all right again.

Dr. Hat suggested to Emily that they go for a picnic, as the summer had finally arrived and the days were long and warm. Emily suggested Michael come with them, though for some reason Dr. Hat looked a bit odd when she raised it. She made formal egg sandwiches and filled two flasks with tea. She brought chocolate biscuits in a tin and they drove in Dr. Hat's car out to the Wicklow Mountains.

"It's amazing to have all these hills so close to the city," Emily said admiringly.

"Those aren't hills, they're mountains," Dr. Hat said reprovingly. "It's very important to know that."

"I'm sorry." Emily laughed. "But then what can you expect from a foreigner, an outsider."

"You're not an outsider. Your heart is here," Dr. Hat said, and he looked at her oddly again. "Or I very much hope it is."

Michael started to hum tunelessly to himself as he gazed out the window. Dr. Hat and Emily ignored him and raised their voices.

"Oh, Hat, you feel safe enough saying that to me in front of Michael as a sort of joke."

"I was never as serious in my life. I *do* hope your heart is in Ireland. I'd hate it if you went away."

"Why, exactly?"

"Because you are very interesting and you get things done. I was beginning to drift and you halted that. I'm more of a man since I met you."

Michael's humming got louder, as if he were trying to drown them out.

"You are?" shouted Emily. "Well, I feel more of a woman since I met you, so that has to be good somehow."

"I never married because I never met anyone who didn't bore me before. I'd like . . . I'd like you to . . ."

"To do what?" Emily asked. Michael's humming was now almost deafening.

"Oh, stop it, Michael," Emily begged. "Hat is trying to say something, that's all."

"He's said it," Michael said. "He's asked you to marry him. Now just say yes, will you."

Emily looked at Hat for some clarity. Hat drew the car to a slow stop and got out. He went around to the passenger side, opened Emily's door and knelt in the heather and gorse on the Wicklow Mountains.

"Emily, will you do me the great honor of becoming my wife?" he asked.

"Why didn't you ask me before?"

"I was so afraid you'd say no and that we'd lose the comfortable feeling of being friends. I was just afraid."

"Don't be afraid anymore." She touched him gently on the side of his face. "I'd love to marry you."

"Thanks be to God," said Michael. "We can have the picnic now!"

Emily and Dr. Hat decided that there was no reason for delay at their age; they would marry when Betsy and Eric were in Ireland. This way Betsy would get to be matron of honor and Michael would be best man. They could be married by Father Flynn in his church. The twins would do the catering and they could all go on honeymoon, with Dingo driving them, to the west.

Emily didn't want an engagement ring. She said she would prefer a nice solid-looking wedding ring and just that. Dr. Hat was almost skittish with good humor, and for the first time in his life he agreed to go to a tailor and have a made-to-measure suit. He would get a new hat to match it and promised to take it off in the church for the ceremony as long as it could be restored for the photographs.

Betsy was almost squeaking with excitement in her e-mails.

And he proposed to you in the car in front of this other man, Michael? This is amazing, Emily, even for you. And you're going to be living around the corner from your cousins!

But can I ask, why is he called Hat? Is it short for Hathaway or was there an Irish St. Hat?

Nothing would surprise me.

Love from your elderly matron-of-honor-to-be, Betsy

Emily still managed all her various jobs: she tended window boxes, she did her stints in the surgery, she stood behind the counter in the thrift shop—which was where she found her wedding outfit. It arrived from a shop that was about to close down. There were a number of pieces that had been display items, and the owner said she would get nothing for them and it was better they went to some charity.

Emily was hanging them up carefully on a rail when she saw it. A silk dress with a navy and pale-blue flower pattern and a matching jacket in navy with a small trim of the dress material on the jacket collar. It was perfect: elegant and feminine and wedding-like.

Carefully, Emily put the sum of money she would have hoped to get for it into the till and brought it home straightaway.

Josie saw her coming through the house.

"The very woman," Josie said. "Will you have a cup of tea?"

"A quick one, then. I don't want to leave Molly too long on her own." Emily sat down.

"I'm a bit worried," Josie began.

"Tell me." Emily sighed.

"It's this money Mrs. Monty left to Charles."

"Yes, and you're giving it to the Statue Fund." Emily knew all this.

"It's just that we're worried about how much it is," Josie said, looking around her in a frightened way. "You see, it's not just thousands . . . it's hundreds of thousands."

Emily was stunned.

"That poor old lady had that kind of money! Who'd have thought it!" Emily said.

"Yes, and that's the problem."

"What's that, Josie?" Emily asked gently.

Josie was very perturbed. "It's too much to give to a

statue, Emily. It's sort of different from what we had thought. We wanted a small statue, a community thing with everyone contributing. If we give this huge sum we could have a huge statue up straightaway but it's not quite the same. . . ."

"I see. . . ." Emily hardly dared to breathe.

"It's such a huge amount of money, you see, we wonder have we a duty to our granddaughter, for example. Should we leave a sum for her education or to give her a start in life? Or should we give something to Noel so that he has something to fall back on if times get bad? Could I retire properly and could Charles and I go to the Holy Land? All these things are possible, I know. Would St. Jarlath like that better than a statue? It's impossible to know."

Emily was thoughtful. What she said now was very important.

"Which feels right to you, Josie?"

"That's the trouble. They both seem to be the right way to go. You see, we were never rich people. Now that we are, thanks to Mrs. Monty, could we possibly have changed and become greedy like they say rich people do?"

"Oh, you and Charles would never go that way!"

"We might, Emily. I mean, here am I thinking of an expensive tour to the Holy Land. You see, I tell myself that maybe St. Jarlath would *prefer* us to spend the money doing good in other ways."

"Yes, that is certainly a possibility," Emily agreed.

"You see, if I could only get some kind of a sign as to what he wanted. . . ."

"What would God have wanted, I wonder?" Emily speculated. "Our Lord wasn't into big show and splendor. He was more into helping the poor."

"Of course, the poor can be helped by a statue re-minding them of a great saint."

"Yes . . ."

"You're going off the idea of the statue, aren't you?" Josie said, tears not far from her eyes.

"No, I'm all in favor of the statue. You and Charles have been working on it for so long. It's a *great* idea, but I think it should be the smaller statue you originally thought of. Greatness isn't shown by size."

Josie was weakening. "We could give one big contri-bution to the fund and then invest the rest."

"From what you know about St. Jarlath, do you think he'd be happy with that?" Emily knew that Josie must be utterly convinced in her heart before she abandoned the cracked notion of spending all this money on a statue.

"I think he would," Josie said. "He was all for the good of the people and if we were to put a playground at the end of the crescent for the children, wouldn't that be in the spirit of it all?"

"And the statue?"

"We could have it *in* the playground. Call it all 'St. Jarlath's Garden for Children.' "

Emily smiled with relief. Her own view of God was of a vague, benevolent force that sometimes shaped people's lives and other times stayed out of it and let things hap-pen. She and Hat argued about this. He said it was a man-ifestation of people's wishes for an afterlife and helped put more sense into the time we spent on earth. But today Emily's God had intervened. He had ensured that Charles and Josie would help their son and their granddaughter. They would build a playground to keep the children safe. They would go to see Jerusalem and, most merciful of all, it would be a small statue and not a monstrosity that would make people mock them.

This was coming at a very good time for Noel. His exams were soon and he had looked strained and overtired in the past few days.

"Once you and Charles have agreed, you should tell Noel," Emily suggested.

"We'll talk it over tonight. Charles is out walking dogs in the park."

"I have a lovely lamb stew for you," Emily said. She had actually cooked it for Hat and herself but this was more important. Josie must not be given *any* excuse to put off telling Charles about her decision. Josie was easily distracted by things like having to put a meal on the table.

Emily would make something else for herself and Hat.

They did their roster every Sunday night. A page was put up on the kitchen wall. You could easily read who was minding Frankie every hour of the day. Noel and Lisa each had a copy as well. Soon Frankie would be old enough to go to Miss Keane's day nursery: that would be three hours accounted for each day. Only the name of who was to collect her would be needed for the mornings.

Lisa would take her to Miss Keane's and a variety of helpers would pick her up. Lisa wasn't free at lunchtime. She had a job making sandwiches in a rather classy place on the other side of the city. It wasn't a skilled job, but she brought all the skills she had to it. It paid her share of the groceries, and little by little she told them her ideas.

A gorgonzola and date sandwich? The customers loved it, so she suggested little posters advertising the sandwich of the week, and when they said it would be too expensive to do them, she drew them herself. She even designed a logo for the sandwich bar.

"You're much too good to be here," said Hugh, the young owner.

"I'm too good for everywhere. Weren't you lucky to get me?"

"We were, actually. You're a mystery woman."

He smiled at her. Hugh was rich and confident and good-looking. He fancied her, but Lisa realized that she had got out of the way of looking at men properly.

She had forgotten how to flirt.

She did other things to keep busy.

She joined Emily in the window box patrol and learned a lot about plants as well as about the lives of the people in St. Jarlath's Crescent. Feeding plants and repotting—it was a different world, but she picked it up quickly. Emily said she was a natural. She could run her own plant nurseries.

"I used to be bright," Lisa said thoughtfully. "I was really good at school and then I got a great job in an agency . . . but it all drifted away . . ."

Emily knew when to leave a silence.

Lisa went on almost dreamily, "It was like driving into a fog, really, meeting Anton. I forgot the world outside."

"And is the world coming back to you yet?" Emily asked gently.

"Sort of peering through the foggy curtains."

"Are there things you meant to do before and didn't get to do?"

"Yes, a lot of things, and I'm going to do them. Starting with these exams."

"It will concentrate the mind," Emily agreed.

"Yes, and keep me away from Anton's . . . ," Lisa said ruefully.

She knew very clearly that if she went back to the restaurant they would all greet her warmly. Her absence would not need to be explained. They would assume she had just had a hissy fit and had now come to her senses. April would look put out and Anton would look at her lazily and say she was lovely and the days had been lonely and colorless since she had gone. On the surface nothing would have changed. Deep down, though, it was all changed. He didn't love her. She had just been available, that was all.

But as she had said to Emily, there were still a lot of things that had to be done about other aspects of her life. One of these was meeting her mother.

Since she had discovered that her father brought prostitutes home, Lisa's meetings with her mother had been sparse. They met for coffee every now and then and they had lunch before Christmas. A dutiful exchange of gifts was made and they both engaged in a polite fiction of a conversation.

Her mother had asked about Lisa's design work for Anton's.

Lisa had asked about Mother's garden and whether she had decided on having a greenhouse or not. They had both talked a lot about Katie's salon and how well it was doing. Then, with relief, they had parted.

Nothing dangerous had been said, no forbidden roads had been opened up.

But this was no way to live, Lisa told herself. She must urge Mother to do what she had done herself and cut free from the old bonds.

She telephoned her mother immediately.

"Lunch? What's the occasion?" her mother asked.

"There's no law that says we can only meet on special occasions," Lisa said. She could tell that her mother was confused.

"Let's go to Ennio's," she suggested, and before her mother could find a reason not to go, it was all settled. "Ennio's, tomorrow, one o'clock."

Di Kelly looked well as she came into the restaurant. She wore a red belted coat with a white polo-necked collar underneath. She must be fifty-three but she didn't look forty. Her hair showed that all that brushing had not been in vain, and all that walking had ensured that she was trim and fit.

She did not, however, look at ease.

"This is nice," Lisa said brightly. "How have you been keeping?"

"Oh, fine. And you?"

"Fine also."

"And have you any news for me?" her mother asked with an interested expression on her face.

"What kind of news, exactly?"

"Well, I wondered if you were going to tell me that you and this Anton were getting married or anything. You've had him out on approval for long enough." She gave a tinkling laugh, showing she was nervous.

"Married? To Anton? Lord, no! I wouldn't dream of it."

"Oh, sorry, I thought that that was what this was about. You were going to ask me to the wedding but not your father."

"No, nothing as dramatic as that," Lisa said.

"So why did you invite me, then?"

"Does there have to be a reason? You're my mother and I'm your daughter. That's reason enough for most people."

"But we aren't like most people," her mother said simply.

"Why did you stay with him?" Lisa had not intended to ask this as baldly as it came out.

"We all have choices to make. . . ." Her mother was vague.

"But you couldn't *choose* to live with him, not after you knew what he was doing." Lisa was full of disgust.

"Life's a compromise, Lisa. Sooner or later you'll understand that. I had options: leave him and be by myself in a flat or stay and live in a house I liked."

"But you can have no respect for him."

"I was never very interested in sex. He was. That's all. I didn't enjoy it. You saw we had two separate beds . . ."

"I also saw him bringing that woman into what was your bedroom," Lisa said.

"It was only a couple of times. He was very ashamed that you saw. Did you tell Katie?"

"Why does that matter?" Lisa asked.

"I just wondered. She hardly ever calls. He thinks it's because you told her. I said she had stopped calling a long time ago."

"And did it not upset you that both your daughters feel a million miles from you?"

"You are always very courteous—you've invited me to lunch to keep up the relationship."

"What relationship? Do you think my asking you did the clematis grow over the garage and you asking me whether Anton's is doing well is a relationship?"

Di shrugged. "It's as good as most."

"No, it's not. It's totally unnatural. I live with a little baby girl. She's not yet one and she is loved by so many people you wouldn't believe it. She will never be left alone, bewildered, like Katie and I were. It's natural for people to love children. You were both so cold. . . . I just hoped you'd tell me why."

Di was quite calm. "I didn't like your father very much, even before we were married, but I hated my job more and I had no money to spend on clothes, on going to the cinema, on anything. So I have a part-time job which I like and I thought it was a fair exchange for marrying him. I didn't realize the sex thing was going to be so important, but, well, if I didn't want it, then it was only fair to let him go out and get it."

"Or stay in and have it," Lisa interrupted.

"I told you that was only two or three times."

"How could you put up with it?"

"It was that or start out on my own again and, unlike you, I had no qualifications. I have a badly paid job in a dress shop. As it is, I have a nice house and food on the table."

"So you'd prefer to share a man that you admit you don't like very much with prostitutes?"

"I don't think of it that way. I think of it as cooking and cleaning a fine house. I have a garden which I love, I play bridge with friends and go to the cinema. It's a way of living."

"You've obviously thought it through," Lisa said, with some grudging acceptance.

"Yes I did. I didn't expect to tell you all this. Of course, I didn't expect you to ask." Her mother was self-possessed now and eating her veal Milanese with every appearance of enjoyment.

Maud was serving in the restaurant but realized that this was a very intense conversation, so she steered away from personal chat. She moved gracefully around the room and Lisa saw Marco looking at her approvingly as he poured the wine for customers. That was what love and marriage was about—not this hopeless, downbeat bargain that her parents had made. For the first time ever, Lisa felt a wave of sympathy wash over her.

For both of them.

Faith stayed in the flat several nights a week now. She was able to look after Frankie and put her to bed on the evenings that all three of them studied. It was a curious little family grouping, but it worked. Faith said she found working like this so much easier than doing it alone. Between them they went over the latest lecture and talked it out. They made notes on what to ask the lecturer next week and they revised for their exams in August. They all felt that it had been worth doing, and now that graduation was in sight they began to imagine how it would all work out for them when they had letters after their names.

Noel would immediately seek a better position at

Hall's, and if it wasn't forthcoming then he would have the courage and qualifications to apply somewhere else. Faith would put herself forward as a manager in her office. She was doing that work in all but name and salary, so they would have to promote her.

Lisa? Well, Lisa was at a loss to know what her qualifications would lead to.

At one time she had hoped to be a partner in Anton's. But now? Well, she would have to return to the marketplace. It was humiliating, but she would have to contact Kevin, the boss she had left when she went to work with Anton. That was last year when she had been reasonably sane and good at her job. She picked up the phone with trepidation.

"Well, *hello*!" Kevin was entitled to be surprised and a bit mocking. For months now Lisa had avoided him if ever they turned up at the same function; he had not been a customer in Anton's. It was very hard to call him and tell him that she had failed.

He made it fairly easy.

"You're on the market again, I gather," he said.

"You can crow, Kevin. You were right. I should have listened. I should have thought it out."

"But you were in love, of course," Kevin said. There was only a mildly sardonic tone to his voice. He was entitled to have a lot more I-told-you-so.

"That was true, yes."

If he noticed the past tense he said nothing.

"So he didn't pay you in cash—I'm guessing. Did he repay you in love?"

"No, that's in pretty short supply these days."

"So you're looking for a job?"

"I was wondering if you knew of anything? Anything at all?"

"But this may just be a lovers' tiff. In a week's time you could well be back with him."

"That won't happen," Lisa said.

"Right now I can only offer you a junior place. Somewhere to settle for a while. I can't give you a top job. It wouldn't be fair on the others."

She was very humble now. "I'd be more grateful than I could tell you, Kevin."

"Not at all. Start Monday?"

"Can I make it the Monday after? I'm working in a sandwich bar and I'll have to give them notice . . . get someone else for them."

"My, my, Lisa, you *have* changed," Kevin said as he hung up.

Lisa went and told her boss immediately. "I'll find you another sandwich maker in a week," she promised.

"Hey, I want much more than that. I want a market adviser and a graphic designer as well." Hugh laughed.

"That may take longer, but anyway I wanted to tell you."

"I'm sorry to lose you. I had ferocious designs on you, actually. I was biding my time."

"Always a mistake," she said cheerfully. "Now, Hugh, if you are to have any business at all, put your mind on sandwiches—what about a mild tandoori chicken wrap? They'd love that."

"Let's go out in a blaze of glory for your last week."

Lisa made the spicy chicken sandwiches and in be-

tween times texted Maud and Simon to look for a replacement. One of their friends would be able to do it
without any problem. They had found somebody in a
couple of hours.

"Send her up to me and I'll train her in," Lisa suggested.

The girl was called Tracey. She was eager-looking but
covered in tattoos.

Tactfully, Lisa offered her a shirt.

"We wear these here buttoned at the wrist," she said.
"Hugo is very insistent about that."

"Bit of an old fuddy-duddy, is he?" Tracey asked.

"Bit of a young fuddy-duddy; definitely a looker," she
said.

Tracey brightened. This job might have hidden benefits.

Lisa was amazed at how quickly she managed to adapt to
a life that didn't center around Anton's. Not that she didn't
miss it; several times a day she wondered what they might
all be doing and whether Anton would use any more of
her ideas to beat the downturn in business. But there was
plenty to occupy her, and on most fronts it was going very
well.

Lizzie found the days endless. The savage, raw pain of grief
was now giving way to a gnawing ache, and the void in her
life was threatening to consume her.

"I'm thinking of getting a little job," she confided to
the twins.

"What work would you do, Lizzie?" Simon asked.

"Anything, really. I used to clean houses."

"You'd be too tired for that nowadays," Simon said practically.

"You could work at managing something, Lizzie," Maud suggested.

"Oh, I don't think so. I'd be afraid of the responsibility."

"Would you like to work in Marco's restaurant? Well, his father's restaurant. They're looking for someone to come in part-time to supervise sending the laundry out and take in the cheese delivery and to sort yesterday's tips out from the credit card receipts. You could do that, couldn't you?"

"Well, I might be able to, but Ennio would never give me a big responsible job like that," Lizzie said anxiously.

"Of course he would," Simon said loyally.

"You're family, Lizzie," said Maud, looking down with pleasure at her engagement ring.

Ania's baby was due in a couple of months and there was great excitement in the heart clinic, mainly because Ania's period of bed rest was over and she was back at work, but under constant supervision.

"I feel much safer here," she said piteously, so they let her stay, even though everyone jumped when she took a deep breath or reached up to take a file out of a cabinet.

Clara Casey said that Ania had been so upset by her miscarriage that they must all be on hand to help her the moment there was the remotest sign of the baby. Clara knew the girl was apprehensive—far from home, from her mother and sisters. Her husband, Carl, was, if possible, even more excited than Ania. He took to hanging around the clinic himself in case there should be any news.

Clara was very tolerant. "Oh, work round him," she told the others. "The poor boy is distracted in case anything goes wrong this time."

Clara herself was fairly distracted by matters on the home front: Frank Ennis and his son. The relationship had been prickly from the start, and hadn't improved much during the boy's visit. Des had gone back to Australia and they kept in touch from time to time. Not often enough for Frank, who put great effort into writing weekly e-mails to the boy.

"You'd think he'd do more than send a postcard of the Barrier Reef," Frank grumbled.

"Look, be grateful for what you get. My daughter Adi only sends a card too. I don't know where she is and what she's doing. It's just the way things are."

Then came the word they had not expected.

I find myself thinking a lot about Ireland these days. I know I was rough on you and didn't really believe you when you said you didn't know what your family had done, but it took time to get my head around it all. Perhaps we should have another go. I was thinking of spending a year there, if that wouldn't put you out. I've been in negotiations about jobs and apparently my degree and diploma would be recognised there.

You must tell me if this is something you would be happy with and I would find myself an apartment, rather than crowd you out. Who knows, during my year there we might try the father-son thing and see how it goes. In any case, I'd like to meet Clara and even my nearly stepsisters?

They were both silent when they read the letter. It was the first time Des Raven had shown any sign of wanting a father-son relationship. And also the first time that he had any thought of meeting Clara. . . .

The results of the examinations had been posted on the college notice board. Noel and Faith and Lisa had all done well and the diploma would be theirs. They celebrated with giant ice creams at the café beside the college and planned their outfits for graduation day. They would be wearing black gowns and there would be pale-blue hoods.

"Hoods?" Noel asked, horrified.

"That's just what they call them—they're just the bits that go over our shoulders, to mark us out as different, not engineers or draftsmen or anything." Lisa knew it all.

"I'm going to wear a yellow dress I have already—you won't see much of it under the gown. I'll spend the money on good shoes," Faith said.

"I'm going to get a red dress and borrow Katie's new shoes." Lisa had it sorted as well. "Now, Noel, what about you?"

"Why this emphasis on shoes?" Noel asked.

"Because everyone sees them when you go up on the stage for your parchment."

"If I polished up these ones?" He looked down dubiously at his feet. The girls shook their heads. New shoes were called for.

"I'll get you a pale-blue tie from one of my brothers," Faith promised.

"And I'll iron your good shirt—any money there is, spend it on shoes," Lisa commanded.

"It's a lot of fuss about nothing," Noel grumbled.

"Nights of lectures, hours of study—and you call it nothing!" Lisa was outraged.

"And what about the photos to show Frankie?" Faith asked.

"I'll get the damn shoes!" Noel promised.

The day of the graduation in September was very bright and sunny. That was a relief: there would be no umbrellas or people squinting into the rain. Frankie was excited to see them all dressing up.

She crawled around the floor, getting under everyone's feet and mumbled a lot to herself about it—words that didn't make much sense until they identified "Frankie too."

"Of *course* you're going too, darling." Faith lifted her up in the air. "*And* I have a lovely little blue dress for you to wear. It will match your daddy's tie and you'll be the most beautiful little girl in the whole world!"

Noel looked very well. He was much admired by the women, who dusted flecks off his shoulders and examined his new shoes with cries of approval. Then Emily arrived to take Frankie in the buggy wearing her new dress, and they all set out for the college.

Frankie behaved perfectly during the ceremony. Better by far than other babies, who cried or struggled at crucial times during the graduation. Noel gazed at her with pride.

She was indeed the most beautiful little girl in the whole world! He had done all this for her—yes, for himself too, but all this work had been worth it for the chance to make a life for her.

The new graduates filed onto the stage and the audience raked through the ranks until they found their own. The graduates also searched the audience. Noel saw Emily holding Frankie and he smiled with pleasure and pride.

Lisa saw her mother and sister both dressed up to honor the day; she saw Garry there and all their friends.

Then she saw Anton.

He looked lost, as if he didn't belong there. She remembered writing down this date in his diary months back. It didn't mean anything to her that he was there and it had all been her own fault. Anton had never loved her. It had all been in her mind.

The president spoke warmly about the graduates.

"They had to give up a lot of social life to do this course. They missed television and cinemas and theaters. They want to thank you, their families and their friends, for supporting them on this undertaking. Each and every graduate here today has gone on a journey. They are different people to the people who started out with a leap of faith. They have much more than just mere letters after their names. They have the satisfaction of having set out to do something and seen it through.

"I salute them all on your behalf."

There was tumultuous applause at this, and the new graduates all beamed from the stage. Then the presentation began . . .

They had planned a special lunch in Ennio's together with Noel, his family, Emily and Hat, Declan, Fiona and the Carroll parents. Faith would bring her father and three of her five brothers. Lizzie was working there as a supervisor, and she had reserved a big table for them; Ennio would give them a special price; the twins and Marco would be serving. Lizzie would even sit down and join them for the meal.

Lizzie had found the job a great help. For whole sections of the day she didn't stop and think of Muttie with that sad, empty look that broke her neighbors' hearts. Here it was too busy, too frenetic. There was too much shouting to leave any time to go over all she had lost. Ennio was always there with a coffee or a word of encouragement. She met new people, people who had never known Muttie. It wasn't really any easier, but it was less raw. Lizzie would admit that much, and the twins were there for her every step of the way. Lizzie was a religious person. She thanked God every morning and every night for having arranged things so that Maud and Simon came to live with them.

Ennio had said they should have a banner over the table—*FELICITAZIONI—TANTI AUGURI—FAITH LISA NOEL*: that would be alphabetical order, so nobody could be offended.

"What does it mean?" Faith asked.

"Congratulations, best wishes," Marco said excitedly.

They were a mixed group, including the two babies, but they all got along very well and there was no pause in the conversation. More and more food and wine kept coming to the table. And finally a great cake arrived, iced in the shape of a mortarboard and scroll.

People at other tables gathered round to see it.

"It was iced by Maud," Marco said proudly.

"And everyone else." Maud tried to shrug it off.

"But mainly by Maud," Marco insisted.

And then there was sparkling wine for the toast and a glass of elderflower cordial for Noel. The health of the three successful scholars was drunk to and they were cheered to the echo.

To everyone's surprise, Noel stood up.

"I think that, as the president said earlier, we owe a huge debt of gratitude to our families and friends and that we three should raise a toast to you also. Without you all, we wouldn't have been able to do all this and have this great graduation day and feast. To our families and friends," he said.

Lisa and Faith stood up and all three repeated the toast:

"To our families and friends."

Chapter Fourteen

Ania's baby was almost born in the heart clinic—not quite, but almost. It was too soon.

Her waters broke during one of the healthy cookery demonstrations and they got her into the maternity wing of St. Brigid's in the shortest possible time. Later that night the news went around: a baby boy, born prematurely and taken into the special-care baby unit. Everyone was concerned for Carl and Ania: it was going to be a traumatic time for both parents. They had been so anxious throughout the pregnancy, and the worrying wasn't over yet. They were staying with the tiny baby by his incubator; Carl would come down to the clinic later and tell them what was happening.

Clara Casey called her ex-husband and asked him to drop by her house.

"Don't like the sound of this," Alan said.

"Haven't I done everything you ever asked me: had

two babies for you, left you free to follow your heart? I gave you a divorce when you wanted it. I never asked you for a penny."

"You got my house," Alan said.

"No. If you remember, the house was paid for by a deposit from my mother and every month by a mortgage which *I* earned. It was always my house, so we won't go down that road again."

"What do you want to talk about if I come over?" He sounded sulky now.

"Various things . . . the future . . . the girls . . ."

"The girls!" Alan snorted. "Adi's off in Peru doing God knows what . . ."

"Ecuador, as it happens."

"Same difference. And as for Linda, she won't speak to me if I do get in touch."

"That's because when she told you that she and Nick were going to adopt, you said that you personally would never raise another man's son yourself. That was helpful. . . ."

"You're hard to please, Clara. If I *am* honest it's wrong, if I'm not honest, it's wrong."

"See you tomorrow," Clara said and hung up.

He looked older and shabbier than before. A succession of new ladies later, he was now temporarily without a partner. Alan, who always prided himself on having women iron his shirts, looked vaguely down at heel.

"You look wonderful," he said, as he said to almost every woman almost all the time. Clara ignored him.

"Coffee?" she suggested.

"Or something stronger even?" he asked.

"No, you can't handle drink like you used to. You start crawling over me when you've had a couple of glasses of wine, and I certainly don't want that."

"You liked it well enough once," he muttered.

"Yes, that's true, but in those days I believed everything you said."

"Don't nag, Clara."

"No, of course not. I'm just showing you some courtesy here. Frank is going to be moving in here next week."

"But you can't let him!" He was shocked.

"Well, I have every intention of doing so. I just thought you should hear it from me, that's all."

"But, Clara, you're much too old for this," he said.

"Imagine, you were once considered quite charming and dashing," Clara said.

Emily had the spare room in Dr. Hat's house beautifully decorated, and she planned a series of outings to entertain Betsy and Eric. She had this ludicrous wish that they should love Ireland like she did. She hoped that it wouldn't rain, that the streets would be free of litter, that the price of everything would not be too high.

Emily and Hat were at the airport long before the plane arrived.

"It only seems the other day since you came out to meet *me* here," Emily said, "and you brought me a picnic in the car."

"I had begun to fancy you seriously then, but I was terrified you'd say it was all nonsense."

"I'd never have said that." She looked at him very fondly.

"I hope your friend won't think I'm too old and dull for you," he said anxiously.

"You're my Hat. My choice. The only person I ever even contemplated marrying," she said firmly. And that was that.

Betsy was bemused by the size of the airport and the frantic activity all around. She had thought the plane would land in a field of cows or sheep. This was a huge, sprawling place like an airport back home. She couldn't believe the traffic, the highways and the huge buildings.

"You never told me how developed it all is. I thought it was a succession of little cottages where you knew everyone who moves," she said, laughing. In minutes it was as if they had never been parted.

Eric and Dr. Hat exchanged relieved glances. It was all going to be fine.

Emily was going to be given away by her uncle Charles.

Charles and Josie had finally come to the conclusion that a children's playground and a *small* statue of St. Jarlath would fit the bill. They had been to see a lawyer and settled a sum for Noel and one for Frankie. They had even arranged for Emily to have a substantial sum as a wedding gift so that she wouldn't start her married life with no money of her own. It wasn't a dowry, of course, and Charles said that so often that Emily began to wonder.

Noel knew nothing about his inheritance. Charles and Josie had been waiting to talk to him on his own. There was always someone with him—Lisa or Faith or Declan Carroll. They could hardly remember the days before Frankie was born, when Noel was a man always by himself. Now the two of them were always the center of a group of people.

Finally they found him alone.

"Will you sit down, Noel? We have something to tell you," Charles said.

"I don't like the sound of this." Noel looked from one to the other anxiously.

"No, you are going to like what your father has to say," Josie said with a rare smile.

Noel hoped they hadn't seen a vision or anything, that St. Jarlath hadn't appeared in the kitchen asking them to build a cathedral. They had seemed so normal recently, it would be a pity if they had had a setback.

"It's about your future, Noel. You know that Mrs. Monty, may God be good to her, has left us a sum of money. We want to share this with you."

"Ah, no, Dad, thank you but that's for you and Mam. You did the dog minding—I wouldn't want to take any of it."

"But you don't know how much she left," Charles said.

"Is there enough to take you to Rome? Or even Jerusalem? That's wonderful news!"

"There's much more than that—you wouldn't believe it."

"But it's yours, Dad."

"We've made arrangements for an educational policy for Frankie, so that she'll never lack for a good school. And there'll be a lump sum for yourself, maybe the deposit on a house so you'd have your own place and not have to rent."

"But this is ridiculous, Dad. It would cost a fortune."

"She left us a fortune. And after a lot of thought we are spending it on a children's garden with a small statue, and on our own flesh and blood."

Noel looked at them wordlessly. They had sorted out everything that was worrying him. He would be able to have a proper home for Frankie and maybe, if she'd have him, for Faith. Frankie would get a top-class education. Noel would have his rainy-day security.

All because his father had been kind to Caesar, a little King Charles spaniel with soppy brown eyes.

Wasn't life totally extraordinary?

On the morning of the wedding, before they set out for the church, Charles made a little speech to Emily.

"By rights it should have been my brother doing this but I hope I'll do you credit."

"Charles, if it were up to my father, he wouldn't have turned up, or if he had, he would have been drunk. I much prefer having you."

Father Flynn married them. Emily could have filled the church five times over, but they wanted only a small gathering, so twenty of them stood in the sunlight as they made their vows. Then they went to Holly's Hotel in

County Wicklow and back home to St. Jarlath's Crescent. Then the honeymoon continued for the two couples; Dingo Duggan got new tires to make sure that they got to the west and back.

They stayed in farmhouses and walked along shell-covered shores with purple-blue mountains as a backdrop. And if you were to ask anyone who they were and what they were doing, a hundred guesses would never have said that they were two middle-aged couples on honeymoon. They all seemed too settled and happy for that.

Two days after Emily's wedding, Father Flynn heard from the nursing home in Rossmore that his mother was dying. He got down there quickly and held her hand. His mother's mind was far from clear but he felt that by being there he might be of some comfort. When his mother spoke it was of people long dead, and of incidents in her childhood. Suddenly, however, she came back to the present day.

"Whatever happened to Brian?" she asked him.

"I'm right here."

"I had a son called Brian," she continued, as though she hadn't heard him. "I don't know what happened to him. I think he joined a circus. He left town and no one ever heard of him again. . . ."

When Mrs. Flynn died almost the whole of Rossmore turned out for the funeral. At the nursing home, the staff had gathered together the old lady's belongings and gave them to the priest. They included some old diaries and a few pieces of jewelry no one had ever seen her wear.

Brian looked through them as he came back in the train. The jewelry had been given to her by her husband, the diary told, but they had not been given in love but out of guilt. Brian read with pain and embarrassment that his father had not been a faithful man and he had thought he could buy his wife's forgiveness with a necklace and various brooches. Brian decided to give the jewelry to his sister Judy with no mention of its history.

He looked up the date of his own ordination to the priesthood in the battered diary. His mother had written:

This is simply the best day of my life.

It somehow made up for her thinking he had joined a circus.

Ania's family were on their way from Poland to be with her as she and Carl watched over baby Robert. He was so tiny, they could have held him in the palms of their hands; instead he was lying in an incubator attached to monitors and with tubes in and out of his tiny body. Ania watched carefully as the breathing monitor showed how Robert was having difficulty breathing on his own and how the machine was breathing for him. She was able to hold his tiny hand through the holes in the incubator. He looked so small, so vulnerable, so unprepared for the world.

Back at home, they had a nursery prepared, waiting for them to come home as a new family. The room was full of gifts given to them by friends and well-wishers. There were baby clothes and toys and all the equipment for a newborn child. Carl silently wondered if baby Robert would ever get to use it.

On the third day, Ania was able to hold her baby in

her arms. Unable to speak for the emotion, her face was wet with tears of hope and joy as she held him, so tiny, so fragile.

"*Maly cud*," she whispered to him. "Little miracle."

The honeymoon had been a resounding success. Emily and Betsy were like girls, chattering and laughing. Hat and Eric found a great common interest in bird-watching and wrote notes each evening. Dingo met a Galway girl with black hair and blue eyes and was very smitten. The sun shone on the newlyweds and the nights were full of stars.

It was over too soon for everyone.

"I wonder if there's any news when we get back? I wonder how Ania's baby is doing. I do hope he's going to be all right," Emily said as they drew closer to Dublin.

"You're really part of the place now," Betsy said.

"Yes, isn't it odd? I never had a real conversation in my life with my father about Ireland or about anything else, but I do feel that I have come home."

Hat heard her say this and smiled to himself. It was even more than he had hoped.

When they did get back they heard the astounding news that Frank Ennis had moved in with the elegant Clara Casey, who ran the heart clinic, and, wait for it . . . he had a son. Frank Ennis had a son called Des Raven, who lived in Australia and was coming to Ireland.

Fiona could talk of nothing else. It had completely wiped her own pregnancy off the list of topics. Clara *living with* Frank Ennis—didn't people do extraordinary things. And Frank had a *son* she hadn't met yet. Imagine.

Their first chance to celebrate properly as a family came when Adi came back from Ecuador with her boyfriend, Gerry. Des had wanted to go back to Anton's. "It will be like starting over," he had said. This time, there was no need to plead for a table, even though they were nine: Clara, Frank and Des; then Adi and Gerry; Linda came with Nick. Hilary from the clinic and Clara's best friend, Dervla, made up the party.

The restaurant was half empty and there seemed to be an air of confusion about the place. The menu was more limited than before and Anton himself was working in and out of the kitchen. He said that his number one, Teddy, had gone, as he needed new pastures. No, he had no idea where he went. Des Raven was very courteous to his new almost-stepsisters. He talked to Adi about teaching; he spoke to Linda about some friends of his who had adopted a Chinese baby; he talked easily of his life in Australia.

Clara asked Anton's advice about what they should eat.

"There's a very good steak and kidney pie," he suggested.

"That's the men sorted, but what about the rest of us?" she asked. She noticed he was tired and strained. It couldn't be easy running a restaurant that looked as though it might be on the way down.

"Small, elegant portions of steak and kidney pie?" he suggested with a winning smile.

Clara stopped feeling sorry for him. With a smile like that he would get by. He was a survivor.

Frank Ennis, in his new suit, was in charge of the table.

He poured wine readily and urged people to have oysters as the optional extra.

"I talk about my son a lot," he said proudly to Des.

"Good. Do you talk about Clara a lot?" he asked.

"With respect and awe," Frank said.

"Good," intervened Clara, "because she wants to tell you that her clinic needs some serious extra funding. . . ."

"Out of the question."

"The blood tests take too long from the main hospital. We need our own lab."

"I'll get your blood tests fast-tracked," Frank Ennis promised.

"You have six weeks for us to see a real difference; otherwise the fight is on," Clara said. "He is amazingly generous in real life," she whispered to Dervla. "It's just in the hospital that his rotten-to-the-core meanness shows."

"He's delighted with you," Dervla said. "He has said 'My Clara' thirty times during this meal alone."

"Well, I'm keeping my name, my job, my clinic and my house, so I'm doing very well out of it," Clara said.

"Go on out of that, playing the tough bird—you're just as soppy as he is. You're delighted at this playing-house thing. I'm happy for you, Clara, and I hope that you'll be very happy together."

"I will." Clara had it all planned out. Minimal disturbance to their two lives. They were both people who were set in their ways.

Lisa was surprised when Kevin asked her out to lunch.

She was in a junior position in the studio. She didn't

expect her boss to single her out. In Quentins she was even more surprised that he ordered a bottle of wine. Kevin was usually a one-vodka person. This looked like something serious. She hoped he wasn't going to sack her. But surely he wouldn't take her out to lunch to give her the push?

"Stop frowning, Lisa. We're going to have a long lunch," Kevin said.

"What is it? Don't keep me in suspense."

"Two things, really. Did Anton pay you anything? Anything at all?"

"Oh, why are you dragging this up? I told you it was my fault. I went in there with my eyes open."

"No, you didn't. Your eyes were closed in mad, passionate love, and fair play to you, you're not bitter, but I really need to know."

"No, he paid me nothing, but I was part of the place, part of the dream. I was doing it for *us,* not for him. That's what I thought, anyway. Don't make me go on repeating all this. I *know* what I did for months . . . it doesn't make it any easier having to talk about that."

"It's just that he's going into receivership today and I wanted to make sure you got your claim in. You are a serious victim here. You worked for him without being paid, for God's sake. You are a major creditor."

"I haven't a notion of asking him for anything. I'm sorry it didn't work for him. I'm not going to add to his worries."

"It's just business, Lisa. He'll understand. People have got to be paid. It will be automatic. They'll sell his assets— I don't know what he owns and what is mortgaged or leased, but people have to be paid, you amongst them."

"No, Kevin, thanks all the same."

"You love clothes, Lisa. You should get yourself a stunning wardrobe."

"I'm not smart enough for your office? Is that it?" She was hurt, but she made it sound like a joke.

"No, you're too smart. Much too smart. I can't keep you. I have a friend in London. He's looking for someone bright. I told him about you. He'll pay your fare to London. Overnight in a fancy hotel, and you don't want to know the salary he's offering!"

"You really *are* getting rid of me and you're pretending it's a promotion," she said bleakly.

"*Never* have I been so misjudged! I'd prefer you to stay and in a year or two I could promote you, but this job is too good to ignore and I thought that anyway it might be easier for you."

"Easier?"

"Well, you know, there'll be a lot of talk about Anton's. Speculation, newspaper stuff."

"Yes, I suppose there will. Poor Anton."

"Oh, God, don't tell me you're going back to him."

"No, there's nothing to go back to. There never was."

"Ah, now, Lisa, I'm sure he *did* love you in his own way."

She shook her head. "But in ways you're right. I couldn't bear to be in Dublin while all the vultures were picking over the place."

"You'll go for the interview?" He was pleased.

"I'll go," Lisa promised.

Simon said it was time they talked about New Jersey. The amazing inheritance they had got from Muttie meant that

Maud and Marco could put a deposit on their own restaurant and Simon could go to New Jersey and eventually have a place of his own.

"I'll miss you," Maud said.

"You won't notice I'm gone," he assured her.

"Who'll finish my sentences?"

"You'll have Marco trained in no time."

"You'll fall in love and live out there."

"I doubt it, but I'll be home often to see Lizzie and you and Marco." Maud noticed he didn't include their parents. Father was on his travels and Mother had only the vaguest idea of who they were.

As if he read her mind, Simon said, "Weren't we so lucky that Muttie and Lizzie took us in? We could have ended up anywhere."

Maud gave him a hug. "Those American girls don't know what's coming their way," she said.

It was a day of many changes.

Declan and Fiona and Johnny moved house. It was only next door but it was still a huge move. They arranged that Paddy and Molly Carroll should be part of it all so that they would realize how nothing had really changed. They would be next door; when Johnny was old enough to walk he would know two homes as his own. And as for the new baby? That would be born into a two-house family.

The house had been painted in a cheery primrose color that brought sunshine into every room. They would think about proper color schemes later, but the most important thing was to make it bright and welcoming.

Johnny's room was ready and waiting for his crib. Declan and Fiona would have room for their books and music.

They would have their own kitchen at last.

The time with Molly and Paddy Carroll had been happy, but it couldn't go on forever. They had both looked forward to and dreaded the day when they would have to move to somewhere with more space: this had been an ideal solution.

They walked the few steps between the houses carrying possessions and stopping for a pot of tea in one house or the other so that it underlined how much together they were still going to be. Dimples came in and walked around the new house and seemed to approve. Emily had brought window boxes already planted as a housewarming gift.

Dr. Hat and Emily decided to open a garden store. There was still plenty of room beside the thrift shop. Now that so many residents of St. Jarlath's Crescent had begun to take an interest in beautifying their gardens, there was no end of demand for bedding plants and ornamental shrubs. They went up and measured it. It was now no longer a wish, but a reality; they would do it together, and it would be yet one more thing they could share.

In the disturbed world of Anton's restaurant the staff were making their plans. They would not open next week. Everyone knew this. April sat around the place with her notebook, suggesting places for Anton to do interviews on the difficulties of running a business during a recession. Anton felt unsettled. He wasn't listening. He wondered what Lisa would be saying.

It was the day that Linda and Nick decided to stop talking about adopting a baby and do something about it.

For Noel it was a good day also.

Mr. Hall had said that there was a more senior position in the company that had been vacant for some time. He now wanted to offer it to Noel.

"I have been impressed by you, Noel. I don't mind saying that you did much better than I would have thought at one stage. I always hoped you'd have it in you to make something of yourself, though I confess I had my doubts about you for a while."

"I had my doubts about myself," Noel had said with a smile.

"There's always some turning point for a man. What do you think yours was?" Mr. Hall had seemed genuinely interested.

"Becoming a father," Noel had said without having to stop and think for a second.

And now he was at home with Frankie helping her take her first independent steps. There were just the two of them. She still liked the comfort of something to hold on to, and every now and then she suddenly sat down with a surprised look on her face. She had been making great efforts to tear up the cloth books that Faith had given her, but they were proving very resistant. She was frowning with concentration.

"I love you, Frankie," Noel said to her.

"Dada," she said.

"I really do love you. I was afraid I wouldn't be good enough for you but we're not making a bad fist of it, are we?"

"Fst," Frankie said, delighted with the noise of the word.

"Say 'love,' Frankie. Say, 'I love you, Dada.' "

She looked up at him. "Love Dada," she said, as clear as a bell.

And to his surprise he felt the tears on his face. He wished not for the first time that there really was a God and a heaven because it would be really great if Stella could somehow see this and know that it was all working out like she had hoped.

Chapter Fifteen

Noel and Lisa planned a first birthday party for Frankie. There would be an ice cream cake and paper hats; Mr. Gallagher from Number 37 could do magic tricks and said he'd come along and entertain the children.

Naturally, Moira got to hear of it.

"You're having all these people in this small flat?" she asked doubtfully.

"I know—won't it be wonderful?" Lisa deliberately misunderstood her.

"You should do more for yourself, Lisa. You're bright, sharp, you could have a career and a proper place to live."

"This *is* a proper place to live." Noel was at the washing machine in the kitchen so didn't hear.

"No, it's not. You should have your own apartment. You'll need one soon anyway, if Noel's romance continues," Moira said, practical as always.

"But meanwhile I'm very happy here."

"We have to stir ourselves from our comfort zones.

What are you doing here with a man who is bringing up some child that may or may not be his own?"

"Of course Frankie's his own!" Lisa was shocked.

"Well, that's as may be. She was very unreliable, the mother, you know. I met her in hospital. A very wild sort of person. She could have named anyone as the father."

"Well, really, Moira, I never heard anything so ridiculous," Lisa said, blazing suddenly at the mean-spirited pettiness of Moira's attitude. Wasn't life the luck of the draw? They could have got a very nice social worker like that woman Dolores who came to Katie to get her hair done at the salon. *She* would have been delighted with the way Frankie had turned out and would rejoice at such a successful outcome. But no, they were stuck with Moira. Thank God Noel had been in the kitchen while stupid, negative Moira was talking. It was just a miracle that he hadn't heard.

Noel had, of course, heard every word and he was holding on by a thread.

What a sour, mean cow Moira was, and he had just begun to see some good in her. Not now. Not ever again after such a statement. He managed to shout out a cheerful good-bye as he heard the door. He wouldn't think about it. It was nonsense. He would think about the party instead. About Frankie, his little girl. That woman's remarks had no power to hurt him. He would rise above it.

First he must pretend to Lisa that he hadn't heard. That was important.

Moira walked briskly along the road away from Chestnut Court. She was sorry she had spoken to Lisa like that. It was unprofessional. It wasn't like her. She had been thrown by Lisa's apparent freedom to get on with it and then, of course, she had her own worries about her father and Maureen Kennedy. Still and all, it was no reason to run off at the mouth about Noel. Mercifully, he was in the kitchen at the washing machine and didn't hear. Lisa was unlikely to bring the subject up.

Why did worries never come singly?

Moira's brother had written to say that their father and Mrs. Kennedy were getting married. Mr. Kennedy was now presumed dead after fifteen years' absence, with no contact being made and his name not found on any British register. They would marry in a month's time and a few people were being invited back to the house. Everyone was very pleased, her brother wrote.

Moira was sure they were, but then they didn't have to cope with the fact that Mr. Kennedy was alive and well, living in the hostel and on Moira's caseload.

"Father, it's Moira."

He sounded as surprised as if the prime minister of Australia had telephoned him.

"Moira!" was all he could say.

"I hear that you're getting married again. . . ." Moira came straight to the point.

"Yes, we hope to. Are you pleased for us?"

"Very, and is everyone okay with you getting married, what with . . ." She paused delicately.

"He's presumed dead," her father said in sepulchral

way. "The state gives a declaration of death after seven years and he's been gone years longer than that."

"And . . . um . . . the Church?" Moira said.

"Oh, endless conversations with the parish priest, then they went to the archdiocese, but there's a thing called *presumptio mortis* and each case is argued on its merits, and since this boyo hasn't had an address or a record of any sort, there isn't any problem."

"And were you going to invite me?" It felt like probing a sore tooth. She hoped her father would say it was very small and, considering their age and circumstances, they had restricted the numbers.

"Oh, indeed. I'd be delighted if you were there. We both would be delighted."

"Thank you very much."

"Not at all. I'm glad you'll be there." He hung up without giving her the date, time or place but, after all, she could get those from her brother.

Frankie's birthday party was a triumph.

Frankie had a crown and so did Johnny, since it was his birthday too. Apart from the two birthday babies there were very few children coming to the party, but lots of grown-ups. Lizzie was helping with the jellies and Molly Carroll was in charge of the cocktail sausages. Frankie and Johnny were much too young to appreciate Mr. Gallagher's magic tricks but the grown-ups loved him and there were great sighs of amazement as he produced rabbits, colored scarves and gold coins from the air. The children loved the rabbits and searched fruitlessly in the magician's top hat to know where they had gone. Josie suggested a rabbit hutch in the new garden, and the idea was received with great enthusiasm.

Noel was glad the party went well. There were no tantrums among the children, no one was overtired. He had even arranged for wine and beer to be served to the adults. It hadn't bothered him in the least. Faith and Lisa cleared up and quietly put the unfinished bottles in Faith's bag.

But Noel's heart was heavy. Two chance remarks at the party had upset him more than he would have believed possible.

Dingo Duggan, who always said the wrong thing, commented that Frankie was far too good-looking to be a child of Noel's. Noel managed to smile and said that nature had a strange way in compensating for flaws.

Paddy Carroll said that Frankie was a beautiful child. She had very fine cheekbones and huge dark eyes.

"She's like her mother, then," Noel said, but his mind was far away. Stella had a vibrant, lively face, yes, but she didn't have fine cheekbones and huge dark eyes.

Neither did Noel.

Was it possible that Frankie was the child of someone else?

He sat very quietly when everyone had gone; eventually, Faith sat down beside him.

"Was it a strain having alcohol in the house, Noel?" Faith asked.

"No, I never thought about it. Why?"

"It's just you seem a bit down." She was sympathetic, and so he told her. He repeated the words that Moira had said: that he was naïve to believe he was Frankie's father.

Faith listened with tears in her eyes.

"I never heard anything so ridiculous. She's a sour, sad, bitter woman. You're never going to start giving any credence to anything she would say?"

"I don't know. It's possible."

"No, it's not possible! Why would she have chosen *you* unless you were the father?" Faith was outraged on his behalf.

"Stella more or less said that at the time," he said.

"Put it out of your head, Noel. You are the best father in the world and that Moira can't bring herself to accept this. That's all there is to it."

Noel smiled wanly.

"Here, I'll make us a mug of tea and we'll eat the leftovers," she said.

Moira went to visit Mr. Kennedy in the hostel to make sure he was getting all his entitlements. He had settled in well.

"Did you ever think of going back home to where you were from originally?" she asked him diffidently.

"Never. That part of life is over for me. As far as they're all concerned I'm dead. I'd prefer it that way," he said.

It made Moira feel a little bit, but not entirely, better. She was being unprofessional, and when all was said and done she had nothing left but her profession. Had she fallen down on that too?

She also regretted her outburst to Lisa when she questioned Noel's paternity of Frankie. It had been unforgivable. Fortunately, he hadn't heard it, or at any rate he was polite when she talked to him, which was the same thing.

———

Noel couldn't sleep, so he got up and went to the sitting room. He got a piece of paper and made a list of the reasons that he was obviously Frankie's father and another list of reasons that he might not be. As usual, he came to no conclusion. He loved that child so much—she must be his daughter.

And yet he couldn't sleep. There was only one thing to do.

He would get a DNA test.

He would arrange it the next day. He tore up the sheets of paper into tiny pieces.

That was all there was to it.

Noel didn't want to approach either Declan or Dr. Hat about the DNA test. He had asked at the AA meeting if anyone knew how it was done. He made it seem like a casual inquiry for a friend. As always, the assembly was able to find an answer. You went to a doctor, who took a swab of your cheek and sent it to a laboratory—couldn't be more simple.

Yes, all very well, but Noel didn't want Declan to know his doubts. He couldn't ask Hat either, since Hat was family now that he had married Emily. So it would have to be someone totally new.

He wondered what advice his cousin Emily would give him. She would say, "Be ruthlessly honest and do it quickly." There was no arguing with that.

He looked up a doctor on the other side of the city. It was a woman doctor, who was practical and to the point.

"It will cost you to have this test done. We have to pay the lab."

"Sure, I know that," Noel agreed.

"I mean, it's not just a whim or a silly row with your partner or anything?"

"It's nothing like that. I just need to know."

"And if it turns out that you are *not* the child's father?"

"I will make up my mind what to do then."

"You have to be prepared to hear something you don't want to hear," she persisted.

"I can't settle until I know," he said simply.

And after that it was straightforward. He brought Frankie in and swabs were taken. He would know for sure in three weeks.

Even though he had been told that it would take three weeks, Noel watched the post every day. The doctor had promised to let him have the results as soon as she got them. They had agreed that phones could be unreliable or too public.

Better to send it in a letter.

Noel examined every envelope that arrived, but there was nothing.

Lisa went to London and came back thrilled with a job offer.

He had never felt time moving so slowly. The days in Hall's were endless. His need for a drink after each day was so acute that he went to an AA meeting almost every evening. Why could it take so long to match up bits of tissue or whatever DNA was?

He would look at Frankie sometimes and feel covered

in shame that he was doing this to her—that he wanted so much to know.

Noel had a long history of being in denial. When he was drinking, he denied the possibility that anyone would ever discover this at work. When he stopped drinking he banished all thoughts of comfortable bars from his head and memory. Mainly it worked for him, but not always.

It was the same now. He banished the possibility that Frankie might *not* be his child. He just would not think what he would do then. The fact that Stella might have lied to him or been mistaken and the heartbreaking possibility that Frankie might not be his little girl but somebody else's—it was too big to think about. It had to be left out of his conscious mind.

Once he knew one way or the other, it would be easier. This was the worst bit.

The letter arrived at Chestnut Court.

Lisa left it on the table as she went out; in the silent flat Noel poured himself another cup of tea. His hand was too shaky to pick up the envelope. The teapot had rattled alarmingly against the teacup. He was too weak to open it now. He had to get through this day without shaking like this. Perhaps he should put the letter away and open it tomorrow. He put it into a drawer. Thank God he had shaved already; he could never do it like this.

He dressed very slowly. He was pale and his eyes looked tired, but really and truly he might pass for a normal person, not someone with the most important secret of his life tidied away, unopened, in a drawer. A person who would give every single possession he had for a pint of beer accompanied by a large Irish whiskey.

How amazing that he looked perfectly normal. Now, looking at him, you might think he was a perfectly ordinary man.

Lisa was startled to find him there when she arrived back with Dingo Duggan and his van. She was going to take her possessions down to Katie and Garry's.

"Hey, I thought you'd be at work," she said.

Noel shook his head. "Day off," he muttered.

"Lucky old you. Where's Frankie? I thought you'd want to celebrate a day off with her."

"She went with Emily and Hat. No point in breaking the routine," he said flatly.

"You okay, Noel?"

"Sure I am. What are you doing?"

"Moving my stuff, trying to give you two lovebirds more room."

"You know you're not in the way—there's plenty of room for all of us."

"But I'll be going to London soon. I can't clutter your place up with all my boxes."

"I don't know what I'd have done without you, Lisa, I really don't."

"Wasn't it a great year!" Lisa agreed. "A year when you found Frankie and when I . . . well, when I let the scales fall from my eyes over so many things. Anton for one, my father for another . . ."

"You never said why you came here that night," Noel said.

"And you never asked, which made everything so restful. I'll miss Frankie, though, desperately. Faith is going to send me a photo of her every month so that I'll see her growing up."

"You'll forget all about us." He managed a smile.

"As if I would. This is the first proper home I ever had." She gave him a quick hug and went into her bedroom to check the boxes that were going to be driven over to her sister's.

"Give Katie my love," Noel said mechanically.

"I will. She's dying to tell me something—I know by her voice."

"It must be nice to have a sister," he said.

"It is. Maybe you and Faith could arrange a little sister for Frankie one day," she teased.

"Maybe." He didn't sound very confident about it.

Lisa was relieved to hear Dingo arriving to carry the boxes. Noel was definitely not himself today.

Katie did indeed want to tell Lisa something. It was that she was pregnant. She and Garry were overjoyed and they hoped Lisa would be pleased for them too.

Lisa said she was delighted. She hadn't known that this was in the plan at all, but Katie said it had been long hoped for.

"Two career people? Highfliers?" Lisa said, in mock wonder.

"Yes, but we wanted a baby to make it complete."

"I'll be a terrific aunt. I don't know anything about having a baby but I sure as anything know how to look after one."

"I wish you weren't going away," Katie said.

"I'll be back often," Lisa promised. "And this baby will grow up in a family that wants a baby—not like the way you and I grew up, Katie."

Emily and Hat were surrounded by seed catalogs, trying to decide from the huge amount on offer. Frankie sat with them and seemed to study the pictures of flowers as well.

"She's just no trouble," Emily said fondly.

"Pity we didn't meet earlier—we could well have had a few of those ourselves," Hat said wistfully.

"Oh, no, Hat, I have much more the personality of a grandmother than a mother. I like a baby who goes home in the evening," she said.

"Is it dull for you here with me?" he asked suddenly.

"What do you mean?"

"Back in America you had a busy life, teaching, going to art exhibits, thousands of people around the place."

"Stop fishing for compliments, Hat. You know that I'm besotted with this place. And with you. And when we push this little pet back up to Chestnut Court I will make you the most wonderful cheese soufflé to prove it."

"Lord above, life doesn't get much better than this," Hat said with a sigh of pleasure.

The flat was very silent when Lisa and Dingo had departed with a chorus of good-byes.

Noel opened the drawer and took out the letter. Perhaps he should eat something to keep his strength up. He had eaten no breakfast. He made himself a tomato sandwich, carefully adding chopped onion and cutting off the crusts. It tasted like sawdust.

He pulled the envelope towards him.

When he saw it all confirmed that he was Frankie's father, then everything would be all right. Wouldn't it? This hollow, empty feeling would go and he would be normal again.

But suppose that . . . Noel would not allow himself to go down that road. Of course he was Frankie's father. And now that he had eaten his tasteless tomato sandwich, he was ready to open the envelope.

He took the letter from the drawer and slit it open with the knife he had used to make his sandwich. It was stilted and official, but it was clear and concise.

The DNA samples did not match.

A hot rage came over him. He could feel it burning around his neck and ears. He could feel a heavy lump in his stomach and a strange light-headedness around his eyes and forehead.

This could not be true.

Stella could not have told him a pack of lies and palmed off her child on him. Surely it was impossible that she had made all these arrangements and put his name on the birth certificate if she had not believed it was true.

Perhaps she had so many lovers she had no idea who might be Frankie's father.

She could have picked him because he was humble and would make no fuss.

Or possibly Frankie's real father was so unreliable or unavailable that he could not be contacted.

Bile rose in his throat.

He knew exactly what would make him feel better. He picked up his jacket and went out.

Moira was having a busy morning at the heart clinic. Once the word had got around that she was an expert on finding people entitlements, her caseload had increased. It was Moira's belief that if there were benefits there, then people should avail themselves of them. She would fill in the paperwork, arrange the carers, the allowances or the support needed.

Today Mr. Kennedy was coming to the clinic for his checkup; she would see him and make sure that he was being properly looked after. And unexpectedly Clara Casey had asked if Moira could spare her ten minutes on a personal matter.

Moira wondered what on earth it could be. The gossip around the clinic had said that Dr. Casey had moved Mr. Ennis into her home, but surely Clara didn't want to discuss anything quite as personal as that.

Just after midday, when Moira's stint ended officially, Clara slipped into her office.

"This is not on the clinic's time, Moira. It's a personal favor on my time and yours."

"Sure, go ahead," Moira said. A few months ago she might have said something sharper, something more official, but events had changed her.

"It's about my daughter Linda—she and her husband are very anxious to adopt a baby and they don't know how to set about it."

"What have they done so far?" Moira asked.

"Nothing much, except talk about it, but now they want to move forward."

"Fine—do you want me to talk to them sometime?"

"Linda is actually here today. She came to take me to lunch. Would that be too instant?"

"No, not at all. Do you want to stay for the conversation?"

"No, no—but I do appreciate this, Moira. I've realized over the last months you are amazingly thorough and tenacious. If anyone can help Linda and Nick, you can."

Moira couldn't remember why she had thought of Dr. Casey as aloof and superior. She watched as Clara ushered in her tall, handsome daughter.

"I'll leave you in good hands," Clara said, and mother and daughter hugged each other. Moira felt an absurd flush of pleasure all over her face and neck.

At lunch in the shopping precinct Linda was bubbling over with enthusiasm.

"I can't think why you didn't like that woman—she was *marvelous*. It's all very straightforward. You go to the health board and they refer you to the adoption section and fill in a lot of details, and they come for home assessment visits. She asked did we mind what nationality the child would be and I said of course not. It really looks as if it might happen."

"I'm so pleased, Linda." Clara spoke gently.

"So you and Frank had better polish up your babysitting skills," Linda said with unnaturally bright eyes.

———

Moira left the clinic in high good humor. For once it appeared her talents had been recognized. It was one of those rare occasions when people actually seemed pleased with the social worker.

She had warned Linda about delays and bureaucracy and said the most important thing was to be quietly persistent, keeping even-tempered no matter what the provocation. Linda had been delighted with her, and moreover, Linda's mother had given words of high praise.

This was a personal first.

Her steps took her past Chestnut Court, and she looked from habit at Noel and Lisa's flat. Noel would be at work, but maybe Lisa was there packing her belongings. She was heading off to London soon. Anyway, no point in going in there and talking to Lisa and being accused of spying or policing the situation. She didn't want to lose the good feeling that had come from the clinic, so she passed by.

Emily got a phone call at lunchtime. It was Noel. His voice was unsteady. She thought he sounded drunk.

"Everything all right, Noel?" she asked anxiously, her heart lurching. He should have been there to pick up Frankie. What could have happened?

"Yes. Everything's fine." He spoke like a robot. "I'm at the zoo, actually."

"The zoo?" Emily was stunned. The zoo was miles away, on the other side of the city. She didn't know whether to be relieved or horrified. If Noel was there, then he was safe; but then he was wandering around looking at lions and aviaries and elephants rather than picking up his daughter.

"Yes. I haven't been here for ages. They've lots of new things."

"Yes, Noel, I'm sure they do."

"So I was wondering could you possibly keep Frankie for a while longer?"

"Of course," Emily agreed, worried. Was he drunk? His voice sounded stressed. What could have brought all this on? "And are you at the zoo on your own?"

"Yes, for the moment."

Noel had been over and over it in his mind. For a year he had been living a lie. Frankie was not his child. God knew whose child she was. He loved her like his own—of course he did. But he had thought she was his own child and had no one else to look after her. His name was on the birth certificate; he had loved her and looked after her and fed her and changed her. He had protected her, given her a life surrounded by people who loved her; he had made her his. Did he regret all this? She was a year old, her mother was dead—what sort of start in life would it be if he washed his hands of her now?

Could he bring up another man's child as his own? He didn't think so. She was someone else's child; someone else had fathered her and walked away, got away with it. Should he find out who it was? Would it be a wild-goose chase?

And what sort of man would he be if he ran away now? Could he abandon her when she needed him every bit as much as when she was that tiny, helpless baby he had brought home from the hospital? He pictured the flat that was their home: Frankie's toys on the floor, her clothes warming on the radiators, her photographs on the mantelpiece. Her favorite food in the kitchen, the baby lotions in the bathroom; he knew where she was every minute of the day. He remembered the horror of the night she'd been missing. Everyone had been out looking for her—so many people had been concerned for her safety. She was with Emily and Hat now, and when they went to the thrift shop, they'd take her with them. His own parents knew her as their grandchild. She knew everyone in the neighborhood; they were all part of her life, as she was part of theirs. Was he going to end all that?

But could he bring up another man's child?

He needed a drink. Just the one, so he could see his way clearly.

When Moira called at St. Jarlath's Thrift Shop and seemed surprised to see Frankie asleep there in her pram, Emily kept her worries to herself.

"What time is her father picking her up?" Moira asked. She didn't really want to know; it was just a stance—she always liked them to know that she was in control.

"He will be along later," Emily said with a confident smile. "Can I interest you in anything here, Moira? You have such good taste. There's a very attractive bag here— it's almost a cross between a bag and a briefcase. I think it's Moroccan; it's got lovely designs on it."

It was, as Emily said, very attractive, and would be perfect for Moira. She fingered it and wondered. But before she spent money on herself she must think of a present for her father and Mrs. Kennedy. Maybe Emily could help here too.

"I need a wedding present, something unopened, as it were. It's for a middle-aged couple in the country."

"Do they have their own house?" Emily inquired.

"Yes, well she has a house, and he's living there . . . I mean, going to live there."

"Is she a good cook?"

"Yes, she is, actually." Moira was surprised at the question.

"Then she won't need anything for the kitchen—she'll have all that under control. There's a very nice tablecloth, an unwanted gift, apparently. We could open it to make sure it's perfect, then seal it up again."

"Tablecloth?" Moira wasn't sure.

"Look at it—it's the best linen and has hand-painted flowers on it. I'd say she'd love it. Is she a close friend?"

"No," Moira said. Then she realized that it sounded a little bit bald. "I mean, she's going to marry my father," she explained.

"Oh, I'm sure your new stepmother would love this cloth," Emily said.

"Stepmother?" Moira tried the word on for size.

"Well, that's what she'll be, surely?"

"Yes, of course." Moira spoke hastily.

"I hope they'll be very happy," Emily said.

"I think they will. It's complicated, but they are well suited."

"Well, that's what it's all about."

"Yes, it is in a way. It's just that there's unfinished business, hard to explain but that's what it is."

"I suppose there always is," Emily said soothingly. She hadn't an idea what Moira was talking about.

Moira left with both the briefcase and the tablecloth; she was rapidly becoming one of the thrift shop's best customers.

There was something weighing heavily on her mind. Surely Mr. Kennedy had a right to know that his house existed in Liscuan, that his wife was taking another man in as her husband, and this man was the social worker's father. Moira knew that many would advise her to stay out of it. It would all have gone ahead without a problem if Moira hadn't come across Mr. Kennedy and settled him into long-term hostel care. But there was no denying it. She had met Mr. Kennedy and she could not let it go.

"Mr. Kennedy, you're all right?" They sat in the dayroom of the hostel.

"Miss Tierney. It's not your day today."

"I was in the area."

"I see."

"I was wondering, Mr. Kennedy, are you properly settled here?"

"You ask me that every week, Miss Tierney. It's okay—I've told you that."

"But do you think of your time in Liscuan?"

"No. I'm gone years from there."

"So you said, but would you like to be back there? Would you try again with your wife?"

"Isn't she a stranger to me now, after all these years?" he asked.

"But suppose she got married again? Presumed you were dead."

"More power to her if she did."

"You wouldn't mind?"

"I made my choice in life, which was to go off—she's free to make hers."

Moira looked at him. This was good—but she wasn't off the hook yet. She still knew what was going on. She had to tell him.

"Mr. Kennedy. There's something I have to tell you," she said.

"Don't worry about all that," he said.

"No, please, you must listen. You see, things aren't as simple as you think. Actually, there's a bit of a situation I have to tell you about."

"Miss Tierney, I know all that," he said.

She thought for a wild moment that maybe he did, but realized that he couldn't possibly know anything of life in Liscuan. He had been an exile for years.

"No, wait, you must listen to me . . . ," she said.

"Don't I know it all—your father's moved into the house, and now he's going to marry Maureen. And why shouldn't they?"

"Because you are still her husband," Moira stammered.

"They think I'm dead, and I am as far as they are concerned."

"You've known all the time?" Moira was astounded.

"I knew you at once. I remember you well from back home—you haven't changed a bit. Tough, able to take things. You didn't have a great childhood."

This man, ending his days in a hostel, pitied her. Moira felt weak at the way the earth had tilted.

"You're very good to tell me, but honestly we should just leave things the way they are—that way there's the least damage."

"But . . ."

"But nothing. Leave it happen, let them get married. Don't mention me."

"How did you know?" Her voice was almost a whisper.

"I did have a friend I stayed in touch with—he kept me posted."

"And is he there in Liscuan now, your friend?"

"No, he's dead, Moira. Only you and I know now."

Secrets were a great equalizer, Moira thought. He wasn't calling her Miss Tierney now.

Linda told her mother that Moira was as good as her word. She had made appointments here and introductions there, and the process was now under way. Nick and Linda said they would have been lost in a fog without her. She seemed to find no obstacles in her way. A perfect quality in a social worker.

"I can't understand why none of you like her," Linda said. "I've never met anyone as helpful in my life."

"She's fine at her work," Clara agreed. "But, God, I wouldn't like to go on a holiday with her. She manages to insult and upset everyone in some way."

Frank agreed with her. "She's a woman who never smiles," he said disapprovingly. "That's a character flaw in a person."

"She had the strength of character to refuse to be your

spy when she came to the clinic," Clara said cheerfully. "That's another point in her favor."

"I think she must have misread the situation there. . . ." Frank didn't want to bring disharmony into their home.

It was nine o'clock in the evening when Noel and Malachy turned up at Emily and Hat's house to collect Frankie.

Noel was pale but calm. Malachy looked very tired.

"I'm going to spend the night in Chestnut Court," Malachy said to Emily.

"That's great. Lisa's taken her things so it might be a bit lonely there otherwise," Emily said neutrally.

Frankie, who had been fast asleep, woke up and was delighted to be the center of attention.

"Dada!" she said to Noel.

"That's right," he said mechanically.

"I've been explaining to Frankie that her granny and granda are going to build a lovely, safe garden where she and all her friends can play."

"Great," said Malachy.

"Yes," said Noel.

"Your parents are going to have a sod-turning ceremony for the children's garden on Saturday. The work is going to start then."

"Sure," Noel said.

Wearily, Malachy got them on the road. Frankie was chattering away from her stroller. Words that were recognizable but not making any sense.

Noel was silent. He was there in body but not in spirit; surely people were able to guess something was different, something had changed. Frankie was just the same child she had been this morning but everything else had changed, and he hadn't yet had time to get accustomed to the idea.

Malachy slept on the sofa. During the night he heard Frankie start to cry and Noel get up to soothe the little girl and comfort her. The moonlight fell on Noel's face as he sat and held the child; Malachy could see there were tears on his cheeks.

Moira took the train to Liscuan. She was met at the station by Pat and Erin.

"Who's minding the store?" she asked.

"Plenty of help, good neighbors, all delighted that we're going to your father's wedding." Erin was dressed to the nines with a rose-and-cream-colored outfit, a big pink rose in her hair. Moira felt dowdy in her best suit. She looked at Erin's dainty, girlish handbag and wished she had not brought her own serious-looking briefcase. Still, too late to change now. They would need to hurry to be in time for the ceremony.

There were about fifty people waiting at the church.

"You mean all these people know that our father is getting married?" she asked Pat.

"Aren't they all so pleased for him?" Pat said. It was as simple as that.

And Moira prepared to sit through the whole ceremony, nuptial Mass and papal blessing knowing that she was the only person present who knew the whole story. When it came to the part where the priest asked was there any reason why these two persons should not marry, Moira sat dumb.

The presents were displayed in one of the reception rooms at the Stella Maris, and everyone seemed to think highly of the hand-painted tablecloth. Maureen Kennedy, now Maureen Tierney and her stepmother, drew Moira aside.

"That was really a most thoughtful gift, and I hope now that the situation has been regularized you will come sometime and stay under our roof and maybe we will eat dinner with this beautiful cloth on the table."

"That would be lovely," Moira breathed.

Faith had been away for three days, and when she came back she rushed in to pick up Frankie.

"Have I brought you the cutest little boots?" she said to the baby as she hugged her.

"The child has far too many clothes," Noel said.

"Ah, Noel, they're lovely little boots—look at them!"

"She'll have grown out of them in a month," he said.

The light had gone out of Faith's face. "Sorry—is something annoying you?"

"Just the way everyone piles clothes on her. That's all."

"I'm not everyone and I'm not piling clothes on her. She needs shoes to go to the opening of the site for the new garden on Saturday."

"Oh, God—I'd forgotten that."

"Better not let your parents know you did. It's the highlight of their year."

"Will there be lots of people there?" he asked.

"Noel, are you all right? You look different somehow, as if something fell on you."

"It did in a way," Noel said.

"Are you going to tell me?"

"No, not at the moment. Is that all right? I'm sorry for being so rude—they're adorable shoes; Frankie will be the last word on Saturday."

"Of course she will—now will I get us some supper?"

"You're a girl in a million, Faith."

"Oh, much more than that—one in a billion, I'd say," she said and went into the kitchen.

Noel forced himself into good humor. Frankie was unpacking the little pink boots from their box with huge concentration. Why couldn't she be his child? He sat in the kitchen and watched Faith move deftly around, getting together a supper in minutes, something that would have taken him forever.

"You love Frankie as much as if she were yours, don't you?" he said.

"Of course I do. Is this what's worrying you? She is mine in a way, since I mostly live with her and I help to look after her."

"But the fact that she's not yours doesn't make any difference?"

"What are you on about, Noel? I love the child. I'm mad about her—don't you know that?"

"Yes, but you've always known she wasn't yours," he said sadly.

"Oh, I know what this is all about—it's this ludicrous Moira who started this off in your head. It's like a wasp in your mind, Noel, buzzing at you. Chase it away. You're obviously her father; you're a great father."

"Suppose I had a DNA test and found she wasn't—what then?"

"You'd insult that beautiful child by having a DNA

test? Noel, you're unhinged. And what would it matter what the test said, anyway?"

He could have told her there and then. Gone to the drawer and taken out the letter with the results. He could have said that he had done the test and the answer was that Frankie was not his. This was the only girl he had ever felt close enough to even consider marrying; should he share this huge secret with her?

Instead, he shrugged.

"You're probably right—only a very suspicious, untrusting person would go for that test."

"That's more like it, Noel," Faith said happily.

Noel sat for a long time at the table when Faith left. He had three envelopes in front of him: one contained the results of the DNA test, one had the letter that Stella had left for him before she died and one held the letter she had addressed to Frankie. Back in the frightening early days when fighting to keep away from drink on an hourly basis, he had often been tempted to open the letter to Frankie. In those days he was anxious to look for some reason to keep going, something that might give him strength. Today he wanted to read it in case Stella had told her daughter who her real father was.

Something stopped him, though, perhaps some sense of playing fair. Although, of course, that was nonsense. Stella certainly hadn't played fair. Still, if he hadn't opened it back then, he would not do it now.

What had Stella got from it all, anyway? A short, restless life, a lot of pain and fear, no family, no friends. She never got to see her baby or know the little arms around her neck. Noel had got all this and more. A year ago, what did Noel have going for him? Not much. A drunk in a dead-end job, without friends, without hope. It had all changed because of Frankie. How lonely and frightened Stella must have felt that last night.

He reached out and read the letter she had written to him in that ward. *"Tell Frankie that I wasn't all bad . . ."* she had said. *"Tell her that if things had been different you and I would both have been there to look after her . . ."*

Noel straightened his shoulders.

He was Frankie's father in every way that mattered. Perhaps Stella had made a genuine mistake? Who knew what happened in other people's lives? And suppose somehow Stella was looking out for Frankie from somewhere—she deserved to know better than that the baby had been abandoned at the age of twelve months. Noel had loved this child yesterday, he still loved her today. He would always love her. It was as simple as that.

He reached across the table and put the two letters from Stella into the drawer. The letter with the DNA results he tore into tiny pieces.

It was a fine day for the turning of the sod. Charles and Josie put their hands together on the shovel and dug into the ground of the small waste patch they had secured for the new garden. Everyone clapped and Father Flynn said his customary few words about the great results that came from a sense of community involvement and caring.

Some of Muttie's Associates had come to watch the ceremony, and one of them was heard to say he would much prefer a statue of Muttie and Hooves to be raised instead of some long-dead saint whom nobody knew anything about.

Lizzie was there, with her arm around Simon's shoulders. He was going to New Jersey next week but had promised to be back in three months to tell them all what it was like. Marco and Maud stood together; Marco had hopes of a spring wedding but Maud said she was in no hurry to marry.

"Your grandfather gave me his blessing to marry you," Marco whispered.

"Yes, but he didn't say in the blessing *when* you were to marry me," Maud said firmly.

Declan, Johnny and a visibly pregnant Fiona were there, with Declan's parents and Dimples, the big dog. Dimples had a love-hate relationship with Caesar, the tiny spaniel. It wasn't that he had anything against Caesar—it was just that he was too small to be a proper dog.

Emily and Hat were there, part of the scenery now. People hardly remembered a time when they were not together. Emily was noting everything to tell Betsy that night by e-mail. She would even send her a picture of it all. Betsy too had fallen under the spell of this little community and was always asking for details of this and that. She and Eric had every intention of coming back again next year and catching up where they had left off.

Emily thought back to the first day that she herself had arrived in this street and heard her uncle and aunt's plans to build a huge statue. How amazing that it had all turned out so differently and so well.

Noel, Faith and Frankie were there, Frankie showing everyone her new pink boots. People pointed out to Noel that one of the houses in the Crescent would shortly be for sale—maybe he and Faith could buy it. Then Frankie would be near her garden. It was a very tempting idea, they said.

And as they wound their way back to Emily and Hat's house, where tea and cakes were being served, Noel felt a weight lift from his shoulders. He passed the house where Paddy Carroll and his wife, Molly, had slaved to raise their son, a doctor, and then past Muttie and Lizzie's house, where those twins had found a better home than they could have dreamed of. He blinked a couple of times as he began to realize that a lot of things didn't matter anymore.

Frankie wanted to walk the length of the road, even though she wasn't really able to; Faith followed with the buggy but Frankie struggled hard, holding Noel's hand and calling out "Dada" a lot. Just as they got to Emily and Hat's place, her little legs began to buckle and Noel swung her up into his arms.

"Good girl, Daddy's good little girl," he said over and over. His chest was much less tight, the awful feeling of running down a long corridor gone. He put his other arm around Faith's shoulders and ushered his little family into the house to have tea.

My dear, dear Frankie, my lovely daughter,

I will never see you or know you, but I do love you so very much. I fought hard to live for you but it didn't work. I started too late, you see. If only I had known that I would have a little girl to live for . . . But it's all far too late for those kind of wishes now. Instead I wish you the very best that life can give you. I wish you courage—I have plenty of that. Too much, some might say! I hope that you will not be as foolhardy and as reckless as I was. Instead, may you have peace and the love of good people who will mind you and make you happy. Tonight I sit here in a ward where nobody can really sleep. It's my last night here, you see, and tomorrow is your first day here. I wish we had been able to meet.

But I know one thing. Noel will be a great father. He is very strong and he can't wait to meet you tomorrow. He has been preparing for weeks, getting things ready for you, learning how to hold you, to feed you, to change you. He will be a wonderful dad and I have this very clear feeling that you will be the light of his life.

So many people are waiting for you tomorrow. Don't be sad for me—you have managed to make sense of my life eventually!

Live well and happily, little Frankie. Laugh a lot and be full of trust, not suspicion.

Remember your mother loved you with all her heart.
    —Stella

A WEEK IN SUMMER

Do you know what I think should be banned? Those advertisements for cruise holidays for mature people. You get this suave man in a dinner jacket, hair lightly streaked with gray, looking into the eyes of a woman with a pashmina stole around her slim, firm shoulders, to protect her against the night breezes as they stand on deck together. There is a hint that they have been at it like rabbits all afternoon and that they can't wait for the captain's cocktail party and gala dinner to end, so they can be at it all over again.

Are there people like this or is it just a fantasy dreamed up by an advertising agency, to sell holidays to us middle-aged Americans? Something that will leave the rest of us unsettled and unhappy? In any event, it is not important; it's not relevant to us. We had never had a real vacation. Not even when the girls, Mel and Margy, were children. Brian used to say, in his farming days: "Find me a cow that doesn't need to be milked for three weeks, and then we'll have a vacation."

And when the bottom fell out of the dairy-cattle market, as it did—for Brian, anyway—he was into growing corn in Illinois and flax in North Dakota, and in those days you couldn't take a vacation, either, because there was always something to be planted or watered or reaped or saved. And when the bottom had fallen out of flax and corn—for Brian, anyway—he studied mathematics and became a math teacher at a private school.

Other teachers had vacations. In fact, people were always saying they met teachers on vacations. But not Brian, because there were papers to mark, or courses to do, or students to tutor, and he liked going up to the attic and writing little bits of poetry that he never showed to anyone. But anyway, what with all this . . . hey presto, the vacation was soon over.

Me? Oh, I have worked forever at the same thing. Like my mother before me, I bake things. I used to work as a patisserie chef in a big hotel, but after I met Brian I had to think up something a bit more mobile. Something that could move easily when he did. So now I make cakes and casseroles and pies and deliver them to people's homes. I had to be ready to get up and go to the next place, so it was good to have a craft or trade or skill, whatever you might call it, to take with us.

People everywhere want to eat, and lots of younger women don't have time to cook. You'd be surprised how many deep-dish apple pies I make in their own pottery dishes. They even pretend to their husbands that they cooked it themselves. I have to be very careful about how and when I make my deliveries.

———

Now, I know I could have taken a vacation on my own. There was nothing to stop me from going to Europe or on a cruise or to the Grand Canyon. But that wasn't the point. It wasn't just to be able to say that I had been somewhere. I'm way too old for that. My customers who buy deep-dish apple pie and lamb stew wouldn't think more of me if I said I had been on a cruise to Alaska or on a train through the capitals of Europe. No, I just wanted to travel with Brian, and he just didn't want to go anywhere at all.

I wanted it for Brian and me. Something to remember. Something to look back on during the long evenings when we were on our own.

Mel and Margy were away a lot; there was always something for them to do during the summer holidays, when the school term was finished. There was this camp and that camp; the children loved camp. And because Brian had had so many careers and we had moved so much and so often, we thought it best for the girls to go to boarding school. It would give them more stability and enable them to keep their friends. And, heavens, they had so many friends.

A lot of these friends had parents who were much younger than we were. We are conscious of being older parents. I mean, Brian was forty when we married, and I was thirty-eight. We didn't want to seem too geriatric. All parents live on different planets from their children, they say, and, Lord, I've seen enough of it in the houses where I deliver food. But older parents? That's a solar system even farther away. Anyway, why should the girls hang out around our home, with Brian always so worried about everything, big lines of worry etched into his forehead, and me always up to my elbows in pastry dough? Not much fun with us. And I remembered my own childhood. I didn't want to hang around my house when I was younger, either.

And, of course, I could have gone away with my girlfriends. (All right, we're all in our fifties, but we think of ourselves as girls and we always will.) But I didn't want to spend our hard-earned money on a vacation with them. I wanted to be with Brian. I love Brian. I always have, since the day I met him, with his dreams and poetry and hopes of changing the world. It didn't matter that he didn't earn much of a living or that nobody thought very highly of him. He was the man I wanted; always has been. I can just see him in a tuxedo, like the men in the advertisements. I can see us spending long afternoons in a bedroom, a cabin, a sleeping-car compartment. Wherever. I can see us exchanging a knowing glance that says there will be more of that later on. I'm not sure why I can see this so clearly, but somehow I can. And Brian needs a holiday even more than I do these days. You see, he has just been suspended from his school. It's August now, and he hasn't any position for September, when the school year starts. A man of fifty-seven without a job. And all because he had to speak his mind. And what's more, to speak it at the parent-teacher association.

It was the occasion for congratulating the school for doing so well and for concentrating on the positive side of things. But my Brian had to choose the occasion to tell people that he did not think the war in Iraq was a just war. This was in a community that had already lost two young men on tours of duty. They didn't even wait until the next day to tell him that his services would no longer be needed. The principal came around to our house that night and said he was sorry, but feeling was running too high. "I'll only teach math in the future," poor Brian had promised. "Too late," the principal said.

It hit Brian very hard. He didn't want me to tell the girls. "I don't mind you knowing that I'm an all-time loser," he pleaded, "but I don't want my daughters to know this. Not yet." But Mel and Margy would have to know come September, when Brian wasn't returning to school, I told him. "Hey, honey," he said. "They're not really all that interested in what I do or don't do. Just give me time, Kathleen, just give me a little time. I know I don't deserve it, but I can't breathe properly. This would give me some breathing space."

I don't know why I agreed, but I did. "Right," I said. "I'll trade you. We have a vacation together—just one vacation–and then I'll give you time."

He smiled a horrible smile, as if there was nothing behind it. As if he was an empty head. All the color and life had gone out of his face.

"And maybe you might go to the doctor for a checkup, too," I suggested.

"Don't move the goalposts, Kathleen. A week in summer. You organize it. That's the deal."

He looked wretched. He didn't want a holiday. I loved him to bits. Maybe a kinder person would say forget the holiday. But somehow I thought it would be the making of us.

"A week in summer, that's the deal," I said, and we linked little fingers, the way kids do.

———

He never asked where we were going to go; he made no suggestions. His face was gray; his mind was miles away. Brian was more of a shadow than a man. So I did it all. I found his passport. I checked our savings account to see how much we could spend and then I went to the Snappy Seniors' Travel Agency to discuss dates and venues with one of their Vacation Buddies.

His name was Chester. He was Chief Vacation Buddy in this branch, and he would have been a happy camper no matter where he had been sent on vacation. There wasn't really time, we agreed, for a cruise, if all we had was a week in summer. And anyway, I confessed, Brian wasn't cruise material, as he didn't own a dinner jacket and might get bored. Bored on board ship? Chester was unbelieving. But he had other suggestions.

Perhaps a cultural tour of four European cities via luxury bus? For all that he liked writing poetry, Brian wasn't that interested in museums and art galleries. I couldn't see him standing in line in Paris and Bruges. Culture didn't loom large in his life.

Then what about a beach holiday, if he was anti-culture? A place where the ladies go around topless? Chester asked. I told my new Vacation Buddy that Brian wasn't anti-culture, just that four cities full of it in one week and lots of luxury busing along autostradas and autoroutes might not be his thing. He hadn't been well, and he needed cheering up.

Disneyworld? A theme park? Chester suggested and I refused. He didn't need *that* kind of cheering.

One by one, I rejected: learning to snorkel, bridge for beginners, cooking in France and the gardens of Andalucia. Chester was beginning to despair. Never had he met such an unsnappy senior.

"Suppose it were up to you, ma'am. What would you like to do?"

"But it's not up to me. He's had a shock, you see. He's not well. He needs the holiday."

"But if it *were* up to you, what would you choose?" Chester hated admitting defeat; it just wasn't what Snappy Seniors' Vacation Buddies did. I paused to think. Supposing that Brian would like anything I chose, what would I pick?

"You know, I'd like to go ancestor hunting," I said eventually. "You know, looking in old graveyards and parish records."

Chester was immensely cheered. "Where are his people from?"

"No, not *his* people . . . mine. Brian's father came from a village in Russia that no longer exists."

"Most places are still there in some form," Chester said reprovingly.

"No, truly, the whole population of the village left for the United States. It's my roots I'd look for. A long way back, but I'm sure there's something."

"So where's that, then?" Chester was so relieved he might actually sell me a vacation that he was beaming at me.

"Ireland," I said. "My people were Collinses from Ireland. I don't know where."

"Let's go hunt," Chester said with the enthusiasm that earned him the position of Chief Vacation Buddy of the branch. He tapped at his computer for a while and looked back at me full of smiles.

"Originally from Limerick," he said triumphantly. "But they were driven out by the Anglo-Normans and ended up in West Cork. Which area do you want to start in?"

"Where were they in their heyday?" I asked.

"Limerick, I think. They were lords of the Barony of Conello then."

"Oh, then let's try Limerick."

He was good, Chester was. He didn't want us to spend our whole vacation stuck in a city looking up people who'd been dead for hundreds and hundreds of years. If my husband was ill, if he was difficult to please and in a bit of shock, Chester said this wasn't the kind of restful holiday we needed. Maybe we should consider the neighboring county, County Clare. There are lovely drives around the Burren, unusual plants to see, castles to look at, porpoises and dolphins in the Atlantic, for the days that we don't spend looking up my roots. Plus nice comfortable hotels and good food. Build my husband up it would.

At Snappy Seniors' they wanted us to be happy; it meant repeat business. I felt guilty talking about Brian behind his back. He was such a good man who only wanted the best for everyone, but now he was like an empty shell. No matter how hard Chester and I tried, I feared nothing was going to put a smile on his face or life back into his soul.

The girls came home for two days before heading off to camp.

"You look awfully old, Dad," said Mel.

"I *am* awfully old, Mel," said Brian.

"Not so much old as confused," corrected Margy.

"Oh, I'm confused too, Margy," Brian agreed.

Our two daughters seemed pleased that they had correctly identified everything.

Brian didn't talk much about the vacation because he didn't talk much about anything, really. He just sat there staring ahead.

When the day came, he packed obediently and came along with me to the airport as if it were yet another visit to the supermarket. No enthusiasm. No hope. Nothing but a deal done, a trade agreed, a promise kept.

I had told my customers that I would be away for a week. "A week in summer," I said, as if it were the most normal thing in the world. "Ireland? That's nice," they said without conviction. They would really have preferred me to stay where I was, making passionfruit Pavlovas on their family china for summer parties.

Brian was very quiet on the plane. He pretended to read the airline magazine, but he never turned a page. And then we were in Shannon Airport. It was a bright, sunny day; the fields were small and green; the road signs were in two languages; the rented car was small.

Brian wasn't listening when they asked us who wanted to drive, so I said I would. I learned about the wrong side of the road and to beware leaving gas stations, and roundabouts. And we set off. The other drivers on the road were, well, interesting, I suppose you'd call it. They never used turn signals or anything. They just pulled straight out in front of you. But once you got used to that . . .

I gave Brian the maps and the brochures, but they sat on his lap. In the middle of this lovely early-morning countryside I felt no joy of being on day one of a vacation. I got no feeling of having come home to my roots. I got no indication that this holiday would be the great breakthrough for us. The long, cramped sleepless night on the plane and these narrow windy roads were beginning to take their toll. "Tell me something about Lisdoonvarna," I said, with the false cheerfulness that I hate in others. I could hear the tinny insecurity in my voice. I must have listened to a thousand of these nonconversations between husband and wife. The kind that ended up either as "Yes dear, yes dear" or "What do you know about that?"

Brian and I were never going to be anything like that. Surely. We had fought to get married. My family thought he was a slow starter with his head in the clouds. His family thought I was a bit too brittle and hard-nosed for them. They didn't care that I supported him and put the girls through school. They would have liked a poet or a weaver or some damn thing.

But that had never mattered to Brian or me. We rose above it. We had so much going for us for years. But as we drove through the beautiful County Clare countryside, I thought that all we had going for us might have kept on going—and gone away.

He opened a brochure and read to me obediently, like a child at school, about the Spa Wells and the curative water and the restorative baths. And there was a matchmaking festival in September. "Pity we'll miss that," I joked. "We might have found the love of our lives."

"Nobody would blame you for leaving me, Kathy," he said, "nobody at all."

I was busy trying to negotiate the Lycra-covered back-sides of some cyclists who were hogging the road. It wasn't the moment to tell him that I had never loved anyone else and never would.

At the hotel in Lisdoonvarna they were very nice and wel-coming. Cups of tea, congratulations on our having man-aged to drive there, our first day in a new land. "You'll have a great week," the receptionist said. "The weather looks up and you were so lucky to get the cancellations."

Chester hadn't mentioned any cancellations. I was puzzled. Perhaps somebody hadn't liked something about the hotel. Brian hadn't heard any of it, so I hid my frown of worry, and the girl chatted on happily.

"The nicest couple in the world they are, they nor-mally come here every year and stay for the whole week, but this year they've gone to Australia. They were most apologetic, but the chance came up, you see, and what with them being in their nineties they thought they should go now in case it might be more difficult later."

I felt a pang of sharp envy for these people and an un-reasoning sense of jealousy. In their *nineties* for heaven's sake and had gone to the other side of the earth. We were in our fifties and a week in Ireland was nearly killing us. We could never fill their shoes.

"But have a great rest now," the receptionist urged. "And then you'll be in fine form for the Fáiltiú."

The Fáiltiú? What, exactly, was that? She said it was

the Irish for "welcome." That sounded familiar, though why people were going to welcome us was beyond me.

But it wasn't us, it turned out. It was the start of a summer school of some sort. Everyone went to the Fáiltiú, she said reprovingly.

"We don't want to be difficult, but what is it, exactly?" I asked. She said she thought it might be a reception with some wine and maybe some finger food. We'd have a great time. I looked at Brian's gray, empty face and doubted it but thanked her very much.

We went up, unpacked and lay beside each other in the big, cool bed. The unhappiest couple in the Western world, and it was nobody's fault, really. That was the terrible thing. I sort of slept. I must have, because I dreamed of Margy and Mel when they were toddlers. They were asking me what was going to happen in life, and I was telling them it would all be great. I woke and found Brian sitting in a chair. His eyes were open, but he wasn't looking at anything.

It was six p.m., and outside the window we saw people heading down the road in the early-evening sunshine. Old and young, men and women; they walked in twos and threes, on their own or in laughing groups. Heading towards the Spa Wells on a summer's evening to have a couple glasses of wine and some finger food. "Come on," I said. "We don't want to be late."

"Late?" he replied, astounded.

Anything was better than a long night looking at each other with nothing left to say. Soon I was out of the shower and choosing which dress to wear. Some of the men walking down the road wore collars and ties; some had open shirts. Some of the ladies had cardigans; some had smart suits, flowery dresses; some were in jeans. It looked fairly free and easy.

"I don't know whether we should go to this thing, Kathy. We haven't been invited."

"Oh, come on, Brian," I said. "Didn't you hear the lady at the desk? Everyone is invited."

"We may have to pay," he said, sounding anxious.

"So we pay," I told him.

We discovered that it was going to cost €120 each to sign up for the summer school's week of activities. A bit expensive for a welcome reception, I thought, but then I looked at the brochure. There were all kinds of things: lectures, poetry readings, bus trips, dancing lessons, seminars and debates. And the main thing was, it would be a distraction. We wouldn't be left on our own, facing each other with nothing left to say, forced to admit the emptiness of our lives.

It wasn't men in tuxedos and women in gowns leaning on a ship's railing, but a lot of these people had fairly playful eyes. You got a sense that there might be a fair amount of flirting in this lot, if you know what I mean. If not now, then in the past. They had all been coming here for years and years, apparently, to dance in squares and roam the countryside. They liked it so much they booked in again every year. It was all about Brian Merriman, some poet dead for hundreds of years, but people brought him back to life every summer.

Everyone was very friendly. They told us all sorts of things, like where to go for a swim, where to get cheap lobster, which translation of his poem *Cúirt an Mheán*

Oíche to read. The poem wasn't even in English, for heaven's sake, but there seemed to be a stack of translations of *The Midnight Court,* and everyone recommended a different one. People were full of advice about everything. They said we should drive out and see the Burren— but not to pick the flowers—or maybe go to Doolin and get a boat to the Aran Islands, or go to places we had never heard of. Ballyvaughan, Ennistymon, Lahinch, Corofin: they tripped off the tongue. There were people speaking in the Irish language, which they told us we'd know in no time after a few lessons in the mornings.

So we listened to the opening of the school and to a lecture, and then we discovered that the theme of this year's gathering was marriage. They could have had something less brutally relevant, I thought, but I kept a bright smile, as if I hadn't a worry in the world about marriage and how it seemed to be panning out in our lives.

And then there was dancing. Mainly we couldn't do it at all, because there were complicated things much more intricate than our square dancing at home. Caledonian sets, Ballyvourney sets, all way, way beyond us. But apparently we could learn all that, too, in special dancing lessons every day. By the end of the week we would be whirling with the best. There *were* a few waltzes, so eventually Brian and I took to the floor like everyone else. Everyone in the hall sang the words. "My mother died last springtime, when Irish fields were green. The neighbors said her funeral was the finest ever seen." Brian listened in amazement. "Some topic for everyone to dance to," he said. But at least he was smiling, and I hadn't seen that for a while.

And so it went on for the week. We went to poetry

readings and lectures. We learned about the construction of the Irish language at one seminar and about the courts of Munster poetry at another. We tried to keep up with horrifically fit dancing instructors, and soon we had our own eight and were swinging each other around in great style. We had conversations way into the night with poets, politicians and polka dancers.

If they asked us what we did, which was rarely, I told them I baked for people in their own dishes; Brian said he wrote poetry and had been doing some teaching on the side. Everyone seemed to think this was a completely reasonable thing to do. Nobody asked if there was money in it, or what he had published recently, or what his real job was, or what his ten-year plan was. I may have been imagining it, but, as the days went on, I thought that there were fewer lines etched on his face and that his eyes were brighter.

People kept assuring us that they were pacing themselves. They urged us to pace ourselves, too. This, I think, had to do with not staying up until six a.m. singing, which was a danger. And not starting to drink after the dancing class and forgetting to stop all day, which was another danger. And we heard amazing amounts of gossip. Things that happened some years back, when certain people had more energy than they currently did or had not been as wise as they were now.

One summer a man had lost his false teeth and asked rather sheepishly at reception if any had been handed in. He was discreetly given a set in an envelope. When they didn't fit, he was told that all the other sets in the lost-and-found had been claimed. Once upon a time another man had made so many perambulations to the rooms of different ladies that he never knew which was his own room, and when he went to pay his bill there was nothing to pay, because the hotel had assumed he was a no-show and had relet it.

There was a marvelous woman who told us that it usually took her until November to recover from her indiscretions every third week of August. Another said regretfully that everyone was very old and staid and settled now, and that it was a pity we hadn't met them in their heyday. They looked very much in their heyday to us. A great roaming band of people, old and young, serious drinkers and teetotalers, fit as fiddles or bent over canes, long retired or in their first jobs. Some went to every lecture, took notes and asked questions. Others adjourned to bars, golf courses, lunches in craft shops; or to have healing baths in the Centre, where ropes suspended from the ceiling had helped haul thousands out of the mineral salts over the years.

They talked about any number of subjects: the nature of evil, the joys and problems of being part of a united Europe, the wisdom or lack of it in having a celibate clergy. And because of the theme we discussed marriage at length: whether it was possible to have an equal partnership, what equal meant, if a marriage could last forever and whether it should last forever. My head was in a whirl.

As for Brian Merriman himself—they all talked about him so familiarly that I would not have been surprised to hear that he was up at the Roadside Inn, singing songs, and that we should hurry, in case we missed him. It was a mystery. At home we didn't have gatherings like this. Or maybe we did, and Brian and I had never come across them. These people had come from all over the country, and even farther afield, for this celebration. Their conversation was full of "Do you remember?"s and "Aren't you looking like a two-year-old?"s. I forgot all about looking for my roots. There wasn't time, anyway. The Collins family tree would have to wait for another visit.

The man who ran the summer school was actually called Collins—Bob Collins—a very nice man, approachable when he was free. But he was always talking to someone very important, like a former prime minister of Ireland or an ex-president who had a vacation house down the road. If the social climbers I make carrot cake for back at home only knew the high society we were mixing with, they'd be pea green with envy.

I did get to talk to Bob Collins once. I told him that I was a Collins, too, and was wondering where I should start to research the clan. (He gave me all kinds of tips, but, of course, there wasn't one moment left to do any of it.) "Kathleen Collins?" he said. "You have the same name as Brian Merriman's wife." I don't really believe any of this fate or coincidence thing, though you'd be surprised how many of my clients back home consult psychics. They're always talking about them.

That evening Brian suggested we go out for an hour and watch the sunset. I wish I could tell you how unusual this was in our lives. If ever I suggested a sunset, he would say bleakly: "So the sun goes down and it comes up again. That's what happens." But now he'd heard of a place where you might see dolphins and porpoises or some such, and this other poet he had met told him it was a great place for the soul. It was called Fanore, and he pointed it out to me on a map, the same map he hadn't had the interest or energy to pick up from his lap just a few short days ago. Of course I agreed to go, so we went.

At Fanore I looked at Brian and saw that there were no lines in his face. He was relaxed and happy. If he'd been wearing a tuxedo and leaning against the rail of a cruise ship he wouldn't have looked better. I decided not to tell him about having the same name as Brian Merriman's wife, in case he thought I was being fancy or trying to justify the holiday or something like that. It's usually my instinct to prattle on, but this time I just patted his hand and looked out at the Atlantic Ocean.

"You're very restful, Kathy," he said. "I feel I could tell you anything, even something so crazy you won't believe it."

"Tell me," I said, without the faintest idea of what he was going to say.

"I think we were led here in some way," he said. "I think I am the reincarnation of Brian Merriman."

My heart sank. I thought he was getting better, the depression was lifting, the clouds were parting, and instead he was coming out as clinically insane. "The what?" I asked.

"You know, Kathy, the way they say things don't really die, they come back again. I have come back again. It's as simple as that." He beamed at me like a complete madman.

"How, exactly, a reincarnation?" I asked, hoping I didn't sound too much like Nurse Ratched in *One Flew Over the Cuckoo's Nest*.

"Well, don't you see?" he said, his eyes blazing happily

in the sunset. "My name is Brian Merman; his wife was Kathleen Collins; we have had exactly the same careers, married at the same age as he did; they had two daughters, like we do; he was a flax farmer and won prizes for growing it; I did, too, in Dakota, remember? And, of course, he was a teacher, like me, and, most of all—and here's the whole heart of it—he was a poet."

I nodded dumbly. Was this the time to tell him that when his grandfather had come to the United States from Russia, Merman was as near as Americans could come to pronouncing the family name? No, it was probably not the time. Anyway, I wouldn't have got a word in. He was going on and on: they were born exactly two hundred years apart yet had followed the same path; the first Brian Merriman had been impatient about clergy and the Establishment, just as my Brian had been. It had to mean something. Something amazing. Something very significant.

I had thought it was terrible when he seemed to be suffering from depression, but why hadn't I just left him the way he was? Now he was hallucinating he was a long dead poet who wrote in a different language, a person he had never heard of before last Saturday. And it got worse.

Brian Merriman had died two hundred years ago this very year. That's what this gathering was all about. Did my poor Brian now think this was his fate, too? Had he actually given up on his life on account of all these coincidences? Had he brought me to this beautiful place to say good-bye? Was this the result of all my scheming and plotting and planning with Chester, Chief Vacation Buddy of the Snappy Seniors' Travel Agency? I hadn't helped him at all; I'd only managed to rot his mind.

"Well, Brian," I said with a heavy heart, "you know there are a lot of ways of looking at things."

"Of course there are," he eagerly agreed. "And if we hadn't come here I never would have known it. When he died, the first Brian Merriman that is, there were only a few short lines in the newspaper about him, and he might well have thought that he didn't amount to much. But think, *think*, Kathy, two centuries later there are hundreds and hundreds of us celebrating him, reading his poetry, debating his ideas, studying his life and times."

He hadn't looked so young and hopeful for as long as I could remember. He said that he was going to show people his poetry, that he wasn't going to keep it hidden. It had been the sign he needed, something to prove he wasn't worthless. His arm was around my shoulders, his face nuzzling my cheek in a way it hadn't done for some considerable time. The coy look of a Merriman was in his eye. What the hell, I thought. I know what's changed him: he met a marvelous band of good-natured people who live life to the fullest. If he thinks he's the reincarnation of some guy who walked these roads two hundred years ago, then I'm going to let him think it.

I would write a postcard to Chester before we left. I would tell him that the Snappy Seniors' record is unbroken. He would have our repeat business; we would indeed come back here next year. Of course we would.

I know only four figures of one Clare set. There is much still to learn. Brian has read only one translation of *Cúirt an Mheán Oíche*. We have only skimmed the surface of Clare music and got the barest essentials of dolmens, holy wells and the lunar landscape of the Burren. Imagine leaving all these people and not knowing how their lives turned out. It's more than flesh and blood could bear.

Anyway, this coming back as a butterfly or something else is a perfectly decent theory. Buddhists believe it, and they are gentle people. And, just as there are strong women in the famous poem, I have met many strong women this week. Surely one of them will get a summer school going on Mrs. Merriman, on Kathleen Collins— quite possibly my ancestor. I might be her reincarnation, too. And if she makes me as happy as her husband has made Brian, then we won't be doing badly at all.

Acknowledgments

I would like to thank my editor, Carole Baron, and my agent, Chris Green, who have been hugely supportive and great friends to me during the writing of this book.

WHITETHORN WOODS

When a new highway threatens to bypass the town of Rossmore and cut through Whitethorn Woods, everyone has a passionate opinion about whether the town will benefit or suffer. But young Father Flynn is most concerned with the fate of St. Ann's Well, which is set at the edge of the woods and slated for destruction. People have been coming to St. Ann's for generations to share their dreams and fears, and speak their prayers. Some believe it to be a place of true spiritual power, demanding protection; others think it's a mere magnet for superstitions, easily sacrificed. Father Flynn listens to all caught up in the conflict, as the men and women of Whitethorn Woods decide between the traditions of the past and the promises of the future.

Fiction

HEART AND SOUL

In this insightful, humorous, and compassionate novel, Dr. Clara Casey agrees to take on the seemingly thankless task of establishing a heart clinic with little funding for one year. She has plenty on her plate already—two difficult grown daughters and the unwanted attentions of her ex-husband—but she assembles a wonderfully diverse staff devoted to helping the clinic's demanding, often difficult patients. Much to her naysayers' surprise, the clinic becomes an undeniable success, leaving Clara with a difficult decision: whether she should leave a place where lives are saved, courage is rewarded, and humor and optimism triumph over greed and self-pity once the year has ended.

Fiction

THE MAEVE BINCHY WRITERS' CLUB

In this warm and inspiring guide, beloved author Maeve Binchy shares her unique insight to how a bestselling author writes: from finding a subject and creating good writing habits to sustaining progress and seeking a publisher. Whether you want to write stories or plays, humor or mysteries, Binchy prescribes advice for every step with her signature humor and generous spirit. She has called upon other writers, editors, and publishers to add their voices to this treasury of assistance for budding writers and a refreshing dose of encouragement for longtime scribes.

Writing

ANCHOR BOOKS
Available wherever books are sold.
www.randomhouse.com